Will My Touch Make You Feel Any Less Lonely?

A Novel
by Peter Wodarz

Culicidae Press, LLC
PO Box 5069
Madison, WI 53705-5069
culicidaepress.com
editor@culicidaepress.com

Madison | Berlin | Lemgo

WILL MY TOUCH MAKE YOU FEEL ANY LESS LONELY?

Copyright © 2026 by Peter Wodarz
All rights reserved.

No part of this book may be reproduced in any form by any electronic or mechanized means (including photocopying, recording, or information storage and retrieval) without written permission, except in the case of brief quotations embodied in critical articles and reviews. For more information, please visit culicidaepress.com

ISBN: 978-1-68315-176-0

Our books may be purchased in bulk for promotional, educational or business use. Please contact your local bookseller or the Culicidae Press Sales Department at +1-352-215-7558 or by email at sales@culicidaepress.com

culicidaepress.bsky.social – facebook.com/culicidaepress
threads.net/@culicidaepress – instagram.com/culicidaepress
x.com/culicidaepress

Design by polytekton © 2026

Table of Contents

Book 2 155

Book 1

1 The Bitch, the Bastard, and the Housewife

The young man had a terrible headache. From the sixteenth floor of the Aomori Banking Complex, he sat leaning forward, his elbows on his desk. With his chin resting on his fists, he appeared to be looking beyond his three computer screens out at the Aomori Bay Bridge. Recently opened, the high, impressive rainbow-styled span connected the east side of the city to the west side, below it the always-cold waters of Aomori Bay. But, deep in his reverie, he didn't see it. Though his eyes were wide open, he took in nothing.

She's going to wear that hideous hat again tonight, he mused; and since he wanted to retain the English he had learned in America, he slowly repeated the words, this time out loud: "She's going to wear that hideous hat again. She's going to wear—"

"Ah, Makoto, how goes it? Practicing your English again?" Hayashi, a decade older both in years and in time at the firm, had slipped up behind him unawares. "That will come in handy when we are in Singapore next week." His colleague sounded cheerful, and bored, but the young man didn't turn to greet him. Instead, he sighed, closed his tired eyes, and flatly said, "I am not going out tonight."

"Who said anything about going out?"

"You did."

"When?"

"Right now. That's why you are standing here, bothering me, right?"

"But why not?"

"Because I went out with everyone last night." Slowly, he spun his chair around and looked up at the smiling man. "I've been incredibly hungover all morning, thanks to you. So I am going out with Mariko tonight. We're having a quiet dinner."

"What time?"

"When we finish."

"Where?"

"At a restaurant."

"Why don't you just eat together at home later?"

The young man didn't respond.

"Listen," his older colleague said, sounding disappointed. "Fujisawa-san asked me to look after you. You younger Japanese are different, especially those of you who have been overseas. You try to do things your own way. He's worried." The young man wanted to defend himself, wanted to tell the entire older generation to fuck off, but he knew he couldn't use such language. Even a mild rebuttal would be futile. Once again, he said nothing. He turned his back to his older colleague and stared out the window at the bridge. He saw it now. He noticed the snow too, waves and waves of large flakes falling diagonally.

"We're all a team here. You need to remember that. And part of being on this team is socializing, drinking, being with your colleagues in and out of the office. Doing this is very important."

"Tonight I am socializing with my wife."

"You can socialize with her whenever you want," the other countered, laughing and placing his hand on the young man's shoulder. "How long have you been married?"

"Three months."

"Three months! Wait until you've been married five years. Then you'll be out with us every night!" He chuckled again and fished a cigarette out of the pack he carried in his breast pocket. With a lighter, he lit it and took a long drag. "Okay," he resumed, exhaling and nodding at the quiet determination of his younger colleague. "We'll make an exception. Tonight, the growing shark will have his way. Have a nice, romantic dinner with Mariko-chan. Buy her some pretty flowers. Share a bottle of her favorite wine. But remember, you swim in the ocean with us." To reinforce his point, he placed his hand back on the young man's shoulder and squeezed once very firmly.

After Hayashi walked off, the young man glanced around to make sure no other colleagues could hear. Hunched over, his left elbow on the desk, he lifted the receiver with his right hand and punched the numbers with his index finger. When he was in a playful mood, he often called his wife Mary. She didn't like the nickname. She told him that he must have had a girlfriend named Mary when he was living in New York. He told her he was a virgin when they married, like she was, but she knew he was lying.

"Hi, Mariko," he began, speaking softly, the receiver pressed to his ear. "Unfortunately, I'll be going out with the team again tonight. The Singapore trip. We have a lot to discuss.

"I know.

"I'm sorry.

"Yes, I know. But I have to. I can't say no.

"I should be home before ten."

He set down the receiver gently and once more looked around. Each of his colleagues—some just a few meters away—sat peering into his computer intent on his task. The office floor was strangely quiet. He gave the various numbers on his three screens a quick scan, then looked down at the documents in front of him. He tried to concentrate, but soon his gaze returned to the bridge. He had never seen such heavy snow. He glanced at his watch. Though it was just before three, it was almost dark outside; he could barely see the flashing green and red lights of the bridge towers.

⧗ ⧗ ⧗

As planned, the young man arrived at the Chez Banane forty-five minutes late. He was hoping that the woman he was meeting would have left by then, but when he slipped in behind a young couple, he saw her sitting at the bar. Much to his dismay, she was wearing the brown hat, an old French beret that she felt made her unique. On their second rendezvous, she happily told him the story: she had bought it from an old, nearly toothless woman in a second-hand clothes shop in Montmartre when she was there on holiday three years previously. She had been in Paris—her only trip abroad—for six days. She wore the hat when they met; he didn't have the heart to tell her that the tired-looking, out-of-fashion beret made her look homely.

The bar was nearly full, so it was easy for him to slip in behind the couple and find a small, round table in the back. As he removed his snowflake-covered overcoat and draped it over the back of one chair, a waitress came and took his order. When she brought the whisky a few minutes later, he took a sip, leaned back, watched her. Obviously bored, she sat leaning forward, elbows on the bar, her right hand twirling her pink straw in her nearly finished cocktail. She glanced at the entrance, then down at her watch. She twirled some more. She bent over the glass and took the straw into her mouth.

Feeling exhausted, the late nights of carousing catching up to him, the young man was certain he was coming down with a cold. He reached into his pocket, pulled out a handkerchief, used it to wipe his wet face. As he refolded it and laid it on the table, he couldn't believe that the snow was still falling.

To keep from being noticed, he picked up and pretended to read the small, laminated food menu that lay on his table. Mixed nuts? Dried squid? A toasted ham-and-cheese sandwich? He wasn't hungry. When he set it aside a minute later and glanced back at the bar, the woman had noticed him. As she looked at him over a shoulder, he saw the hint of resentment on her questioning face. Slowly, she pushed herself off her stool, gathered her coat from the back of the chair, walked over to his two-person table. As she approached, he stood and, perhaps unconvincingly, feigned surprise and concern. "Yumiko, how long have you been sitting there?"

"What time were we supposed to meet?" she replied, hugging her coat to her chest with both arms.

"At eight."

"I've been sitting there since eight."

"What time is it now?"

"It's nearly nine."

"But I got here just after eight. This," he said, gesturing to his glass of whisky with his right hand, "is my second drink."

"How could you miss me?" she asked, her narrowing eyes full of suspicion.

"Are you sure you arrived at eight? Perhaps you were a few minutes late and I didn't see you enter."

"I wasn't late. I told you I would be at the bar."

"Did you? I must have forgotten. I've had a long and difficult day."

"Didn't you recognize me?"

"I didn't recognize the hat," he replied, pointing.

"What do you mean?" she asked incredulously. "I always wear this beret, especially when I see you."

"Really? I guess I hadn't noticed."

As the two stood looking at each other, he could see that she was more than a little angry.

"Aren't you going to sit down?" he asked, giving her his let's-be-friends smile. "Here. Let me have me your coat. Let's forget about this unfortunate misadventure. What do you want to drink? Wine? Another cocktail?" He motioned to the waitress, who quickly approached and took her order.

The two sat across from each other, but neither spoke. Even after the waitress arrived and placed her glass of red wine in front of her, the two said nothing. Another minute passed, the silence becoming uncomfortable.

"I'm not well," he offered, feeling that he had to say something.

"What do you mean?" she asked, reaching for her glass.

"I think I am coming down with a cold."

After she took a sip of the wine, she set down the glass, reached across the table, indifferently felt his forehead and then his cheek with the back of her hand. "You don't feel hot."

"That may be. But like I said, I can sense a cold coming on. It's this weather. And probably I have been working too hard."

"Maybe you should tell Mary," the woman suggested sarcastically, leaning back and crossing her arms, all the time her eyes fixed on his. "I am sure," she added, her caustic tone a strong reprimand, "she would take very good care of you."

The young man frowned. "Don't call her Mary."

"Why not? You seem to think Mary is a nice name."

"It is a nice name. But my wife's nickname—among many other things—is something I should have never told you."

"Do you want me to call her and tell her how nice it is?"

"She already knows."

"Perhaps I could tell her other things. I think I should call. I would be doing her a big favor."

"Yeah? What will you tell her?"

"I will tell her about us. I bet she doesn't know. She may not forgive you, and then where would you be?"

"Do you have my number?"

"I do."

"Then why don't you call?" he asked, leaning forward and placing his elbows on the table. "She's home preparing dinner. She's trying awfully hard to be a good wife."

"I will."

"Go ahead. I insist."

Their eyes—his warm and animated, hers cold and calculating—were locked in a competition, the loser being the one who looked away first.

"Do you need some coins?" he asked, his smile a taunt.

She blinked a few times, but she didn't respond.

"Want to use my phone card?" He withdrew his wallet from his inside breast pocket, flipped it open, slid out a telephone card. "Here," he said, offering her the plastic card. "Come on! Take it! I saw a telephone just outside the front door by the elevator." She paused, but then slowly, she pushed back her chair, stood, accepted the card. As she walked toward the bar's front door, he called after her, "It's a new card, Yumiko, so please bring it back." Then, leaning back and sighing heavily, feeling even worse, he lifted his whisky and took another sip.

When she returned a few minutes later, he stood, moved to her side of the table, and politely helped her into her chair.

"So how is Mariko?" he asked, taking his seat and looking into her eyes.

"Mary is fine."

"What is she doing?"

"You were right. She's cooking dinner."

"Really?" he asked, leaning forward and pretending to be engaged. "What is she making?"

"I didn't ask."

"I suppose the two of you didn't talk about the culinary arts."

"No, we didn't."

"You had much more important matters to discuss."

"We did."

"Did you talk about my leaving her for you? You told her that that is what I desperately want, right?"

"Of course."

"And how did she take the news?" he asked, leaning back and smiling. "I hope she wasn't too upset."

"I wasn't there," she said, looking away. "I mean I didn't see her reaction."

"But Yumiko, what did the tone of her voice convey?"

"She told me it didn't matter." After a pause, she added, looking again into his eyes, "She has a lover."

The young man beamed, his broad smile nearly a laugh; he called over the waitress and ordered himself another whisky.

When he held this new glass, the young man took a generous swallow and asserted, "Unbelievable! You don't know how good I feel! I mean I'm glad it's all out in the open." Then, his smile disappearing, he continued in a menacing undertone. "Now I won't have to listen to the phone ring in the middle of the night knowing it's you. Mariko does wonder. And we won't have to meet here anymore at this dump that you call a café. I'll just move into your tiny studio. Won't that be fun! And you won't have to call the office three or four times a day pretending to be a client. Why, you ask? Because I won't have a job to go to. Why won't I have a job? Well, can you imagine the scandal when the president finds out his son-in-law has left his only daughter? That ought to bring a good laugh. They won't even let me clean the toilets! And I keep reminding myself *this* is what you want. Every time we meet you ask when. I keep telling you it's *not* going to happen, that it *can't* happen, but you keep right on asking. No, not asking. Demanding."

The woman sat with her head bowed. The young man took another greedy gulp of his whisky.

"Look at me."

She didn't.

"I said look at me."

Slowly, she raised her head and their eyes met. He addressed her in English: "Don't be a bitch to me, and I won't be a bastard to you."

"What?"

He translated his last sentence into Japanese.

"I am not a bitch," she snapped. "A bitch would have called her and told her!"

"I met you a month after my wedding. What did you say then? You drop your purse, I pick it up, and the next thing I know we're having a couple of drinks. What did you say next? Huh? Didn't you say you knew a place that had a nice view of the bridge? Didn't you say that, or was that a different woman?"

She sat there, mute.

"You know what they say in America? 'Did the cat get your tongue?' Yumiko, did the cat get your tongue?" He reached across the small table and roughly grabbed one of her wrists. "What did you say to me then?"

"I said I knew a place that had a nice view of the Aomori Bay Bridge."

"And then where did you take me?"

"I took you to a hotel."

"Oh," he said bitingly, "weren't you being original! And now since we fucked a half dozen times you want me to leave my wife." He released his grip and leaned back. As she sat before him subdued, her eyes cast down, the young man lifted his glass, took a sip, then a gulp, setting down the empty glass with a loud thud.

"I am going now," he said, standing, sliding first one arm, then the other, into his overcoat. "I won't be seeing you anymore." From his wallet, he withdrew a 10,000-yen note and let it drop to the table.

"I'm going to call," she said, reaching up to grab a sleeve as he passed by. "This time I will."

"It's over," he said, pausing to look down at her, shaking his head. "It never began."

"I will."

"I thought you said you aren't a bitch."

"I'm not!"

"All this talk is growing tiresome," he sighed, placing two hands on the table and leaning over her. "Why can't you just be reasonable? It's over."

"I…"

"You what?"

"We need to talk more. That's all."

"We need to talk more?" He pulled up his chair and sat down next to her. "All right then, do you want to talk here, or do you want to talk at the hotel?"

"What hotel?"

"The one we always go to. I'll fuck you, if that is what you want. But it will be the last time. I am not going to leave my wife. I love her. I don't love you."

"I may not feel like going."

"Good. Then stay here. I am going home."

"I didn't say I didn't want to."

"Mariko, what the fuck do you want from me?"

"My name is not Mariko!" she hissed, pulling back her head as if she had been slapped.

He had made a genuine error. Closing his eyes, he sighed again and rubbed his temple with the thumb of his right hand. "You see," he said, shaking his head, opening his eyes again to look into hers, "I really am ill. How could I call you Mariko? You and she have nothing in common whatsoever. She's not a bitch."

"Asshole!" she said, her voice loud enough for the quiet, hand-holding couple nearby to look up and glance at them. "Let's go!" She stood so quickly that her chair nearly toppled over.

Down on the busy street, the large, white flakes still fell heavily. Reaching out an arm, the young man hailed a cab, and quickly the two found themselves in back, the windows fogging. When the driver asked the destination, and when the young man remained silent, the woman said, "Ikebana-dori." The driver nodded and nudged the cab out into traffic. It was slow going on account of the snow-covered streets and the late-evening congestion.

"Is there a specific address, ma'am?"

"I'll tell you when to stop," she replied.

Ikebana-dori was an entertainment district famous for its snack bars and love hotels. The Endless Pink, the hotel she and he frequented, was located there.

Up in the room, the young man pulled open the heavy drapes and looked out at the bridge, a long line of cars moving slowly in each direction. "You know, the view *is* impressive. Even in this snow. Actually, the falling snow enhances the entire scene. It's lovely. I have to thank you for showing it to me."

"Would you like something to drink?"

"Amazing!" he said, turning to face her where she stood by the room's small refrigerator. "That's the first nice thing you said to me all evening."

When she didn't respond, he left the window and sat in an armchair near the bed. "Please. I'll have a beer."

She removed a can of Kirin from the refrigerator and handed it to him without looking at him. She turned away from him, took off her coat, sat on the edge of the bed with her back to him.

He opened the can and drank half of it; he was examining the outside of it as he spoke. "I thought you didn't want to come."

She opened her purse. She found a small pocket mirror and a tube of lipstick. As she looked in the mirror, she began reapplying the red to her lips. "You think it's funny," she said.

"I didn't mean to," he replied, laughing. "It just came out. Mariko… Yumiko… you have to admit, they're similar."

"They're not."

"Well, I apologize." He looked at the can some more, then brought it to his mouth and emptied it.

As she continued looking in the small oval of the mirror, she removed the beret and touched up her hair.

"So how do you look?"

"I look fine."

"Not beautiful?"

"I'm not an overly attractive woman."

"Really?" He laughed again. "What are your charms then?"

When she didn't respond, he said, "Well, how do I look? You haven't looked at me in a long time."

She didn't turn toward him.

"Do you want me to take off my clothes?"

She said nothing. She was still looking into her mirror and playing with her hair.

"Are you going to take off your clothes?"

"No."

"Then what are we doing here?"

After a moment, she said, "We came here to talk."

"I didn't know there was something to talk about," he replied with a chuckle. He stood and took off his overcoat and threw it on the chair behind him. Then he removed his suit jacket. He moved over to where she sat on the bed. He motioned for her to stand, and she complied. Then he moved behind her, placing his hands on the tops of her slender arms. "Come on," he said, whispering into an ear. "Off with the dress."

"Aren't we going to take a bath first?"

"Not tonight," he said, his mouth still at her ear.

"It's been a nice summer, hasn't it?"

"I don't understand what you are saying."

"You blossomed like a flower." He was speaking in English.

"You spend a year in America. You work there. You speak English. You think you're so smart."

"But all flowers fade." He began massaging her shoulders and neck.

"Shut up."

"Even the most beautiful ones fade."

"I'm not listening."

"The seasons change and the flower dies." He moved his hands down and cupped her apple-sized breasts through the fabric. "Take off your clothes." He whispered this last sentence in Japanese.

She reached her two hands behind her and unzipped the dress; with both hands, he pushed it off of her shoulders and let it fall to the floor. She turned to embrace him, but he held her in place. He walked them over a few feet to the left so they stood in front of a wide floor-to-ceiling mirror. As he stood behind her, he ran his hands over her slim body. Then he pulled down her stockings, the lavender bra and panties the only items left. She leaned back into him.

"Like a rabbit." Again, he spoke in English.

"I don't know what you're saying."

"Of course you don't."

He pulled down her panties, and she stepped out of them; he unclasped her bra, letting it fall to the floor. He massaged and kissed her back and shoulders and neck and breasts before he led her over to the bed, positioning her so she lay on her back in the middle, her head resting on a large pillow. He found her purse, which she had left at the foot of the bed. With his shoes still on, he crawled onto the bed and straddled her waist. He shook out the contents of the purse next to her. He brushed through the various items until he found the lipstick. He took off the cap and threw it on the floor. He twisted it so the red tip stuck out. As he smiled down at her, she returned the smile. He grabbed her right breast. Over the small, erect nipple and on the white that encircled it, he wrote the letter "B." He followed it with an "i." Their eyes met. She smiled again. On the space between her breasts, just above her fast-beating heart, he drew a "t." Then he grabbed her left breast and followed the "B-i-t" with a "c" and an "h." When he was finished with his artwork, he sailed the lipstick across the room. Looking down at the word on her chest, she asked, "What does it mean?"

"Quiet." He slid off her and slowly brought her right hand down between her legs.

"I want you to masturbate," he explained, moving her slender fingers for her until she did it on her own. He bent down and whispered in her ear, "Yumiko, don't stop." He got off the bed and stood looking down at her and her half-closed eyes, her face beginning to twist in pleasure.

"I'm going to go outside and come back in again. Pretend you don't know me. I'm just some guy who came to the wrong room. I'm an overworked, exhausted stockbroker. It's been a long day. I want to sleep. I need to sleep. But instead, I find you, the most enchanting woman in the world." The woman's smile grew; her dark eyes twinkled.

"Are you wet?"

"Yes."

"Does it feel good?"

Breathing faster, she closed her eyes and nodded.

"I didn't mean to be rude to you earlier. Please forgive me."

"I forgive you."

"Do you want me inside you?"

"Yes. Yes, I do."

"Tell me that is what you want."

"I want you inside me."

"Don't stop."

He glanced around the room; he saw what he wanted. He went over to the bedside lamp and switched off the light. In the dim half-darkness, the only light coming through the window, he gathered the few items and walked to the door. Before he opened it, he called to her, "Yumiko, please don't stop. Do it for me." Outside, he let the door close quietly; then he took the elevator down to the street and caught a cab to his apartment.

When she heard the sound of the key in the lock, the young man's wife bounced up from the living room sofa and darted to the entryway to greet him. "You're late, as usual," she teased as she helped him remove his overcoat and suit jacket. She folded them neatly over her arm. When he slipped off his shoes, she gathered them and placed them in their space on the shoe rack by the door.

"Things took a little longer than expected."

"What things? You mean drinking and talking with bar girls?"

"Yes, that's what I mean."

"Was Father there?"

"Not this week."

"Your dinner will be ready in a minute." After she placed his items on hangers in the small closet, she slid on her stockinged feet into the couple's kitchen / dining room space. She pulled open the refrigerator door and removed various containers. As he passed by, he saw the small table was already set for one—a small plate, a pair of chopsticks, an empty beer glass.

In the living room—on the TV a police drama—he sat on the sofa and again rubbed his temple. His wife brought him a warm *oshibori*; she had heated the small, damp towel in the microwave.

"I'm not hungry," he reported, but she was already back in the kitchen.

He called out to her, "I said I'm not hungry."

She didn't respond.

When he finished wiping his face and neck with the towel, he glanced over his shoulder and watched as his wife busily set out the various dishes—a small plate with a piece of cold mackerel, a bowl of colorful *tsukemono*, another teeming with *edamame*. He noticed that she had gained some weight since they married, and he smiled. With the remote, he thumbed off the TV, stood, made his way to her. With her back to him, she was spooning some rice from the cooker that sat on the counter. He approached her, and from behind, he slid his hands around her slim waist and held her.

"What are you doing?" she asked, one hand holding the half-full bowl, the other the plastic rice spoon. "Your rice is going to get cold."

"You know what this is?" he asked, his hands caressing her abdomen. "Do you know what they call this in English?"

"You've had too much to drink. And you need a bath." She squirmed to free herself, but he held her. He pulled up her blouse and slid his hands under the fabric so they touched the bare skin of her abdomen.

"They call this a pot belly," he told her, using English. He repeated the words and then translated them into Japanese. "You're going to have to start going to the gym with me."

"I don't think so."

He buried his face into her thick hair and kissed the back of her neck. "Why not?"

"This pot belly is not going away. At least not for a while."

"It's the kind that's going to grow, huh?"

"Yes."

"I see."

The phone rang. He kissed the back of her neck again and then released her. The phone rang a second and then a third time. "That's going to be for you," he said.

"How do you know?"

"Just answer it. Then we'll talk."

She set down the bowl of rice and the spoon and dashed into the living room. She picked up the handset. "*Moshi moshi*," she said. "*Hai, so desu*," he heard her say. Slowly, the young man entered the living room. He leaned back into the sofa and waited.

With her back to him, she stood just a few feet from him, listening intently. Then she whirled around and faced him. In her left hand she held the body of the phone; in her right she gripped the handset. A short cord, the cable curled, stretched between the two pieces of plastic. After a half minute, his wife dropped her right hand to her waist. From the handset, the young man could hear the animated voice of the woman he had abandoned in the hotel room.

"You had better hang up."

His wife didn't move. The woman on the phone said more, and then silence, as if she were waiting for an answer, prevailed.

"Why don't you hang up now?"

Before him, his wife stood stunned. She looked down at the body of the phone and then at the handset as if she had just realized she was holding them. She looked back at him and squinted.

The blow surprised him completely. The body of the phone crashed down on his forehead with a bang. There was one more strike before he reached up his hands to cover his face and head.

At first, she used only the body. Then she used both the body and the handset. However, one was too heavy and awkward to hold, the other too light. Still, she swung at him with both, first one, the other. Somehow, the two separated. The body banged to the floor, but she gripped the handset firmly in her right hand. She tired momentarily, but every time her husband brought down his hands, she struck more blows. Eventually, she ran out of energy. Collapsing to the floor in front of him, she covered her face and began sobbing, her body shaking uncontrollably.

The young man brought down his hands from his face and examined them. As he rotated them, he saw that a couple knuckles were badly bruised and bloodied; he touched the bridge of his nose and felt that it too was bleeding. No longer caring, he wiped it on the sleeve of his white dress shirt. He glanced at his watch, an expensive gift that she had given him on his birthday, and saw a spider web of cracks on the glass. He leaned forward slowly, his head just a foot from hers. "She's the bitch," he said, speaking in English. "I'm the bastard, and you're the—"

"Goddamn you!" she yelled, jumping to her feet. "Why do you speak in English? You know I don't understand." Still gripping the handset, now cordless, in her right hand, she towered over him.

"I'm sorry."

"No, you're not!" She whacked him again with the handset. When he didn't lift his hands to cover himself, she struck him again.

"Aren't you going to protect yourself?"

"No."

This response angered her, and with renewed energy she began again, the *bang! bang! bang!* of the handset on his battered face. "Fucker!" she screamed, panting. Her intensity was brief yet furious. When she was spent this second time, she stood over her husband and stared at him with intense hatred.

He looked up at her; blood leaked from his nose and from a cut just above his left eyebrow.

"Are you finished?"

"No," she replied, her eyes aflame, her breathing fast.

"I'm waiting."

"What are you waiting for?"

"I'm waiting for you to finish."

"Finish what?"

"Finish beating me."

"I'm not beating you."

"What are you doing?"

"I'm standing."

"Why are you holding the phone?"

"I don't know."

"Why don't you give it to me?" As he reached out, she passed him the handset.

"Look," he reported, pointing to the handset being cordless. "Someone broke the phone. It looks like I'll have to buy a new one tomorrow. It's a good thing I am getting my bonus this month." As he examined the handset with mock concern, she knocked it to the floor. Quickly, he reached up and grabbed her wrists. She resisted, doing her best to release his grip, trying to strike him with her fists, but he was much stronger. He twisted and pulled her so she sat on his lap. "Stop it," he said when she continued to struggle. He hugged her and held her arms pinned against her small breasts. "I said stop it," he whispered. Her struggle slowly ebbed. She began to sob again. "It's over," he said, burying his face into the back of her head. "I did something incredibly stupid. Mariko, you have to believe me. Please listen. I can't tell you how sorry I am."

In a T-shirt and pajama bottoms, the young man lay on his back with a cold, wet towel covering his face. From where he rested on their bed, he could hear his wife in the bathroom, the faucet running lightly as she brushed her teeth. Then she used the toilet. She entered the bedroom and lay next to him. She had left the hallway light on. He thought about getting up to turn it off, but he felt as if he couldn't move. They lay silent side by side for a very long time.

"Are you going to see her anymore?"

"Of course not," he replied, sighing heavily. "I told you. I saw her just a handful of times. I ended it."

"But you were with her tonight. She said so."

"Yes, but nothing happened. I may have lied to you before, but I am not lying now. It's over."

"I don't believe you."

"Then don't."

"I'm trying to hate you."

"Then do. I deserve it."

His face and hands and head ached terribly; he didn't feel like talking anymore. After he lifted the small towel and looked to see how much blood was on it, he repositioned it. He tried to bring on sleep, but after a minute, she propped herself up on an elbow, pulled off the towel, looked at him, her face cold, indifferent.

"Did you have sex with her tonight?"

"Of course not."

"How do I know?"

"I stole her clothes."

"You mean she was naked?"

"I made her take off her clothes."

"What did you do with them?"

"I threw them into the bay. I had the taxi stop on the Bay Bridge. The driver thought I was insane. At first, he wouldn't stop. I had to pay him an extra 10,000 yen." He turned his head and looked into his wife's eyes. "I am insane. You're insane too."

From the faint glow of the hallway light, he saw the anger, the still-questioning eyes.

"Where were you?"

"At a hotel."

"And you took off her clothes?"

"No. I told her to take off her clothes."

"And she did?"

"Yes."

"Then you took them and walked out the door, just like that?"

"More or less," he replied, nodding, "that's what happened."

For a minute, she looked at him incredulously; she seemed to be pondering the incredible nature of the story.

Eventually, she said, her voice softening, "You look awful."

"I feel awful."

"I hit you pretty hard, didn't I?"

"Yes, you did. But I deserved it. And well, you always hit me hard."

"Liar! I never hit you before in my life!"

"You hit me when we make love. That is, when you are on top of me." She considered him for another minute before lying down again, two sets of eyes focused on the ceiling.

"Can I have the towel back?"

"No."

"Can we sleep now?"

"No."

"I'm dead tired, Mariko-chan."

"I'm thinking."

"Okay," he said, his heavy eyelids closing. "You think about whatever you're thinking about, and I'm going to think about sleep."

"Do I really hit you when we make love?"

"Sort of."

"Does it hurt?"

"Of course not."

"Did it feel good when I hit you tonight?"

"In a way."

"But it hurts now."

"Yes. It hurts a lot."

"I'm sorry."

"Me too."

"But it was your fault."

"I know."

"Then don't do such awful things!" she shouted, leaning on her side again to look at him. "And don't speak English anymore! And don't call me Mary!" She blurted out these final sentences and quickly rolled over to her other side, her back now to her husband.

The young man had nearly fallen asleep, but then he remembered what his wife had told him. "When is the baby due?" he asked.

"I'm sleeping," she replied, sounding wide awake.

Slowly, painfully, the young man hoisted himself up. His feet found the floor, and he left the room. He made it as far as the bathroom, where, with cupped hands, he drank greedily from the faucet. Then he pissed, the sound loud as the urine splashed in the bowl. As he returned to the bedroom, he switched off the hallway light. Under the comforter, his wife remained in the same position, the length and contours of her body a small mountain range. With a groan, he lay on his back next to her.

After his eyes adjusted to the darkness, he rolled over on his side, reached out a tentative hand, touched her forearm.

"Don't touch me," she snapped, slapping away the hand and sliding a few inches farther away.

"How long are you going to be angry?"

"I told you. I'm sleeping. Leave me alone."

"I was just wondering."

He tried one more approach. "What's your father going to say when he sees me next week?"

She remained silent.

"Mariko," he sighed, "please forgive me. What I did was stupid and incredibly selfish, but I am not going to do it again."

Only a foot separated the newlyweds, but to the young man, the space felt like a wide valley. A minute later, in half sleep, his brain not fully functioning, he sensed his wife moving, then standing. What was she doing? Was she going to strike him again? A second later, he had his answer: she yanked off the thick duvet and left the room with it. As he lay on his side of the bed, his body now uncovered, he immediately felt the cold.

2 Rick's Café Americain

"How many times do I have to tell you? You don't have to sleep with them. You can if you want. Some are more than willing. But that's not your job. Your job is to make them happy. Flirt with them. Flatter them. Make them feel special. Above all, take their fuckin' money!"

"I don't know," the young man replied, looking away.

"What don't you know? You're the one who works at a fuckin' record store for minimum wage. A Waseda student! Minimum wage! I can't believe it! What's wrong with you?"

"I do it for the music."

"Fuck the music. You need some money. Come for just one night. Come see what happens. I guarantee, a smart, good-looking guy like you will take home a bundle. If you don't like it, you can bail."

The young man had a general idea of what went on in such places, and he didn't like it. But he went that Friday. Even though he hadn't been officially hired, and even though he did little—sat at a couple of booths, spoke when spoken to, laughed when others laughed—the manager gave him 20,000 yen. At the record store, he was making 430 yen per hour. The next week, he quit Recofan and began hosting at Rick's Café Americain.

"Okay. They always come in a group. There'll be three or four or five or more. If you're at the door, it's your job to show them to a booth. Then, get them some drinks. Push the bottles, not the cocktails. Get the table to buy a bottle or two if you can. Push the champagne especially. We get the bubbly from some *yakuza* guys down in Yokohama. They relabel the garbage. I shouldn't tell you this, but we get each bottle for 1,000 yen. We sell it for 8,888. That's our own special number. Most of these girls don't know much. About liquor. About anything. They just want a good time, and we're here to give it to them.

"We have food, too, but there's no need to push it. It's mostly garbage. But if they want some, by all means, order some. And eat it with them. Sometimes there is a birthday party or some other special celebration, and we have cakes for that. If we don't have one, we'll get one. We can do just about anything."

The manager opened and then passed the young man the large, leather-bound, fold-open menu. On one side were drinks, on the other side food items. There were no prices.

"Now, I don't have to tell you that your primary job is to drink with them. That's the very hard part, not getting drunk. If you get drunk and do anything stupid, I'll bounce you myself.

"Usually, they're all a little juiced before they arrive, but, as I said before, keep the spirits flowing. Keep their glasses topped off. At this point, you know each lady's name. Use it. Use it often. Never forget a name. Moreover, never let the conversation lag. Talk about recent films or music or the temples in Kyoto. Anything. If they want to talk about Honolulu, tell them you lived a block from Waikiki. Above all, ask a lot of questions. They want your attention. Give it to them. They want to feel special. Make eye contact. Touch their legs and arms. Don't go too far, but a little touching is just what the doctor ordered. Believe me, they'll be touching you. If they all had considerate boyfriends, we'd be out of our jobs.

"We do have special rooms," the man continued, reaching out an arm and pointing over his shoulder. "We call them cabanas. There are five of them. They cost a little more than the booths. They have karaoke machines and mirrors and other knick-knacks, if you know what I mean. The doors have locks. If someone, or if the entire party, wants you to join them in a cabana, that's your prerogative. And whatever you do in one is up to you. Just remember not to get lost in one. When things get busy, you'll need to help the others, and they will help you in turn. We all work as a team. You understand?"

The young man nodded.

"Usually, there will be two of you working a booth, but on busy nights, you may be on your own. And when the repeat customers come, the ones who request you, you'll be a porn star on an all-day shoot. We have cocaine if you need it."

The man paused, lifted his cola, took a sip.

"Okay. The important stuff: payment. Once you get the group settled in a booth and drinks ordered, you need to get a credit card. After a minute or two, you'll sense who the leader is. Try to get one from her. She may ignore you or pass you off to another, but we need a card.

"Don't do anything with it. Don't set it on the table like it's someone's business card. Just pocket it discreetly and make a toast or something, anything to distract them. But I'll need to see it at some time, the sooner the better, to record the name and number. I'll get it back to you somehow, and you get it back to whoever gave it to you.

"At the end of the evening, when they tell you they want to go, first and foremost, talk them into staying. One more drink. One more bottle. If you see one of them yawning, give her your full attention. And if one of us comes and tells you that one of your booths wants to skedaddle, get over there. Do anything to get them to stay.

"If they are first-timers, and if they insist on leaving, you present them their bill, which you get from me. Do it very discreetly. Again, focus on whoever appears to be the leader. Give it to her.

"Now say it's 39,000. What you do is this. When you bring it, say, 'Hey, listen.' A soft touch on the arm or thigh goes a long way at this point. You'll learn. Say, 'This is much more than I thought it would be. I can talk to the manager. Let me get this down a bit.' Again, you are doing this only for the first-timers, but pretend to be their dearest friend and then disappear for five minutes. Come find me. Let me know what you think is a reasonable number, one that you can get them to pay in cash. I'll write you a new bill. When you return to them, say, 'I took care of it. Well, most of it.' Then give them the new bill. Make sure they have seen the old number and this new number. Get them to pay this new bill in cash. You can keep it. That money is yours.

"If you get them to pay in cash and they ask about their credit card, tell them there will be no charge. Just get them to pay half of what they owe, or as much as you can, in cash, and then once they're out the door, we bill the card for the full amount. If someone raises a stink later, I can refund the full amount, if necessary.

"Another option—the best option—for the first-timers is for them to open an account. It can be a group account or an individual account. Most of our repeat clientele have one. Tell them about the 20% discount we offer if they do that. But don't push too hard. It's best not to talk about money at all.

"Any questions?"

"Those with an account. How do they pay?"

"At the door, I'll give you a little signal if they are repeat customers. Soon you too will know who's who. Don't even bring up paying with them. That's my job."

The manager leaned back and lit a cigarette; he seemed to enjoy talking about the specifics. "Some of these ladies are very wealthy," he said, inhaling deeply, letting the nicotine work its magic. "Paying a million or two is absolutely nothing," he said, exhaling. "Some of them have very rich husbands. They, the husbands, that is, can be a problem. Or their fathers. So we don't charge them too much. I can drop a zero, and I have, just as fast as I have added one. It's the single, naive ones we're after. The prettier they are, the better. And if they have a company job, we got them. If they can't pay money, they can pay in other ways," he said, chuckling. "You watch any porn?"

"No."

"Don't lie. Well, let's just say that quite a few industry newcomers got their start because they owed someone money."

Within a month, the young man was one of the most sought-after hosts, pulling in 400,000 – 500,000 in a month, double what his mother was making standing at the supermarket cash register all day on her aching feet. And he could, more or less, drink and eat as much as he liked. When they closed at dawn, the manager opened the kitchen and the beer taps. Often, the young man stumbled out into the Kabukicho streets at six or seven completely fucked, a small collection of recently-acquired 10,000-notes in his wallet. As he rode the train back to his dormitory, the sun was rising, and briefcase-carrying salarymen and school children in their sailor uniforms were starting their long, tedious days.

Further, he often received expensive watches and neckties and money on the side, for he did sleep with a few select customers. While the cash he received was never explicitly for "services rendered," it was clear that the spending money and presents and over-night trips to *ryokan* in Hakone would end if he wanted out of the relationship. And it did. In this regard, he had to be tactful. The older ones often got too attached. That—their clinging jealousy— was a problem. Once, one had wanted to give him a Porsche. So when he ended a relationship with one of his repeat customers, and if she stopped coming to Rick's, the manager wanted to know why. But there was never any shortage of ladies at Rick's. And there was always another one, or usually, several at a time, whom the young man kept on the sly. Each one believed that she was the special one, and of course, she thought this because he treated her like the special one.

⧗ ⧗ ⧗

Most of his fellow hosts ran through their money like it was water that they needed to consume, but the young man soon had over 3,000,000 yen in a brokerage account, and he put his studies at Waseda to good use. During the mornings and afternoons—if he wasn't out with one of his customers playing tennis, having lunch, visiting the Bunkamura—he was learning how to make money in the stock market. He could sleep through most of his classes, and he often did. But he was attentive in his economics courses, sitting up front, taking meticulous notes, asking specific questions about company balance sheets and the differences between common and preferred stocks. He focused a great deal on stock valuations, reading just about any magazine or newspaper article or book on the subject that he could find. Further, he signed up for intensive one-on-one English classes, soon learning that the most lucrative markets were overseas. When he felt he wasn't progressing fast enough, he found an American girlfriend; and even though she was six years older and chubby and constantly complained about her life in Japan, and even though he saw her only once a week at tops and she wouldn't go down on him and she always made him wear a condom, he made her feel that she too was the very special one.

And there was money to be made, certainly. The Japanese economy was a forest fire burning at its peak. Everybody, it seemed, had loads of money. Most couldn't spend it fast enough.

"You won't believe this! You know chubby Watanabe-san, right? She owes over 2,000,000. She's in here every Thursday. Sometimes Friday too. Her old man is loaded. But, of course, he doesn't know. If he did," Satoshi laughed, "he'd probably have her locked up.

"Well, dig this. She's giving head in Cabana 5! We told her we'd knock off 100,000 for each guy she sucks off. But here's the kicker.

35

She has to swallow. If she doesn't swallow, it doesn't count." Satoshi laughed some more and cuffed the young man on the shoulder.

"Can you believe it? I think she's already taken down six or seven loads. Shinji has gone twice. Even Duan, the Cambodian cook, has gotten one! You should have seen his smile when he got back to the kitchen. Pure Buddhist nirvana!" Satoshi began to push the young man down the hallway to the infamous Cabana 5. "Go," he insisted. "Get yours!"

"I wish I could," he replied, shaking his head and pivoting to return to the main room. "But I'm running a marathon. I got three booths tonight."

"What the fuck? That's nothing. I do three or four booths every Friday."

"Yeah, but two are regulars. I've got my hands full."

"And that stupid bitch Watanabe has her stomach full!" Satoshi struggled to get the words out he was laughing so much.

Nakamura was the most challenging customer. Incredibly, the first time she came, she came by herself on a Tuesday. They all wondered, who would come to such a place alone? On a Tuesday, no less? To complicate matters, she was completely sober and ordered a gin tonic. That first night, the young man and Satoshi guided her to booth number three and sat with her.

"I always wondered what this place was like," she said, glancing around. "I've walked by a dozen times. Where's Sam?"

"Sam?" Satoshi asked. "Who's Sam?"

"You haven't seen the film?"

"What film?"

"Nakamura-sama," the young man asked, ignoring his colleague, "do you think Rick did the right thing when he put Elsa on the plane?"

"My young man," she responded, the question garnering her full attention, "that's the ending that makes the film so wonderful.

Now if there were some gin in this drink, we could talk more about it.

"You," she said, turning to Satoshi, "go get me a new drink, and make sure there is some gin in it this time."

"I am very sorry, Nakamura-sama," the young man said after his colleague left. "We have a new bartender, and he may have made a mistake. I'll speak with him later."

"Don't try to con me. I know how these places work. Now," she said, placing a hand on his thigh, "get a little closer and let's talk about something interesting. After all, I have all the time in the world."

She was that kind of customer. She could have been forty, but she was probably fifty, even fifty-five. She wore too much makeup, and her polka-dot dresses were from the previous decade. Much to the young man's dismay, she always requested him. And she always complained about the watered-down drinks and haggled openly— and loudly—over her bills. She could never leave soon enough; they were never sorry to see her go.

Wearing party hats, oversized party glasses in various dayglo colors, tight dresses, high heels—twirling the noise makers they had brought with them—the five young ladies were guided to booth number four, which one had reserved months previously. Passing on the champagne, they ordered whisky. Two bottles. They vowed to drink both. Shouting over each other, obviously already tipsy, they promised that they weren't going home until the sun rose.

Quickly, a tray with glasses, two ice buckets, two bottles of water, two bottles of Johnnie Walker materialized. But, it seems, the items hadn't come fast enough. Standing impatiently while the others took their places in the semicircle booth, one unscrewed the cap to one of the bottles and took a generous swig. "What the fuck is this?" she asked—her voice loud and full of contempt—as she wiped her mouth with the back of her hand. "Do you know who we are? This isn't Johnnie Walker!" To make her point, she made a big show of pouring out the entire bottle into one of the ice buckets.

"Manager!" she yelled, one bare arm in the air. "Take this rubbish back!"

"Fuck you all!" another shouted, standing to support her inspiring friend, and the chant was started. "Fuck you all! Fuck you all!" they all yelled, beating the table and laughing uproariously.

Though the young man was occupied with guests in booth number one, he saw the commotion and wasn't surprised when the manager rushed over and touched his shoulder, the signal to go and calm the approaching typhoon. He politely excused himself from the six middle-aged ladies—"Don't go! Don't go!" they yelled, reaching out hands to pull him back—zigzagged his way through the crowd, and stood next to the woman. A quick glance told him she was an experienced drinker—perhaps experienced in other ways too—and obviously the group's leader. With her, he felt, he had to be careful.

"What do you want?" she asked, squinting her eyes as she considered him.

"Good evening, ladies," he said, smiling and bowing slightly.

"Who sent you?" another asked.

"Nobody. You ladies just arrived. You were by yourselves. I thought you would want some company."

"Ah, he's a fucker," the leader said to her friends. "He can't be trusted. Where is the whisky?"

"It's on its way," the young man replied. "We didn't know you wanted the premium. I apologize. I can't tell you how sorry I am. For our best customers, we offer only the best."

She wagged her index finger in front of his face. "Don't fuck with me," she sneered.

When the new bottles arrived, the young man, still standing, quickly—and adeptly—poured five glasses, added water and ice, gave each a twirl with a metal stir stick. With both hands, he presented each glass to each young lady individually. "Thank you very much for coming to Rick's," he said when he had finished. "It's an honor to celebrate with you on this special occasion. It's not only the end of a year, but it's the end of a decade."

"I didn't tell you to put ice in mine," one whined, setting down her glass. "I don't want ice."

The young man raised his hand, and one of the servers quickly brought a new glass. When he had finished pouring out this new drink and presented it, the leader looked down at her friends. Swaying slightly, she belched loudly, then laughed at herself. "What should we drink to?" she asked.

"To the new year," one shouted and raised her glass.

"It's too early, dimwit," the leader said disdainfully. "It's not even eleven."

"To erections!" another offered, raising her glass.

"To erections!" they all shouted. Those sitting stood, they clinked their glasses, and they began guzzling. Incredibly, each one emptied her glass, much of the golden liquid spilling out of the corners or their mouths or down their chins. One banged her tall glass a little too hard on the table, and the side of it cracked.

"God, I love a good stiffy," the leader shouted over the noise, for Rick's Café Americain had perhaps reached its apex. Every booth was packed, and as the midnight hour approached, chaos ruled. Who could say what was going on in the back cabanas?

"But guys these days, all they want to do is come on your tits. What the fuck is that?"

"Or on your face. I was sucking a guy last week who…"

The conversation raced on like this. Sitting at one end of the half-circle booth, the young man poured glasses and served them. He hardly had a chance to say anything. He had never heard beautiful ladies—any ladies, for that matter—express themselves so frankly and so openly. Finally, when there was a brief lull, he asked the leader, "May I drink with you ladies?"

"No, you may not," she replied curtly, bringing her finger into play again.

"Ah, let the idiot have one," another countered. "He looks thirsty."

"Okay," she replied with a hiccup. "But just one."

"I'll pour it for you," offered the one sitting next to him. She leaned over the table so her cleavage was right in front of him. As she began pouring the whisky, she looked him in the eyes. "Like what you see? Have a good look. That's all you're going to get." She continued pouring the whisky until it ran over the glass. "Drink that, asshole," she said, sitting back down and offering him a self-satisfied smirk.

As their boisterous drinking party carried on, the young man tried his best to enter the conversation, but he was rebuffed at every opportunity. His best lines and inquiries fell flat, or they were seen for what they were, just patronizing come-on lines.

When the leader stood and staggered off to the ladies' room, he took advantage of the change in seating, sliding over to the young lady who sat hunched over, her shoulders sagging, in the middle of the booth. She was the quiet one, a follower. Though she appeared to be the same age as the others, she was not like them. He could see that. She lacked the swagger and experience that her more confident friends possessed. She came from money, yes. Those were genuine Mikimoto pearls around her neck. He knew that. But they all had money.

"And what is your name?" he asked, leaning in so he could better hear her.

"Go away," she slurred, looking straight ahead, her eyes not focusing. "I don't want to talk to you." With two unsteady hands, she held her half-full glass in her lap. When he saw that it was about to tip, he reached out a hand, took it from her, and set it on the table. Like one in a trance, she didn't seem to notice.

"Don't mind her," one of her friends shouted, laughing. "She's drunk."

"I am not drunk," the young lady claimed, barely getting the words out before slumping over, the side of her head bouncing on the table edge before finding rest on her friend's lap. This friend, still laughing, pushed her away, and the pretty young lady slid, like water over the edge of a table, from the leather of the booth to the floor. "It's her first time drinking," her friend yelled to the young man, sliding closer to him, motioning for him to refresh her drink. "I should say, it's her first time getting drunk. But she'll be okay. Let her sleep."

As the young lady lay on the floor in her sleeveless satin dress, the party raged on around her. When she vomited twenty minutes later, no one noticed. A minute before midnight, two of the ladies climbed onto the table and were dancing, the table wobbling precariously, the thumping music loud and obnoxious. And then came the *five! four! three! two! ONE!* "Happy new year!" the bacchanalians all shouted, setting off the poppers they had brought with them, the confetti flying everywhere. One sailed one of her heels across the room, and another threatened to remove her dress. "Should I? Should I?" "Do it! Do it!" her friends answered, starting another chant, at this point all of the voices hoarse from the hours of shouting. All the while, the young lady under the table lay with the right side of her head and face covered in vomit. At least the vomit was hers.

When a kind of exhaustion set in, they all sat again, the makeup on their sweaty faces smeared, their hair disheveled, most of the party hats and party glasses discarded. One of the ladies gripped the young man's arm, her head resting on his shoulder. "Lick my pussy," she whispered, lifting her head to tongue his ear. As he placed his hand high on her black-stockinged thigh, he glanced under the table. What he saw—the young lady on the floor, her mouth open, the vomit—bothered him, and he wondered why he had forgotten about her and why her friends hadn't done anything to help her.

"Lick my pussy," she purred again.

"Listen," he replied, freeing his arm and pushing the woman away gently. "I am going to take your friend to the bathroom."

"What did you say?"

"Your friend," he said, leaning into her ear and pointing. "On the floor. Look."

"What about her? She's a stuck-up bitch."

"I am going to take her to the bathroom."

"Let's take her picture first!"

While this friend asked the others for a camera, the young man leaned over, his head under the table, and tried to rouse the young lady. She was a little tall, but she had a slim body, so it was easy for him to get two hands on her waist and to pull her out from under the table. A small handbag with a long strap hung over her neck. He slipped one of her thin arms under the strap as he got her to her feet. The friend had found the camera and pointed it at them, but before she could take the picture, the young man knocked it to the floor. He then threw the young lady's arm over his shoulder and half-carried, half-dragged her through the crowded club and down the dark hallway past the cabanas to the small men's room. Inside, one of the other hosts, a guy named Kenji—disliked and distrusted by most of the others—was fucking a young woman from behind in front of one of the two sinks. Kenji, his pants at his ankles, had her dress up over her waist, and he smiled when he saw his colleague, thinking perhaps that he had come to do the same. The woman, more than likely too drunk to resist, had her little hands balled into fists on the counter. She was moaning, asking him to stop, but Kenji didn't stop. There was only one stall, the door thrown open, and a lady, not a man, her knees on the floor, was inside throwing up.

The young man slumped the young lady over the open sink, and while he gripped the back of her dress and held her and her handbag in place, he reached over his other hand and grabbed some paper towels from the dispenser. Then he turned on the tap by her head. He massaged a little water into her hair and began wiping out the vomit. He cleaned her face and neck too. Meanwhile, Kenji, watching himself in the wide mirror, seemingly quite happy with his performance, banged away.

Gently, the young man, his arm now around the woman's waist, did the best he could. Was it the cold water? Was it the loud, hard *slap! slap! slap!* of one naked body on another? Whatever it was, the young lady started to come to, and when she saw and heard what was happening only a few feet away, she groaned, terror filling her barely-opened eyes.

"No, no, no," he said, trying to reassure her. "I'm not going to hurt you."

It's doubtful the young lady comprehended or even heard what the young man had said. She tried to strike him, but in doing so, she fell to the bathroom floor, bruising both knees and an elbow. From behind, the young man lifted her and half-carried, half-walked her out into the hallway, some vomit and confetti still remaining in her matted hair. He stood her up and placed his hands around her neck to hold her up. He could have easily strangled her, but instead he placed his mouth next to her right ear. "Listen," he said, speaking slowly, "you need to leave! You have to get out of here!"

Her head dangled and she drooled saliva from one corner of her mouth, but she nodded. With one bare hand, he wiped her face, then wiped that hand on the side of his white dress shirt. He leaned into her ear again. "Home!" he said, the word nearly a shout. "I'm going to get you home!"

With a strong arm gripping her waist, he rushed her out the club's front door, out to the elevator, down to the street below. While he stood at the edge of the narrow, one-way street—struggling to hold her up with one arm, struggling with his free hand to open her handbag and get the hand inside—he kept glancing down the street, on the lookout for an empty cab. Mumbling something unintelligible, she threw both of her long, slender arms around his neck, her head slumped on his shoulder. "You're going to be okay," he reassured her, holding her up as she leaned on him. "Don't worry.

You'll be home soon. I promise." At last, he found her wallet and, inside, her driver's license. He looked at the name, her birthdate, then the address. Nishi Azabu. Sure enough.

Three cabs, then another, had already passed, but each had passengers. Miraculously, a fourth appeared, and when the young man saw the red light that declared it was vacant, he danced her out into the middle of the narrow street, forcing the cab to stop. Through the windshield, he made eye contact with the driver. When the back door opened, he brought her over and laid her gently onto the seat. He tried to get her to sit up, but she promptly fell over, her head hitting the opposite door with a thud. He noticed that she wore only one small heel, but at this point, what could he do? He lifted her legs onto the seat and pushed the door closed.

Opening the front passenger door, he turned his attention to the driver. "Old man," he began, leaning his head inside and looking the man in his eyes, "I have a golden memory. I have your name and your cab number," he said, pointing to the man's photo and permit on the dash. "The young lady taking a rest in your cab is a very important lady. You got that? If anything happens to her, I will have your balls hammered. I know the right fellows. Believe me. I know."

When the young man saw that the driver understood, he passed over her license. "You take her to this address. If you're not there in twenty minutes, I will have the right fellows and their hammers and you down in an alley in Hamamatsucho. And if you touch her in any way, even cop a squeeze, I will know. You understand?"

"I understand, sir," the old man said and bowed his head.

"Do you?"

"I do," he replied, looking frightened.

"Good." The young man reached into his right front pocket and pulled out his roll of money. "Here. Take this," he said, counting out five 10,000-yen notes, more than ten times what the fare would be. "Mind what I told you. Get her home safely." Before shutting the door, he glanced one more time at the pretty young lady who lay in the backseat, more drool oozing from her open mouth, a small trickle of blood coming from a knee. With an angry-sounding "Happy new year" to the driver, he shut the door. The cab moved forward. He watched it until it slowed and turned right.

The young man looked down at his shirt, on it a large stain from her vomit. It was on his tie too and had soaked through to his undershirt. Instead of going back up to the club, he started walking. Drunk revelers around him—small groups of three or four—were laughing and calling out and stumbling. Others slept on the sidewalks, their heads lying on the cold concrete. As he walked, he had to avoid broken glass and piles of stepped-in vomit. Even though he too had consumed more than he usually did, his experience with the young lady—the entire evening's sordid escapades—had sobered him. Adrenaline coursed through his body.

He didn't have a jacket. It hung in the backroom at Rick's Café Americain. Soon, he was shivering. He turned a corner and stumbled upon a crowded Family Mart—the nervous staff cowering behind the counter, fearful of the boisterous customers—and bought two cans of hot milk tea. Since the subways had stopped running, he would have to take a cab back to his dormitory. Finding a free one for the young lady was a stroke of luck; finding another for him would be nearly impossible.

The next afternoon, after he woke just after three, the young man showered and dressed. The dormitory—the entire campus— was eerily quiet, most of his fellow students having gone back to their hometowns for the winter break. He knew the student union would be closed, but he was ravenous. He wanted something warm, a steaming bowl of *ramen*, perhaps. But if he wanted more than convenience-store food, he would have to find a place. He would have to walk.

As he sauntered out the campus gate and down the wide sidewalk, a large, black Toyota Grande Mark II with tinted windows pulled up alongside him. The driver's window dropped. "Makoto Tanaka," the rough-looking fellow in the seat said, placing his elbow on the door, "we need to talk."

The young man stopped. He looked at the face for a long time. He looked at the car. He thought about running. Was the campus security guard at his post? He couldn't recall seeing him.

"I can sense what you are thinking," the man said. "It wouldn't be wise. You can jump in the back seat and have a cordial chat with us. Or we can chase you down. I don't feel like running." The young man held back for a moment, but then he pulled open the back door and sat down on the leather seat.

The driver put the car in park and turned so he could look into the young man's eyes. "You had an eventful New Year's Eve, didn't you?"

When he said nothing, the man continued, "I can't tell you everything. We are, in a sense, her minders. Her father pays us to follow her. She knows about us, and last night she gave us the slip. You, Makoto Tanaka, saved us. And you saved her well-established family from a lot of embarrassment.

"Now, the old man doesn't know that we lost her for a few hours, but he knows she was in your club. Let's just say he wasn't pleased to know where she had been. And when she turned up in the condition she was in last night, the sight nearly gave him a heart attack. She is, after all, his only child."

The driver pulled out a cigarette from a pack that sat on the dash. He lit it with a lighter that he fished out of his jacket pocket. He took a long drag.

"I was there," he said, exhaling, "when the cabby brought her. A young guy. With glasses. I talked to him for a very long time. You understand? A very long time. You, Makoto Tanaka," he said, gesturing with the lit cigarette, "were very generous."

He took another long suck on the cigarette. When he exhaled, he blew the smoke out his open window. "I have to ask you some questions," he said, looking long and hard at the young man. "Did you or anyone touch her?"

"No."

"You understand what I mean?"

"I do."

"Are you certain?"

"I was with her from when she passed out. And I saw her into the cab. Nothing untoward happened."

"You sure?"

"Absolutely."

"What about the driver?"

The young man shook his head.

"What time did you get her in the cab?"

"It was after midnight."

"You have to be more precise."

"Twelve-thirty. Twelve-forty tops. And the cabby was an old guy. No glasses. I have his name and cab number if you want it."

The driver glanced over at his companion and took another long pull. When he exhaled, once more he was looking long and hard at the young man.

"So we did some checking, Makoto Tanaka. We made some calls. We talked to our friends. It's not easy doing this on a quiet New Year's Day, but, like I said, the old man has his connections. Believe it or not, he too went to Waseda. You may not have much in common, but you have that."

The driver took a final pull before he tossed the still-lit butt out onto the sidewalk.

"He wants to meet you. We'll be in touch. Now get the fuck out."

3 "I Have Six Things on My Mind. You're No Longer One of Them."

Prefab Sprout's *Two Wheels Good* was released in 1985, the same year as New Order's *Low-Life* and Lloyd Cole & the Commotions' *Easy Pieces*. Everything But the Girl's and The Smiths' self-titled releases came out a year earlier. A year later, 1986, saw the release of Felt's *Forever Breathes the Lonely Word* and Cocteau Twins' *Victorialand*.

Though they had been rather expensive, the young man owned these records, many others too. He listened to The Jazz Butcher, This Mortal Coil, The Housemartins, The Colourfield, even more obscure acts like The Monochrome Set, Microdisney, and Stockholm Monsters. If it had been released on Factory or Cherry Red or Rough Trade or Creation or 4AD, chances are he had it in his collection. He prized them all. He prized his faded The Fall T-shirt, too.

By the time he was nineteen, he owned hundreds of such albums. The exotic-looking covers attracted him, and with song titles like "I Don't Owe You Anything," "All the People I Like Are Those That Are Dead," and "Suffer Little Children," the young man was smitten. And even though he had trouble understanding the lyrics, he found the music soothing. The songs spoke to him, and, alone in his tiny room, he listened intently. He had friends—

sure, and millions lived in the vast Tokyo metropolis like he did—but he felt more intimate with these song makers than he did with those around him.

"You come here a lot," the young clerk said with a smile as he passed over the counter the three records he wanted. "You should work here."

"Is that possible?" he asked, laying a 5,000-yen note in the tray that sat on the counter.

"I don't know why not. I can. And I don't know anything about music."

"Who do I talk to?"

"The manager, Sunagawa-san. He's that guy over there." The apron-wearing clerk pointed to a skinny, middle-aged man in a black Ramones T-shirt who was going through a stack of used LPs. She passed over his change, bagged up the young man's purchase, and handed it to him.

"It doesn't pay much," the manager said when he stood before him. "I overheard you talking to Ryoko. But I can offer you a 25% percent discount on anything in the store. And you get dibs on stuff that comes in, whether it's a promo or used. For example, look at this. It's from the States. Incredible shit. It's the *Let It Be* release from The Replacements. I sold my only one last week to some punk from Tachikawa, but some English teacher just brought this in this morning. Must be very hard up to let this gem go."

The manager had the album out and was examining the grooves very closely. After a half-minute, he put it on a turntable behind him and set the needle. "Fabulous!" he said as the song began, the sound of the jangling acoustic guitar and then later the singer's pained voice filling the small shop. With his eyes nearly closed, the manager sang along, the music and lyrics to him clearly meaningful. "Look me in the eyes and tell me I'm satisfied. Are you satisfied?" For a minute, he ignored the young man and became lost in the song. Then, reaching out a hand to turn down the volume on the hi-fi system, he returned from his the-music-took-me-there trance. "Any questions?" he asked, looking at the young man.

"No."

"You speak English? We get a lot of foreigners."

"Some."

"Are you satisfied?"

The young man laughed. "On some days, I guess."

"When can you start?"

"Sunday?"

"Great. We open at eleven. Be here then. Welcome to Recofan!"

Of all the women the young man had been with, Aki was the diamond. Since she was eight years his senior, and since she was well educated (she had degrees in psychology from Tokyo University and San Francisco State) and had a good-paying job, he had no idea what she saw in him, a third-year student who studied economics and who worked part-time at a record store.

But he knew what he saw in her. She walked around her apartment naked; she drank whisky; she masturbated. Quite unlike all of the other women he had slept with, Aki was uninhibited. When he was too aggressive down below with his tongue or fingers or way off mark, she would tell him and then show him exactly what to touch and how much pressure to apply. Once, she even stopped him mid-coitus. "What the fuck are you doing?" she asked, looking and sounding aggrieved as she stared up into his eyes. When she saw the hurt look on his face, she sighed and assumed a more soothing tone. "Makoto, listen," she began, lifting both hands and caressing his cheeks, "You are a little bigger than usual, and sweetheart, that's a good thing. It is. But don't just stick it in and start slamming," she explained. "That's not what any woman wants. Start off slowly. Make it last. The longer the better. Can you make me come first? That's what you want to do. That's your goal.

50

In essence," she concluded, the evening's lesson coming to an end, "giving pleasure is more important than receiving. Keep that in mind."

At times, the young man found himself a little confused. After all, there were no-sex evenings when Aki wanted to be held and soothed (he had to admit she had a difficult job). But on other occasions she wanted to be licked, fingered, fucked. "C'mon, Tiger!" she would assert, rolling over on her hands and knees. "Jungle time. Let me hear you roar!" But she always told him what she wanted. Communication was her thing. From Aki, he was getting a real education, one that he could try out on his other special and not-so-special girlfriends.

Even better, she had her own apartment in Shibuya, and when she went off in the morning to the private high school where she counseled troubled kids, he could stay as long as he desired, for she had given him a key. If he wanted to skip class and sleep in, he rolled over and buried his head in her soft pillows. If he wanted to go out and do fuck all, he could. And he could bring over his records and play them as loud as he wanted. In the dormitory, he had to contend with computer nerds and other geeks who ate *ramen* from Styrofoam bowls in their rooms.

Aki even had a car. Sure, the young man could take the train out to Saitama, catch a bus, and borrow his mom's if he needed wheels. But getting to his childhood home took over ninety minutes, and driving back into the city center was always a drag. Then he somehow had to get the car back to his mom. With Aki, they could be spontaneous. If the sun was out on a July Sunday morning, he could call the rugby manager or Sunagawa, or both, and say he was sick. He and Aki could be in the car and on the expressway in twenty minutes. The long beaches of Kamakura were only an hour away. And Aki, a small, colorful butterfly tattoo on one shoulder blade, looked stunning in her pink bikini.

So why, after only seven months, would he want to throw away such a diamond? Who knows what he was thinking?

⧗ ⧗ ⧗

The young man had been wanting to say something all night, but there was never a good moment. She was in such a good mood; she had had a breakthrough, she had told him during dinner, with one of her most pressing cases, a teenager who had attempted suicide six weeks previously. And he didn't want to tell her at her place. He couldn't do that. That would be too much, he felt. So, he had to act; the waiter was bringing the check.

"Aki-chan," he mumbled, "I wonder if we should see each other anymore."

"What?" She reached into her wallet, took out a 10,000-yen note, placed it on the check the waiter had just brought to the table. "You can take this," she said to him.

He waited until the waiter left with the check and money before he continued. "I was thinking we should take a break."

"A break?" Aki looked across the table at him. "A break from what? I see you only once or twice a week as it is."

"I'm just so busy."

"What are you busy doing?"

"Well," he replied, looking down at his hands, "we have a big match next weekend in Osaka. I have to train. And I have my studies."

"What are you talking about? You don't go to half of your classes."

"I have a lot going on," he insisted.

The waiter brought the change. "Thank you," she said, glancing up at him and smiling. After he bowed and left, she turned back to the young man, his eyes still lowered.

"So anyway," she asked, her tone a kind of rebuke, "you want to take a break. A short break, or a nice, long break?"

"A long one."

"Is there something wrong with my pussy? Not tight enough anymore?"

"Aki!"

"Look at me."

The young man raised his eyes, and for nearly a minute, the two stared at each other.

"You know, Makoto," she said at last with a sigh. "I think you have issues with intimacy. You told me about your father. When did he leave? When you were ten? And you say you are not close to your mother. Why? What's wrong with you?"

She waited, on her face a questioning look of concern, but he just looked at her.

"And that music you listen to. It's morose. 'I've got six things on my mind. You're no longer one of them.' What kind of love song is that?"

"Aki, I am not one of your high school students who needs counseling."

"No, you're just an immature idiot. I see that now. Or perhaps I am the dumb one." As she stood, she paused and looked at the young man as if she were going to say more, but instead she turned and walked out of the restaurant. He glanced at his watch. The change from the dinner—over 6,000 yen in bills and coins—sat in its tray on the table where the waiter had left it. He looked at it. Then he stood up and pocketed it. If he rushed, he could still meet Ryoko. He would be only an hour late.

On the Yamanote train to Ebisu, he recalled that he had left a pile of records in Aki's apartment. He had left his favorite jacket, too. He would miss them dearly, but all those things, like Aki, could be replaced.

4 The Morning After

The eleven of them, the trading and commodities teams, were gathered in the conference room. Akiyama, Hayashi's secretary, was there to serve coffee and take notes.

"Gentlemen, I would like to begin. First, let me explain why I look the way I do. I am sure you want to know why.

"I was at the doctor's this morning. Nothing is broken. There are a few cuts and bruises, hence the small bandages. But I shall be fine in a week, ten days tops. Actually, I am fine now.

"As many of you know, I played rugby when I was at Waseda. And I did a little karate when I was in New York. In other words, I am used to being knocked around.

"Last night I had a disagreement with a certain individual. I thought I could acquit myself, but this certain individual, as you can see, got the better of me. I bear the other party no ill will. To be honest, I deserve to look this way, even worse.

"That's all I would like to say about the matter.

"In front of you, you will see today's agenda. As you all know, Murakami, Abe, and I are leaving for Singapore this Saturday. There is much at stake. We need to renew these contracts. That's the primary goal of the trip.

"When we are gone, the Sakura team, under Hayashi's leadership, will consider our best options. We think the market has bottomed out, so they will be looking for opportunities. But if any of you have any other ideas, you are welcome to speak to him. Do so before you commit any capital over 10,000,000.

"In regard to the yen's falling below 160, Hayato has something to say about that."

Hayato stood and bowed to the young man; then he bowed to the others. He spoke for fifteen minutes, as he had been directed. The meeting continued until noon.

5 The Minders Have Lunch and Discuss What They've Learned and How to Proceed

"What should we tell the old man about the kid?"

The two minders had ordered *ramen* and *gyoza* in a dive near Takadanobaba Station. For the past week, they had been out conducting their research.

"Well, we have to be careful. If we're too hard on the little shit, and if he finds out, he could squeal. I don't think the old man will keep us around if he finds out we were never in the club with her."

"Do you remember how she looked when the cab pulled up?" the other asked, laughing at the recollection. "I think she had wet herself."

"She had. And she had vomit in her hair. For a moment, I thought it was cum."

"Fuck. Don't remind me," he chuckled. "I nearly crapped my pants."

"Don't laugh too much. We were lucky we were there and not where she ditched us, the little cunt. You, asshole, were the one who lost her. I was in the can."

"What the hell kept you? You were in there forever."

"I had the shits."

With her usual fanfare, the proprietress placed two bowls of steaming *ramen* on the bar in front of her only customers. She followed the *ramen* with two small plates of *gyoza*. "*Dozo go-yukuri*," she said with a warm smile.

As the two slurped the noodles noisily and chomped on the *gyoza*, neither man spoke. From behind her counter, the proprietress took pleasure watching them eat. If one took a swig from his small glass, she quickly poured more from the large bottle. When they finished, one leaned over on his stool slightly and blasted a fart.

"Yuji-kun," she said, blushing, "how can you do that in my shop? Shame on you!"

"I am sorry, Setsuko-san. It's the garlic. It gives me gas. But goddamn if you don't make the best *ramen*. I can't get enough of it. It's like a high school girl's pussy."

The woman frowned. "You will scare away my customers with talk like that."

"You don't have any customers."

"That's true. Business has been slow. We used to get a lot of students from down the way, but I guess they are too hoity-toity for us these days. Another beer?"

"Another bottle won't hurt us."

"Make it two," his companion chimed in. After the proprietress placed two large bottles of Asahi on the counter, she popped each open both with an opener that hung from a piece of string that she had around her neck and refilled their glasses. She removed the empty bowls and plates and set them in a deep sink behind her.

"Okay, lover," one of the men said to her, "put some tissue in your ears."

The compliant woman turned around and adjusted the volume on a small transistor radio that sat high on a shelf above the sink. Quietly, she began singing along to the soft *enka* music. Next, she turned on the faucet. She waited for the water to get warm and then started in on the dirty dishes.

The man pulled out a cigarette and lit it. He took a deep drag before he spoke. "What kind of jerk-off Waseda senior works as a host? He should be graduating soon. He could get himself expelled."

"They all do these days. There is a load of money to be made. A shitload. If I were younger and had a little charm, I'd do it myself. But he hasn't been there for a week. He never went back. At least that's what the manager says. I fucked with him yesterday. Had his drawers nice and tight. We don't have to worry about him. He claims he never saw her, and I believe him."

"No pictures, right?"

"No. Nothing. Seems the place does not allow them."

The man squinted and took another drag. "You reckon he has his eye on the little cunt?"

"Who knows? I doubt it. Don't think he's that smart. May not know what she's worth."

"Yeah, but he's a crafty fucker. There's something going on." He took one last pull on the cigarette before stubbing it out in a glass ashtray.

"Well," his companion continued, "he has no money. That's for sure. He used to work at a record store in Shibuya. But he gave that up to work at the club about seven months ago. His old man left when he was ten. Ran off to Osaka with a little chickadee. His mom lives out near Saitama. She works in a supermarket. Clerk. She's been there forever. Not a bad-looking bird. But she never remarried. Never recovered, it seems, from the loss of the first one. And who wants used goods? Anyway, she lives in a little one-room flat not far from Yono Station."

"Beaver?"

"Plenty, it seems. But nothing serious. You can't fault a guy for wanting to get laid."

"And the kind who want money?"

"You would think with his looks, getting a piece wouldn't be a problem. But I can trace him too many times, too many places. Why? Who the fuck knows. Sometimes he goes with his rugby buddies. That part I can understand. But he's been known to go solo. At his age, that's the troublesome part."

"Any habits of the pharmaceutical kind?"

"No. As you know, most of the guys who work in those places are jacked up on something. Speed freaks. A lot of that white powder these days. Got to have something to keep the hours they keep. But as far as I can tell, he's clean. Shibuya, Shinjuku, even as far as Yokohama, there've been no buys."

"You sure you talked to the right fellows?"

"I'm sure."

"Well," the man sighed. "The meeting with the old man is this Saturday. We're supposed to gather the little shit at eleven and bring him over to The New Otani. They'll be having lunch. Tonight, when we see the old man, let's just keep it simple. We'll relate what we know about the family. Let's mention a visit just to keep it realistic. I'm sure the old man will understand. Probably did a little of that when he was younger. Who hasn't?"

His companion poured himself a last glass of beer and downed it. "After all this dirty talk, I could use a little cleaning. Should we go get soaped up?"

The man looked at his watch. "Why not? The little cunt won't be leaving campus for another two hours. And since her little adventure, she's been keeping pretty close to home. Whatever happened dried up that little pussy."

His companion laughed heartily. "God, she was a mess! Scared herself to tears. Even Yoshiko started crying when she ran out and saw her. I nearly cried myself."

The two stood, set a few banknotes on the counter, grunted a couple of goodbyes, then left to go get soaped up.

6 A High School Math Teacher Advises One of His Students

"You should try. The exam is free. If you pass, you will be accepted."

"But how will I pay? It costs a fortune to go there."

"We can cross that bridge when we get there. The most important thing is passing the exam."

The teacher looked at his skeptical student.

"You told me once your father died. This sounds cruel, but your father's death may be a good thing. Waseda will consider your family's financial situation. Scholarships are available for disadvantaged students."

"Actually, it's worse than that. He ran off."

"He's not dead?"

"He could be. I haven't seen him since I was ten. I don't think he has contacted my mother either. I am sure she would have told me."

"Well, I don't think that changes things much. Take the exam. If you get the right score, you get in. It's that simple."

After a pause, the teacher added, "You have the talent. There's no doubt about that. And with a degree from a school like that, you'll be set for life."

7 Singapore Business Trip

Instead of one this time, he wanted two. Why not? he mused. After the long flight from Narita, he needed more than a drink and a bath. And how about that stunning JAL flight attendant? All he could do was look at her and imagine. In what hotel was she now? What little sounds did she make when she was being touched? Did she trim? As he shaved, he had a fantasy that he could get the two to wear flight attendant uniforms, but that was probably out of the question.

Yes, he had made a promise to his wife. But that had been a long week ago. A sexless week. Naturally, she was still cold and distant, still quite angry. Who could blame her? The revelation must have come as quite a shock. Had she really no idea? Better not to think too much about it. Thankfully, his paramour hadn't called again or caused any headaches at the office; she could have made his professional life a mess. What had he been thinking? Over several tiny cups of *sake*, he pondered the question for hours on the flight. In any case, he didn't want to push matters with his wife. He knew he deserved the icy winds that were presently blowing from her. With kindness, with consideration, with time, she would come around. He could wait. But a guy could jerk off only for so long.

He joined the others in the hotel restaurant at seven. After fresh sea bass and other delicacies and drinks, they took two cabs; there was no need for all four to squeeze into one. The local guy, Kawasaki, knew where to go. After they arrived, he explained the local rules. Then he added, "Keep your wallets in your pockets where they belong. Everything has been taken care of. Will two hours be enough?"

"Plenty," they all replied, nodding to each other.

"Gentlemen," he smiled, "enjoy yourselves."

The two Chinese were lovely, large-chested, energetic, and since both spoke and understood reasonably good English, he could explain to them exactly how he wanted them to lick his balls, something he could never imagine asking his wife to do. The two hours went by very pleasurably. Later, back in his king-sized bed at the Conrad, he slept well. The next two days, the company business went smoothly. With the contracts signed, the company was set to make a lot of money. The three even had time for a leisurely round of golf at the Sentosa Country Club.

The night before he departed, he went back by himself and got the same two ladies. They were happy to see him.

At the airport the next morning, each man picked up souvenirs for his wife. The young man bought his a colorful tablecloth and some pearl earrings; he paid with his company credit card. On the plane, after a nice meal and a half bottle of *Vieux Château Certan*, he slept soundly for four hours.

8 A Brief Scene with a Shady Character

To get to the men's room, the young man had to walk past the bar. A hands-holding couple sat at one end, their heads bowed toward each other, in front of one a glass of red wine, in front of the other some kind of cocktail in a tall glass with a stemmed cherry floating at the top. He envied them their happiness. On the other end, a shady character sat brooding in front of a half-consumed mug of beer—a pack of cigarettes, a lighter, a tray of mixed nuts there in front of him, his ashtray nearly filled. As the young man passed, the shady character glanced over his shoulder and made eye contact with him.

In the bathroom, the young man stood in front of the urinal and unzipped. He had just started when the shady character entered. His large penis already pulled out and held at the base, he started urinating on the young man. He sprayed the back of his legs and his black dress shoes; leaning back, the arc a yellow rainbow, he was even able to get some of his urine on the back of the young man's white dress shirt.

"What the…?" he yelled, jumping to his left, his own urine streaking the wall.

"Sorry," the shady character growled, his voice insolent. "Couldn't wait." When he had finished, he zipped up and stood glaring at the young man. He too zipped up, but it seemed some of his own urine had splashed onto his hands, so he did so awkwardly, on his face a frown. With two fingers, he carefully reached into his left front pocket and withdrew a white handkerchief. He shook it out, wiped his hands on it, and then tossed it in the direction of the overflowing trash can. When he finished, the two men, one at least a dozen years older than the other, stood looking at each other.

"I am ready to go if you are," the older man said, sizing up his adversary. "I'll let you throw the first punch. Go ahead. Hit me as hard as you can."

When the young man didn't respond, the shady character sighed. "That's what I thought." He seemed disappointed that there wouldn't be a fist-to-face fight.

"Your Tokyo best buds asked me to have a little chat with you. They would have come themselves, but they have been busy.

"I congratulate you on your marriage and on your business success. We… You don't mind if I use the first-person plural, do you? Your Tokyo best buds and I have been good friends for years. We go back a long way.

"We are a little concerned. To be frank, more than a little. At home sits your beautiful wife. She spends a lot of time looking at her watch. We wonder what she might be thinking. That kind of contemplation ages a lovely woman. We wouldn't want that now, would we?

"Of course, she might be the understanding type. We are too in some respects. We can understand your having a little after-work tipple with your colleagues, like you're doing this evening. It comes with the job description. Perhaps a rub and tug as well. But we wonder if there is anything to be done so that beautiful wife of yours can stop looking at her watch so frequently. Any suggestions?"

The young man started a reply, but then stopped. Looking defeated, he shook his head, his eyes falling to the tiled floor.

"Nothing to say?

"Nothing at all? Well, let me say it then. You have to break it off. Your Tokyo best buds and I will give you a few days. If we don't see crystal-clear results, I will shit on you. If I drink too much beer, I get the runs. And it's not a pretty sight. I would hate for any of it to get in your eyes or ears or nose or, God forbid, your mouth. You understand?"

The young man nodded.

"Good."

The shady character stepped over to the sink. "I forgot to wash my hands," he announced, turning on the faucet. He generously applied soap and rubbed his hands together under the running water for a long time. As he washed them, he looked over at the young man. "Your Tokyo best buds told me I would feel dirty around you. I do. Can't seem to get this dirt off. One fuckin' month. That's all it took, huh? What a charmer you must be."

When he finished rinsing his hands, he shook the excess water off and casually walked over to the young man, his scarred, rough-looking face inches away from the other's. He looked into his eyes with a fierce hatred. Then he grabbed the wide end of the young man's tie and used it to dry his hands.

9 A Father and His Only Son Have a One-sided Conversation

"Your teachers say you're bright, that you'll be somebody someday," the father said. "What do they know?" He picked up his burger and took another bite. Slumped on his plastic seat, the skinny boy just looked across the table at his father.

"Aren't you going to eat your apple pie?"

"Why can't I have a hamburger too?"

"You just ate a few hours ago at school, right? You shouldn't be hungry. What, you think money grows on trees?"

The father could see that his child was about to cry.

"See," the father said. "That's why you are a loser. You cry too easily. You should be happy that I bought you anything at all." He stuffed a few French fries into his mouth and chomped on them; then he sucked noisily on the straw of his Coke.

"You know, your mother is a loser too. I am doing you both a favor by taking a long hike." He took another large bite of his burger. As he chewed, he held the half-eaten burger and looked at it.

"This burger is pretty good," he reported to his son with his mouth full. "Just the right amount of ketchup and mustard." He took in some more fries and then licked his fingers.

Next to the two sat a mother and her two children. She spoke quietly and kindly to them. Each family member had a burger. And on a napkin in the middle of the table sat a small mountain of fries. Whenever the children wanted some, they could help themselves.

"If you are not going to eat it, I will." The father set down what remained of his burger, reached across the table, grabbed the apple pie. He opened one end of the thin, cardboard container and let the still-warm pie slide out into his hand. He took one big bite, then another. The pie was gone.

"Loser," he said, his mouth full as he chewed. "A couple of fuckin' losers. The two of you are going to be losing all your life. Meanwhile, I will be winning."

Even though the father had not finished eating his burger and fries, he gathered his tray, stood up, and walked over to the trash receptacle. He dumped everything, even the plastic tray, into it and walked out the door.

10 A Young Man and an Old Man
Meet and Have a Long Talk

In the hotel lobby, the young man walked up to the old man and bowed. The old man stood there, accepting the bow.

"I must say I sincerely appreciate what you did for my daughter." Now it was the old man's turn to bow. With his arms at his sides, he did so slowly and with great formality.

"I did nothing out of the ordinary," the young man responded. "You, certainly, would have done the same."

"I'm not so sure. At your age, I probably would have a good laugh at the poor girl. But it appears you didn't laugh."

"She needed a little help. That's all."

"It appears she found a guardian angel." The old man extended his right hand. The young man offered his. The two shook hands, and the older man held the younger's for a long time.

"Let's eat," he finally said. "I've reserved a table." He guided the young man down a wide flight of stairs to a restaurant where the two were met by a *kimono*-clad hostess. She too bowed slowly and deeply. Then she turned and shuffled down a dimly lit passageway, the two men following. She slid open a *shoji* door and showed them into a private room with an intimate view of the hotel's expansive interior garden.

After they sat, and after each refreshed himself with an *oshibori*, a warm hand towel brought by a *kimono*-clad waitress, another similarly dressed waitress arrived with a tray. On it were two large bottles of Kirin, already opened, and two plates of *sashimi*. This second waitress held the tray as her colleague set the beer bottles in the center of the table. Then she set a plate of *sashimi* in front of each man. Having said nothing to their guests, the two bowed themselves out of the room, sliding the *shoji* door closed.

"I hope you don't mind," the old man said, lifting one of the large bottles and filling the young man's small glass. "I ordered for us." The young man picked up the other bottle and filled the old man's small glass.

The old man raised his glass. The young man raised his.

"*Kampai*," they both said.

"As you know, sir, there are believers and skeptics. Optimists and pessimists, if you will. Presently, I am one of the latter. Most say the market has legs, that it will go higher, perhaps as high as 45,000 or even 50,000. I don't think so. I think the horse has run its race."

The old man picked up his coffee cup and looked long and hard at the young man. "What makes you think so? There is a lot of money at stake. One might lose a lot of money if he pulled out now."

"One could lose a lot if he stayed in too long."

The old man sipped his coffee; then he set the cup down.

"As you know, sir, there have been bubbles in the past. They come and go periodically, often skipping a generation. Have you ever read John Kenneth Galbraith's *The Great Crash, 1929*? Forgive me if I sound condescending, but it's a seminal work. It's had a profound effect on me.

"Of course, I read the Japanese translation. I have been working on my English, but it's not good enough yet. Someday soon I want to read it in the original.

"Well, as I just said, this work has had a great influence on me. What happened in the United States in 1929 *could* happen here. I think it *will* happen. Actually, I think it *is* happening. Will Japan experience 25% unemployment? Will the crash be that bad? I don't think so.

"The most recent high was what? Just under 39,000 a few days before New Year's. Right? That was three weeks ago. It's gone down a little since then. It may go back up and reach a new high, but I don't think so.

"Forgive me. Maybe I am talking too much."

The old man glanced at his watch. "I can't believe it's already four. Where have the hours gone? I must say this has been a most entertaining afternoon. I look forward to our next meeting."

"I do too, sir."

"Are you sure you can find our office?"

"It won't be a problem."

"I can have my fellows pick you up, as they did this morning."

"That won't be necessary."

"Once again, let me sincerely thank you. I am referring to my daughter. The same two fellows who picked you up this morning assist my daughter from time to time. They tell me you were very generous with the cab driver. Very generous."

With his right hand, the old man reached into his suit jacket and withdrew an envelope. He set it on the table and slid it toward the young man.

"That's not necessary, sir. Please."

"Yes, it is."

The young man bowed his head and picked up the envelope with both hands. Then he slid it into his suit jacket pocket.

"Someday soon, I would like you to meet her. We don't talk about that evening. I don't think she can recall much. A little too much youthful exuberance, it seems."

"If our meeting would bother her in any way, I insist it doesn't take place."

"I insist that it does. I don't think it will bother her at all."

The old man pushed his chair back and stood. The young man followed his lead. The old man slid open the *shoji* door and let the young man pass through first. They made their way down the dimly lit passageway. At the entrance, the two waitresses and the hostess, each in her colorful *kimono*, bowed deeply as the two men walked out into the bright hotel interior.

The three team members shared a taxi from the airport, the young man being the last to alight. When he keyed in and entered, the apartment was dark and cold. He thought perhaps his wife was sleeping. But when he turned on the light in the kitchen, he saw the unsigned note on the small table. "Gone to Tokyo for a few days," he read.

He set down his travel bag on the floor and placed the bag containing the presents he had bought for her on one of the two chairs. Thinking about how to proceed, he checked his watch; it was after eleven. Calling the house in Nishi Azabu at this hour, he surmised, would not be a good idea. What if she were not there? In that case, such a call would be highly suspicious. What would the maid think if he asked for his wife? Worse, what would he say if his father-in-law answered? Then again, what if she *were* there? Wouldn't she be expecting a call? He was the guilty party, after all, and he couldn't risk looking indifferent or cold.

He went into the dark living room, picked up the new phone, and dialed. "If someone else answers," he thought as he heard the first ring, "I will hang up."

But she answered after six rings. "I thought it might be you," she said indifferently.

"I miss you. When are you coming home?"

"I told Father yesterday. He was very happy, of course. But he insisted I see our family doctor here. So I flew down this morning. I have an appointment tomorrow morning. Yoshiko is taking me."

"I wish you would have told me. I was just at Haneda a few hours ago. I could have taken the train in and spent the night with you."

"I called your hotel yesterday. Actually, I called several times. But the front desk said you were out. At least no one answered your phone when they put the call through."

"When did you call?"

"It doesn't matter."

"Yes, it does. I never got any message. It irritates me that we pay so much to stay there and then something like this happens. What if something had happened to you?"

"Something has happened to me." After a pause, she added, "I'm going back to sleep."

"When can I call you tomorrow? How early?"

She sighed. "My appointment is at 9:45. Afterwards, I was thinking of seeing a lawyer. I should be home after lunch. Call me then." Before he could reply, she hung up.

The young man gently replaced the receiver. He sat down. It seemed he was staring into emptiness. But actually, he was looking across the valley. He saw his wife on the other side. It was difficult to see her clearly. Was she walking away from him? He had a lot of work to do, but the valley could be crossed. No, he knew it *had* to be crossed. He had little time; he had to get to her.

12 A Short Chapter with Some Important Numbers

The Nikkei, Tokyo's leading stock market index, stood just over 13,000 in January 1986. At the end of 1988, it had reached 24,000. It found its high of 38,916 on December 29, 1989. So, it had nearly tripled in value in three years. By the end of 1991, the index was below 25,000. It fell further, finishing 1992 at 16,924. And it dropped even lower in the years that followed.

13 A Young Man and a Young Woman Meet

There was a large gate before a driveway that ran up to the house. At six promptly, he pressed the white button on the intercom attached to the gate. After a few seconds, a female voice responded, "*Hai!*"

"Tanaka *desu.*"

The gate buzzed and slowly slid open. After he passed by, it reversed direction as he began walking up the slight incline to the house. In the twilight, to his left, he could see a garden and an old man in a uniform kneeling and carefully pruning a small *bonsai* tree. The man stood and bowed to him. The front door opened, and a maid in uniform hurried down the driveway to greet him. Behind the maid stood her employer in the doorway. He smiled and waved. "Come on up," he said in English.

The young man paused and bowed to both the maid and the man. The maid bowed as well.

"I thought I should speak English since you will be leaving soon. Are you excited?"

"I am very excited. I will do my best. I promise you."

He bowed again, and then the two men shook hands firmly.

"I hope so. We'll need your knowledge and expertise. The year will go by very quickly."

In the spacious *genkan*, the young man slid off his shoes and donned a pair of slippers that had been set out for him. He followed the older man down a wide hallway into a spacious living room. Glancing to his right, he could see a large kitchen and a dining area; to his astonishment, he saw that the long, rectangular table had chairs for ten people. The kitchen itself was as large as the apartment he grew up in. To his left he saw a studio of some kind; the walls were filled with large family photographs.

"Let me take you to what I call the garden room. It's through here." The young man followed the other into the studio, where the older man stopped. "Mrs. Ueda is no longer with us. Did I tell you? No, perhaps not." He pointed to a large picture of his wife. "She left us ten years ago. No, it's been longer. Cancer." The two men looked at her photograph. With just a hint of a smile, the young woman in the photograph had wavy, late-1960s hair. But the colorful *kimono* she wore could have been from any decade. Down below was a smaller photograph of a pretty girl in a high school uniform.

"Best not to dwell on the past," he said after a moment. He turned, slid open a door, and passed through into another large room three steps down. The young man followed him.

"As I said, I call this the garden room. Have a seat," he said, gesturing to some cushions that lay on the *tatami* floor. There were six or seven of them around a small, low table near some very large, floor-to-ceiling windows. While the young man remained standing, the other turned to the windows and began sliding them open. "It's nice out," he said. "Let's get some fresh air in here."

When he finished, he turned to the young man. "Mariko is upstairs in her room doing whatever young ladies do these days," he said, laughing. "She has her suspicions."

The maid arrived carrying a tray with three full glasses and a pitcher. Carefully, she set each item on the table. The glasses were full of ice and some clear liquid.

"Yoshiko, I won't be staying. You can take one of the glasses back with you." The maid picked up one glass from the table and bowed herself out of the room.

"I'll see you on Tuesday, Makoto. At the office. Be there at nine. We'll talk more then. I'm going to get some work out of you before you leave. Of course, you'll be paid." The two men shook hands again before the older man left.

Alone in the room, the young man approached the open windows and looked out at the substantial garden. He couldn't imagine that such surroundings could exist as part of someone's home. The home itself, for him, was beyond comprehension. And he had seen only parts of the first floor. Out in the garden were a few soft lights pointed up at the trees, and he could hear running water. Maybe there were *koi* too. Incredible, he thought.

He heard a soft cough and turned. Just inside the doorway stood the pretty young lady he had helped at the club. She wore a long, green skirt, a white sweater, white socks. She slid the door closed behind her, took the three steps down, approached the table, and dropped herself on a square cushion. She pulled another cushion onto her lap. Then she reached out, picked up one of the glasses, took a sip.

"Water," she reported, looking up at him. "Is that okay? I can ask Yoshiko to bring something else, if you want."

"Water is fine," he replied, sitting down on a cushion across from her.

"There's a little bit of lemon in it," she said after he lifted his glass and took a drink. "Yoshiko knows I like it that way."

"I like it that way too."

During the awkward silence that followed, both lifted their glasses and sipped more.

"I can't believe Father is letting me sit alone with a boy. He's rather protective. He pays these two losers to follow me when I go out, especially at night. But if I really want to, I can lose them. That's why I call them the losers."

The young man smiled.

"You find it funny that Father pays two men to follow me? I am twenty years old."

"No. Just your description of these guys. I can almost picture them."

"Well, I pretend that I don't know that they're there. It's a little game we play. But one time I really needed their help. I wish they were there with me that night."

"What happened?"

"It's too embarrassing to tell. I mean it's really bad," she said, emphasizing the word "really."

"In junior high school, I once dove into a pool and lost my swimming trunks. I forgot to tie them. Is it that kind of bad?"

"Worse. Maybe I'll cry if I tell you."

"Maybe I'll cry too then."

The young woman looked at the young man for a long time. Neither spoke. Then she looked down and played with the cushion in her lap.

"I was at a club with some friends," she began. "I shouldn't say 'friends' because, believe me, we're not friends anymore. I drank too much. I mean, I *really really really* drank too much."

"We've all done that. It's part of coming of age."

"No, I vomited, and somehow the vomit was in my hair. And I peed in my undies. Actually, I peed in the back of a taxi. Yoshiko— she's like a mom to me—had to fetch me from the taxi and bring me into the house and bathe me."

"That is bad."

"See? I told you I shouldn't have told you. Now I am crying." She held up the back of her right hand to her eyes and dried them.

"The scary part—and believe me, it's terrifying—is I don't remember much."

"Maybe that's a good thing."

"No, it's awful. Not really knowing, I mean."

"Have you ever heard of The Smiths? They're a band from the UK. They have this song, 'Heaven Knows I'm Miserable Now,' which, in Japanese, is '*Kamisamawa ima bokuga mijimenano o shitteiru*.' Something like that.

"I'd sing it, but I'm not a singer. In English, it goes like this, 'I was happy in the haze of a drunken hour, but heaven knows I'm miserable now.'

"Into Japanese, I'd probably translate it as '*Yopparatte, morotoshite iru tokiwa shiawasedatta. Keredo, kamisamawa ima bokuga mijimenano o shitteiru*.'"

"God," she sighed, her wet eyes still glistening. "That's just how I felt. I was sick for three days."

"The song is much more than about drinking and being hungover. In some ways, it's about life. You get what you want but then you're not happy. Do you know what I mean?"

"I guess so. I have everything. But sometimes I wonder if I'm happy."

"I hope you are happy now."

"You mean right now?"

He nodded.

"I'm okay," she replied, looking at him and laughing a little.

"In any case, please don't feel bad. I understand about the drinking too much." He paused. "By the way, it's a good song. Maybe I can play it for you sometime."

She looked past him out into the garden. "The funny thing is, I do remember this guy. At the club, I mean. I'm pretty sure he was the one who helped me into the taxi, not my so-called friends. I think he even tried, at one point, to wash the vomit out of my hair. In some ways, I would like to meet him."

"What would you say?"

"I don't know. 'Thanks' doesn't seem enough. That's for sure."

"Why don't you publish an anonymous letter in the newspaper, 'To the Guy Who Washed Vomit Out of My Hair'?"

"That's not funny," she said, frowning.

"I apologize. I didn't mean to make light of your experience. It's just…"

"It's okay."

"Please forgive me."

"I can't believe I told you. I don't even know you."

"I appreciate that you did. Thank you very much."

She closed her eyes and shook her head, as if in doing so she could cast off the unpleasant memories. When she opened them, she looked at him. "Father tells me you are going to work for him, but first you will study in New York."

"That's our agreement. I leave in five weeks."

"Are you excited?"

"I am."

"How long will you be gone?"

"A year. At least that's the plan. As you probably know, your father has an office there. I am going to work there, take some classes, learn more about the American markets."

"Are you going to be rich someday, like Father?"

"I wouldn't mind."

"Believe me, being rich is not all that it's cracked up to be."

"I wouldn't know."

There was a knock at the door. It slid open a half a foot. "Mariko-chan, your father says it's time."

The two women saw the young man to the *genkan*, where he slipped on his shoes. As he bowed to the two before he stepped out the door, the maid returned the bow and held hers longer. The young woman just stood there, her right hand casually resting on her hip. With her left, she offered a wave.

14 Across the Valley, Part 2, or,

a Day Full of Adventures

Just after seven, the young man called, hoping he wouldn't have to talk to his wife. He just wanted to call, talk to Yoshiko, the maid, and leave a message, so he was pleased when he heard her voice. "Oh, Makoto-san!" she said warmly after he introduced himself. "Congratulations! You are such a happy, handsome couple! I hope the first one is a boy."

"Thank you."

"Would you like me to wake her? I think she is still sleeping."

"No, don't bother her. But when she wakes, please tell her I miss her. I wish I could be there this morning when she goes for her check-up."

"Don't you worry," the old lady insisted. "I'm going with her. I know all about these things. I have three daughters of my own and five grandchildren. It's best you men don't intrude."

When he got to the office just after eight, the first thing he did was tell the front desk receptionist to order some flowers. "Here is the address," he said, passing her a small piece of paper. "They need to be there before noon. Spend at least 10,000. Put them on my expense account."

"Do you want to add a message?"

"'Miss you.'"

"That's all?"

"That's all," he replied, looking around. "Anybody else here?"

"No."

At 8:45, after he had checked all of his messages and correspondence, he returned to the receptionist. "Are the flowers on their way?"

"They are supposed to be there by ten."

"Good."

He looked at her more closely. It seemed he was seeing her for the first time. "I don't know you," he said.

"I started last week."

"Do you know who I am?"

"Yes."

"Who am I?"

The young lady stood up and looked him directly in the eyes. "You are Tanaka Makoto. You are one of the leading stockbrokers. I just sent your wife flowers." She then bowed deeply and held the bow.

One of the phones started ringing. "You had better answer that," he said, pointing. She took her chair and lifted the handset.

He returned to his desk, again glancing at his watch. All he could do was wait. In the meantime, he considered making a few trades.

At 11:35, he left the building with a colleague. The two went to a Chinese place for lunch. After they found a table and ordered, the colleague gave the young man a knowing look. "Goddamn that Kumamoto-san is something else!"

"Who is she?"

"The front desk girl. She's new. Hayashi fired the old bag we had and got this new lollipop." He added, "I'd love to give her a lick."

"I hadn't noticed."

The colleague looked at the young man. "Are you fucking with me?"

"Singapore. You know. Just got back. Still a little tired."

"Yamamoto told me everything went smoothly."

"Things went fine."

"Something must be wrong for you not to notice that delicious dessert. You are off your game."

"I'll check her out when I get back."

Back at his desk, he looked again at his watch: 12:40. He waited. "Another ten minutes," he thought. "Don't call too soon."

Twenty minutes later, he returned to the front desk with an armful of file folders and asked the new receptionist if anyone had booked the conference room. He would have more privacy— and time, if needed—if he called from there. Looking down at a schedule book she had open before her, she reported that it was not reserved.

"I have some documents I need to peruse. I need some privacy. I'll be in there for thirty minutes, maybe an hour."

"Would you like me to bring you anything?"

"Actually, yes. Can you come in about fifteen minutes? I'll need you then. There are some papers you and I need to go over."

After he slipped into the conference room, he sat, then picked up the handset and dialed.

"Hi," he said. "How did everything go?"

"You mean at the clinic? Or at the lawyer's?"

"Mariko."

"What?"

"I wish you wouldn't be that way."

"I wish I weren't pregnant."

"Don't say that."

"Okay. Everything is fine then. The baby is due in July."

"That's wonderful."

"The doctor says I am too skinny. I have to eat more."

"Then let's have a big meal to celebrate."

"I have more news."

"Yes?"

"I am looking for a place," she said and paused. "Here in Tokyo."

He sighed heavily.

"It's for us," she continued. "Since I'm pregnant, Father wants us here. You are going to be transferred. Father is going to tell you this afternoon, so you had better act surprised. I wasn't supposed to say anything."

"Mariko, I miss you terribly."

"Shouldn't you be working?"

"Work can wait."

After a long pause, she said, "So anyway, I've started the apartment hunting. I'll send you some faxes of the floorplans."

"Did you get the flowers?"

"I did."

"Last night was awful without you."

"The lawyer says I should give you another chance."

"Please do. I am very, very sorry."

"Sometimes I wonder."

"I am. Please forgive me. What I did was incredibly selfish."

There was a long moment of silence.

"You're supposed to say, 'I won't do anything like that again.'"

"I won't do anything like that again."

"Okay," his wife sighed, sounding tired. "Thanks for calling. Call me when you get home tonight."

"Let's eat dinner together."

"What?"

"I will buy a *bento* on my way home. You buy one too. Then when I get home, I'll call. How about seven? We can talk and eat together."

"You are not supposed to talk with your mouth full," she said with a small laugh. "Didn't your mother teach you any manners?"

"You are my teacher now. I need your guidance."

When she didn't respond, he said, "I love you."

"I guess I love you too."

"Seven, then."

Slowly, he replaced the handset. Once more, he was looking across the valley. He saw his wife more clearly now. She was standing and looking back at him. He felt more confident, and once again the future looked promising. But his reverie was broken by a soft knock on the door. It opened slightly, and he saw her pretty face. "Please come in," he said, and she did, closing the door behind her. As he stood, he gestured to the chair next to his. "Kumamoto-san, won't you sit down?"

"Mori-san is covering for me. I can stay only a few minutes."

"I was hoping you could stay longer," he said, smiling and helping her into her chair. "But I understand. I don't have much to say. I simply wanted to welcome you to the firm. Everything going okay?"

"Yes," she replied, nodding. "I like working here."

"That's wonderful," he said, looking into her coffee-black eyes. "I hope you and I can be friends. From now on, please call me Makoto. Please know that if you have any questions—any questions at all—you can ask me."

15 The Young Man and the Old Man Meet Again

"As I said before, I think a year should suffice. You'll go over on a working visa, but you won't be trading right away. For that, you need a license, which will require taking some courses and passing an exam. Of course, you can do your research. Pass on your suggestions to Nomura. He can make the requisite purchases. Your usual commission will apply." The old man had left his door open. When Kobayashi, his secretary, knocked, he waved her in. She set an armful of files on his desk and left without saying anything. The old man opened the first one and glanced at its contents. Lifting one page, then another, he remained silent for several minutes as he read the documents.

"And your English?" he asked without looking up.

"It's getting better."

"You've been meeting with the tutor?"

"Several days a week."

"Do you think you can understand the lectures then?"

"Yes, sir."

"As I said, you will be taking classes. From what I gather, they are intense. Everything will be in English. After you arrive, we can get you another tutor if you think having one would help."

"I think I can get by without one. Please let me try."

At last, the old man closed the file and looked across his desk at the young man.

"I haven't decided yet. But I am thinking of placing you in our Aomori branch when you return. It's our smallest and newest office. Will that posting be a problem?"

"No."

"Of course, much can happen in a year. So don't count on anything. If you do end up there, the assignment will be temporary. A year or two. That is, if all goes well.

"But we seem to be getting ahead of ourselves. First things first. New York. Kobayashi is working on your visa and ticket. You've given her everything that she needs?"

"Yes, sir."

"And I hear you've been in touch with Nomura. I spoke to him a few days ago. He will be meeting you and getting you set up."

"That's right."

The old man stood.

"Would you like me and Mariko to attend the ceremony this Saturday?"

"I would rather not inconvenience the two of you."

"I think Mariko would be upset if you didn't include her."

"Actually, she told me she would like to attend, so I invited her. I had no idea that you would like to go too. Please forgive me."

"I go every year. I am on the alumni board."

"Then, sir, it would be an honor if you accompanied Mariko."

"I think the three of us could have a nice dinner afterwards. That is, if you have no other plans."

"Please forgive me," the young man replied, smiling awkwardly. "Mariko and I were going to go to McDonald's afterwards."

"McDonald's?"

"It's kind of a joke between the two of us. The other day, she told me that she has never been to a McDonald's. I hope you are not offended, but I found that kind of odd. I thought everyone, especially kids, had been to McDonald's."

"I've never been myself," the old man said with a chuckle. "But let's pass on McDonald's. The three of us can go another day. On Saturday, let's go somewhere a little more accommodating. I am rather fond of *sushi*. Mariko is as well."

"That would be wonderful," the young man said, standing and bowing.

As the two left his office and made their way down the hallway to the main doors, the old man continued. "I've been following the market closely, very closely. Of course, that's what I always do. But since we had lunch last month, I've taken a renewed interest in it. As you predicted, Makoto, it seems to have peaked."

"The very good days may be over."

"I am very sorry to see them go. But if the party is indeed over, we had better be good guests and leave. Wouldn't you say?"

"Those are my sentiments. It's never good to overstay one's welcome."

As the two reached the office's front doors, Kobayashi was standing there with an umbrella. "It's raining," she reported, passing the umbrella to the young man.

"Saturday, then."

"Saturday."

The two men shook hands. Then the young man bowed to his superior. He bowed to his secretary as well. He excused himself and took the elevator down to the street level. As he exited through the tower's revolving doors, he found that it was indeed raining. He opened the large, expensive umbrella and walked to the subway station.

16 One Alone, Two Together

While one lay alone in a soft, cozy bed in the affluent Nishi Azabu neighborhood and fretted about her precarious future, a future that would soon include an infant, two others snuggled in a post-coital embrace and ruminated on theirs, this future perhaps being more exciting since it was full of risk and adventure.

"Haruka, I have some incredible news."

"And what might that news be?" she asked, looking up into his eyes.

"I am being transferred. It's a big move for me. It came sooner than I expected. Not that I dislike Aomori, but I will be in Tokyo, and the opportunities there are endless."

"I heard. Mori-san told me. I wish I could go with you."

"Actually, you can, that is if you want to. This promotion means I am entitled to my own assistant. I know it's been only a week," he said, kissing the side of her forehead as her head rested on his shoulder, "but I want you to be that assistant."

"From what I have heard," she replied, holding and examining a few strands of her long, unkempt hair, "Tokyo is awfully expensive."

"I don't know what your salary is now, but I think I can double it."

Once more, she tilted her head to look into his eyes. Then slowly, she moved one leg, then the other, then her entire naked body, sliding herself on top of him. She pushed herself up with her arms, straddling him, looking down at him with a blossoming smile. When he reached up a hand to cup a breast, she shook her head, intercepting the hand with one of hers. Soon she had both of his hands pinned above his head with hers, their fingers interlocked. Dangling the ripe fruit of her breasts in front of his face, she casually brushed both her hair and her hardening nipples across his nose, across his forehead, across his cheeks. Every time he raised his head to take one in his mouth, she lifted herself up so he couldn't.

"Are you going to abandon me in Tokyo?"

"Why would I do that?"

"Maybe it's in your nature," she replied, brushing the nipples again in a circular motion.

"You are too fascinating, Haruka, for me to cast you aside."

"Yeah?"

"Yeah."

"I wonder if I can trust you."

"You can."

At last, she disengaged the fingers of her right hand, reached down, and guided him into her.

At the same hour the two made love, slowly at first, then with wild abandon, the one alone in Nishi Azabu felt more and more distressed, blinking back the stinging tears. When the two finished and collapsed happily exhausted, they soon fell into a deep sleep, their warm bodies entwined. Meanwhile, the one alone lay in the dark room with her wet eyes open, the fear and distrust growing in her fragile heart. When she woke with a start a few hours later, she saw that the morning sunlight was trying to peek through the curtains. While the other two woke refreshed—with more than enough energy to please each other again—the one alone felt as if she had not slept at all.

17 The Young Man Takes His
Date Out for a Special Treat

As the two stood in line, they looked up at large, colorful pictures of the illuminated menu.

"What should I get?"

"A hamburger. Or a cheeseburger. Some fries. A Coke. And you have to have an apple pie for dessert."

"They have apple pie?"

"You bet."

The young woman glanced around the crowded restaurant. "I can't believe how clean it is." When the two reached the counter, she took his arm with both of her hands and whispered into his ear, "You order for me."

"Like I said, when I was a child, coming to McDonald's with my mother was a treat. The apple pie was always the best part. Sometimes I ate it first."

He passed her the cheeseburger. "If you don't like the cheese, you can have mine. Mine doesn't have cheese." As she slowly peeled off the paper wrapper, he dumped out the two orders of fries onto the tray. As he helped himself to some of the fries, she took a small bite of her burger, chewing slowly.

"So?"

"There's something crunchy inside," she reported, swallowing.

"You might have gotten one with a cockroach. That sometimes happens. This part of the restaurant may be clean, but the kitchen is filthy."

Her mouth fell open. Slowly, she set her burger down on the tray.

He picked up one of the Cokes and punched in a straw through the hole in its plastic lid. "Here," he said, passing the drink to her. "Wash it down with this."

Obediently, she sucked on the straw.

"I wouldn't worry about the cockroach. It's just some extra protein. And it's gone now anyways." He took a big bite of his burger. "Mmm," he said with his mouth full. "Mine has one too. Crunch crunch." He took another large bite.

"I am joking," he said, swallowing and then laughing. "It's called a pickle. It's a kind of vegetable." He lifted the top bun off his half-eaten burger and showed her the green pickles. With his thumb and forefinger, he picked one up and ate it. He stuffed some more fries into his mouth. He found his Coke, punched in the straw, took a big swig.

"Now be a good girl and finish your meal," he said.

"You're right. The apple pie was the best part."

"I told you. Would you like another one?"

"Can you order them separately?"

"Wait here," he said. He stood and went to the counter. A few minutes later he returned with another tray; on it sat two warm apple pies in their cardboard packaging.

18 The Young Man Visits the Dentist and Ponders, What Is to Him, a Weighty Concern

The new hygienist showed the young man into the room. She appeared to be much younger than the hygienist he was used to. Since she wore a medical mask, he couldn't see her face; but he could see that she was short and a little chubby, and beneath her white uniform she had large breasts. Her brown hair was done up in a bun. He sat down in the dental chair.

She asked the usual perfunctory questions. He had no pain and no sensitivities. He was there to have his teeth cleaned. That was all. After she noted his answers on a chart, she rolled her chair over, leaned over him, and attached a turquoise paper bib over his dress shirt and tie.

"Okay," she said. "Chair going back." A few seconds later, the young man's head was at the same level as the hygienist's waist. She asked him to rotate his face slightly to the right. As she directed a bright light onto his face, she asked if he wanted her to cover his eyes with a small towel. "I can get by without it," he told her.

"Open, please." She leaned over and looked around inside his mouth with a small, round mirror. Just a few inches separated their faces. She was tantalizingly close. He liked her fresh smell and the downy hair on her forehead. He found that he was incredibly attracted to this new hygienist.

She began the cleaning. As she picked up and set down her various tools and used them on his teeth, he had the very distinct sensation that her breasts were touching his right arm. Were they? Or was he imagining this? He moved his elbow ever so slightly. Yes, it seemed they were resting on his forearm! Was she so engrossed in her work that she hadn't noticed? Or could she be doing this on purpose? Was he letting his vanity get the best of him?

After she finished cleaning the top row of his teeth, she pulled back and asked if he was okay, and in reply, he nodded. "Your teeth look very nice," she reported. "You can rinse now." He leaned his head and shoulders to his left, found the cup of water, took a sip. After he swished for a few seconds, he spit the water into the small, circular sink and replaced the small cup, a weight-sensitive machine automatically refilling it. He leaned back, and, with an earnest look in her eyes, she bent over him and continued her cleaning.

The heavy breasts were there again. He was sure of it. What the fuck is wrong with me, he asked himself. Every day he interacted with young women in uniforms—flight attendants, bank clerks, waitresses, the university girls who worked at the local donut shop. Why, he asked, do I want to have sex with them all? This can't be normal. Perhaps I need help, he thought. As he lay there with the hygienist's breasts touching his right elbow, he closed his eyes and contemplated all of the beautiful women in the world. He found himself getting an erection.

19 "Maybe You Don't Believe My Heart Is in the Right Place."

When the young man walked out of the station, he saw her waiting near the famous Hachiko statue. She wore a lovely all-yellow, sleeveless dress. With her two hands, she held the strap of a small, black handbag. She smiled as he approached.

"I reserved a private room," he said. "*Shabu shabu.* You told me on the phone that you like it."

"I do."

"I hope you are hungry."

"I am."

"Me too."

"It's not too far. We can walk. But first I thought I would buy you some music." The young lady—her dark-brown hair just touching her shoulders—took the arm of the young man, and off they went. It was a beautiful spring evening; there wasn't a cloud in the soft-blue sky.

The young man was no fan of Tower Records, but if he wanted to buy her any music, he thought he had better avoid buying used items. And since she had no record player, he had to go with CDs. After they walked through the automatic glass doors, they found the elevator and took it up to the seventh floor.

She followed him as he slowly made his way down the first aisle. He had hoped to find the 2-CD set, *Girls Girls Girls*, but all the store had was *Imperial Bedroom*. He grabbed it. Nearby he saw *Garlands*, *The Pink Opaque*, and *Victorialand*; he chose the latter. "One more," he said, leading her to another aisle. He was disappointed to see *Hatful of Hollow* was also not in stock. He had to go with *The Queen Is Dead*.

"This should do. Shall we go?"

"What kind of music is this?" she asked, looking down at the three CDs he held.

"Please," he replied as they got to the counter. "Just give it a chance. Promise?"

"I promise."

He paid, and the two took the elevator down to the street level.

As they were exiting the store, the young man recognized one of the other customers; this older man seemed to be considering the recent J-Pop releases displayed near the entrance. For a few seconds, the two men made eye contact, but then the young man looked away.

Out on the street, the young lady took her date's arm with both of her hands and leaned into him.

"Did you see that guy?" she asked as they walked.

"What guy?"

"That guy in the store. The guy by the front door."

"No."

"He's one of the losers," she said, for some reason whispering.

"Losers?"

"I told you. My father pays these two guys to follow me."

"Why?"

"He's just protective, I guess."

When the young man said nothing, the young lady pulled his arm, forcing him to stop. "You don't mind?" she asked, looking into his eyes.

"That we're being followed? No, not really."

"But it's creepy."

The young man reached down and took his date's hand, intertwining his fingers with hers. "Let's not think about them," he said, giving her a tug, and they continued on their way.

After their *shabu shabu* feast, the young couple sat on the *tatami* in their private room. Under each was a thick, square cushion.

"Did you get enough?" the young man asked, looking across the low table at her and leaning back on his hands.

"Yes."

"We can order more."

"No."

"It was nice, wasn't it?"

"It was very nice. Thank you."

"It's very nice being here with you, Mariko."

"My friend Hitomi says I should be careful."

"Careful? Of what?"

"You." She paused, biting her lip and looking down at her hands. "She says you may be after my money."

"Your money?" he asked, chuckling. "Are you rich?"

"Father's money will be mine someday," she replied, her lifted eyes meeting his. "Surely, you must know that."

"You think I am here because I want his money?"

"I don't know what to think," she said, trying to repress a smile. "This is our third date, and you haven't tried to take off my clothes or anything like that, have you? Not even a kiss. Tonight was the first time you took my hand."

"I didn't know you wanted me to take off your clothes," he said, smiling back at her.

"I didn't say I wanted you to," she said, her smile becoming a blush. "Not yet at least."

"Actually, at this point in time, I think I have more money than you do. A lot more."

"That's what Father says."

"So, to show you that I am not using you, that I have absolutely no ulterior motives, I will let *you* pay for dinner tonight," he said, laughing. "And you have to pay more—a heck of a lot more—if you want me to take off your clothes."

"Father told me you saved him a lot of money."

"I hope I did."

"I don't understand such things. I mean, sure, you and he play the stock market. I get that. But what does that mean? And why do you care about him? Why do you care about me, for that matter? Don't you find me boring?"

A frown replaced the young man's smile.

"I don't know how to kiss," she added, looking down again at her hands. "I kissed my arm once. I mean I tried."

"Not knowing how to kiss is not a bad thing," he replied. "You can always sign up for a kissing class."

"And kiss strangers? That's not funny." Her dark, shiny eyes began to swim, and a few tears slid down her unblemished cheeks.

"Mariko, my God, what's wrong?" he asked, leaning forward. "Why are you crying?"

"I told you," she replied, her soft voice full of despair. "I don't know what happened to me that awful night. I can't remember. Don't you understand? Maybe something very bad happened. Maybe some guy, maybe the cab driver…. Oh, God," she moaned, covering her mouth with her hand and looking away.

"Please, Mariko."

"Maybe if you knew," she sobbed, "you wouldn't want to be with me, like you are tonight."

"Mariko, don't be ridiculous." The young man reached into his dress shirt pocket and withdrew a light-blue handkerchief. He shook it out and handed it to her.

"How do you know?" she asked softly, dabbing her eyes and composing herself. "You weren't there. Believe me. There was nothing ridiculous about what happened."

"Listen," he said, reaching across the table with both of his hands. "May I?" After she placed her hands in his, he continued, "I have something important to tell you."

"What?"

"Actually, it's a favor. I mean a very big favor. I need your help.

"I was planning on kissing you tonight. Later, that is.

"I mean kissing with lots of tongue. I was going to nibble on your ears too. Maybe squeeze your tits and grab your ass as well. I have been thinking about doing such things all day. And when I saw you tonight, when I saw how stunningly beautiful you are, I couldn't help myself. Tonight was going to be the night. I was going to risk everything.

"But now that you have been crying like this, now that you've told me you don't trust me, the mood is off. It's all wrong, very wrong. There'll be no kissing, no fondling, nothing at all. I don't know if there ever will be."

"I never said I didn't trust you."

"Let me finish. Please.

"This is what I have to say. Nothing untoward happened that night. I don't know how I know, but I do. I know. Okay? So the favor I am asking is this. Don't think about that night. There's no need to. You promise?"

With her head bowed, the young lady nodded. She disengaged one hand, lifted the handkerchief to her eyes, and started to cry again.

"I want to see you every day," he said, giving the hand he held a firm squeeze with both of his. "I think about you every hour. If you need time to trust me, I have time. I have days and months, years even. But if you are going to cry like this, if you are going to be unreasonable…"

The young lady tried to say something, but she couldn't. The young man waited. After a long minute passed, he said, "I don't want to make you unhappy."

"I am not unhappy."

"Good," he said, releasing the hand. "Now give back my handkerchief," he added with a laugh. "Your father probably has a dozen silk ones. It happens to be the only one I have. And it's not fair. Supposedly, I am the thief, the one with nothing, yet you, with everything, are stealing from me."

The young lady smiled. Instead of passing it to him, she folded the handkerchief neatly, opened her handbag, and placed it inside.

"Give it to me," he said, holding out his hand.

"No."

An hour later, at dusk, when the two stood before the gate to her home, he took her face with both of his hands, his thumbs delicately massaging the soft skin below her chocolate-brown eyes. Then he leaned in and kissed her, kissed her energetically and a little roughly before he tongued one of her ears and bit the lobe lightly. Next, he gently licked the side of her neck before he kissed her some more. Finally, he slid his hands down her long, slender arms to her waist and leaned forward so their foreheads and noses touched.

"Beautiful young lady," he began, his voice a whisper, "may I have my handkerchief back?"

"No."

After another long kiss, he asked, "And why not?"

"You haven't kissed me enough."

A few minutes later, when she got to her room, she found that she was shaking. She stepped into her bathroom and examined herself in the mirror—her face flushed, her lips a little sore, her dark eyes two diamonds shining brilliantly.

Out on the street, the young man made his back to the subway entrance. He saw the two minders at the street corner. One stood outside and leaned against the side of the Toyota Grande Mark II smoking a cigarette. The young man waved to them casually before he descended the steps to the Hibiya line.

⧗ ⧗ ⧗

The young lady had forgotten about the small plastic bag that contained the three CDs. In the morning, they lay on her cluttered desk where she had placed them the night before. She wasn't much interested in music—though she had told him otherwise—and she never applied herself much in her English classes. Moreover, she had never heard of Elvis Costello, The Cocteau Twins, The Smiths, the words and the letters that formed them meaningless to her. But she had been kissed, kissed a little roughly, and she had liked those kisses and the tingling sensations they brought. At that point in her life, receiving such kisses was all that mattered.

20 The Minders Meet with the Young Man and Talk About the Little Cunt, and Then the Three Have an Early Dinner

The young man and a few of his teammates walked off the rugby pitch, one tall fellow carrying the ball under his arm. They exited the gate that enclosed it and were about to walk across the road that separated it from the main campus when he saw the black Toyota Grande Mark II off to his left. One of the minders, the driver, was leaning against the car smoking. Instead of walking across the road and returning to his dormitory with the others, Makoto waved them off and sauntered over to the car.

"Let's go for a ride," the man grunted, flicking his half-smoked cigarette onto the pavement. As the young man opened the back passenger door and climbed in, the driver took his seat, started the car, hit the gas.

"So pretty boy," he began, throwing the other a glance through the rearview mirror, "you'll be graduating soon, huh?"

"In a week."

"You must feel good. All those long hours in the library have paid off."

"I feel fine."

"Any more rugby? Still training, it seems."

"No. We were just kicking the ball around."

"Off to New York in two weeks then."

"That's about right."

"We'll be there to give you a ride. We rather enjoy the long drive out to Narita. Allows us to get a bit of the fresh country air."

"That's not necessary."

The driver threw on the signal and made a left. He seemed to be driving around western Tokyo aimlessly.

"You and the little cunt have been seeing a lot of each other lately."

The young man winced. "I wish you wouldn't use such words," he said, his voice a little louder and his eyes meeting the other's in the mirror.

"Did you hear that?" the driver asked, giving his companion a sideways look. "I don't know if I like his tone."

"He certainly doesn't sound very friendly. I'd say a north wind was blowing, and I thought winter was over."

"Pardon me, scholar," the driver said, glancing into the rearview mirror again. "I didn't know your ears were so sensitive. You don't want to talk about the gash between her legs? Perhaps you've already gotten your fingers wet." The man's companion turned and leaned back over the seat and made a rude gesture with his hand and tongue.

"Tell him what you saw last week," the driver said.

"You mean when I brought the old man his mail?"

"Yeah."

"Well, I peeked into the dining room as I passed by," he reported, turning to look at the backseat passenger. "She was at the table. I caught her practicing on a banana. I was amazed at how much she could take in. She has a talent, it seems!"

"You can pull over now," the young man said, shaking his head and frowning.

"More of that cold wind. You had better turn on the heater."

"We're not done talking," the driver growled. "I have more to say." He made a right and was silent for a minute. As he drove, the two exchanged icy glances through the rearview mirror.

"Actually, lover boy, I am glad to see you respond this way. That angry look on your face tells me she must mean something to you. I'm glad to see it. Let me just say that after all these years, she means something to us. I've grown rather fond of her. I mean that. She's the daughter I abandoned many years ago." He made another right turn before he continued.

"So if you poke and run, as is your tendency… Ah, fuck, what have I done?" he asked, banging the steering wheel in mock anger. "I wasn't supposed to use foul language." The driver once more glanced at his buddy. "And did I just say the word 'fuck'?"

"You did," his companion said. "It fuckin' drives me fuckin' crazy when you use words like that."

"I apologize," he said with a sigh. "It's in my nature, I guess."

At a red light, he stopped, and the crosswalk filled with people. As they waited, the driver kept his eyes focused on the small mirror.

"Are you listening?"

"I am."

"Good. As I was saying, then, if you do anything before you fly—scratch her delicate heart in any manner—I will find you, bend you over the hood of this car, and fuck you with a baseball bat."

After a pause, he continued, "That's the point I am trying to make, pretty boy. I think I made it." The light turned green, and the car edged forward.

"You hungry?" the driver asked his partner.

"Starving."

"Let's go get some *ramen* then. And since the three of us are best buds now, and since we understand each other clearly, we'll go together. Scholar boy, we know a nice place not too far from here. And even though I'd say you're a little underdressed, I think we'll get in."

21 The Young Man Takes His Sweetheart Out for *Ramen* and *Gyoza*

As the apron-wearing proprietress prepared the *ramen* and *gyoza*, she overheard what the handsome boy whispered to his date. "I've eaten in a lot of dives, but this place is the best."

"I must admit. I have never been in a place like this. It's…" As the pretty girl in her stylish dress sat on her stool next to him, she looked around at the faded beer posters tacked to the dirty walls and at the sooty ceiling above her. Plastic crates of empty beer bottles were stacked near the front door. She was searching for the right word. "Charming," she said, finding it.

"Shall we have beer too?"

"I don't know if I should. I haven't had any alcohol since that night, the night we're not supposed to talk about. It's been over two months. Why don't you go ahead."

"Excuse me," he said, speaking to the back of the old woman. "I'll have a beer too. Asahi, please."

"Draft or bottle?" she asked.

"Bottle."

The proprietress turned away from the gas stove and squatted down in front of the small refrigerator she kept. She grabbed one of the large dark bottles and a small glass, one of many, that she also kept in the refrigerator. She turned and placed both on the counter in front of the boy. She picked up the bottle and popped off the top with an opener that hung from a piece of string that she had around her neck. As she poured the boy's glass, the pretty girl blushed and said, "I'll have a glass too, please."

"Of course you will," she said with a smile.

22 The Young Lovers Meet One Last Time. Who Knows When They Will Meet Again?

In the afternoon, the day before his departure, the two sat together in a quiet cafe.

"You looked very handsome at graduation."

"Thank you. You look wonderful today, as always."

"Thank you."

"Would you like more tea?"

She shook her head.

"More cake?"

"No."

"Are you sure?"

She nodded. Were the normally chatty couple having trouble finding something to talk about? It seemed they were.

"As you know, I took a lot of pictures. I will send them once I get the film developed."

"Thank you."

"I wonder how long they will take to arrive."

"Maybe a week. That's all."

"That's a long time."

He looked at her. She looked down at her hands. When she looked up again, she said, "I hope we are not running out of things to say."

"We can write. We talked about that. And call."

"You promise?"

"I promise. The year will go by quickly. And then we can meet again like this."

"Like this?"

"I hope so. We are not saying goodbye today. At least I am not."

She reached into a small Takashimaya shopping bag—thick brown paper, with handles—she had brought with her. From it, she withdrew a small, bow-wrapped box and passed it to him. Slowly, he undid the bow and opened the box. He smiled when he saw what it contained: six handkerchiefs, each one a different color.

"I still want the one I gave you," he said with a laugh.

"You can't have that one."

"Never?"

"Never."

As he replaced the top of the box, there was another awkward moment.

"You can have this, though." She reached into the bag again and pulled out two unwrapped plastic packages: one contained white, lined paper, the other envelopes. Each envelope had red and blue edges and a *Par Avion* stamp on the lower left corner.

"Now you have no excuse."

"I am very sorry, Mariko," he said. "I don't have anything for you. How thoughtless of me!"

"One more," she said. One last time she reached into the small bag; then she handed him something small wrapped in white tissue paper.

"Now I feel very bad."

"You should."

Carefully, he undid the small piece of tape that held the tissue paper in place. As he unwrapped the tissue, he smiled again when he saw what the present was: a beautiful blue, black, and white *kokeshi* doll, hand painted, no doubt.

"Wonderful!"

"She kind of looks like me. Don't you think?"

"She does. Thank you!"

"Wherever you go," she added with a playful smile, "I will be watching you."

"It's just music," he said, sounding confused. "What's the point?"

The young man looked at his older colleague. He had no idea how to respond.

"How many records did you say you have back in Tokyo?"

"Close to a thousand."

"So that means if you listened to one a day, it would take you almost a thousand days to listen to them all. That's nearly three years."

"I guess so." The young man had never thought of his record collection that way.

"And now you want to know where you can buy more?" the other asked, lifting his square-bottomed tumbler of whisky and taking a sip. "Well," he said, "I guess they must mean something to you."

"They do."

"The only thing that means something to me is making the right trade at the right time. That and cozying up to a frisky sea lion, if you know what I mean."

The young man chuckled. "At least we have that in common."

His colleague took another sip and then gave him a long look. "I am glad to hear you say that. You are too serious. I mean way too fuckin' serious. When you got here last week, I didn't think you'd ever laugh. I thought you were some spy the old man had sent to see what was going on. We all had our doubts. Serious fuckin' doubts."

"Really? I apologize. I guess I was a little overwhelmed."

"Sure. It's a new country, a new language, a new way of doing business. And that awful jet lag. We understand. But who asks the receptionist for a key to come in at 7:30? And who wants to stay after the closing bell? What the fuck?

"In any case," he continued, answering a question that the other had posed earlier, "I have no idea where to buy the albums you want. And the stereo equipment? Ask Fujimoto. He's been here a couple of years. He might know." He finished his whisky and stood. "C'mon. The place I told you about is in Chinatown. We'll take a cab."

The first album the young man purchased in New York was Durutti Column's *Circuses and Bread*. He was drawn to the enigmatic cover, it was on the Factory label, and he was intrigued by the song titles, especially "Street Fight," "All That Love and Maths Can Do," and "Blind Elevator Girl (Osaka)." So, he had the album. In his unfurnished studio apartment, he took it out of the sleeve and examined it under a light. For a used album, it looked very clean. Gently, he returned it to its sleeve, then looked at the lyric sheet. "All I ever wanted was your time," he read. "All you ever gave me was tomorrow."

"You again?" the old woman said, smiling mischievously as she lit a cigarette. She was missing several teeth, and her no-bra, nipples-pointing-at-the-floor breasts sagged nearly down to her waist. "You too much," she said and laughed.

"I'll have Dandelion. Give Buttercup to my friend."

"Dandelion not here tonight," she said forcefully, waving her hands in front of the two men. "You take Buttercup. She an angel. She wait for you. I give Sunshine to your handsome friend."

"I've had them all," the older colleague said to the other reassuringly. "They all are buys. You don't need to do any research before you invest."

He reached into his pocket and pulled out a wad of folded-over twenty-dollar bills, which he passed to the old woman. "For both of us," he said. "It's all there."

"I know you," she said, coughing as she exhaled. As she pocketed the money without counting it, a small, white poodle at her feet barked once. The old woman bent over and picked up the dog, and, as she cradled it, she led the two men down a dimly lit hallway. "You here," she said to one and opened a door. "Don't you fucky-sucky too long," she said to him as she closed the door behind him.

"You over here." She opened another door further down the hallway, gesturing for the young man to enter, which he did. On the edge of the bed sat a young, bored-looking woman—bright red lipstick, dark-red panties, a matching negligee. From the doorway, the old woman said something to her in Mandarin. The young woman nodded. The room glowed comfortably with lighted candles, and behind the young woman was a large, well-lit aquarium with several colorful fish. "I knock in one hour," the old lady said to the young man. "You finish. Okay?"

"Okay," he replied, nodding. "One hour."

On her small, bare feet, the young woman stood and made her way to the young man. Without saying anything, she slid off his suit jacket, folded it neatly, set it on the arm of a chair. Then she stood in front of him and slowly unknotted his tie, pulling it off his neck and laying it on top of his jacket. As she worked on the long line of buttons to his dress shirt, he ran his hands through her long, shiny black hair. He had never felt such soft hair before. After she removed his dress shirt, she lifted herself to her toes and began tonguing one of his ears; then she unbuttoned his belt and trousers and slid her small hand into his boxers.

"I'll buy this receiver and those speakers," the young man said to the salesman. "And," he added, pointing to the other side of the room, "I want that Technics turntable you have over there."

"You need speaker wires too?"

"Yes."

"Fifty feet good?"

"What?"

"How long you want the wires? Fifty feet is our longest."

"Sure," he replied, not really understanding how long one would be.

"You got it."

After the young man paid the $1,245, in cash, the salesman helped him get all the boxes into the trunk and the backseat of a taxi, but when the cab pulled up in front of his apartment twenty minutes later, he realized there was no way he could carry all of the boxes in one trip by himself. He was afraid that if he left a box or two on the sidewalk, someone would steal them. After all, this was Queens, not Tokyo. As he removed the boxes from the cab and set them on the sidewalk, the driver just sat there, both hands on the wheel.

"Forty-five," he said when he had finished.

"Can you help me? I want to carry everything up to my apartment."

"Nah, man. I can't just leave the cab here in the middle of the street. And my shift is over. Sorry. Forty-five."

The young man pulled out his wallet, found a fifty-dollar bill, gave it to the driver. After he sped off, he looked at the five large boxes, frowning. The elevator was too slow. He couldn't risk leaving two or three boxes, even for a few minutes. Instead, he decided that he would just move each one a few feet at a time. That way, he could keep his eye on all of them.

As he reached down to grab the biggest box, the heaviest one, the one that contained both Pioneer speakers, he heard a female voice. "You want help?" He turned to see a young woman. She was a little tall, and she had her long, brown hair tied in a ponytail. She was wearing some kind of dark-blue uniform, with matching visor, and a black backpack hung from her shoulders. As he looked into her brown eyes, he noticed the tiny pieces of silver attached to her teeth. It was the first time he had ever seen someone wearing braces.

"Yes, please," he said, a little surprised. "Can you wait here?"

"Sure."

"I mean, I am going to carry this box to my apartment. Can you watch the others when I am gone?"

"Of course," she said and smiled, showing him again the silver, which, to him, looked like railroad tracks.

"Thank you very much." The young man slid over the biggest box to the apartment's front door. He pulled it open and pushed the box in ahead of him. Then he had to use his key on the second door. When he got that one open, he glanced back at the young woman. She smiled again and waved.

The elevator to the fourth floor seemed to take longer than usual, but eventually it shuddered into its position and the door slid open. He lifted the big box and carried it down the hallway to 4E. When he had it inside, he hurried back down the hallway to the elevator, but just as he was about to push the call button, the elevator started moving back down to the small lobby. He—and she—would have to wait a few more minutes.

When he finally got back outside, he saw that a light drizzle had started to fall. The young woman had stacked the remaining four boxes and was holding an opened umbrella over them.

"You had better hurry," she said, glancing at the darkening sky. "Why don't we move them into the lobby?"

"That's a great idea!" he found himself saying, a line from one of the English-language textbooks he had used back in high school.

There was a small awning over the apartment door. The young man moved quickly, grabbing a smaller box and the plastic bag that contained the speaker wires and setting them under the awning where the pavement was still dry. After he had moved the three other boxes, she closed the umbrella and followed him. When he got the first door open, she held it for him. He got everything inside the entrance. When he got the second door open, she held that for him too.

"I am very sorry," he said, once they were inside the lobby. "Can you wait one more time?"

"No problem."

"Really? Are you going to be late somewhere?"

"It doesn't matter. I don't really like my job." The statement—a person in his country would never confide such a thing to a stranger—startled him. Once more, he looked at the young woman. "Okay," he said with a smile. "Just please wait." He punched the elevator call button. After the doors slid open, he hoisted two more boxes; from his right dangled the bag with the speaker wires.

When he got these items up the four flights and inside his door, his eyes searched his empty apartment. He wanted to give something to the young woman, a small gift to repay her for her kindness and patience. But the small refrigerator was empty, as were the shelves in what he would call his living room. He had no furniture either, just a box spring and a one-sheet, one-blanket mattress in the back part of the studio. The only thing he saw was a half-eaten Hershey's bar that sat on the kitchen counter; that wouldn't do. Then he recalled the small doll his girlfriend had given him. He went to where he had set it next to a lamp on the mantle of the no-longer-in-use fireplace. He picked it up and considered it for nearly a minute. Then he set it back down and turned and headed to the door. But before he got there, he returned and grabbed the blue, black, and white doll.

Down in the lobby, he was happy to see the young woman and his two boxes.

"Did you just move here?"

"Yes."

"I thought so. You speak kind of funny. Where are you from?"

"Japan."

With both hands, he presented her the doll. "This is for helping me," he said, bowing his head slightly. Then he added, "I am sorry to have troubled you," another line from the textbook.

"What is it?" she asked, holding the small doll in her two hands.

"We call it *kokeshi*. It's traditional Japan."

"Thank you," she said as she studied it more closely. "It's cute."

There was an awkward silence as the young woman slid off her backpack, opened it, and placed the colorful wooden doll inside. Then she zipped up the backpack and shouldered it, the two looking at each other.

"Do you have McDonald's in Japan?" she asked.

"Yes."

"That's where I am going. I work there," she said, pointing to her visor. "Can't you tell?"

"Pardon me?"

"The uniform."

"Yes."

The young woman laughed.

"This is my uniform," she said slowly. "It sucks, but I have to wear it."

"Okay," the young man said.

"You don't work at McDonald's, do you?"

"Excuse me?"

"You are way too polite. I said, where do you work?"

"I am a stockbroker." It was a sentence he had been practicing for many months. He was sure not to leave out the article.

"A what?"

"A stockbroker."

"A stockbroker? Like on Wall Street? That sounds exciting. It certainly sounds way better than what I do."

116

The young woman glanced down at her watch. "Listen," she said. "I am late. I mean *really really really* late. Why don't you come later? It's not far from here. I work until seven. Go out," she turned and gestured with her arm, "and turn right. McDonald's."

Once he got all of the items out of their boxes, he needed another twenty minutes to connect all of the wires. Then he found the album, took it out of its sleeve, placed it on the turntable. He carefully set the needle and sat down on the polished hardwood floor next to the turntable.

What he heard was not what he had expected, not even close. The mixture of haunting violins, gentle guitar and piano, drum machine, background noise, the occasional voice—all was mostly devoid of emotion, which meant that, paradoxically, it contained more emotion. But if the music wasn't what he had expected, it was incredibly beautiful nonetheless.

When he got to the second song and heard its refrain, "All I ever wanted was your time. / All you ever gave me was tomorrow," his body tingled, and the tears came suddenly.

The young woman smiled when she saw him. "Hey," she said, the braces again to him a novelty, "I didn't think you'd come."

"Why not?" he said, returning the smile. "I like McDonald's."

He ordered a burger and some fries and a Coke. She turned away, gathered the items, and set them on the tray. After he handed her a new-looking twenty-dollar bill, she pushed a few buttons on the register and the till opened. She put the one bill inside and withdrew several others, most of the notes dirty and crumpled. She gathered some coins too. "Your change, sir," she said. He held the tray in one hand, his change in the other. As she smiled, he began to wonder if she was younger than he thought. Since other customers were waiting, and since he didn't know what else to say other than "Thank you," he turned to search the crowded restaurant for a seat.

After some late-hour *sushi*, the two colleagues moved from their table to the bar, where they ordered *sake*.

"So did Sunshine spread a little sunshine in your life?" the one asked the other with a chuckle, cuffing the man on his shoulder.

"She did," he replied with a smile.

"I hope she spread more than just sunshine."

"Indeed. And how was your girl? What was her name?"

"Buttercup."

"Incredible," the other said. "Where do they come up with these names?"

The young man returned the next day, a Sunday, for lunch. Again, the place was crowded, and there were several workers at the front counter, but he saw the young woman. He waited in the line that formed in front of her.

When he stood before her, he ordered the Big Mac set. "Apple pie, too, please," he added.

The young woman nodded. "I thought you were an apple pie kind of guy." She smiled, jabbed some bottoms on the register with her index finger, and then turned to gather the items. After he paid, after she passed him his tray, other customers stepped up. He turned and found a seat in the back. Since he hadn't eaten any breakfast, he unboxed the Big Mac right away and took a big bite. He looked out the window at the passersby, people of all colors and sizes and ages. So, this is New York, he thought. He took another bite of the burger, then ate some fries.

With his mouth full, he glanced up to see the young woman, her hands clasped in front of her.

"Everything okay?" she asked, again smiling.

He nodded, raising his right hand to give her a please-wait gesture. As he chewed hurriedly, then swallowed, he wiped his fingers on a napkin.

"Do you like *sushi*?" he asked quietly.

"What's that?"

In his letter to his girlfriend that evening, he reported that he had had an eventful weekend. On Friday, he had gone to a *sushi* restaurant and had bonded with one of his more senior colleagues; on Saturday morning, he had bought a stereo system—which included a turntable—got it to his apartment, and got all of the components connected. Further, he had found a local McDonald's. "I ate your apple pie," he wrote. "Sorry."

He ended this long paragraph with this observation: "While New York is dirty, and perhaps a little dangerous, it certainly has its charms."

After the two sat at the counter, the *kimono*-clad waitress— using a small pair of silver tongs—handed each of them a rolled, cold, wet hand towel from a tray she held.

"We call this *oshibori*," he explained, saying the word slowly. As he unrolled his and used the refreshing cloth to wipe his face and hands, she watched, then did as he had done. "It feels good, doesn't it?"

"I like it," she said and nodded, folding it into a small square and setting it on the counter, again mimicking him.

"So, you never ate Japanese food before?"

"No."

"Why not?"

"I don't know," she replied, shrugging her shoulders.

"You look nice," he said.

"Thanks. You look very professional. Did you make a lot of money today?"

"What kind of question is that?" he asked with a laugh.

When the waitress returned, he ordered for them. Since she was Japanese, it was easy to tell her exactly what kind of *nigiri* he wanted and how many pieces and how much *wasabi* should be added. Speaking Japanese to her, he was very specific. He even ordered some items that were not on the menu. And to ensure she would enjoy the meal, he ordered some *tempura* as well. And of course, he ordered himself a large bottle of Kirin.

"And what do you want to drink?" he asked his companion in English.

"I don't know," the young lady replied, giving a lost look to the waitress. "Coke?"

When the waitress left, he picked up his *ohashi*. "Do you know how to use these?"

"No."

"Let me teach you," he said, loosening his tie.

After a few solo visits, the young man worked out an arrangement with the old woman. Once or twice a week, he would call and have a woman sent over. It cost a lot more, but he didn't mind. He would get a long massage, a blow job, a fuck—whatever he wanted, often all three—in the comfort of his own place. And then, after a hot shower, feeling refreshed, he would open a bottle of wine and study.

A week later, they returned at her request. She was more adept this time with her *ohashi*. "See?" she said, showing him. "I have been practicing. At school. I use two pencils."

"I see. I am very impressed."

With her *ohashi,* she lifted another piece of *maguro nigiri,* dipped it in the soy sauce and *wasabi,* and put it into her mouth. She smiled as she chewed slowly.

"You don't mind the *wasabi?*"

"I like it," she said, swallowing and nodding her head. "*Oishii desu!*"

"Shall I order more?"

"*Hai!*"

She sat engrossed from the beginning. The opening song, the boat-sized cars crowding the narrow streets, the leading actress' taste in fashion and her eccentric speech and mannerisms—the young man could see that everything about the film brought her joy. This was a new New York for her. And her excitement pleased him.

"I can't imagine wearing such clothes," she said, genuinely stirred. "What's her name again?"

"Audrey Hepburn."

"She's the most beautiful woman in the world," she claimed with obvious sincerity.

"Have you seen Grace Kelly?"

"Who is she?"

So that is how it all started. Unexpectedly, she had buzzed him on a Sunday evening just after her shift ended, intending to say hello. He had just slid the video into his bought-that-day VCR and had pushed play. Though he had seen the film three or four times, he rented it again.

"You want to come up?" he said into the intercom. "I am watching a movie."

There was a long pause, but then she answered with an "Okay."

As the two sat on his small sofa, she blurted out questions whenever she had one. "What kind of name is Sally Tomato?" "Do you think Holly was really married to Doc?" "Doesn't 'mad' mean 'angry'? How can Holly be mad about Jose if she is going to marry him? What does she mean?"

"Just watch," the young man replied, observing her more than he did the film.

At the end, when Holly tossed Cat out into the pouring rain, she cried. She cried loudly, so loudly that he too found himself fighting back tears, the only light coming from the TV screen. In the last few scenes, she had been leaning forward and clutching a small pillow. He reached over a hand and rubbed her back. She looked from him to the TV screen and then back to him, her face and eyes full of genuine pathos. Even after the credits were rolling, she buried her face in the pillow and couldn't stop crying.

So, that is how it all started, the Sunday-evening movies. After *Breakfast at Tiffany's*, they watched *Sabrina* and then *Charade* and later *To Catch a Thief* and *Rear Window* and *North by Northwest*. She loved them all. Of course, they watched *Casablanca* and *Chinatown* and *Citizen Kane* too, even Fellini's incredible *8½* and *La Dolce Vita*. Even though he had seen them all, each Sunday he would rent one and they would watch it together happily.

"I don't get it," she said as the two stood shoulder to shoulder in front of the painting. "Picasso is way more famous than this guy. What's his name? Chagall? How can you say he's a better painter?"

"Being famous doesn't necessarily mean that you are good. Look at all the music you hear on the radio. Is it any good? Not much of it is. Even a lot of good bands have put out some very bad albums. A lot of popular films are awful too."

With curious eyes, the young woman examined the painting more closely. "What am I missing?"

"I am not saying Picasso is bad. I like most of his works. I do. He *is* a great artist. But I like Chagall more. I would argue that Chagall has more emotion. Much more emotion. Step back now.

Just let the colors touch you. See how the bright red of what she is wearing is set off by her pale skin, the white clouds, and the dark buildings in the background?"

"I want some pajamas like she has."

The young man laughed. "They're not pajamas."

"But why is there another head? It's kind of weird, isn't it?"

"That's a very good question. Who knows? But you have to decide for yourself. Don't let anybody tell you what to think or do." For the first time in their relationship, the young woman took his hand, interlocking her fingers with his. Without saying more, they considered the painting for another minute, then strolled into the next room, where more modernist works hung on the walls.

After he had made them a salad and some carbonara pasta, the two sat at his table. The dirty dishes and pans and glasses sat in the sink. Though his older colleague had spent weeks explaining the various regulations to him in Japanese, he wanted to read it all in English. But he found the terms and definitions very technical, and he often had to consult a dictionary. She was reading—and highlighting certain terms and their definitions—a thick biology textbook. After a few minutes, she looked up. "Teach me more Japanese."

Without looking up, he said in a fake-serious voice, "*Watashi wa totemo isogashii desu. Hottoite kudasai!*"

"What does that mean?"

"It means I'm busy. Leave me alone."

"How do you say, 'Be nice'?"

"*Yasashiku shite kudasai.*"

"Say it again."

"*Yasashiku shite kudasai.*"

She tried repeating the phrase. "How did I do?"

The young man turned a page. When he didn't respond, she poked his hand with the tip of her yellow highlighter, but still he didn't say anything or look in her direction. She drew some stars on his arm with the highlighter. When he ignored that, she returned to her book.

A few minutes later, she looked up again. "So, what exactly do you do?"

"What?"

"Your job."

"My job? You know. I buy and sell stocks."

"But what does that mean?"

"You really don't know?"

"I want you to teach me. Please. I want to know what you do."

"If a company issues stock," he began, taking a deep breath, "that means it wants to raise money. One stock certificate is a share in a company. Buying one means that a person trusts that company. That person thinks that company is a good bet. Basically, he wants to invest in that company. The company is supposed to use that money to improve its goods or services. At the same time, the buyer wants the stock price to go up. When it goes up, that's a very good thing. He can sell the stock and make money. When it goes down, it's bad. It's like… Well, anyways, a buyer wants the stock to go up.

"For example, I have been looking into this tech company called Cisco Systems. It's based in California. Now it's trading at just over eight dollars a share. On my advice, my firm purchased about ten thousand shares last week. I can't speak directly to our clients. Not yet, at least. That's why I have to pass this exam. But when I have a recommendation, I tell my colleagues. If they agree, they can purchase the stock—for us, or for a customer. Even though it's technically illegal, right now I still get the commission. Anyway, with a little luck, I can pass in the next month or two. You understand?"

"A little."

"Do you want me to explain more?"

She nodded, reaching out a hand to place in his.

"Sometimes a company pays what's called a dividend. That means the company gives the owner of the stock some money. Usually, dividends are paid every quarter. That means every three months. So, if a person owns one share and the dividend is fifty cents, that individual gets fifty cents four times a year, sometimes more, sometimes less. The dividend depends on the company's profits."

"Fifty cents? That's not very much."

"Yes, but if a person owns one thousand shares of that company, then that person makes five hundred dollars. That may not seem like much, but say the stock rises in value in the same time period. A person might make fifty cents per share—or more—and if the stock rises 20%, then he can celebrate. He can sleep well at night. He can buy—"

"You own that much?"

"A thousand shares? Of course. Sometimes more. And the firm I work for owns even more. We buy and sell thousands and thousands of shares every day for our clients. If we make money for them, we make money for ourselves.

"Actually," he continued, chuckling a little, "if the stock loses value, we still make money. They—the clients—pay commissions. But our customers can't lose too much. That's obvious. In any case, we are a small firm, but we have very wealthy clients all over the world. London. Toronto. Singapore. The Middle East. Of course, here in New York. And Tokyo too. We are very selective, our commissions are high, and we make a lot of money."

"How long are you going to stay here?" she asked, looking him in the eyes. "I mean, how long are you going to stay in New York?"

The question—and what it implied—surprised him. Looking into her earnest eyes, he saw that they began to swim, and one unwiped tear slid down her cheek.

"What's wrong?"

"You're twenty-four," she moaned. "I'm only sixteen."

"You'll be seventeen next month."

"Still. You know so much about everything. About films. About art. About money. Even cooking. I know nothing. And I don't give you anything."

"You helped me with the salad tonight."

"That's not funny," she said, withdrawing her hand.

"Come here," he said. After she stood, he reached over and pulled her onto his lap. "You give me everything," he said, embracing her with both of his arms and rocking her gently. "And you know how much I like your long, brown hair, your brown eyes, most of all, your smile."

"But I told you—"

"We can do those things when you are ready."

"What if you find someone else?"

"Find someone else? Why would I do that?"

"Cause you have certain needs. All guys do, don't they? You won't believe what the guys at work say."

"I'm older and more mature."

"I want you to be happy."

"Who says I'm not?" he asked, squeezing and rocking her again. Then he turned her so they faced each other. "Listen," he said, caressing her face with both of his hands. "My plan is to stay here in New York as long as I can. We have an office here. You know that. If I can pass the test and get my license, I can stay. And if I continue making the firm money, I can do what I want. Okay?"

"Okay."

He kissed her forehead, then used his fingertips to brush away her tears.

"I have to go," she said after a minute. "My mother will be upset if I'm not home by ten."

Slowly, she gathered her books and colored pens from the table and put them in her backpack. At the same time, he grabbed a jacket and his keys, his plan to walk her to the subway station. There, he hugged her and kissed her forehead again before she went through the turnstile. He watched her descend the stairs until she disappeared. Then he returned to his apartment and made a call.

He found his musical tastes expanding. Since a lot of used albums could be had for just a few bucks, he bought a lot. Sometimes he left a store with seven or eight or more. Most of it was dreck, but he had to admit, almost every album had a good song or two, sometimes an incredible song, and every year had its good releases. And while he still looked mostly for present-day indie, he found that the early seventies Neil Young and Van Morrison touched him. He also liked *Wish You Here* and *Animals* and *In Through the Out Door*. He was attracted to some of the noisier stuff too—the Pixies and Lemonheads and Ramones. He kind of laughed when he first heard "I Wanna Be Sedated," but he understood the sentiment. She liked the Ramones too. In her more playful mood, she used to dance around and shake her head and sing along to "Sheena Is a Punk Rocker."

He lay on his back, his head resting on a pillow; she lay next to him, her head resting on his shoulder. He was naked; she wore one of his white T-shirts over her bra and panties. The bedside lamp cast a soft glow onto their young bodies.

"Why don't you touch it?"

Slowly, the young lady raised herself up onto an elbow, reached down a tentative hand, pushed it with two fingers. "It's hard," she reported.

He laughed.

"I mean really hard."

"Put your hand around it."

"Like this?"

"Yes, like that. Now move your hand up and down."

"Like this?"

"Yes."

"How long does it take?"

"That depends."

"Should I go faster?"

"Just a minute," he said, stopping her. He pushed himself off the bed, walked across the apartment to the bathroom. He returned with a small bottle of body lotion. "Use some of this," he said, passing her the bottle and lying back down. She looked at the label, then set it on the bed next to her. Sitting up, she gathered her long hair with both of her hands and used an elastic band to secure it in a bun at the top of her head. Picking up the bottle again, she squeezed out some lotion into her hand, then lay next to him. As she stroked him, she paused and looked up at him. "Can we turn off the light?"

"Of course," he replied, reaching over a hand to do what she asked.

In the darkness, she resumed stroking him. "Does it feel good?"

"It feels very good."

"Am I doing it the way you want?"

"Yes."

"I am really sorry I don't want to have sex yet."

"That's okay. I understand."

"Please wait."

"I can wait."

A few days after her seventeenth birthday, the two—one dressed in a fashionable business suit, the other in her school uniform—entered the Fidelity Asset Management office on Park Avenue just after three. "We need to open an account," he told the receptionist.

"Of course, sir. Please have a seat. One of our representatives will be with you shortly."

A few minutes later, the two sat in a private office, two chairs in front of a large desk. The young man withdrew his wallet from the inside of his suit jacket, and from it he removed some currency. As he held it in his left hand, he counted out ten $100 bills with his right. He laid them on the desk in front of the representative.

"The young lady wants to open an account."

"A savings account?"

"A trading account."

"Wonderful," the representative said and turned to the young woman. "You are wise," he continued, reaching into a desk drawer to gather the appropriate forms, "to begin investing at your age."

When he had them on his desk, he paused, looking from her to the young man.

"There may be a slight problem, however. A trading account requires a minimum balance of $2,500. That amount can be waived if a new client commits to setting up a monthly bank transfer from his or her employer. The money can also come from a savings account. If you commit to transferring a minimum of $100 a month, we can begin with $1,000. Are you working? Or do you have funds in another account?"

"I work at McDonald's."

"I see," he said, again glancing from her to the young man. After an awkward pause, the young man reached into his wallet and counted out another twenty $100 bills. "Let's begin with $3,000," he said, leaning forward and laying the bills on the desk.

"Of course, sir," the representative said, beginning to write. "An initial investment of $3,000. For the young lady."

Looking up, addressing her, he asked, "Do you have any identification? A driver's license?"

"No."

"How old are you?"

"Seventeen."

"Date of birth?"

"September 14, 1973."

"May I ask, sir, what your relationship is to the applicant? Are you her guardian?"

"I am her financial advisor."

"I see. Wonderful." He looked at the young woman again. "May I have your first name?"

"Mary."

24 The First Few Letters

"1990 April 14

"Hi," she began.

"I can't believe you're in New York now. What's it like?

"You left last night. At midnight when I went to bed, I thought, 'He's on the plane now.'

"This morning, I asked Father if you flew business class. He just laughed. I guess that means you didn't.

"I started my French class this afternoon. '*Bonjour, Monsieur Tanaka. Comment allez-vous?*' That's about all I know.

"The last few weeks mean(t) a lot to me. I enjoyed eating *ramen* in that dirty, disgusting place (wink!!!!). And McDonald's was fun too. I am a big fan of cockroaches now (smiley face). I had no idea they were so delicious. And walking home in the rain was kind of romantic, wasn't it? At the gate, I'm glad you have been kissing me (finally!!!).

"Of course, I understand if you forget about me. I think I am easy to forget.

"I hope you will be my good friend, at least.

"If you find a girlfriend, I understand. Please tell me if you do. I will be sad, but I won't be angry.

"I am at the post office now. How should I end? Well, you said you were going to write to me. I hope you do.

"Mademoiselle Mariko"

In reply, the young man wrote the following:

"*Bonjour* Mademoiselle Mariko,

"*Je vais tres bien, merci*!
"I wrote you a couple of postcards last week. Did you get them?
"I was in a hotel for the first few days. I was able to walk to the office. There are only six of us here. All we do is work. My night class starts next week. It's strange, but I think my English is good. I like speaking English. And I am surprised at how much I understand.
"My apartment is in a neighborhood called Queens. I take the subway. I can't tell you how much the subway here is different from the one we have in Tokyo. Let's just say ours is cleaner. It takes me about 45 minutes to get to the office. I can't sleep on the subway. It's too crowded, and I am afraid somebody might rob me.
"I don't plan on looking for a girlfriend. Actually, can you keep a secret? I have someone in Tokyo who caught my eye. She's lovely. I like her big, brown eyes, her long, thin arms. But I don't know how to proceed. Can you give me some advice? I want her to be my sweetheart, but I am here. She is there. She comes from a very rich family. I don't. And of course, I am shy. I think about her a lot.
"I have to read a manual about 8,000 pages long. I am exaggerating only a little. Your father wants me to have broker licenses in Japan and in the States. The Japanese exam will be a cinch. But the test here will be my burden. I have to prepare. I had better go.

"*Au revoir*, Makoto."

In reply, the young woman excitedly dashed off a two-page letter. Here is part of it:

"In regards to that *belle femme* you wrote about, you *have* to tell her your *true* feelings. I mean if you *really really really* want *her* to be *your* girlfriend, I think she will *wait* for you. But *how does she know* if you don't tell her? *SO YOU HAVE TO TELL HER!!!!* Actually, you had better call her. If you are too shy, you can give me her name and number. I will call for you."

The young man's response was brief, but it included this important passage:

"You are a dear friend, Mademoiselle Matchmaker. Thank you for your willingness to make this important call for me. Her name is Ueda Mariko. Her number is 06-5687-4431. Please tell her that I think of her constantly. I don't know what I will do if she rejects me."

With great joy and enthusiasm, the young woman wrote another long letter, which included these lines:

"I spoke with this Ueda Mariko. She seems to be as sweet as you claim. Whether or not she's as beautiful as you assert, well, I have my doubts. In any case, we had coffee.

"Please sit down. I have some very bad news. Her heart is already taken, and I mean TAKEN. She has a BOYFRIEND in New York City, USA. He's smart and handsome and, at times, funny and romantic. He's going to be rich someday. Very rich. You don't stand a chance against a guy like that."

"I am crushed," the young man wrote at the beginning of his letter. There was no salutation. "I still think about her." He continued in a much larger font than usual.

"What should I do now???"

He wrote these three sentences on a large piece of paper and mailed it without signing it.

In thirteen days, he received this response: "She has a cute friend. Do you want to meet her?" This short missive too had neither a salutation nor signature.

"No," he wrote on another large piece of white paper. "I know I am being selfish, but if I cannot be with her, I would rather be alone."

The airlines carried these letters—and many others like them—across the dark-blue Pacific and across the North American continent. The young woman became a familiar face at her local post office. And she spent many evening hours poring over every sentence from her guy in New York City.

And then there were the phone calls. Many of them. Once, at a Sunday breakfast, the old man was about to chide his daughter about this lavish expense, but he decided against it.

"How is your French coming along?" he asked instead.

"What?"

"You seem to have a lot on your mind these days," he said slowly. "I thought you were worried about your end-of-term exams."

"I will do my best, Father," she replied, blushing deeply.

25 New York City Has Its Charms, Part 2

One Sunday afternoon, the two sat at the kitchen table. He had made them a late breakfast—scrambled eggs, toast, blueberry yogurt, freshly squeezed orange juice.

As she wiped her mouth with her napkin, he asked, "Did you get enough?"

She nodded.

"What?"

"Nothing."

He looked at her. "What is it? Tell me."

"Do you want me to massage you again?"

"Sure," he replied. "That would be very nice. But later. Let's do the dishes first."

"So, this is it." He laid the newspaper on the table in front of her. "The *Wall Street Journal* is also very helpful, but this is the one you want, *Investor's Business Daily*."

"What do I do?"

"You read it."

"All of it?"

He laughed.

"As you can see," he said, opening the newspaper to random pages, "there are numerous articles, all related to business. Company profiles, tips, a lot of incredible data. Sometimes we contact the companies ourselves and ask our own questions, but usually, that takes too much time, and often they won't give us the information we request."

She sat looking at him.

"So how much do you have in your account?"

"Three thousand, right?"

"Okay. And what stock do you want to buy?"

"McDonald's?"

"No," he said. "We'll stay away from that one."

"Why?"

He ignored her question.

"Think about things you do every day."

"You mean like poop and pee?"

He smiled.

"Let's try again. What kind of computers do you use at school?"

"I don't know."

"Do you use the computers every day?"

"Pretty much?"

"So?"

"I should buy something related to computers?"

"That would be wise."

Once again, he opened the newspaper. "Here is an index of all the companies listed on the various exchanges. It's in alphabetical order. Let's find the NASDAQ," he said, paging through until he found the section he wanted.

"Here. Look at this company, Microsoft. It makes software. I may be wrong, but I bet your school is using Microsoft software. What did it trade at last Friday?"

"What do you mean?"

"Look here. See this? That's what's called the ticker symbol. Every company listed has one. For Microsoft, it's MSFT. And see these numbers?" he asked, his index finger on the paper. "These are the highs and lows for the previous day, and these numbers are the highs and lows for the past year. This number is the last recorded dividend. And this number is what percentage the stock has gone up or gone down for the year. What did Microsoft do last Friday?"

"It went up 3/4," she reported.

"And what about in the last year?

"It's gone up."

"Is that good?"

"That's very good, right?"

"It is. So maybe Microsoft would be a good buy."

"Can't you just do it for me?"

"No. The account is in your name. Call tomorrow morning. Speak with Mr. Carlyle. He's the man we opened your account with last week. Give him your account number and password. Tell him you want to buy $2,800 of Microsoft. Okay? There'll be a commission for each trade, so always keep a little cash in your account."

The old woman sent a short, chubby, busty Korean this time. As she removed her clothes, she told him her name was Amy. It was the first time he had ever tit-fucked a woman. She insisted on it. "Do that first," she said in native-sounding English, squirting a bunch of baby lotion on her cantaloupe-sized breasts—each areola the size and texture of an oatmeal raisin cookie, each protruding nipple as large as the tip of his index finger. "Anything after that you can do." After she wiped the lotion all over, she dropped to her knees in front of him, and then, just like that, he was doing it. As she pushed together her soft breasts, she kept on shouting, "C'mon! C'mon! Harder! Faster! C'mon!" As he tried to keep up with her, he noticed that she was panting, and she sounded and looked angry; but he soon saw that she took great pleasure in having her tits fucked. When the lotion started to give out, she drooled spit down on his erection as he buried it again and again in the space between her breasts. "Ohhhh!" she moaned and closed her eyes as he thrust. "Ohhhh!" After he came, he staggered back to the bed, sitting on the edge, leaning back on his hands; but she remained on her knees, wiping his cum all over her breasts, then greedily licking each sticky finger. Still breathing heavily, she crawled over to where he sat and grabbed his going-soft penis as if it were the hilt of a sword. "Give me this!" she panted, stroking it aggressively. When she tried to take him into her mouth, he had had enough. "No," he said, pushing her away. "No more."

At The Saint Agnes Academy, the all-girls Catholic high school Mary attended, she played on the soccer team. A starter, she was a quick and aggressive forward. And even though she didn't score often, and even though her team usually lost, the young man enjoyed watching her play. She played tennis too. The two of them played once or twice a month at the club where he worked out. Afterwards, they would change and meet in the pool and swim laps together. Then, later, at his apartment, he would cook pasta and the two would listen to music and study.

He glanced up from his papers. Was she?

"What's wrong?"

She set down the paperback she was reading and looked at him, her face full of genuine sadness. With the backs of her hands, she wiped away the tears.

"Robinson killed a mommy goat."

"A goat?"

"It's an animal. Like a sheep."

"Why did he kill the goat?"

"He ate it. I mean, he was hungry," she said, more tears streaking her cheeks, "so he killed it and ate it."

"Come here."

Slowly, she stood and walked around the table. After he pushed back his chair, she sat on his lap.

"But that's not the sad part," she sobbed, rubbing her eyes. "There was a kid."

"A kid?"

"We call a baby goat a 'kid.'"

"And?"

"After Robinson shot the mommy and it died, the kid just stood there. It didn't run away or anything. It's like it had no idea its mother was dead. When Robinson took the dead mommy goat back to his cave, the little one just followed."

Remaining silent, he looked off, as if he were trying to process what she was relating.

"Later," she explained, "Robinson tried to feed the kid. He felt bad for what he had done. But the kid wouldn't eat the grass. It needed its mother's milk. So the kid died too. Isn't that terrible?"

He nodded slowly. Then he brought her head to his chest and hugged her. "I am very sorry," he said, rocking her. "I don't know what to say."

He glanced at his watch. "Don't you have to go? It's almost ten."

"I told my mom I was staying at Carolina's."

"Yeah?"

"You're not angry, are you?"

"Why would I be angry?"

"I'm still not ready."

"That's okay."

He looked back down at his papers.

A minute passed. "You know," he said without looking up, "if you snore, I'm going to kick you out."

"I don't snore," she said with a laugh.

"How do you know?"

"Believe me, I know."

She reached over and put her hand on his arm.

"Can I have some of your wine?"

"No." But he slid his glass across the table so it stood in front of her. Slowly, she picked it up and took a sip. She licked her lips and then took another sip.

"Want more?"

She nodded.

The two of them ran into his older colleague and his wife in the foyer of the theater one Friday evening. In her Shakespeare class, she had read *The Taming of the Shrew*. And since it was playing at the Barbican, she had asked him to take her.

In the crowded lobby, the young man felt a firm hand on his shoulder. He turned to see his colleague. "Hey," the grinning man said, just a foot away. "Good to see you! You remember Junko, right?"

"Of course. What a surprise!" Though the two men had seen each other just a few hours previously, and though the young man, in parting, had insisted to his colleague that he was going to stay home for the evening, the two men shook hands warmly.

"A Shakespeare connoisseur!" the one declared enthusiastically, pumping the hand. "I had no idea. How charming!" The three exchanged a few more pleasantries, and since they were speaking Japanese, and since the young man had not yet introduced her, the young woman he was with stood there at this side. What was she wearing? Her school uniform—a long, pleated, plaid, blue-and-green skirt; a white blouse; white socks; black loafers. In her hands, she held the Penguin paperback edition.

This young scholar, looking uncomfortable, most of the time her eyes cast down, remained mute until she was finally addressed. "And what do you do?" the other woman asked her in English.

"I am a student."

"I see!"

"This is Mary," the young man said, placing his hand on the small of her back. "Mary, this is my colleague, Mr. Nomura, and his wife, Junko. What a surprise it is to see them! I had no idea they would be here."

"And we you," the husband said, still grinning mischievously.

"Mary is studying Shakespeare and, believe it or not, Japanese. *So desu ka?*"

"*Hai. So desu.*"

"*Kanojo wa totemo kirei!*" the wife declared, but the student had no idea what the older, more sophisticated, well-dressed lady had said.

"Your vocabulary must be getting better day by day," the husband said to her in English. "You have a very good *sensei*."

"I am doing my best."

"I am sure you are."

He looked at the young man and switched back to colloquial Japanese. "A drink afterward?" he asked with raised eyebrows. "What do you say? This lovely surprise needs an explanation."

"I don't think so," the other responded, also in Japanese.

Leaning into his younger colleague, he said, "I can't imagine why not."

A bell rang.

"*Sayonara,*" Junko said to the student and bowed.

"*Sayonara.*"

The two couples parted to take their seats.

"How do you say, 'I love you'?"

He looked up from his papers. "*Anata ga daisuki desu.*"

She kept looking at him.

"And if you really mean it, you can say, '*Anata ga honto ni daisuki desu.*'"

"Say it again."

"*Anata ga honto ni daisuki desu.*"

"One more time."

He said it again, more slowly. As he did what she asked, he noticed she was writing each word down in her small, new-vocabulary notebook.

"Look! Look!" she said, waving a piece of paper as entered the apartment and relating the incident with evident pleasure. "I got my first statement! Do you know what it says? I now have $3,345.34 in my account!"

"*Sugoi!*"

"*Sugoi desho?* I'm gonna buy more when I get paid next week!" She set the statement on the table and unshouldered her backpack. "And look what I brought," she said, unzipping the heavy bag. She reached in and pulled out the *kokeshi* doll the young man had given her more than half a year previously. "I think she belongs here with us," she said as she walked over to his bed. "How about on the nightstand next to the lamp?" And that's where it went.

26 The Young Man's 38th Letter, and the Young Woman's Reply

"1990 December 2

"Dear Sweet Apple Pie," he began, "I miss you terribly."

Then he wrote, "I was wondering if you are busy next summer. As you know, I will be back in early May. I was thinking the two of us could do something special in June or July, like go to McDonald's, get our hair cut at the same time, or get married. Perhaps we could do all three on the same day. What do you think?"

Then below this opening paragraph he drew four boxes and wrote a statement next to each box. It seems that she, in her reply, had to check one of the boxes. Next to the first box he wrote, "Not in a million years!!!!!" Next to the second box he wrote, "I'm busy. Let me get back to you." Next to the third box he wrote, "Give me warm apple pie!!!!!" Next to the final box, he wrote, "Yes."

It was a short letter. He finished by writing, "Please reply soon. Love, Makoto."

On December 18, he received a reply. On the white sheet of paper that he had sent her, she had checked the "Yes" box and then added "!!!!!!!!!!!!!!!!!!" after the "Yes." Also, she had written "Yes!!!!"

and "*Hai*!!!!" and "*Oui*!!!!" in various colors all over the page. There were many smudged lipstick kisses too. At the bottom of the page, she wrote, "I want warm apple pie too!!!!" He was happy to have this reply.

"Do you want me to use my mouth this time?"
"If you want to."
"Do I have to swallow?"
"You can if you want."
"I'll try."

It was a cold, dark evening, and he lived in a relatively nice neighborhood, so he was quite surprised to see a young woman, her face buried in her hands, sitting on the concrete outside the entrance to his apartment. Then he noticed the plaid skirt, the black loafers, the black backpack. When she looked up and he saw her tear-stained cheeks, her red, swollen eyes, he reached out his hands, and she took one, then the other, his from-the-pockets warm, hers cold and trembling. "Mary, what's wrong?" he asked, pulling her up, using both of his hands to rub hers.

"My mother knows."

"Your mother knows?" he asked, looking into her eyes and freeing a hand to push a few strands of hair off her wet face. "About us?" She nodded and began sobbing.

"Let's get inside," he said, guiding her to the door.

As they rode the elevator to the fourth floor, his arms thrown around her in a tight embrace, she explained. "A letter came," she began, still sniveling. "From Mr. Carlyle. I told you I used most of my last two paychecks to buy more stock. He sent some kind of confirmation letter. I wasn't home when it arrived. She opened it. She wanted to know where I got all the money." Once more, her sobbing overwhelmed her.

Once he had her inside, he guided her to the bed and sat her down on the edge. He slid off the heavy backpack, set it on the floor, sat beside her. He removed next her school-uniform blazer and draped it over the backpack. "And what did you tell her?" he asked, pulling the thick comforter from the foot of the bed and wrapping her in it.

"I told her you gave it to me!" she wailed, her voice rich with pain and confusion. "When I told her you were my boyfriend, she called me a slut!"

"A slut? What is a slut?"

"A whore!"

"What is a whore?"

"God! Are you stupid, or what? A whore is a girl who has sex with a guy before she is married. Or she has sex with men for money! She says I am going to go to hell!"

"You are not a whore, and you are not going to go to hell."

"I know, but…" The pained expression on her face pleaded for help.

"Do you want me to talk to her?"

"Are you crazy? She'll scratch your eyes out! And anyways, what would you tell her?"

"Tell her the truth. Tell her that you are my girlfriend. Tell her that nothing has happened, that you're still a virgin."

"If she won't believe me," she groaned, "what makes you think she will believe you?"

"Well, what do you want to do then?"

"I don't know."

146

"You're shaking."

"I know."

"Have you eaten?"

She shook her head.

"Here," he said, lifting off the heavy comforter and positioning a pillow. "Lie down."

"I'm scared," she said as he slipped off her shoes one at a time and set them on the floor. "She told me never to come home again."

"She was just upset," he replied, trying to reassure her. "She didn't mean it." He stood and shook out the comforter so it covered her completely. Then he pulled it back a little to expose her head.

"No" she sobbed again, looking up at him as he tucked the edge around her face. "You don't understand. I have never seen her that mad."

"Well, stay here then."

Still trembling, still sobbing, she rolled over on her side, pulled up her knees, stared out blankly. "Just rest," he said, petting the side of her head, and she nodded. He glanced down at his watch, saw that it was just before eight. Leaning down and whispering into her ear, he asked, "What would you like to eat?"

"Nothing," she replied softly, still looking out at nothing, the thundering of her heart becoming softer. He stood there, looking down at her. Slowly, she joined her hands, palms pressed together, and placed them under the side of her head. Finally, exhaustion closed her eyes, and he was pleased to see that quickly she fell into a deep sleep.

At his small kitchen table, the young man poured himself a glass of wine. He had some important papers to go over, but he had trouble focusing. As he sat and analyzed each document—just the one lamp, brought from the nightstand, on—he kept a close eye on her, all the time wondering where his life was headed. After twenty minutes, he got up and walked over to her where she lay on the bed fast asleep, her mouth half open, her head sunk deep in the soft pillow. Gently, he sat down, placed his hand on her forehead, found that it was hot. She moaned and, in her sleep, tried to push away the hand and then the comforter. He waited, and when she had finished fighting whatever it was she was fighting, he pulled it back up so once more it rested just under her chin.

When his phone rang just before ten, he got up from the table and carried it over to the street-facing windows, the long cord trailing after him. As he maintained his vigil on one, he quietly talked to the other, in Japanese, for nearly an hour.

He looked up from his papers. "What?"

The young woman shook her head.

When he looked up again a minute later, she was still looking at him. "What is it? Are you getting hungry?"

She nodded.

"*Sushi?*"

"Would you mind?" she asked, her face reddening a little.

"Why would I mind?"

"Isn't it far? And a little expensive?"

He frowned.

The young woman smiled. Closing her textbook and straightening her back, she spoke slowly, "*Sore onegaishimasu!*"

Once or twice a week, after work, the young man stopped by the Village to check out the record stores. CDs were taking over, but there was still a lot of good vinyl, most of it used, to be found. He was particularly fond of Galaxie 500, especially the band's *This Is Our Music* release. As they two studied, he would sing to her, "I feel alright when you smile." She loved the album as well. "This is *so* New York," she had said, nodding in approval.

One Thursday evening in early December, she buzzed him unexpectedly. "Can I come up?" she asked. A half minute later, he opened his door. "I ran all the way," she reported, nearly out of breath, dropping her backpack to the floor and walking past him to the shelf that contained his records. "Turn off the lights!" she insisted, her back to him as she fingered through them. "Turn off the lights!" He found the switch on the wall and did as she requested. From outside the window, a soft glow emanated through the windows that faced the street below. He glanced out and noticed that it was snowing, the first snow of the season. She found the album, withdrew it from its plastic sleeve, looked at the track list. Then she set it on the turntable. As she set down the needle, she asked, "Did you buy more candles?" He shook his head. When he heard the first gentle strums of the guitar and then Naomi's voice, he smiled. She came over and leaned into him. He held her as she sang along, "Listen, the snow is falling. Listen, Makoto, the snow is falling everywhere."

The test was much easier than he had expected. In many ways, he had overprepared. But it was over. He had passed. He was now a fully licensed broker in the United States of America.

He had gotten his results Tuesday morning. He told his colleague right away, and, perhaps a bit unreasonably, he insisted on speaking to clients directly. "Let me talk to the old man first," he replied. "He would be upset if we proceeded without his acquiescence."

The phone call from Tokyo came just after the closing bell. The young man was about to leave when he was called back to his desk. "Well done, Makoto!" he heard the old man say. "*Omedeto gozaimasu!*"

"Thank you. You are up very early, sir. I apologize."

"Don't you mind. You must be elated."

"I am."

"Was it difficult? No. Not for a man with your talents."

"You overestimate me, sir."

"I doubt that. I must say that in less than a year, you've made our humble establishment a lot of money. A lot of money. And the markets haven't been to our advantage."

"I am doing my best."

"I greatly appreciate your dedication."

"Thank you."

"I have been thinking. Perhaps you could return before the New Year. The three of us—you, Mariko, and I—could have a little celebration. Would you mind?"

"Not at all."

"I think Mariko will be very happy to see you again. I understand the two of you have been corresponding a little."

"I hope you don't mind, sir."

"Not in the least. So we agree then. I'll speak to Kobayashi. She can arrange the flight. Let's make it first class this time. We have a suite at the New Otani. We can put you up there for a week or so, at least through the holidays."

"How long would you want me to stay?"

"Permanently. I need you here, Makoto. In Tokyo. Maybe in Aomori. We'll see. If you need to speak to our North American clients, you can do so from here by telephone. You may lose a little sleep from day to day, but that comes with your promotion."

Later that same night, she had been using her mouth. But she stopped after a minute. "I think I am ready," she said. The room was dark, but with the faint light creeping in through the windows, he could see enough to watch her slip off her panties and undo her bra. It was the first time she had been naked in his presence. Even when she had used the toilet or had taken a shower, she had kept the bathroom door closed and locked.

"Ready?" he asked, propping himself up on an elbow. As she lay on her back next to him with her arms at her sides, her thighs nearly touching, he looked down the length of her.

"To do it," she replied, the words coming quickly. "To make love."

"Now?"

"Yes. But we have to use protection. You promise?"

"Of course."

"Show me the protection."

"You want me to turn on the light?"

"No. But just let me feel it before you put it on."

"Mary, I don't have any condoms," he lied. "I had no idea you were going to surprise me like this. I'm very sorry."

He waited, but she said nothing.

"Are you okay?"

"No."

He reached out and took her hand. "We can do it this weekend. Saturday night. I'll get some condoms. And I'll get more candles. We'll make it our special night."

Turning away from him, she reached to the floor and picked up her panties.

"Leave them off," he said, arresting her hand. "We can use our mouths. We can do it at the same time. It's not the same, but it still feels good. I'll start. And then I will show you."

"You had better be careful."

"I know."

"It's probably a good thing you passed on your first try and are going back."

The young man picked up his heavy glass. He swirled the whisky and then took another sip.

"How old is she?"

"Seventeen."

"Fuck. You could be in a lot of trouble if her parents talk to the authorities."

"There's only one, a mother, and I'm pretty sure she won't say anything. The girl once confided in me. She told me that her mom is undocumented. She's a hotel maid. Works like eighty hours a week. She's a Filipina."

"So that's all she is, a girl?"

"I didn't mean it that way."

"What is she to you then?"

"What am I supposed to do," the young man asked, sounding both angry and confused, "bring her to Tokyo?"

"Why don't you ask the old man if you can stay here longer? Stay a couple of months. Break it off slowly."

"I thought about that."

"And?"

"Well, there's one good thing. I never slept with her. We've done other things, but she's still a virgin. I'm 100% sure of that."

"You never nailed her?"

"Don't talk like that."

Looking astonished, his older colleague let out a long sigh. "Fuck," he said, leaning back in his chair. "Fuck, fuck, fuck. You are one interesting fellow. I don't know what to say."

That Friday, the Friday before the Christmas break, she was called down to the front office.

"Mary," the school secretary said. "This came for you." She handed her a large Federal Express envelope. "The gentleman here needs you to sign. Please hurry. He's been waiting." Leaning against the chest-high counter, the uniformed delivery man held out a pen and with it pointed to a line. The young woman accepted the pen and signed her name.

Book 2

1 The Minders Greet the Young Man at Narita and Give Him an Update on the Little Cunt

"Well, well, well, look who has arrived, Mr. Makoto Tanaka. JAL flight 619 from JFK. Right on time. You don't look very happy to see me."

The young man glanced around. "Where is Mariko?"

"She's probably sleeping off last night's debauch. When the cool cat is away, the mischievous mice will play."

"You don't say."

"No luggage?"

He shook his head.

The two stepped outside of the terminal to where the man's underling had the black Tokyo Grande Mark II idling at the curb.

"You driving, boss?"

"I think I had better. I haven't had as much to drink this morning as you."

When they got to the expressway, the driver looked up at the rearview mirror. "We kind of missed you," he reported. "But I must say we have been rather busy."

"You bet, boss."

"The little cunt has been up to all kinds of mischief."

"She has indeed! What goes around comes around, right, boss?"

"Lost her prized virginity the weekend you left. Got drilled by a gas station attendant. Hey, fuckface, are you listening to me? Why don't you have the respect to look at me when I have something important to say?"

"Knocked up too," the other man added. "Can you believe that?"

"Yeah, it's always a shame. First time a girl spreads and she gets the stoppage. Yoshiko helped her get the dam all cleared up. She's running again. A regular lioness in heat. Though, of course, I reckon she's not as tight as she once was."

"What the fuck is wrong with you guys?"

"Did he just say something?"

"I think he's tired. Must have been a very long flight. I hear it's a bitch. He sounds a little ungrateful too. That's what too much success will do to a person."

After the driver lit a cigarette, he looked into the rearview mirror again. "Well, he didn't have much success with our friend Amy, now, did he? He's on the other side of the world and he thinks we don't know what he's been up to. She was mightily disappointed. She expects at least an hour of good, solid fuckin', I mean a lot of suckin' and grindin', the kind of action the little cunt likes, but what did you give her, five minutes?"

"Well, boss, not a lot of guys can stand an hour with Amy."

"Amy is not the one on my mind. I've been thinking about a certain high school student. A lovely young lady who's had her head and heart mightily fucked with. What's her name?"

"Mary."

"Yeah. She's the one I'm worried about."

2 The Sound of the Buzzer, Part 1

Just before eight, he heard the buzzer. He got up from the note he was writing and went to the intercom.

"Yes?"

There was no answer.

He had a bad feeling, so he went out and took the elevator down to the lobby. He saw that someone had taped an envelope—chest high—to the outside of the glass security door. He opened the door and saw that the envelope, a greeting card, had his name on it. Next to his name was a sticker of a large, smiley face. He opened the envelope and looked at the front of the card. "Just between you and me, I think YOU'RE a fox!!!" was written there in large letters. The saying was part of the card's message, but he wasn't sure what it meant. When he opened it, he saw that she had written "*Ohayo!!!*" on the left side, the blank side, of the card in large letters. And next to the word, she had drawn a yellow sun with lots of sunshine emanating from it. On the other side of the card was more of the card's message: "You wanna FOX around with me???" Below that, she had written "I can't wait for tomorrow. I hope I don't disappoint you. *Watashi wa anata ga honto ni daisuki desu!!!*" She had filled the white spaces of the card with many little hearts and stars, all of which were drawn in a variety of pleasing colors. And she had signed her name in *katakana,* "マリ."

3 What the Large Envelope from Federal Express Contained

She saw the sender's name on the envelope. She said nothing to the driver or the secretary. She just turned, walked out of the office, went upstairs to the library, found the bathroom in the back. Why would he send her such a missive? Weren't they going to be together tomorrow evening? Hadn't they talked about…? She ripped open one end of the large envelope and turned it upside down. Two keys, a handful of new $100 bills, and a letter fell out. Tears filled her eyes, and her legs had no strength. With a groan, she dropped to the black-and-white tiled floor. For a moment, she couldn't see, and her breathing was fast and heavy.

After a few minutes, she rubbed her eyes and face against her long white sleeves. Then, with unsteady hands, she picked up the letter. This is what she read:

My dear Mary,

I've been called back to Tokyo very unexpectedly. As I write, a car is waiting for me.

I hope to return to New York soon, but I may not be able to for a few weeks, maybe months. This is why I am giving you my apartment keys and some money. The rent is paid through the end of April. My office will take care of the utilities.

I've left everything as it is. Please take care of the records especially. Play them as often as you like.

I know that you and I had a special evening planned for tomorrow. I hope we can share that evening when I return.

Continue to be the wonderful woman you are. I miss you already. *Anata ga honto ni daisuki.*

Makoto

ps. I will call you soon!

4 A Young Man Doesn't Remember the Words He Said and the Emotion with Which He Said Those Words

He stopped by the front desk after he returned from lunch.

"A Yokoda Nami called. From Japan Airlines."

"In regards to a booking?"

"No."

"Client?"

"I don't think so. We have no file on her."

"Give her to Ito."

"She had your private number."

"She did?"

The receptionist nodded. "I politely told her she could speak to any one of our representatives, but she wanted to speak only with you."

Makoto reached out and took the small piece of paper. He looked at the name and the number. "Maybe someone referred her," he said and returned to his desk.

When the markets closed for the day a few hours later, he called. He let the phone ring four, five, six times. He was about to hang up when he heard a female voice.

"*Hai.*"

"Tanaka Makoto *desu*."

"Ah, it's you. I was taking a nap. I arrived this morning from London."

"Welcome home."

"You said you were going to call."

"I know. I apologize. I can't tell you how busy I've been."

"That's a likely excuse. It's been three weeks."

"I am very sorry. If it matters, I am calling now."

"That's a laugh. I called you first."

"You did. Thank you." He added, "Actually, I did call a few times. But no one answered."

"You didn't leave a message?"

"No. I dislike answering machines. I never know what to say."

"I don't have an answering machine."

When he didn't reply, the young lady said, "You know, I waited two hours."

"You did?"

"I did."

"What are you doing now?"

"I told you. I was sleeping. But then someone—a not-so-careful liar, and, I fear, a womanizer—called and interrupted my beauty sleep. I am thinking I should hang up."

"I wish you wouldn't."

"You don't remember, do you?"

"To be honest, I don't."

"Three weeks ago, you flew from New York to Tokyo."

"I did."

"We met then."

"I had a lot to drink. Probably too much."

He heard her sigh.

"Are you a drunkard too?" she asked.

"I don't think so. I had some very bad news that morning."

"That explains the crying."

"I was crying?"

"Just a little. But don't worry. There were only two of you in the first-class cabin. You didn't eat. You just drank and drank and drank. And then after we dimmed the lights, you wept, as I said, just a little. Only I noticed."

"Nami, you have the advantage. I can't recall what I said, what I did. Please forgive me."

"Nothing?"

"Very little."

"Do I have long or short hair? Am I tall? Or short?"

"I have no idea."

She laughed a little. "You told me that I was the most beautiful woman you had ever seen."

"You must be rather lovely for me to have said that."

"You told me you were falling in love with me."

"I think I am. Even though I am sitting at my desk, even though I am completely sober, I feel incredibly attracted to you. I can't wait to see you again."

"You said such words before. You insisted on seeing me that evening. You wanted me to wear my uniform."

"I did?"

"Yes. And then I waited. I waited two hours."

"It seems, Nami, I was holding a prized diamond. But being a fool, I tossed it into the sea. May I have a second chance?"

"Not tonight. I return to Heathrow tomorrow. I have to be at Narita at 5:30. I need to sleep.

"I'll be back Sunday night. If you still want to meet, call me then. I am off on Monday. In the meantime, if you miss me, you can call and leave a message on my answering machine."

5 The Sound of the Buzzer, Part 2

Ｓhe was startled to hear the buzzer. Hoping it might be him, she jumped up and ran over to the intercom.

"Yes?"

"Mary?" she heard through the light static. "My name is Mr. Nomura. I'm Makoto's colleague, his friend. We met at the theater about a month ago. Shakespeare. Do you remember?"

"Yes, I remember."

"May I come up? I would like to talk to you."

She pushed the red button to open the security door. When the elevator opened a minute later, she was in the hallway waiting for him. "He hasn't called," she told the middle-aged man. "Why not?"

"Let's go inside."

"When is he coming back?"

"I have a lot to tell you. That's why I'm here." At the table, he removed his suit jacket and draped it over the back of one of the two chairs. Then he pulled the other one out and sat down. As he loosened his tie, he glanced up at her, on her young, pretty face a look of concern.

"Would you like to sit?"

"No," she replied, shaking her head.

"Okay," he said, glancing around the long, rectangular studio, the far end in semi-darkness. There wasn't much furniture, but from what he could see, everything was tastefully decorated. The three large art posters—a Monet, a Degas, a Chagall, spaced evenly on one wall—added color and style.

"It's been four days," she said, taking a step closer to where he sat. "He said he would call. His note's on the table." The man glanced down to where the young woman was pointing. He picked up this piece of paper and read it. When he finished, he set it back on the table.

"He's not coming back, is he?"

Without looking at her, the man shook his head. "In all honesty," he said, sighing heavily and looking down at his hands where they lay on the table, "it was good that he left when he did. If he hadn't, he might be in jail now.

"You may not understand. Makoto is in a lot of trouble. He's made some unauthorized trades. He's lost the firm—and some of our clients—a lot of money. In a sense, he's a thief." Before he continued, he paused to look up at her. He spoke slowly. "He's selfish. He wants things that don't belong to him."

Squinting at him with disbelieving eyes, the young woman contemplated what she had been told. "That doesn't sound like Makoto," she replied. "He would never do such things."

"Sometimes we don't know the people we are close to."

"No," she said, shaking her head. "No." Her eyes began to swim, and a large tear, then another, slid down her cheek.

"Well," he said, sighing once more, "if he comes back to America, he'll be arrested for certain. And unless we can get the money back, and soon, he may be arrested in Japan."

Biting her lower lip, the young woman was breathing fast, clenching and unclenching her fists. Feeling her pain and confusion, the man couldn't bear to look at her. He stood up and made his way over to the windows that faced the street below. On the ceiling above him was a triangle of faint light from a streetlamp; otherwise, this part of the studio—just a small sofa that sat before a TV on a stand—was dark. On the windowsill, he found a small plant.

He picked it up and, for a minute, considered it. Was it a *bonsai* tree? He wasn't sure. For a moment as he examined what he held in the semi-darkness, he forgot about her. But then he heard her sniveling. He returned the plant to its place on the windowsill and turned. "Is there anything to drink?" he asked.

When she didn't answer, he stepped back into the lighted part of the studio. "I said, is there anything to drink?"

"You mean alcohol?" she asked, rubbing and wiping her eyes with the heels of her hands.

"Yes."

"Next to the stereo," she said, pointing and sounding more composed, "he has some whisky."

Slowly, the man walked over to the stereo and the shelves that held it and other items. In addition to the high-end stereo components, he saw dozens of records and a few paperbacks, in English, by Kundera. Then he reached up and grabbed the half-consumed bottle and looked at the Hibiki label. He turned around, walked back to the table, set it down. Then he turned to the sink and, above it, the few cabinets. He opened one, then closed it. He opened another, found a glass. He sat back down again, uncorked the bottle, poured himself a glass. He took a sip and looked at the young woman. She had moved to the bed and was sitting on the edge of it, leaning forward, her elbows on her knees. Her wet, red eyes were open, but it seemed she was gazing at nothing. The man lifted his glass, took another sip, looked away.

"I kept the apartment clean, just how he likes it."

"I'm sorry. What?"

"I kept the apartment clean."

"I see," he said, glancing around, then back at her. "Good for you. But like I said, he won't be coming back. That's why I'm here. To tell you.

"That's the very bad news," he reported, swirling the amber liquid before setting the glass on the table. "He's gone. You have to accept that.

"But there is some good news. And I think it's very good news."

"Can I talk to him?"

"I doubt it. He's hiding somewhere in Japan. Even I don't know where. Please, let me finish.

"As you know, he was kind enough to pay the rent through the end of the lease, which is the end of April. The money may not have been his, but it's gone now, so we won't worry about it.

"I'll take care of the utilities. Water. Heat. Electricity. Even the phone. If you have any problems, you can call me." The man found his wallet, pulled out a business card, placed it on the table.

"All in all, you have this rather nice place until then. At the end of April, you can take any of these things you want. I'm talking about the bed, this table, the stereo, the couch, the TV. Everything. It's all yours. I'll have some fellows stop by to remove whatever you leave behind." The man lifted the glass and took another sip.

"I know you love him. And I am very sorry about what has happened. But let me be clear. The guy's an asshole."

"Are you going to see him?"

"I might," he replied, standing, placing the glass on the table, then reaching for his suit jacket. "I might be going back to Tokyo this spring."

She stood and went around the corner of the bed to the nightstand. "Give him this," she said. She walked over to where he stood and handed him the blue, black, and white *kokeshi* doll.

6 The Old Man and the Young Man Meet Yet Again

"So how was the flight?"

"Long. A little tedious."

"It's never easy crossing the ocean. But JAL has some fine cognac in its first-class cabin. Did you have any?"

"Actually, I think I drank too much coffee. That's why I couldn't sleep well."

"That's too bad. Good thing we're mostly off this holiday week. I don't ask you to come in at all."

"Thank you."

"And your jet lag?"

"Just a little. The hotel has a wonderful pool, and I find a swim just before going to bed helps. That's what I did last night. Thank you for the suite, sir."

"My pleasure." The old man nodded and looked at his watch.

"So let me tell you what I have in mind. First, Aomori. The clients there aren't as savvy as some here. Many are first-time investors. They may have a lot of questions, but with your good looks and charm, you should be able to win them over. Of course, keep your big ideas coming. The technology is getting better each year. We can trade very quickly now.

"In any case, let's say a year or two. We'll need your expertise overseas from time to time. Hong Kong. Singapore. Maybe even London. You'll need to be ready to travel at a moment's notice.

"Any questions?"

"Yes, sir. Actually, I have a formal request for you to consider." With these words, the young man stood. "As you know, Mariko and I have grown—"

"Sit down," the old man interrupted.

"—very close in the past year." The young man remained standing. "If I may be so forward, sir, I ask to marry her."

The old man looked at him. "And what has Mariko said? Have you asked her?"

"No, sir. I wanted to ask you first. She's given me a hint or two that she might say yes, but again, I respectfully request your permission."

"She's given a hint or two, huh?" he asked, laughing. "That hussy! Well, take her off my hands then. I've been trying to get rid of her for years."

The young man bowed deeply.

"Would this autumn be too soon?"

"Anytime would be fine, sir."

"Good. We'll aim for this September. Maybe October. Now I have a favor to ask you," the old man said, standing and smiling. "Don't say anything until I talk to the hussy myself. Nothing. Go hide yourself for a few hours. You understand? I have a little surprise for her. It will be a good story in the years to come."

"Yes, sir."

"Two more requests. Grandchildren and golf. You do play golf, don't you?"

7 Young Lovers Are Reunited

The view was quite impressive. From the spacious one-bedroom suite on the 34th floor, he looked out at the city as the sun set. He was terrifically hungover, and exhausted, and he wanted to tumble into the king-size bed, but since he had brought no clothes—not even a clean pair of underwear or socks—he thought he had better go out and buy some items. And some warm food would certainly help. As he made his way to the door, he heard the phone. He walked back to the living room and looked at it. Finally, after eight or nine rings, he picked up the receiver.

"Hi," she said.

"Hi."

"So. You're here."

"I am. I just checked in. Just got to my room."

"I thought you might have called by now."

"I apologize. Like I said, I just walked in the door. I had no idea where the phone was until I heard it ring."

"I am sorry I didn't come. Father wouldn't let me go by myself, and I certainly didn't want to go with the losers."

"That's okay."

"Do you want me to come now? We could meet somewhere and have dinner."

"Mariko, I can't tell you how tired I am. I left in such a hurry. I had so much to do the last few days. And I didn't sleep on the plane. Can we meet tomorrow for lunch?"

She sat across from him in a lovely blue dress, her long coat draped over the empty chair next to her. "I was a little disappointed you didn't want to see me last night."

"Please forgive me. Can you believe I went to bed just after eight? I fell into the deepest sleep. If you hadn't called this morning, I might still be sleeping."

"Did we get enough?"

"I think so," he replied, looking down at the shopping bags at his feet. "I can always buy more in the next few days."

"I can't believe you came back with nothing. Not one suitcase? Not even a carry on?"

"Nothing. Just the suit I was wearing. It's like I am making a clean start. Goodbye New York. Hello Tokyo."

"What did you do with the doll I gave you?"

"That," he said, looking into her eyes, "I still have. I carried it in my jacket pocket. It's in the hotel."

During the awkward silence that followed, she looked down at her hands, which rested in her lap.

"It's funny," she said, finally, looking up. "When you were away, I had so much to say to you, so many questions to ask. But now I don't know what to say. I feel nervous all over again."

"I do too. I guess sometimes it's easier to say things in writing than to do so face to face. Do you want me to return to New York? We could write more letters."

"No. But I like the idea of writing more letters."

"And I like the idea of sitting across from you and looking at you. You look exquisite."

The two lovers looked at each other and were silent again. She picked up her fork and took a small bite of the piece of pumpkin cheesecake the two were sharing. He picked up his mango juice and took a sip.

"I'm waiting."

"Waiting? For what?"

"More compliments."

"I like what you've done with your hair. It's much longer."

"And?"

"You gained a little weight."

"That's not a compliment!"

"Actually, I think you were a little skinny last spring. I like the way you look now."

"Well, I think my boobs are a little bigger. What do you think?"

"I wasn't going to say anything about them. I didn't want to be too direct. You might think I am some kind of weirdo. But yes, they too look very nice."

"You are awful," she said, smiling. "I am going to tell Father."

"Did you say anything to him?"

"No."

"Thank you. As you and I discussed on the phone, let me speak to him first. As you know, he's rather traditional. He would expect me to come to him first. And then if he says anything to you, you'll have to pretend to be surprised."

"I'll do my movie-star best."

"There's always the chance he'll say no. Have you thought of that?"

The confused look on her face told him that she hadn't thought that his request would be rejected.

"I come from a broken family, Mariko. My father ran off when I was ten. Who knows where he is now and what he is up to? And my mother is a clerk at a supermarket. I may have gone to the best university in Japan, but that's all."

She looked at him. He looked at her.

"I'll ask him this afternoon. He wants to see me. Just know that I will never forget about you if he says no. But you will have

172

to forget about me." When she heard these words, her eyes filled with tears.

8 A High School Girl Earns Spending Money

Naturally, the high school girl was quite apprehensive, but she had heard about it, and a couple of her friends had already done it. They reported nothing unusual, mostly much older men who were ugly and lonely. "Imagine having sex with your granddad," one of them laughed. "It's easy!" Mostly they talked about the money and what kinds of clothes and cosmetics they could buy with it.

Her first was a college history professor. When she entered the large hotel lobby just after five, she saw a few staff members busily checking in a long queue of guests. She was nervous, but as she walked past, her eyes looking straight ahead, no one stopped her. She found the bank of elevators, and after one arrived, she punched the button for floor 35.

When she entered the room a few minutes later, the heavy curtains were closed, very little light leaking in at the edges. The fifties-looking man who opened the door wore a white T-shirt and black pants and black socks. Slightly overweight, he had a few strands of thin, salt-and-pepper hair combed over his bald head. He wore dark, thick-framed glasses. "I want you to leave your uniform on." As she slipped off her brown loafers, that's all he said.

In the dim darkness, she slid past him, reached out a hand, found the bed. Bunching up her pleated skirt at her waist, she lay on her back, her head on the firm pillow. Then she slid down her panties. She balled them up and held them in her left hand.

As she waited, she could sense the man was taking off his trousers, maybe his shirt and socks too. Then he was doing something and taking a long time doing it. Her eyes were slowly adjusting, but still, she couldn't see well. At last, she felt the man's hand, then his body, on the bed. The hand found her thigh, but he didn't try to touch or massage her. Next, he crawled on top of her, one of his hairy legs, then the other, between hers, the thin T-shirt he still wore smelling like a well-used ashtray. Turning her head to avoid his bad breath, she was happy he didn't try to kiss her. With his left hand, he roughly began squeezing her right breast through her school blazer and white blouse and bra. With his right, he seemed to be directing his erection into her. But he was having trouble. The more he tried, the more rigid she became, her legs and arms stiffening. Though he was not inside her, the man began thrusting. He was breathing very fast. Then, with a shudder, he collapsed on top of her. A half minute later, he rolled off her.

In the darkness, she could barely make out the bathroom door. She waited a minute, then got up and went inside and closed the door behind her. She switched on the light and slipped her panties back on. She checked herself in the mirror. She examined her uniform too, pressing her hands to the wrinkles in her skirt. She turned on the faucet, wet her face, waited for her heartbeat to return to normal.

When she opened the bathroom door, she found the room still dark, the man still on the bed, a forearm thrown over his eyes as he lay on his back. "The money is on the desk," he said, not moving to look at her. "Thank you. Thank you very much." As she made her way to the door, the high school girl paused at the desk to collect the four bills. Outside in the hallway, as she hurried to the elevators, she felt bad, but she felt a little excited too.

The man—young, handsome, extremely well-built—pulled open the door and stood there with a towel around his waist. "Well, what do we have here?" he asked with a leer, looking her up and down. Without another word, he grabbed a wrist, yanking her into the room, and before she could say anything, before she could remove her backpack, he dropped the towel and pushed her down to her knees. Then he forced his large, semi-erect penis into her mouth. Grasping her head with both of his hands, he shoved it in and out as it grew firmer and longer, at times pushing so deep that she gagged. After a couple of minutes, her small hands beginning to resist, he half-stepped, half-shuffled backwards towards the bed, all the while his hands gripping her head, so she had to crawl across the floor on her hands and knees with him still in her mouth. On the TV, an early-evening baseball game was playing, the cheering fans at times drowning out the two announcers. He sat on the edge of the still-made bed with her on her knees in front of him, his hands still holding her head. For a minute, he seemed to be watching the game and her at the same time. "That feels good, doesn't it, when I stick it all the way in." But it didn't feel good. She gagged again.

A batter grounded into second, the third out, and as the two teams changed positions, he turned his full attention back to the girl. Pulling her to her feet, he got the backpack off and dropped it to the floor. He undid the button to her jeans, pulled down the zipper, slid them down to her ankles. When she stepped free of them, he turned her around and pulled down her white panties. When they fell off an ankle to the floor, he picked them up and sniffed them. Then he turned her again, brought up his right hand, rubbed and inserted two fingertips. With his left hand, he lifted her right leg so he could better see her and know exactly where he wanted to massage her. Her eyes moist, the tears forming, she wanted to leave, or at the very least she wanted darkness, but it seemed there was no turning back, and in the well-lit, curtains-open hotel room, she had no way to hide her deep shame.

With rough hands, he positioned her on the bed so he could watch the game and do what he wanted to her. Sitting next to her, he lifted her head and shoved his erection back into her mouth. Then he began to work on the buttons to her blouse. When he had them undone, he threw open the pink fabric and pushed up her bra. "Nice tits," the man said, rubbing them, shaking them, squeezing the nipples roughly. Just then, the sharp crack of bat meeting ball brought his eyes back to the TV, the ball sailing high and deep and bouncing off the center field wall. Pausing what he was doing, he watched intently as the batter tried to stretch it to a triple but was thrown out sliding.

"Fucker," the guy said, standing.

As she caught her breath, one hand at her mouth to check the oozing saliva, he lifted her and turned her over. As she lay on her stomach, he unclasped her bra and slid both it and the blouse off. Next, rotating her again so she lay on her back, down went his head. With it buried between her legs, he could lick and suck and finger and, if he raised his eyes, watch the game at the same time. And that's just what he did; for her, more unsettling minutes passed. When a Toyota commercial came on, he got to his knees. Using her elbows to lift her torso, the girl tried to slide away from him and off the bed, but with his strong hands and arms, he grabbed her by the waist, yanking her back to the position he wanted. Finally, pushing apart her legs, placing his hands on the back of her thighs, pushing them until her knees were nearly in her face, he penetrated her.

"Feels good, doesn't it?" he asked, thrusting quickly.

Grimacing, her eyes closed, she nodded, her pillow-less head nearly hanging off the edge of the bed.

"What's your name?"

"Sakura."

"Come on. Don't give me that bullshit. What's your real name?"

"Sachiko," she answered, lying again.

"You in high school?"

"College." He was penetrating so quickly and so deeply that she found it nearly impossible to speak.

"Fuck!" he said, his smile widening. "This feels fabulous! How about you? Feeling good?"

Though she nodded again, the tears leaking from her eyes gave another answer. Not wanting to see him and what he was doing—not wanting to see anything—she covered her face with both of her hands.

"Nice and tight," he reported, thrusting, looking down at her, pushing aside her small hands. "Just the way I like it."

As the man spoke these last words, he slowed his pace and, a half minute later, pulled out. The girl thought he was going to finish—was hoping desperately that the end had come and that she could soon dress and leave, with or without what she had been promised—but he simply turned her over and lifted her so she was on all fours. With his left hand squeezing a breast, he used the fingertips of his right to rub her before he penetrated her again. He started thrusting hard and fast. For her, this banging went on for several agonizing minutes, her knees and elbows beginning to chafe and burn from the bedspread. But he didn't seem close. He grabbed her breasts, he watched the game, he banged away. When a batter hit into a double play, he shouted at the TV, "You dick!"

Feeling no joy, only pain, the girl thought what he was doing would never end. When she said, "It hurts," he simply ignored her. "It hurts," she said again and again. And then finally, "Please stop!"

A minute later, his hard thrusting at a frenzy, the young man pulled out and quickly threw her onto her back. Climbing on top of her, he exploded on her face, three jagged lines of white, sticky ejaculate running from her forehead to her neck. Then, his left hand at the back of her head, he raised it and forced his erection once more into her mouth. There, he squeezed out the last bits of semen. As he slowly withdrew, he covered her mouth with his right hand and made sure she swallowed what was inside. "That's a good girl," he said, looking down at her and laughing.

As she lay there, her utter degradation and humiliation complete, heavy, salty tears burned her eyes. If the man noticed, he certainly didn't care. As she used a corner of the bedspread to wipe clean her face, he leaned back on an elbow and checked out the baseball game. When she saw that he seemed occupied, she tried to slide off the opposite side of the bed, but, placing a firm hand on her bare stomach, he held her in place. "We're not done yet," he said, glancing from the TV to look at her. "You want your money, don't you?" To emphasize what he had said, he reached over his two hands, pried open her legs, inserted the two fingertips again. She tried, with both hands, to get him to stop, told him that she wanted to leave, but there was little she could do. He was that much larger and that much stronger. Ignoring her, he stood and stepped around the corner of the bed to where her head lay, his groin once again just inches from her face. And the awful, sordid episode described here went on for yet another half hour.

The second time ended the same way it had the first time. After he made her swallow, after he wiped off his waning erection on her aching breasts, he jumped off the bed and sauntered into the bathroom. He seemed to have the stamina and vigor of a dozen young baseball players. When she heard the blast of the shower, she rolled off the bed and fell to the floor. Nothing like this had ever happened with the three high school boys she had been with. Nothing then had lasted more than an awkward minute or two. And for certain, no one had ever done what this man had done. As she lay on the prickling carpet, she began to sob. She was hot and sweaty and incredibly sore and swollen, and she had scrapes and scratches on her knees and elbows and back. But gathering her strength, she pushed herself up and tried to dress as quickly as she could. As she put on her bra, she looked in the mirror by the doorway and saw that she had dried cum and bite marks and bruises on her breasts and neck. And her rubbed-raw knees pained her extremely when she pulled up the denim over them one leg at a time. Of course, hurting in other, more sensitive places, she found that she could barely stand and walk. Her hands still shaking, she was tucking in her blouse when the young man emerged from the bathroom, standing before her completely naked. She was terrified that what had taken place in the previous hour was going to happen yet again.

"Aren't you going to take a shower?" he asked, a large towel gripped in one hand, rivulets of water running down his muscular thighs and calves.

"No," she replied, her voice barely a whisper.

"Suit yourself," he said.

After he dried himself, he dropped the towel to the carpet and slipped on a pair of tight, black underwear. "Did the Giants score?" he asked, turning from the TV to her.

"I don't know."

As he stepped into a pair of tan trousers—first one leg, then the other—he asked, "Want to go get a bite? I'm starving."

"No, thank you."

Standing in front of her, he pulled on a white T-shirt.

"What's wrong?"

Finding it hard to swallow, blinking back the tears, she said nothing.

"I suppose you want your money."

She nodded.

"What the fuck is wrong with you? Why are you crying?"

He reached out to touch her face, but she stepped back.

"Little slut, what were you expecting?" he asked, his voice loud and threatening. "Didn't you have a good time?"

Shaking his head in disgust, he grabbed his thick black wallet from where it sat on the desk next to the TV.

"Am I not going to pay you?" he thundered. She just stood there, her eyes on the floor, more hot tears streaming down her cheeks.

"If I didn't have someplace to be," he said, looking at her in anger, "I'd fuck you for another hour, and only then would you have something to feel sorry about."

Opening his wallet, he took a step toward her. "Listen," he said, withdrawing three bills. "You weren't very good. I was the one who had to do all the work. I know when we talked on the phone, we agreed on 50,000. But that's too much. Here's 30,000. Take it or leave it."

Slowly, she reached out a tentative hand to accept the money he offered. When she had the three bills, she folded them and slid them into her jeans pocket. Backing away from him, she reached down to gather her backpack from the floor. As she made her way to the door, the young, muscular man said with a harsh laugh, "You bitch! You are one lousy fuck!"

9 What a Father Has to Say to His Only Daughter

"Mariko, come here!" her father yelled, sounding angry. He had been drinking red wine quietly and ruminating since he had come home just after seven. The bottle he had opened was nearly empty. The dutiful daughter turned off the TV and joined him at the dining room table.

"Did I say you could sit down?"

"What have I done, Father?" she asked, rising slowly.

"Too much, it seems. That young punk of yours had the audacity to ask me to marry you today. Can you believe that? He did so in my office, of all places. He's a sly fox, that one. He's after the hens in the hen house!"

"About whom are you speaking?"

"Don't give me that naïve look. I'm talking about Makoto!"

"I'm very sorry, Father," she said, tears forming in her eyes. "I thought you wanted me to see him. After all, you were the one who introduced me to him."

"I did, huh? What do you think I am, a whoremaster?"

The maid came rushing from the laundry room. "Ueda-sama! Please!" she implored, throwing her arms around the young lady and embracing her. "Don't say such unkind things!"

"You shut up," he shouted, banging the table. "Both of you listen to what I have to say." He looked at the two women and smiled mischievously, but the woman the smile was directed at had her face buried in the other's bosom. "That rogue is planning on asking you, Mariko, tomorrow. If you say no to him, you had better find a new home to stay in. Did you hear what I said?"

"No," she said almost inaudibly, shaking.

"Look at me." He banged the table again and waited until his daughter turned his way. "I said that fool is planning on asking you tomorrow. What are you going to say to him?"

"I don't know."

"You don't know? Well, let me repeat myself. If you say no to him, you had better find a new home to stay in."

"Father, I…"

"Oh, sir," the old woman said angrily. "You have always been playful, but this joke is too much. Shame on you!"

The old man was beaming. "Yoshiko, soon it will be just you and I in this old house. You had better watch out. I just may ask *you* to marry *me*!"

She held and rocked the young woman. "There, there!" she said, petting the back of her head. "There, there! Stop crying. He was only being cruel."

"Father," the young woman asked, still confused, "do I have your permission?"

"You have."

The young woman looked from him to the maid and then back to him. She saw that both were smiling. But she also saw that the old woman was fighting back tears of her own.

"Stop sniveling, you idiots!" the old man said kindly, emptying the bottle into his glass. "There's going to be a wedding this fall, and it seems you're both invited."

10 At the Live and Let Live, Part 1

The place was crowded, and since he had no idea what she looked like, he squeezed himself in at the bar and ordered a pint of Guinness. When his beer arrived, he took a big swig, then turned and surveyed the noisy, smoky pub. He checked his watch. He was five minutes early.

Fifty minutes later, he was on his third pint. He had to use the restroom, but he had found an empty stool, and he didn't want to give it up. And what if she arrived when he was in the men's room?

It irked him that she was late. Probably on purpose, he surmised. He laughed at himself, got the attention of one of the bartenders, ordered another pint. When he turned back to the crowd, he was almost face to face with a tall, slim, well-dressed woman. She looked at him; he looked at her. He lifted himself off the stool. "Hi," he said, smiling. "It's very nice to see you again."

The attractive woman looked at him and squinted. Ignoring him, she slipped past him and, at the bar, ordered two pints of Harp and a glass of red wine.

"I apologize," he said to her as she waited. "I thought you were someone else."

She didn't reply, didn't look his way.

"I thought you were someone else," he said again, raising his voice and touching her arm gently. "Please forgive me."

Looking at him out of the corner of her eyes, the woman bowed her head slightly.

"Are you with friends?" he asked, but again, she didn't reply.

When her three drinks arrived, she placed them in a triangle and, with two hands, carefully lifted them. She turned away from him and disappeared back into the crowd.

11 The Three Sit Down and Discuss the Menu, the Entertainment, the Order of Events, Among Other Important Matters

"Place a bottle of Macallan on each table. And, of course, beer and *sake* too," the old man told the hotel event planner and her younger assistant.

"Of course," the woman replied and made a notation on her notepad.

"And we'll begin with sashimi—*maguro*, salmon, *hamachi*, *ebi*, some *tamago*. And for the first main course, let's have filet mignon."

"Father, is this my wedding or your wedding?"

The old man smiled happily. "By all means," he said to his daughter, "please proceed."

An hour later, the three were trying out the various cakes the hotel offered. The young woman preferred the white, the old man preferred the white-and-dark swirl, and the young man had no preference. He claimed to like all four options. "You must like one better than the others," his fiancée said, a hint of irritation in her voice.

"Really. They are all very good. You can choose."

After spending over ninety minutes with the event planner and her assistant, the young woman felt frustrated, and she had a slight headache. The process of choosing this or that was, to her, tedious, and her fiancé never seemed to have an opinion. He simply let her choose, but she was tired of choosing. She looked at him. "It would be nice if you told me what you wanted."

"I want what you want."

"See," the old man beamed and slapped his knee, "their first argument!"

The daughter glared at her father. The two event planners looked down at their hands and waited patiently.

"By the way, Makoto," the old man continued, speaking in a voice that all could hear, "I have something rather interesting to relate."

"Yes?"

"Recently, I received our latest report on expenses for our New York office. As you can imagine, with the markets in decline, I have to make sure we are not spending money needlessly. Well, get this! We are still getting utility bills for your apartment.

"The rent I can understand. There was nothing we could do about the lease. But why should we still be getting utility bills? And for more or less the same amounts as when you lived there? It's very curious. It's as if someone were still living there."

The young man sat there stunned. He looked at the old man. With a furrowed brow, his fiancée looked at him.

"In any case, don't worry about it. I called and spoke to Nomura directly. It seems he's been staying there off and on. You know, he's a rascal through and through. Seems he and his wife have been having some disagreements. He's probably got a girl on the sly."

The old man turned to his daughter. "You'll know about those disagreements someday. Couples can't always agree on what to eat, can they? And often they don't see eye to eye on more important matters."

"We never argue, Father."

"Is that so?" the old man asked with a grin.

After another hour, the event planner and her assistant walked with the three to the hotel entrance. Outside, the black Toyota Grande Mark II was waiting; the driver, wearing the same tired black suit he always wore, stood next to the car. When he saw the five approaching, he opened one of the back doors.

"Of course, Ueda-sama, if you have any questions or concerns, or if you want to change anything, by all means, do not hesitate to contact me. We will do everything that you request. We serve at your pleasure." With those words, the two women bowed deeply to the young woman. Then they bowed to her father and the young man.

"See?" the old man said to the young man, a twinkle in his eye, speaking loud enough for his daughter to hear. "That's how a woman should speak to her husband."

"I see."

The daughter shot her father a fierce look. She didn't seem to be too happy with her fiancé either.

"Are you sure you don't want a ride?"

"No, sir. We're going in opposite directions. I can get to the office faster by taxi. I have an hour or two, and there are still some items I want to attend to."

"Suit yourself."

As the driver helped the old man and his daughter into the car, the old man called out, "Don't forget about golf on Saturday!"

"I wouldn't miss it, sir. I can't tell you how much I look forward to our weekly competition."

12 The Prestigious Keiyo Country Club, Part 1

After he returned to Tokyo and found temporary accommodation, after he established a working routine, after the wedding date was set and the various plans—the honeymoon, the move to Aomori—were in motion, the young man took up golf. He was fitted for a set of Mizuno irons and woods, and with the sound advice of the club pro, he was soon hitting consistently long and straight. He was a natural athlete, and he picked up the game—the grip and swing, the etiquette, the terminology—quickly. Much to the chagrin of his soon-to-be father-in-law, he became, after a few months, competitive in their weekly foursome. And after a round, if he wasn't pleased with his score, he often returned to the range and hit another thirty, forty, fifty balls. On other occasions, he would spend thirty minutes on the putting green.

His fiancée wasn't happy that he spent most of his Saturdays—some Sundays too—at the club in Chiba, and she sometimes complained. "You know it's part of business," he would reply. "We often play with clients. And how can I say no to your father?"

To her, he made it sound like the weekly round was a burden. But he quite enjoyed the golf and the country club's atmosphere and facilities. He would sign for his round, for a dozen balls, for dinner, for another bottle of whisky, and he never saw a bill. And after a round, he could shower, soak in the *onsen*, get a massage, even a haircut. It seems he was growing accustomed to living well. If he was late meeting his fiancée, he always had a plausible excuse.

13 At the Live and Let Live, Part 2

"I am very sorry. Because of the snow, we were on the tarmac for several hours. We didn't fly until after seven, more than three hours late. We didn't get to Haneda until after ten. I had no way to contact you."

"There's no need to apologize, Nami. I understand. These things happen. I do hope we can meet sometime soon."

"You sound angry. Or disappointed."

"Not at all. Of course, I wanted to see you. And I still do."

"How long did you wait?"

The two talked for a few more minutes, and though she couldn't commit to a specific day due to her complicated, ever-changing schedule, she promised to call him the next Thursday evening.

After he hung up, he thought about finding yesterday's newspaper to check Hokkaido's weather; but then his phone rang again. In regard to the reception, his fiancée had yet another suggestion, and she wanted to know what he thought of it.

The place was crowded. Since he had no idea what she looked like, he squeezed himself in at the bar and ordered a pint of Guinness. When his beer arrived, he took a big swig, then turned and surveyed the noisy, smoky pub. He checked his watch. He was ten minutes late.

Twenty minutes later, he found himself getting upset, and he thought about leaving, but he ordered a second pint. When he turned back to the crowd, he was almost face to face with a tall, slim, well-dressed woman. "Hi," she said, smiling warmly. "It's nice to see you finally."

"And you," he said, returning her smile. "What would you like?"

"Some wine, please."

"Red? White?"

"White."

"Of course." Raising a hand, he got the attention of one of the bartenders. As they waited for her drink, she looked around. "I like this kind of place," she said, nodding. "It's cozy. And it has a wonderful name."

"It's a little crowded. Smoky too. Sorry about that."

"You don't smoke?"

He shook his head.

"Cheers!" he said when her glass of wine arrived. "I thought I would never see you."

"I apologize for canceling last week," she said after taking a sip. "I had to cover for another attendant."

"Of course. I quite understand."

"You're not angry?"

"Why would I be angry?"

"I stood you up twice. And I was late tonight."

"But you're here now. And you look stunning. Now I know why I said the things I did."

"Have you ever been to London?"

"Not yet. But my work may bring me there soon. It's a city I have always wanted to visit."

"This pub reminds me of London. As I told you, Narita-Heathrow is one of my regular routes. I do it once, sometimes twice, a week."

"Maybe someday you can show me around. I would like that. But with you as a guide, I am not sure if I would see much of the city."

"I don't know what to say to that."

"Should we be quiet for a few minutes and just look at each other?"

She shook her head and took another sip.

"You know, that day, when I met you, I was substituting for a colleague. I don't normally do the JFK route."

"It seems some kind of incredible fate has brought us together."

"If that is what you want to call it."

"And now, after weeks of phone calls, after missed chances, here we are."

"Why were you crying? Do you mind my asking?"

"Crying? On the plane?"

"Yes."

"I don't know. It must have been the alcohol. I get sentimental at times. A sad song, a character's death in a novel, drink… it makes me sad, I guess. Don't you cry sometimes?"

Without answering the question, she looked away, glancing around the crowded pub. "It would be nice to sit. I have been standing all day."

"I am sorry. I had no idea it would be this crowded. I sometimes drop by after work for a pint. Normally, it's not this bad."

She took another sip, her glass nearly empty.

"May I order you another?"

"I would like to stay. Talking with you like this is better than talking on the phone. But as I told you this afternoon, I can't stay long. I fly again in the morning. I should be going."

"Am I going to see you again? Do I have to wait another month?"

"I hope not. I mean, it would be nice to see you again. It's a shame we're both so busy."

"We need to be patient, it seems."

"How about Saturday?"

"Are you free? Please tell me you are. I am going to play golf in the morning, but I am free in the evening. Do you like *shabu shabu*? I know a nice place in Shibuya."

"That sounds wonderful."

"Are you sure?" he asked, pointing to her nearly empty glass. "Just one more? A quick one?"

"If you insist."

"I do. And then I will walk you to the station."

14 Off to Sendai!

Rashly, the young man called in sick from the station. Instead of walking to the office in Ebisu, he got back on the Yamanote train, transferred to the Keikyu at Shinagawa, arrived at Haneda just after nine. He looked up at the large departure board. He had forty minutes before boarding.

At the ticket counter, he handed the representative his JAL Gold Card and a credit card and told her where he wanted to go.

"One way?"

"No. The plane is returning to Haneda, yes?"

"It lands in Sendai at 12:20. Let me see," she said, punching her keyboard. When she looked up, she reported, "It is scheduled to depart Sendai, coming back here to Haneda, at 1:40."

"I want a return ticket then."

The representative looked at him. "Sir, you will be in Sendai less than forty minutes. Are you sure—"

"That's all I need. I am going to collect a signature."

"I see." She began punching her keyboard again.

"And I changed my mind. Let me pay in cash."

"Of course.

"Sir, the business class cabin this morning has many vacant seats. Would you like 4A? 4B? That would place you close to the cabin door. You would be one of the first off in Sendai."

"I am not feeling well. Place me far away from others, if that is possible."

"Of course."

The representative punched her keyboard some more. And after she collected the 36,400 yen, she printed his boarding pass and handed it to him.

"Here you are, sir. Gate 86. After you pass through security, please refresh yourself in our lounge before you board. You have a few minutes. I wish you a safe and pleasant flight."

He avoided the lounge. He began to realize that what he was doing was rather foolish. And though the chance of seeing anyone related to his business—a colleague, a client, a known competitor—was highly unlikely, he decided to play it safe. He found a bathroom near the gate and washed his hands and face. Then he bought a Coke and a golf magazine from a kiosk. A few minutes later, he stood back from the gate and watched as the boarding commenced. There weren't more than two or three dozen passengers. Still, he waited. He wanted to be the last to board. After the final boarding call, he waited another minute, then slowly made his way to the gate. He handed his boarding pass to the agent. Then he made his way down the gangway. He had no idea where on the plane she would be. But when he turned the corner of the gangway and stood before the cabin door, there she was. The blue blazer and skirt fit her tightly. A fashionable red and dark blue scarf was tied around her neck, and she wore a blue cap as well.

The young man stood before her and smiled. Gradually, her mouth fell open. He waited, but she just looked at him, paralyzed.

"'Welcome,'" he said softly. "That's what you're supposed to say."

"Welcome," she replied unenthusiastically. Then she added in an undertone, "What are you doing here?"

"I wanted to see you. I couldn't wait until Saturday. I hope you're not upset."

One of her colleagues approached. It was time to close the boarding door, she reported, all of the passengers being on board. He walked past the two women and turned left. As they began to close the large door and secure it, he found his seat.

There were two other businessmen in the business-class cabin. Both sat on the opposite side of the plane from him. One was engrossed in a newspaper; the other, his head leaning back, already had his eyes closed.

"Here you are." As he looked up, she handed him a warm *oshibori*.

"Thank you."

She looked over at the two other passengers. When she saw that they couldn't hear, she leaned over him slightly and said playfully, "I am not giving you any alcohol. Don't even ask!"

"You're all the alcohol I need today. My God! You look fabulous. I hope you don't mind. After we talked last night, I just had to see you."

When the plane began to roll back from the gate, she whispered, "I have to go."

As the plane taxied to the runway, the young man was incredibly pleased to hear her voice give the safety announcement. First, she spoke in very formal Japanese, reminding the passengers to take their seats, to buckle up, to do this or that during an emergency. Then she gave the same announcement in tentative, ungrammatical English. He listened intently and then smiled when she, at the end, said, "Please relax your flight."

She came as often as she could. After they reached 10,000 feet, she brought him a glass of orange juice and a small plate with a tuna sandwich cut diagonally, then later a glass of hot tea. They talked softly. When the plane began its descent, she brought him another warm *oshibori*. The seventy-minute flight went by very quickly.

In the departure lounge before the return flight, he bought her a chocolate bar. He boarded last again. This time when she saw him at the boarding door, she smiled warmly and said "Welcome!" loudly and bowed deeply.

"Can you help me find my seat?"

"Follow me, sir," she said, glancing at his boarding pass.

He was dismayed to see that there were six or seven more passengers now in the business-class cabin, but at least the seat next to his was unoccupied. He sat down, secured the seatbelt. Soon he heard her voice once again giving the safety announcements.

He saw her much less on this flight. She and her colleagues had more passengers to attend to. But he was able to pass her the chocolate bar; she dropped it into a pocket on the apron she wore during the drink service. And he enjoyed another sandwich and some apple juice. Later, he got up and made his way to the bathroom. In the small space there outside the door, he stretched a little. Then she came up the narrow aisle from the economy class cabin. She was followed by a mother and a toddler. He stepped aside, and she pushed open the bathroom door. After the mother and her daughter entered, the young man—in his fashionable business suit—and the young woman—in her handsome uniform—stood side by side. She looked at him and smiled, but she said nothing.

When they landed at Haneda, what could he do? He got up to deplane with the others. He looked at her as he made his way to the door, but since other passengers surrounded them, he said nothing. Making eye contact, she cheerfully said, "*Arigato gozaimasu!*" and bowed. But then she was saying that—and bowing—to all of the passengers. She and the plane would soon be boarding new passengers and taking off for Fukuoka.

In the arrival area, he looked at his watch. It was just before three. On the plane, he had thought about going in, but there was no need to at this point. He remembered he was supposed to meet his fiancée for dinner. Since he was sick, he would have to cancel. He found a pay phone, inserted his card, dialed the number. "I'm not sure what it is," he said when she asked. "Maybe something I ate. I just feel lousy. I am going to go back to bed.

"No, it's okay. There's no need to bring me anything. I'll see you tomorrow. What would you like?

"Let's have *sushi* then.

"Okay. Call me later."

At his apartment, he fell into a deep sleep. Just before eight, she called. He had been having a pleasant dream, about what he couldn't remember since he had woken up suddenly. But as they talked, he felt incredibly refreshed. "I feel much better," he reported. "It's incredible what sleep can do. So how was your day? Did you have any adventures?" The two talked for twenty minutes.

The other called from her hotel room in Fukuoka just before ten. He was watching the news and drinking a can of Asahi.

"I nearly fell over when I saw you this morning."

"You looked a little surprised."

"You are a fool!" she said, laughing into the phone.

"What are you doing?"

"I just took a bath. I washed my hair. I brushed my teeth. I did all kinds of girly things to look nice tomorrow."

"What color are your pajamas?"

"Red and blue."

"Wonderful."

Playfully teasing each other, the two talked with warmth and ease for over an hour. When the other called again, and again, and yet again, she wondered why the line was busy.

15 A Short Chapter with Some Apologies and a Lot of Lies

"I am sorry about this morning. I didn't mean to sound irritated."

"Well, who knew we would have to choose the color of tablecloths and napkins?"

As they sat on the park bench by the river, she leaned into him. "I'm tired," she said. He lifted his arm and gently placed it on her shoulders.

"Did you get your work done?"

"I did."

"Was it exciting?"

"About as exciting as choosing whether or not we want our guests to have three or four main dishes."

"Is that really how you feel?" she asked, lifting her head and turning it to look into his eyes.

"No, Mariko. I was just joking."

"It didn't sound like a joke."

"I apologize."

Later, the two rode the subway to Hiroo. Slowly, the two walked hand in hand to her gate, and after they exchanged a few kisses, he caught a cab to Shinjuku to get soaped up at his usual place.

He returned to his monthly sublet a couple of hours later. As he keyed in, he heard the phone ringing.

"Where did you go?"

"What do you mean?"

"When I suggested we have some wine, you told me you were tired. You told me you were going to go to bed early. There was no answer when I called."

"Maybe I was in the shower."

"But I called several times."

"Actually, I went for a drink."

When she didn't respond, he sighed and then continued, "Mariko, I made a bad trade today. I lost the company—your father—a lot of money."

"Why didn't you tell me?"

"What was I supposed to say?"

"I don't know."

"That's why I said nothing. It's part of what we do. I am sure your father will understand, but still…"

"I'm sorry."

"I'm sorry I lied to you, and I am sorry I wasn't home when you called."

16 Tearfully, a Young Woman Makes a Confession

When the young man walked out of the station, he saw her standing near the famous Hachiko statue. She wore a lovely blue dress and a white cardigan. With her two hands, she held the strap of a small, red handbag. She smiled as he approached.

"I reserved a private room," he said. "I hope you are hungry."

"I am."

"Me too. I haven't eaten since this morning. Shall we? It's not too far. We can walk." The young lady took the arm of the young man, and off they went. It was a beautiful spring evening; there wasn't a cloud in the soft-blue sky.

After their *shabu shabu* feast, the young couple sat on the *tatami* in their private room. Under each was a thick, square cushion.

"Did you have enough?" he asked, looking across the low table at her and leaning back on his hands.

"Yes."

"We can order more."

"No."

"It was nice, wasn't it?"

"It was very nice. Thank you."

"It's very nice being here with you, Nami. I rarely see you, but when I do, I feel so happy."

"You are always so nice to me. Please don't talk like that." The young woman's brown eyes began to swim, and a few tears slid down her cheeks.

"Nami, what's wrong?"

She didn't respond. She just looked at him as if she were in some great emotional pain. "Tell me. Please."

She sobbed, "I've been wanting to tell you."

"Then do."

As she looked at him, more tears fell down her cheeks.

"I think I know. You have a boyfriend?"

Her face twisting in pain, the eyes narrowing, she nodded and began crying harder.

"I see." The young man reached into his dress shirt pocket and withdrew a handkerchief. He shook it out and handed it to her.

"I thought I loved him," she said, touching the handkerchief to her face and eyes. "But then I met you. You—"

"It seems you and I have two insurmountable problems. You love another, and I—"

"I didn't say I love him. I said I *thought* I loved him. But since I met you, I realize I don't. You and he are so different. At first, I was certain you were some kind of playboy who would just take advantage of me. That's why I was somewhat cold and indifferent during our first meetings. I purposefully came late. I purposefully left early. I was testing you."

"Maybe we should go," he said, after a pause.

"Oh God," she moaned. "I knew I shouldn't have said anything." She raised a trembling hand to her mouth and looked at him with pleading eyes.

"Please, Makoto!" she implored when he said nothing. "Don't be angry. I am going to break it off. He means nothing to me. I know that now."

"Then why did you tell me?"

"I wanted to be honest. You have been so kind, so attentive, so patient. I feel terrible. I feel like I have been lying to you."

He chuckled a little.

"Why are you laughing? It's not funny."

"I am not laughing at you. I am laughing at us, I guess. The incredible fate that brought us together now seems to be driving us apart," he said, leaning forward, placing his elbows on the low table.

"You have someone you've been seeing. You may or may not love him."

"I don't love him," she insisted. "And I told you I am going to end it."

"Okay. But I have some news too. At the end of October, I will be moving to Aomori. It's a temporary assignment. Probably I'll be back in Tokyo in a year or two.

"But I hardly see you now, what with your schedule. You live here, but then you don't. You spend most of your time away. That's your job. I understand. But when I am living in Aomori, I wonder how I will ever see you."

"I fly to Aomori occasionally. I was there two weeks ago."

"And how long did you stay? Twenty minutes? An hour?"

"I was overnight there last month. And you know I can fly for free. I can come on my off days. And now we talk almost every night. We can do the same, can't we? We just need to be patient."

"I don't know."

"Please, Makoto! Can't we at least try?"

"I should become a pilot for JAL," he said, laughing. "But doing so would take years, I imagine. I guess I should just ask you to marry me." She had stopped crying, dabbing at her eyes one last time with his handkerchief; then she folded it and placed it in her handbag.

"Come on," he said, chuckling some more as he pushed himself off the *tatami*. "I need something strong. Let's go and get a drink."

17 The Prestigious Keiyo Country Club, Part 2

As the days grew longer, as the one spent more hours at the office, as he played golf more often, the other found herself at home alone more and more. This other had graduated, and without her classes to attend, she had little to do. Since she applied to no companies, she had no job interviews to prepare for. She assumed she would be spending more time with him, but instead, she felt neglected. Was he avoiding her on purpose? Had he other things on his mind? She wondered. He was always off, it seemed, doing things by himself. It pained her to acknowledge that she needed him more than he needed her. In contrast, he seemed to need no one. He had his work, which he enjoyed, and his independence, which he enjoyed even more, and both irked her.

So, when she found that she could take lessons at the club, she decided to take up tennis. If he was going out on a Saturday or Sunday morning, she could accompany him. How convenient! She imagined that after his round, and after her lesson, the two could have lunch and work out the minor changes she wanted to make regarding the reception. And didn't they need to speak about the apartment in Aomori and the furniture they would need? They did. She had floorplans to various units; didn't he want to see them? In sum, she felt they had a lot to discuss. So tennis—being at the club at the same time—was a way to bring them together more often.

What could he say when she told him? "Wonderful," he said, doing his best to sound enthusiastic. "I had no idea you were interested in tennis." He played tennis too, and played well. But at this point in his life, he wasn't interested in tennis. Since he played his first round, golf had all of his attention. Nevertheless, he gave up a Sunday round one beautiful May morning to play tennis with her, but perhaps "play" is the wrong word. Since she hadn't held a racket since junior high school, and since she was not athletic, she had trouble making good contact with the ball. Even after a few lessons, most of her shots fell into the net, went long, or simply bounced off the edge of her racket.

"You're supposed to hit the ball back to me," he yelled at one point with a playful smile, but she didn't like his joke.

Despite her lack of talent and experience, he was patient. During their many breaks, when the numerous yellow balls needed collecting, he would jog over to her side of the court and show her how to grip the racket, how to bend her legs, how to swing. "Step into the ball, like this," he explained, showing how to move her body. Later, when she grew tired of volleying, he taught how to toss the ball for a serve. When she wasn't making the correct motion, he used his hands to position her body.

"Like this."

"Are you trying to get fresh?" she asked flirtatiously as he had his hands on her waist.

"Keep your eye on the ball," he replied.

"It would be easier to do if you would stop touching me."

But she liked being touched, and she liked touching him, and she liked having him close. And she knew she looked cute in her stylish red tennis skirt and white polo shirt. He and she were having fun together, and for a few minutes, he even forgot about the round he had given up.

"Are we done?" she asked.

"What? Are you tired? We have the court until ten."

"What time is it?"

"Just before nine."

"That's all? It feels like we've been hitting much longer. And it's starting to get hot, isn't it?"

Her instructor sauntered over, a large basket of balls in one hand, several rackets in the other. "Hi, Mariko," he said warmly. "I hope you don't mind. I was watching from the clubhouse. I like what I see—lots of improvement!"

"This is my fiancé, Makoto," she said, emphasizing the word. "He works with Father." The two men nodded at each other and shook hands.

"Well, I just wanted to stop by and say 'Hello.' I am giving a lesson on the court next to yours at nine. See you next Thursday."

After the instructor walked over to his court, the young man asked, "Shall we?"

"Let me go to the bathroom first," she answered, walking off slowly in the direction of the clubhouse.

The instructor's student was late, so he came over and asked the young man if he wanted to hit. Glad to play with someone more at his level, he readily accepted the offer. But he soon saw the instructor was very talented. He had to be in his late forties, the young man surmised, maybe even older, but he was quick and nimble, and it seemed he could hit just about every ball back, even when the young man had volleyed well. Five—then ten—minutes went by. The student didn't show; neither did his fiancée. The two hit harder. For every winner he hit, the instructor hit five. Soon, the young man, exhausted, called out for a break.

"You play rather well!" the instructor said as the two sat on a courtside bench. "You should play more often."

"I don't know," the other replied, still catching his breath. "I would like to, but lately golf has all of my attention."

"That's what I hear. Kawasaki-san tells me you are a natural."

"I wouldn't say that. But he's been a great help. With his suggestions and guidance, I am improving, little by little."

"Still, you shouldn't forget about tennis. It's a worthy pastime. We can play whenever you want. I am here most days."

"Thank you. I will keep that in mind."

"Ah, here is Mariko," the genial instructor said, standing. "Shall the three of us hit? It looks like Higashi-san is not coming this morning."

The three—the young couple on one side of the court, the talented instructor on the other—hit until ten. As they walked off, the young man promised to play with him the next Thursday evening. If he caught the 5:48 train, he would arrive at the club just after seven. And since his fiancée had a lesson at six, the two could return to the city together. It seemed all parties were satisfied, one probably more satisfied than the others.

18 With Her New Admirer, a Young Woman Sees a Bright Future, One Full of Promise and Adventure

"**I** did it."

"You did it."

"Yes."

When he said nothing, she continued. "I broke it off. We met yesterday for coffee. I had nothing with him. I am certain of that. But now with you, I have something, something more. It's a miracle."

"Are you happy?"

"Incredibly!"

"That's very good. I am happy when you are happy."

"Last Saturday, at the hotel, when I insisted we don't make love, you didn't push me. You didn't seem angry or disappointed. I told you I needed time. I still do. But I am more confident of you now."

"Please stop, Nami. I have something to tell you. It may not be good news."

"Yes?"

"I just found out this morning. I won't be here all of next week." He paused, then continued in a serious tone. "Eight days, actually. I leave Saturday night and don't return until the following Sunday. I know I promised to cancel golf and be with you all day Saturday.

We talked about going to Hakone. But I can't do that now. I am very sorry."

She was quiet. Finally, she asked, "Where are you going?"

"You won't like it. It's a place called London. Have you heard of it?"

She said nothing for a half minute. It took her that much time to realize that his words and serious tone were just another example of his playful manner.

"I don't like it at all," she said, at last.

"I knew you wouldn't."

"So, you leave Saturday evening at 7:15. JAL 519 to London Heathrow, I presume? You will arrive in London Sunday morning."

"You are correct."

"I hope you don't expect me to come see you off."

"Would that be asking too much?"

"Yes, it certainly would. As you know, I have to go to Narita myself on Sunday. Going two days in a row is too much. You are rude, sir, to make such a request."

"I have more bad news."

"And what might that be?"

"The office has given me all of Monday off to recuperate. What am I going to do in London all by myself?"

"A full day in London, huh? Nothing to do?"

"That's right. On Friday too I am mostly free. At least I think so."

"You don't know anyone there?"

"I am afraid I don't. As you can imagine, I am going to be very lonely."

"No friendly face?"

"None."

She said nothing. He waited. For nearly a minute, neither spoke.

"How soon could you be ready for some sightseeing? Where shall we begin? You must guide me."

"Did you put together this trip because you knew I was going twice next week?"

"Maybe."

"You have the power to do things like that?"

"Maybe."

"Well, then, aren't you supposed to be working? How can you make your company any money with all of this meaningless chit-chat?"

"We'll talk more tonight," he said, laughing. "We have a lot to plan. If you are not too tired, it looks like you and I will have two full days in London next week."

"Yes, it just so happens that I'll be there on those days that you are off. Some would say it's a miracle," she added, "but I have my doubts."

"*Sayonara*, Nami."

"I'll call after nine. I should be in my hotel room by then."

19 Ah, London!

"I know I have been saying this all day. But I can't believe we are here together."

"You were an incredible guide. We saw a lot today—Big Ben, Tower Bridge, St. Paul's, Hyde Park. Thank you very much!"

"You're welcome."

"I hope we can see more on Friday."

She nodded.

The two sat at the counter of The Mad Bishop & Bear near Paddington Station. It was just before five, and the pub was beginning to fill.

He lifted his Guinness. She lifted her gin and tonic. "Cheers!" he said, touching his glass to hers. "To us."

"To us," she said.

"Are you happy?"

She nodded.

"That's very good. I am happy when you are happy."

"I think I have heard something like that before."

"I mean it."

After she took another sip, she asked, "And what are you going to do tomorrow?"

"I have never been to Oxford. I thought I would take the train there. You should call in sick."

"I thought you were here on business," she said, ignoring his suggestion.

"I am. Sort of. Tomorrow night I am having dinner with Mr. Hansberry and his wife. They have an account with us. It would be nice if you were there too."

"I see. And what are you going to talk about?"

He reached over and grabbed the small glass bottle of tonic water that the bartender had placed next to her glass of gin. He checked the label. "Just as I thought," he said, pouring what little remained into her glass. He examined the empty bottle, rotating it several times to read the label. "You see this tonic water? It's made by Cadbury Schweppes."

She nodded.

"It's one of the biggest drinks companies in the UK—in the world, for that matter. It has…"

She placed her elbow on the bar and then leaned her head on her hand. She looked at him, blinking her eyes sleepily.

"Am I boring you?"

She reached over and took the small bottle of tonic water from him and placed it in front of her. Then she reached over and lifted his pint of Guinness. She took a sip and then nodded her approval; but instead of placing it back in front of him, she set it down in front of her.

"I have three," she said, pointing with her eyes. "What about you?"

"At this present moment," he replied, smiling, "I have nothing to drink. But I have other things."

"Like what?" she asked, lifting her gin tonic and taking a sip.

"I have a beautiful woman sitting next to me. She's young and funny—and a bit of a thief. Her presence should count for something. You see, finding a woman like the one who is sitting next to me is rather difficult, but I can always order another pint."

"Try it. See what happens."

He got the attention of the bartender and ordered another pint. She continued to sip her drink and look at him out of squinted eyes, but the two said nothing as they waited. The bartender was busy, and pouring a Guinness took time and skill. When he was finished, he placed the pint in front of the young man; after he turned his back to serve another customer, she reached over and took it.

"This is mine. Now I have four. Well, I guess three. An empty bottle doesn't count, does it?"

"You should be careful."

"Why?"

"You don't want to drink too much."

"Don't you want to get me drunk?"

"Not really."

"I see," she said, nodding. Then she picked up the new pint and took a long drink. "It's creamy," she reported, licking her upper lip. "I like it."

"Can I have some?"

She nodded again and closed her eyes.

He reached over and picked up the pint. After he took a drink, he asked, "Are you okay?"

"I am tired, so incredibly tired," she said, opening her heavy eyelids and looking at him. "I feel like heavy snow is falling on me."

"We did a lot. Actually, you did a lot. You flew for over ten hours. Then you met me."

She closed her eyes again, her head still resting on her hand.

"Why don't we go to my room? You will feel better after a nap. Then we will get you to your hotel."

With her eyes closed, she said, "I still need time."

He reached out and massaged her back and neck. "We have a lot of time, Nami. I am not asking you to do anything you do not want to do. But a short sleep will do you well."

She sat with her eyes closed, quiet for a long time. Her breathing slowed. At last, she opened her eyes. "Okay then. Let's go."

In the small hotel room, there was only a narrow single bed.

"Come here," she said as she pushed him toward the bed. "Just hold me." She pushed him down and lay down next to him, resting her head on his chest. He did as he was told, slipping his arms around her. Soon she fell asleep. It took him another minute, but soon he too was sleeping.

An hour later, she woke with a start. She sat up and placed her feet on the floor. For a half minute, she rubbed her eyes and looked around the room as if she didn't know where she was.

"Do you feel better?"

She looked down where he lay on the bed. "What are you doing here?" she asked, falling over into him. After a pause, she continued, "Yes, I do. I really do. Thank you."

"Good."

Her breathing slowed; he thought she fell asleep again. But after a few minutes, she said, "I have to go."

"Okay."

But she didn't move. She just lay there.

Outside, the sun was setting, and the light from the window was waning. "Aren't you going to get up?"

"No."

"Are you going to fly tomorrow?"

"No."

"Am I going to see you Friday?"

"No. Wait. You tricked me."

She pushed herself up.

"Let me walk you to the train."

"That would be nice." But instead of standing, she looked down at him. Slowly, she unbuttoned her blouse, then slid it off her long, thin arms. She reached behind with both hands and unclasped her bra. She slid it off and let it fall to the floor. She looked down at him, her long hair falling over her breasts.

"Nami, I don't mind waiting."

She shook her head.

After the two made love, they slept for another hour. Then they dressed. Hand in hand, her head resting on his shoulder, the two lovers walked back—in the early summer twilight—to Paddington Station. She had to return to her hotel at Heathrow. She had to be back at the airport early in the morning for the flight to Tokyo.

"Friday then?" he asked.

She nodded. But instead of moving toward the turnstile, she stood looking at him.

"I love you, Makoto."

"I love you, Nami."

He reached out and put his arms around her.

"I'll be waiting for you right here. Friday. Okay? If something comes up, if your plane is late, anything, you can call my hotel."

He released her. She turned and went through the turnstile, walked to the second car, then boarded the train. He waited a minute on the platform; then, with a slight tug, the train slowly pulled out of the station.

20 Victory and Defeat at the 1991 Sunazawa Ladies Open

He was a little perturbed that the management shut down the entire course for three weeks before the tournament. The summer heat had abated; it was the perfect time to play 18 or 27 holes. Even the expansive putting green was closed. And he wasn't keen on going all three days, but since the old man had given him the nod to take the Friday off—and since his colleagues spoke enthusiastically of the VIP tent the company provided and the provisions it contained—he caught the first train.

Instead of taking a cab from the station, he thought it would be fun to ride the free shuttle bus the tournament was providing. As the nearly full minibus went through the gate and up to the clubhouse, the sun was rising over the tall pines that lined many of the narrow fairways. As he looked out the bus window, he saw that the fairways and greens were still wet with dew. He knew that the old man and some of his more senior colleagues—perhaps his fiancée too—might have arrived by now in their chauffeured cars, but he didn't go look for them.

For the first two hours, he stood by himself at the number-one tee box and watched the competitors tee off. He enjoyed the pageantry; after each competitor had her name called out, she would bow slightly to the spectators and then turn and look down the fairway. She would crouch down, tee up her ball, and set up her drive. Then came the swing and the little *ding!* sound the metal club made when it struck the ball. Then off they went, three young ladies and their caddies followed by a handset-carrying rules official. At that point, he wanted to be one, that is, a caddie. He would shoulder any weight to be the one she talked to as the two strolled down the fairway. He imagined the compliments, the advice, the intimate encouragement he would give. And of course, he was impressed—even amazed—with their full swings, their accuracy, their distance. They drove longer and straighter than many of the fellows he played with. Mostly, he was attracted to the tight skirts and the tight tops and what those items covered. Certainly, they were not all beauties, but he found quite a few simply stunning. These he gazed at longingly, their firm bodies and their handsome tans from spending hours in the sun. He gazed too at their faces. One even had a soft blue ribbon in her long ponytail; several wore bright red lipstick. On their breasts and sleeves and caps were the various advertisers: Coca Cola, Toyota, Mizuho, JAL. He envied them all; most of them were, like him, in the prime of their lives, and they were getting paid to play! He had other ruminations and fantasies, so much so that just before ten, he went into the clubhouse and found the nametag-wearing teenager.

On Saturday, he did the same: took the first train, rode the bus, stood at the number-one tee for nearly two hours. Then he had another pleasurable fifteen minutes with her, presenting her with a silver necklace when they had finished. What a grand life he felt he was living! Ah, the excitement! Later, at noon, he ate well with the old man and his fiancée, then sat in the VIP tent, sipped whisky, watched the competitors come up the eighteenth fairway. There they were again, just ten or fifteen yards away. As each one examined her putt and judged the break and speed, he again found himself giving advice and encouragement. If he clapped a little too enthusiastically, one can understand why. The leader—after two days of competition—was only 21.

He glanced up at the board. The leaders—the final threesome—had just finished 14. Two were tied at nine under; the third had faltered and was four shots back. He had time. Three days in a row would be like scoring an eagle on the long, par-5 6th. He chuckled to himself at the analogy. He stood up, bent over her, and whispered in her ear, "Mariko, I am going to run inside. Do you need anything?"

"Why?"

"Bathroom."

"But won't they be here soon?"

"Maybe one more hour. I'll be back in a few minutes."

"I should come with you. I need to stretch my legs. A walk would do me good."

"No, please stay. I don't want you to miss anything."

"Are you sure?"

"Of course. I will bring you another bottle of tea."

Inside, each table was set with plate and cutlery and cloth napkin, but the expansive dining room was mostly empty. A few club members sat or stood near the windows and looked out at the eighteenth green, but most of them were outside. It was a lovely early-autumn afternoon, the sky a vibrant blue. Many of the wait staff—even a few of the bartenders—stood at the windows and were watching too. In an hour or two, each would have a dozen things to do, but now they were watching or idly chatting.

He didn't see her at the window. He glanced around the dining room. Maybe she was in the kitchen. He hadn't thought of that. He stood there, not knowing what to do.

"Sir, would you like something?"

He turned and faced the lead waitress. "No, Watanabe-san, thank you. I am okay. I just wanted to stretch my legs."

"Are you enjoying the tournament?"

"It's wonderful. I had no idea it would be this exciting."

"If you don't mind my saying, sir, you and Mariko-san look so charming together. I understand you two are getting married soon."

"We are. Next month. Thank you."

Out of the corner of his eye, he saw her enter the dining room carrying a tray full of dishes—steamed and fried rice, some sautéed vegetables, some kind of stir fry. She made her way to a table by the window and set down each item carefully. She bowed slightly to those seated, turned, and started to make her way back to the kitchen.

"Watanabe-san," he said, "Since I am here, I am going to use the restroom. Please excuse me." He turned and casually exited the dining room. Out in the wide hallway, he hurried a little. He was just a few meters behind her when he quietly called out her name. She turned and faced him, the round tray she held tucked under right arm.

"Miki!" he said again. "Please. I can't stop thinking about you. Can we?"

"We almost got caught yesterday," she replied, frowning. "I got scolded for being gone so long. What if I get fired?"

"You won't get fired. I'll make sure of that."

She said nothing. She just stood there, the tray now clutched to her chest.

"Please."

"I have one more order to bring."

"Okay. I'll wait for you. You still have a key, right?"

She nodded.

"Ah, Miki," he smiled, reaching out a hand to caress her cheek. "The loveliest of flowers!"

He walked past her and down the hallway. The utility closet—full of paper towels and bathroom tissue and cleaning supplies and other such materials—was just past the bathrooms. Since no one was in the hallway, he walked up to the closet and tried the handle, but it was locked. He walked back to the men's bathroom and went inside; he stood just inside the door and used his foot to prop it open a few inches.

A minute went by. Then another. Still another. He grew impatient. At last, he saw her walking slowly down the hallway in his direction. As she walked past the men's bathroom, he pushed open the door a little further and looked at her. From an apron pocket, she pulled out a silver key on a ring and showed it to him. As the two made eye contact, he noticed that she was blushing and smiling mischievously. After she keyed in and entered the closet, he stepped out. He dashed down the hallway, opened the door, stepped inside. He found the lock on the doorknob and turned it. Outside, there was loud clapping and cheering from the gallery.

Inside, it was incredibly dark. He reached out his hands and found her face.

"Oh, Miki, my little nineteen-year-old dream come true, I can't believe how beautiful you are."

"You're the only one who says things like that."

"I can't stop thinking about you. Your smile, your perky breasts, my God! I don't know what to do!"

"Don't you think I am chubby?"

"You are perfect. Too perfect! How many times do I have to tell you that? And this little black-and-white uniform of yours! You are like a doll!"

They kissed roughly for half a minute. Then, showing no patience, he turned her so she faced the door. With his left hand, he lifted her pleated skirt; with his right, he pulled down her cotton panties. When he had them down at her knees, he withdrew the condom he had stashed in his pocket, undid his belt and trousers, and let them fall to his ankles. He slid down his underwear and ripped open the plastic that contained the condom; since he was already quite erect, it was easy to slip it on. Then he pushed her over a little and again he lifted her skirt with his left hand. With his right, he found her and guided himself in; then slowly he buried himself deep inside her. There was more loud cheering from the gallery, he groaned, and that was it.

"Oh, Miki," he said. Panting heavily, he buried his head in her hair.

"Is that it?" she giggled.

"I am sorry. I couldn't wait. That's what you do to me." Gently, he slid himself out of her, turned her around, kissed her forehead. Then he reached down with both hands and pulled up her panties. He slid off the sticky condom and let it fall to the floor.

"Who is that young lady in your tent?"

"Who? Oh, she's the daughter of a client," he replied, kissing and gently biting one of her ears.

"You two seem very close. She was there yesterday too."

"Miki, don't be ridiculous. I have to be nice to her."

Outside there was more noise from the crowd, this time a loud, collective groan.

"Don't you want to watch?"

"I would rather be here with you."

"I waited for your call. You said you were going to call."

"Miki," he whispered into her ear, "last night I was with my client and his family until well past eleven. I tried to get away, but I couldn't, not even for a few minutes. And since you live with your parents, I didn't think it would be a good idea to call so late. Please understand."

"Sometimes I feel like you are just using me. Only once have we gone on a date."

"And where did we go?"

"On a dinner cruise."

"Where?"

"Tokyo harbor."

"Wasn't it romantic? Did you not have a nice time?"

"I did."

"And now it sounds like you are trying to break up with me."

"What? I didn't know—"

"Miki, can't you see how I feel about you? But, please be patient. Please remember how busy I am."

"Are we still going to Disney next weekend?"

"Next weekend, we will do whatever you want, my little Minnie Mouse. And if you want to stay with me, I will book a hotel. A very nice hotel. Actually, I would like that very much."

"You promise?"

"I promise. Saturday, right?"

Just then the two nesting lovebirds—perhaps one loving and trusting much more than the other—heard the unmistakable sound of a key in the lock and the bolt being turned. With both of his hands, he grabbed the doorknob just in time. He could feel someone pulling it from the outside. It took all of his strength to hold it shut. His heart beat fast, and again he was breathing heavily. His trousers and boxers still lay crumpled at his ankles.

Then there was a pause. The person outside locked and unlocked the door several times. Then he or she pulled again. Inside, he held the door closed with all of his might. There was another pause, this one longer. He waited. Then he risked everything. He reached down, grabbed his underwear and trousers, pulled them up. He zipped up the trousers and hurriedly buckled his belt. He had no idea what he looked like, how much of his polo shirt was tucked in, but he smoothed his hair and took a deep breath. Then he opened the door and stepped out. He shut it quickly without saying anything to the terribly frightened young waitress, five months out of high school. The bright light nearly blinded him, but at the end of the long hallway, he saw the lead waitress turn and look at him quizzically. He began walking to her.

"Please forgive me, Watanabe-san. Sometimes I get these terrible headaches. The light bothers me. I need complete darkness. To ease the pain, I stepped into that closet. I needed a few minutes to collect myself. I thought I was going to fall over."

"How did you get in? We keep the door locked."

"I asked one of the janitors. He was passing by. Just a few minutes ago. He had a set of keys."

"A janitor? I wonder who that might have been." She looked at him skeptically. She was about to speak, but he interrupted her.

"I believe there is a first-aid station downstairs. Would you be so kind and guide me there? Perhaps I could get some aspirin. I will follow you."

"Well, I am looking for one of my staff," she replied, looking past him down the hallway. "I haven't seen her in over fifteen minutes. I have no idea where she got off to. She's a sweetheart, but she is not very bright. Rather naïve, I must say."

"Please, Watanabe-san," he said, taking her arm and turning her. "I find myself not feeling well again. It's this way, isn't it?"

At the same time they turned the corner, a young woman poked her head out of the utility closet. The slightly chubby waitress in her black-and-white uniform saw no one—and there was no one to see her—so she slipped out of the closet and returned to the dining room as quickly as she could without running. The crowd outside let out another round of applause, this one louder and more sustained.

As the patient and his guide descended the broad stairway that led to the locker rooms and *onsen*, he said, "Watanabe-san, I can't thank you enough." He was still holding her elbow. "I will put in a very good word for you. This club cannot function without you."

"I do my best, sir."

"You do more than that. Ah, I see we are here." He let go of her elbow and looked at her. "I have been such an inconvenience to you. Please forgive me. But I have one more favor to ask you. Please don't say anything about these headaches to Ueda-san or his daughter. I do not want to worry them. In short, please don't say anything to anyone. I am sure you understand."

"I hope you are feeling better soon, sir." With those words, she bowed to him and then turned. He watched her walk back down the wide hallway through which they had come. He lost sight of her as she ascended the stairs.

He wondered how long he had been gone. Twenty minutes? A half hour? He had lost track of time. As he stood there, he chuckled at his adventures. But then he recalled the left-behind condom. He could only hope his paramour had picked it up.

Instead of going back the way he had come and returning to the VIP tent, he entered the first-aid station. On his way to the locker room, he had walked past this room dozens of times, but now, as he stood there, he couldn't recall what it was used for. Some kind of office, he assumed. But for the tournament it had been converted into this first-aid station. And now the room had no door—just a white sheet with a large red cross on it that hung from the doorframe. Inside, it was cool and quiet; a middle-aged woman in a white uniform sat in a chair reading a paperback. She looked up at him.

"Hi," he quietly said. "I have a headache."

"I see," she said and set down the book. She stood, went up to him, gently placed a cool hand on his forehead. She held it there for a few seconds. Then she removed the stethoscope that hung around her neck.

"May I?" she asked.

"Of course."

"Please sit down."

To his left was a small table and one round stool; he sat on it.

"Would you be so kind as to lift up your shirt?"

When he did what he had been asked, she first put the resonator on his back. "Please take a deep breath." He did so. She moved the resonator. "And one more." She moved it once again, this time to his chest. As she listened intently, she asked a few more questions.

"Any alcohol today?"

"None. But some last night."

"Do you smoke?"

He shook his head.

"Did you eat anything unusual for breakfast or lunch?"

"No."

"Would you mind if I took your blood pressure?"

"Of course not."

The monitor hung on a low hook on a wall. She unwrapped the cuff, placed it around his right bicep, and fastened it. Then she pumped it. As it tightened around the muscles, she began to listen with the resonator. Then she looked down at her watch. When she was finished, she removed it and set it back on its hook.

"When did your headache commence?"

"That's hard to say. Maybe an hour ago."

"And do you feel a great deal of pain? Or just a little pain?"

"The pain was severe, but for some reason, sitting here with you, I am already feeling better."

"I can't find anything amiss. Your heart sounds quite strong, you have no fever, and your blood pressure is normal."

"I see. Well, I guess that is good news."

"Perhaps you would like to lie down for a few minutes. Maybe it will pass. We have several cots," she said, gesturing with her arm. "Maybe thirty minutes of quiet rest—even a nap—would help. Maybe you were overexcited."

"That is a wonderful suggestion," he said, standing. "Thank you, doctor."

The middle-aged woman blushed slightly. "I am not a doctor."

"Through here?"

"Yes. You will find four cots on each side. Presently, there is only one other patient. Please be quiet. I believe she is sleeping."

It seemed the nurse's station was divided into two parts by a white, sheet-like divider that hung from small hooks that were attached to the ceiling. There was the examining room, in which he stood, and behind the divider were the cots. The nurse pulled aside this divider, and he stepped inside.

He found the eight cots, four on each side, as she had related, and the cots themselves were separated by similar white-sheet dividers, again suspended from the ceiling. Slowly, and quietly, he stepped a bit further. The last cot on his left was indeed occupied. A young lady lay on her side with her back to him. She was wearing a fashionable white polo shirt, a pink skirt, white knee-high socks, and—what caught his attention the most—a pink ribbon that was tied around the end of her long, tightly braided hair. Her arms and legs—the skirt high on her muscular thighs—were deeply tanned. He looked down at the floor and saw white golf shoes sitting next to the cot. For half a minute, he just stood and looked down at her. Was she? She had to be. She held a small, white towel to her face.

She must have sensed she was not alone. She turned slightly, lifted the towel, and looked up at him with red, puffy eyes. "Are you a reporter?"

"No."

"Then what do you want?"

"Nothing but your happiness." With a gesture toward her cot, he asked, "May I?"

Squinting, she examined him more closely. She said nothing, but she slid her legs over slightly and gave him room to sit down at the end near her stockinged feet. Then she turned again so she lay with her back to him, one side of her face on a small pillow. As she replaced the towel over her eyes, he eased himself onto the narrow space she had provided. For a half minute, his left hand hovered over her back; then he pushed aside the thick, rope-like braid and placed both of his hands on her shoulders. Gently, he began massaging them and her neck. He waited for her to speak, to say something, anything, but she remained quiet. He massaged, and he waited. Still, she said nothing. He thought she had fallen asleep. Her breathing was deep and regular.

"Who are you?" she asked, at last.

"Who I am is not important. I am here to help."

"I see. And what do you plan to do for me, Mr. Helper?"

"Whatever it is that will make you smile your lovely smile again and clear up the rain clouds that are in your eyes."

She rolled over onto her back and looked up at him. "You don't know me?"

He shook his head.

"I am 61."

"What is 61?"

She laughed ruefully. "Sixty-one is the one who doesn't get to play next year. Sixty-one is the one who, if she *does* want to play again, has to go back to qualifying school. Only the top 60 get to play next year. Based on my performance this weekend, I am 61."

"Then I have a simple solution, 61. How about I blind two or three of your fiercest competitors? If that sounds too extreme, I could simply, and casually, break a leg or an arm or an ankle, force them out of competition for the next year or two. That way you would be number 59 or 58. Please give me your command."

"You would do that for me?"

"Gladly."

"No, thanks," the professional said, sitting up, tossing her small towel on the cot behind her. "Where are my shoes?"

"They are here where you left them."

"Did you clean them?"

"I would have if you would have told me."

"Well, Mr. Helper, I think I have a plane to catch. Or a train. I don't know exactly."

"Destination?"

"Kyoto."

"Your hometown?"

"Yes."

"I can't help but feel, 61, that a kind of fate has brought us together. I came with a headache. May I leave with a telephone number? Or better yet, a rendezvous, say this weekend? Since I am from Tokyo, perhaps you could guide me here and there in your beautiful city. Is it true what young couples say about Kiyomizu-dera at sunset? How about this Saturday?"

For a half minute, she looked at him skeptically. Then she turned and put her feet on the floor. Slowly, with her back to him, the long braid nearly touching the floor, she leaned over, pulled on her golf shoes, tied them. When she stood up, he stood up. When she looked into his eyes, he looked into hers, and waited.

"Saturday?"

"I would very much like to see you then."

"In Kyoto?"

"Yes. I could take the *shinkansen*. It's only a couple of hours."

"It's a little more than that."

"Then it's a little more. I don't mind."

"I'm 32. How old are you?"

"I am old enough. Or young enough. I simply want to see you."

"Okay, Mr. Helper, or Mr. Mysterious, or Mr. Clever Scoundrel. I will see you. Saturday. Saturday at eleven. Kyoto Station. There is a coffee shop called Kurasu. It's on the second floor."

"Kurasu. The Second floor. Kyoto Station. 11:00 a.m."

"That's what I said."

Just then the curtain flew open and a guy—a big guy, strong arms and shoulders, his face dark brown from years in the sun, his green polo shirt stained with sweat, sunglasses propped up on his shaved head—stood in the room. This newcomer looked dubiously at the young man.

"Who the fuck are you?"

"Kenji, this is Mr. Helper. Mr. Helper, this is my brother. And my caddie."

"Mr. Helper?"

"I will tell you later."

"Listen," the new arrival said, turning his attention to his sister, "I know you wanted to be alone for a while, but we need to leave. We can't get to Haneda in time, but we can catch a Nozomi from Tokyo Station at 8:48. We should go now. I have all your gear ready. Otherwise, if we stay, we're going to have to pay for a hotel, money that we don't have."

The 32-year-old, possibly ex-professional golfer reached down and gathered the small towel that she had tossed on the cot. She folded it into a square and handed it to the young man; then her brother pushed aside the curtain, and the two left, the man following the woman. Neither said goodbye.

The young man brought the square to his face and inhaled, the smell fresh, lemony, a hint of salt. Then, with a start, he recalled the people he had been sitting with. Certainly, they would be wondering where he was, and he considered rushing back to them. But he decided against returning. Instead, he sat down on the cot, bent over, untied his sneakers, kicked his shoes off; then he lay down and, shaking loose the square, placed the towel over his eyes, as she had done. Taking a few deep breaths, he felt calm, the quiet, no-window basement room a place of refuge, and soon he fell into a deep sleep.

How long did he slumber? What were his dreams, if any? When he awoke, he sensed that he was not alone. He slid off the small towel and looked up at a concerned face.

"Mariko, what a nice surprise. How are you?"

"I'm fine. Makoto, are you okay?"

"I had this terrible headache. Maybe I was dehydrated. So, I came here." The third time he told the lie, he felt he sounded even more convincing. He looked over at her, to where she sat on a neighboring cot looking at him, the curtain between the two pulled back. He reached out and took her hand.

"I had no idea where you were!" she said, her anger mixed with sadness.

"I am very sorry."

"I looked everywhere for you. Finally, Watanabe-san told me you were here."

"What time is it?"

"It's past six."

"So late? Incredible. So who won?"

"How would I know? And why would I care? When you didn't return, I went looking for you."

"Of course. Mariko, please forgive my selfishness. I don't know what happened. I can't explain. I simply needed some rest. But now, seeing you, I feel much better. Shall we?" With tears in her eyes, she nodded. He sat up and handed her the small, white towel. As he put on his sneakers, she used it to dry her eyes.

Upstairs, a few patrons sat at the bar, but the dining room was empty. He looked out the windows and was astonished to see it was twilight. Under bright, artificial lights, workers were busily dismantling the scaffolding that had been placed around the eighteenth green. Beginning tomorrow, the course would once again be open to members.

At the club entrance, the driver was waiting with the black Toyota Grande Mark II. As he opened the back door for them, the young man looked at him. He saw something in the older man's face, but he had no idea what he was thinking. He drove quickly to the expressway. In the dark backseat, his fiancée reached over and took his hand. In her other hand, she still held the small, white towel. The three drove in silence, and just after an hour, they arrived at the gate to the Ueda residence in Nishi Azabu. When the driver got out to open her door, she whispered to him, "Call me when you get to your apartment." Then, holding her purse and the towel, she slid out of the back seat.

The driver got the car turned around, but he paused at the end of the driveway. "I would drive you to your apartment," he growled, "but I have a date. With Miki. Get the fuck out."

All week he thought about her and her well-tanned face and athletic arms and legs. He could have checked the final scores in last Monday's paper and ascertained her name, but he preferred 61. For as long as he could, he would call her that. And as he considered all of the possibilities, a sense of adventure beckoned him. He couldn't help but feel something incredibly alluring about the entire assignation.

Before Saturday, he had to break two promises. First, he avoided the club all week—no tennis with Abe, the instructor, and of course no golf lessons with Kawasaki. On Thursday evening, he called the too-trusting teenager. Since she didn't know him well, and since she was perhaps new to such strong emotions, she didn't take the broken promise well. After a minute or two of small talk, he related that there would be no Disney. "Miki-chan," he said, trying to explain, "please understand. This trip to Kyoto came up unexpectedly. I live in such a chaotic business world. There are always unforeseen changes. And this topsy-turvy market requires that I give each client extra attention. I hope you understand. I will make it up to you soon. I promise."

She said nothing.

"Miki?"

The phone went dead.

He felt a little guilty, but he opened another can of beer, and then a minute later, he called his flying-here-and-there admirer. He used more or less the same lie. She knew enough about him and his work that what he explained seemed quite plausible. She wasn't angry. And she didn't hang up. But she was disappointed.

"I wish I could join you. Kyoto is wonderful. Will you have a chance to do any sightseeing?"

"I doubt it."

"It's a nice time to visit. Kyoto can be miserable in the summer, but it should be much cooler now, and the leaves should be starting to change."

"That's what people tell me."

"Well, try to call me if you can," she urged.

"I will," he said.

Fortunately, he didn't have to break a date with his fiancée. She would be in Hiroshima with a cousin and an aunt for a pre-wedding weekend getaway. He phoned her last, and the two talked for twenty minutes. After his third beer, he crawled under his sheets and fantasized about his Saturday rendezvous. He hoped that she would wear a skirt. A tight top too. Then he fell asleep and slept well.

He caught the Nozomi 15 at 8:09, which put him into Kyoto Station at 10:34. From the platform, he took an escalator down to the ground floor. The station—recently renovated—was covered in tinted glass, and through it, he could see the blue sky. He felt taller, stronger, more confident. He found himself on another exciting adventure.

He passed through the wicket and stood in the vast lobby. He glanced around and found another escalator and took it up one floor. A minute later, he stood before the coffee shop. Glancing inside, he saw a few open tables, but he loitered outside. He didn't enjoy hot coffee. Moreover, he had been hoping that he would not be the first to arrive. But then he went in, took a table with a view of the entrance, glanced at the laminated menu that lay on the table, ordered an orange juice and a croissant.

At half past eleven, he grew worried. Had he the wrong day? No. He was sure it was today. And the coaster his glass sat on clearly said he was in the right place. She was running late. That's all. Maybe she was hitting range and had lost track of the time, he thought, chuckling to himself. He wished he had brought a guidebook or at least a newspaper. But twenty minutes later, he was beginning to feel annoyed.

"Are you Mr. Helper?"

"What?"

"Are you Mr. Helper?"

Confused, he looked at the same uniformed young lady who had served him his orange juice and croissant over an hour ago. She was probably still in high school. She spoke so softly he could barely hear her.

"I am, I guess."

"I have this for you."

With two small hands, the fingers like pencils, she set an envelope on his table.

"You had this the entire time? I mean, when I came in an hour ago you had this envelope for me?"

She nodded. "I didn't know then you were Mr. Helper. But I was told to give this message to you precisely at noon. Would you like another orange juice?"

"No."

For a few minutes, he sat back in his chair and simply looked at the envelope. He thought about getting up and walking out—just leave it lying there—but then the novelty of the situation got the best of him. He glanced around at the people inside and outside of the coffee shop. Was she watching? Then he picked up the unsealed envelope. The piece of paper inside was folded once. Though the handwriting was neat and feminine, the words frightened him:

Mr. Helper,

I know who you are. And I know what is scheduled to take place later this month. But I won't say anything to her. I would rather not get involved.

I must say I was impressed with your come on. I wish I had your confidence, your *savoir faire*. But I don't like selfish people. I don't like you.

The future is uncertain. But you can change. If you want to change, you can.

Au revoir! *Bon chance*! I hope I never see you again.

He read the letter a half dozen times. Then he set it down on the table. He looked at his hands; he found that they were shaking. His heart beat fast. He felt much more than the strong sting of rejection. Were these her words? They couldn't be, not all of them. Was her caddie brother some kind of detective? Perhaps he was more protective—and more discerning—than he seemed. His mind raced. There were several possibilities. In the end, he reached a simple conclusion: the minders had their dirty hands at work. He was genuinely worried. If they knew about this planned rendezvous, they probably knew about the flight attendant too. He had to be more careful. No, he admitted, being more careful was not enough. He had to choose one over the other. That would be the honorable undertaking. For a few moments, he felt foolish and a little angry. But then he understood he had received the comeuppance that he deserved.

That day, he saw nothing of Kyoto except for the newly remodeled station. The revered temples would have to wait. On the *shinkansen* back to Tokyo, he vowed to be better. He would make amends. But some vows, made in haste, are easy to abandon. The contrite often do not remain penitent for long. Desires resurface. Strong emotions persist. Back in his apartment, he listened to some records, and after a few hours of late-evening, whisky-inspired reflection and music, he had made peace with his transgressions. It helped that he had received a warm call from one; and then later, he had called the other. He looked forward to the plans he had made with each. Though he had lost today, the future, he felt, still glowed brightly. And with those warm thoughts he tumbled into bed and once more slept well.

21 Two Men Meet in Tokyo
for a Drink, Part 1

"**I** mean it," one said, turning to face the man who sat next to him at the bar. "I can't thank you enough."

"Don't worry about it."

"No. I think about what happened a lot. I do. Do you have any idea how she is doing?"

The other shook his head slowly and looked down at his glass. The two were silent for a long while. Each sipped his whisky quietly.

"Anyways, it's very nice to have you here. We didn't expect you."

"Well, the old man paid. Paid for all of us. The kids too. We'll be at the hotel all week. Speaking of which, do you want to do lunch or dinner? I mean, the four of us? Or do you think Junko might say something?"

"What do you think?"

"I can tell her to keep her mouth shut."

"Fuck. I just remembered. I can't believe what you told the old man. I mean about your staying in the apartment because you and Junko were not getting on. I feel very bad about that."

"No," the other chuckled. "That was my mistake. The secretary simply passed on the expenses, as she always does. That's what she's supposed to do. I should have told her to wipe the figures, but I forgot."

"Well, I hope I didn't cause you too much trouble."

"You did," he said with another chuckle. "Lying to your lovestruck high school girl was hard enough, but then I had to lie to the old man. So just remember me when you commandeer the ship. That, Captain, shouldn't be too far along in the future."

"I will. You can count on that."

Again, the two men sat silently, each sipping his whisky.

"Let's pass on lunch or dinner. As you can imagine, I have a thousand things to do before Saturday. Then on Monday we fly to Paris."

"Sure. I understand."

"Shall we?"

The two got up, made their way to the counter by the front door, and settled their bill. As they made their way down the street to the station, the older one placed his hand on the other's shoulder. "Please forgive me if I am out of line," he said, "but you are the envy of many men. Don't fuck it up this time.

"Oh, by the way, she wanted you to have this." From out of a small, fashionable paper bag with the Takashimaya logo on it, he pulled out the blue, black, and white *kokeshi* doll.

22 She Wonders Why

He wasn't ready to talk to her. He looked down at the phone and at the blinking light. Slowly, he picked up the receiver and pushed the button.

"*Ohayo!*" she said, her voice full of warm morning sunshine. "*Genki?*"

"I am fine. A little busy. How are you?"

"Okay, Busy Boy, I have only a few minutes too," she said excitedly. "I have to be on the plane shortly. But after we talked last night, I was thinking. I checked this morning. The flight takes only an hour, maybe a little longer. I was thinking either I could come see you, or you could come see me. For example, BA has a 9:20 a.m. flight. If I caught it, I could be in Paris with you by noon. That would give us at least five or six hours because there is an 8:40 p.m. return flight the same day. I could be back in my hotel room before eleven."

"I don't know, Nami," he began after a pause. "I told you last night. I am traveling with two colleagues this time, my superiors. As far as I know, we have a tight schedule. It's going to be hard to get away."

She was quiet for a while. He waited.

"I thought you would be excited to know that I am going to be in London twice while you are in Paris."

"I am excited. I just don't know if I can come see you."

"Well, I can come to Paris. That is what I am suggesting."

"And what if I cannot see you when you come? If I am conducting business? You'd have to look after yourself, and what fun would that be?"

"What hotel are you staying in?" she asked after another long moment of silence.

"I'm not sure."

"You don't know?"

"The assistant is handling all of the flight and lodging details."

"You're leaving this Saturday?"

"Yes."

"And you'll be gone ten days?"

"Ten days. Two weeks. Something like that. I am sorry to be vague. I don't have all the details at hand. I told you. This trip came up unexpectedly. The old man told me yesterday afternoon. That's why I called last night, to let you know."

"Okay."

"You sound upset."

"No, I'm not. I just thought we could somehow see each other. As I told you, when I got to work this morning, I checked some flights. I thought we could make it work."

"I wish we could."

"Can you call me at least?"

"When I am in Paris? Of course, I'll call you. I should be able to call every day."

After another pause, she said, "I miss you already."

"I miss you too. But I'm not gone yet. And we're still having dinner on Thursday, right?"

"Yes."

"Seven?"

"I may be able to arrive earlier. I'll try. I'll be coming right from Haneda."

"I'll see you then. By the way, I finally developed the film. I'll bring the photos, the ones we took in London. And we'll see if we can do anything about Paris. Maybe we can make something work after all."

23 A Brief Conversation a Few Days Before the Wedding

"The rain sounds lovely, doesn't it?" she said.

"It does."

"I wonder if it's going to rain this Saturday."

"It won't."

"You know, we don't have to wait."

The two sat in the garden room on a rainy Monday evening. They half-sat, half-lay together on the cushions that were scattered on the *tatami*. She had her back to him, and he had his arms around her. They had been kissing, nibbling on each other's neck and ears, but their sore lips told them a break was needed. Still, his hands remained inside her blouse, the fabric pulled up from her skirt. He had undone her bra, and as they lay together, he had been massaging her small breasts and softly pinching her erect nipples.

"No," he sighed, lightly touching his lips to her ear. "We should wait. We waited this long. I know it sounds like a cliché, but waiting will make it special."

She turned her head and looked up at him. "Do you want me to give you oral sex?"

"No," he replied, laughing. "If that eagle-eyed maid comes in and catches us, your father will call off the whole thing."

"I'm not talking about here, dummy. But we could go to a hotel."

"That's okay. I still think we should wait."

"I was just testing you," she said, looking mischievously into his eyes. "Now stop playing with my tits. My nipples are sore."

24 A Proud Father Gives a Speech
at His Daughter's Wedding

At the microphone stood the dignified old man smartly dressed in a tuxedo, a beam of a spotlight directed at him in the large, lights-turned-down banquet hall. "Ladies and gentlemen," he began—but then he faltered. He had been holding a champagne glass, but he set it down, and, with a folded handkerchief that he removed from a pocket, he slowly wiped his deep-set eyes. The bride and bridegroom were standing on a raised platform a few meters away, and they too, like two movie stars at an award show, stood under the bright beam of a spotlight. Both had their heads bowed, the beautiful bride dabbing at her eyes with a cloth napkin. The handsome groom, his hands clasped together in front of him, was looking down at the floor.

"Excuse me," the old man said, needing a half minute to compose himself. He blinked his eyes many times and looked around the room. The guests had completely stopped eating and drinking. Silence filled the hall. Even the numerous hotel waiters and waitresses had paused in their tasks and stood with their heads bowed solemnly. As the guests looked up at him and waited, many gazed with watery eyes.

"Ladies and gentlemen," he said in a loud voice.

"In spite of these womanly tears, I stand before you a very happy man.

"You see my only daughter." With his arm, he gestured in the bride's direction. "Isn't she an angel today? She is.

"With great luck, she met a very nice, clever boy. I am proud to call him my son." Then, with a chuckle, he added, "If only you knew how the two met. But that's a secret."

He paused and smiled. Some in the audience laughed.

"Mariko," he said, turning to his daughter, "I command you to be a good wife and a good mother. Look after your husband and your children as your mother, when she was alive, looked after us. She never wavered in her duties. Never be a disgrace to her," he said sternly. As he spoke these words, the bride openly wept.

"Makoto, I command you this: never neglect your incredible responsibilities as a husband and as a father. I give you a princess today. Let her be your queen. She has a true and gentle heart. Smile upon her. Be always kind and generous. Let her be a rose that forever blossoms in the bosom of your heart."

The groom took a step forward and then bowed deeply to his father-in-law. The bride was still crying.

The old man looked at the two. "That is all I have to say," he said.

He reached for his champagne glass. With an unsteady hand and arm, he raised it. There was a rumbling of chairs as the guests stood and raised theirs as well. The hotel staff rushed around to make sure each guest had a glass and it was full. With a kind smile, the old man waited. This moment seemed to bring him great pleasure. Finally, he looked around at all the guests one last time; then he turned to his right where the bride and groom stood.

"*Kampai!*" he thundered.

"*Kampai!*" the guests shouted. As they downed the champagne and set down their glasses, many started clapping warmly. Cheers rang out. The soft lighting returned, and the sound of a ballad, immensely popular at that time, began to fill the wedding hall.

Glasses were being refilled, and more shouts of "*Kampai!*" could be heard. The hotel staff rushed to bring more bottles—more champagne, whisky, beer—and the next course of dinner. One of the groom's colleagues rushed onto the wedding platform with a newly opened bottle and two glasses. He tried to give the bride and groom each a glass, but the bride, even though she was comforted by the groom on one side and by an old lady on the other, couldn't stop crying.

"Mariko," the old, *kimono*-clad woman said, "shame on you! To be crying at such a joyous hour."

"I know, Yoshiko," the bride replied, struggling through her sobs to get the words out. "I know. But I can't help myself. It's overwhelming. I truly am the luckiest person in the world."

25 Along the River Seine

When he was certain his wife was asleep, he got up and quietly donned a T-shirt, his trousers, his jacket. Without turning on a light, he made his way to the door of the suite and found his shoes. Then he opened the door and slipped out. After he stepped into his shoes, he strode down the long hallway to the elevator, which he took down six floors.

The spacious lobby was empty. Even Marcel, the uniformed doorman, was not at his post. The glass doors slid open, and the young man walked out into the cool, autumn evening. A cab driver parked nearby looked up hopefully from the newspaper he was reading, but the young man looked away and headed down to the river, just a few blocks away. At the stone edge, he looked down at the black, fast-moving water. Then, deciding to make a circle, he turned right and walked along the promenade, and at the first bridge, he walked up some steps, took a left, and crossed the river on a wide avenue. On the other side, he turned left, went down some steps, and continued meandering along the river. As he walked with his hands deep in his pockets, he saw an unlit park to his right with large trees—brown leaves still clinging to some of the branches—and empty benches.

Out of the corner of his eyes, he saw a person approaching him. The figure, a tall, very black woman with beautiful white teeth, emerged from the shadows. He paused to look at her, and she stopped a dozen feet away from him. The two stood looking at each other.

"You Japanese?" the woman asked in heavily accented English.

The young man nodded.

The woman looked around to make sure no other people were around. She stepped forward a few feet. "I give you nice blow job," she said quietly. "I lick your balls and swallow your cum. Four-hundred francs."

The young man said nothing.

"You married, pretty boy?"

"Actually, I'm on my honeymoon."

"What?" she asked incredulously. "And you out late at night looking for a tasty treat? You should be with your wife with your tongue in her sweet oriental pussy. Don't forget to lick the brown hole. She like that too. Then stick your little finger up there. She go crazy."

The young man smiled.

"I clean," the woman assured him. "Just you step over here and we get started. You never forget my sweet lips. Okay?"

The young man considered the offer, but he shook his head.

"Three-hundred francs then."

Out of the shadows, another woman emerged. She was Asian. But not Japanese. He was sure of that. Probably Chinese or Thai. She was tall and had long straight hair and wore thigh-high black boots with heels, a red mini skirt, a fur jacket. The Asian woman said something in French to the black woman and then looked at the young man, on her lips a bright red lipstick.

"She speak no English. You don't need to use the plastic with her."

The black woman asked the Asian woman a question. After she answered, the black woman said, "Five-hundred francs. Anything you want. One hour. No plastic. You understand? No condom. Front hole. Back hole. Mouth. Any hole you want."

The young man reached into his pocket and pulled out the wad of bills he had. He counted out five one-hundred-franc notes and handed them to the Asian woman. She accepted them greedily and then reached out and took his hand. But the young man shook off her hand and withdrew a few paces. He shook his head. He still held the wad of notes in his hand. He counted out another five one-hundred-franc notes and passed them over to the black woman. He turned, walked back to the river's edge, and then continued on his way.

"*Merci*! *Merci beaucoup, mon ami*!" the black woman called out.

Back at the hotel entrance, the cab driver was still reading his paper. He looked up at the young man. Marcel was there smoking a cigarette. As the young man approached, the doorman dropped the cigarette and ground it out with the front of his shoe.

"*Monsieur* Tanaka," he said confidentially, "by all means, do not correspond with the ladies of the evening."

"*Bonne nuit*, Marcel."

"*Bonne nuit, Monsieur* Tanaka."

26 A Very Unusual Eighteen Hours

"Do you like this dress?" the young woman asked.

"I do," he replied, giving the advertisement just a cursory glance.

The young woman sitting next to him was contentedly paging through a thick fashion magazine.

"And how about this handbag?"

He nodded, forcing a smile, but he wasn't thinking about her or the handbag. No. He had more pressing concerns—about another, and more important, about his condition. Was something seriously amiss with him, with his personality? Some deep character flaw that could never be corrected? This honeymoon was supposed to have been a wonderful week together. Of course, he had to appreciate—and he did—that moments of wonder and joy did occur; but over and over again the sinister thoughts intruded, more strongly with each passing day, leading him to the same unsettling conclusion: "Something is terribly wrong with me." This was not the first time he had had such unpleasant thoughts, but now they seemed to overwhelm him. "It seems," he acknowledged with a painful sigh, "that I am doomed to want what I don't have. And if I do possess what I so earnestly desire, then soon thereafter I want something else. Why?" As he glanced around the full cabin at the other passengers, some sleeping, some reading, an older couple chatting amiably, he mused, "Surely, I cannot be the only person who feels this way." For a moment, he closed his eyes, as if in the darkness an answer could be found.

"Will you be upset if I cut my hair like this?" she asked, touching his arm. He opened his eyes and looked down at a full-page photo of a tall, anorexically thin model in a short-sleeve top, cropped just below her small no-bra breasts, her bobbed hair at jaw level.

The young man could take no more. He unbuckled his seatbelt and stood up. "Listen," he said a little curtly, "I am not feeling well. I am going to the restroom."

He ambled back to the two business class toilets, but both were occupied. There was a space next to one bathroom and the boarding door. He stood there and stretched his arms. He massaged his neck and temples. He loosened his tie. He looked down the five rows and saw her turning the glossy pages slowly. She liked fashion more than he had realized.

This young woman—his wife of eight days—was getting on his nerves. It was the first time he had spent eight days with a woman—with anyone, for that matter—and he sorely missed his independence. He hadn't had half a day to himself since the wedding. Even in Paris, when he encouraged her to get out by herself, she refused. One morning, she wanted to go to the Louis Vuitton shop, but he had a hangover and wanted to sleep in. "Take the Metro by yourself," he said as he lay in the spacious bed, the most comfortable he had ever been in. "We did it yesterday. Remember? It's not that hard. Or take a taxi. Have one of the front desk staff write down the address and give it to the driver." But she refused to go by herself. As he fitfully slept, she sat by the bay window and sulked.

The two had to have breakfast, lunch, and dinner together every day. And when they were out eating or exploring the museums or taking in the sights, who did all of the speaking? She had recently studied French for a year, but it seemed she knew nothing. "They speak so fast," she said. "And I get so nervous." He was the one who said "*Bonjour!*" and "*Merci*" and "*Puis-je voir la carte des vins?*" and "*Le-addition, s'il vous plait.*" Much to his annoyance, she just sat there, mute. And of course, since he neither spoke nor understood any French—just a few words and phrases stolen from a small guidebook he had brought with him—the two had to rely on his English. She had studied that language too, but she comprehended very little of what was said as he spoke to surly waiters and indifferent cab drivers. Her often-whispered "What did he just say?" became to him an incredible irritant.

"Sir, we have other restrooms in back." He was shaken from his troubling reflections and unpleasant memories by the soothing voice of a flight attendant, her outstretched arm, the palm flat, gesturing to the rear of the plane.

"Okay. Thank you." He turned and walked back to the middle of the plane, where there were two more bathrooms; but a young mother was standing there rocking a wailing infant, so he continued to the back of the plane. He didn't need to use the bathroom; he just needed space.

At the rear of the plane, he saw the back of a flight attendant in the galley. Busily, she was securing various compartments. When she turned, the two stood face to face.

"Nami! My God, what a surprise!"

"Makoto! You gave me such a fright. I thought you were still in Paris."

"There was a crisis. I had to return. I got in last night. I had no time to call." Quickly, he shoved his hands into his pants pockets. With his thumb, he was able to remove the newly acquired ring.

"Stay here," she whispered. "I'll be right back."

She sauntered up the aisle to the middle of the plane with a duty-free catalog in one hand. As she made her way back, she smiled and held it aloft and asked the passengers if any wanted to make a purchase. This section of the plane was only half full, and since no one bought anything, the two were soon conversing quietly in the galley.

"What are you doing back here? Aren't you in business class?"

"I am. I… There's this woman sitting next to me. She won't stop talking."

"Maybe she likes you," the flight attendant said with a twinkle in her eye. "I am jealous! I wish I could sit next to you in business class."

"I don't like her. Believe me."

"Hey," she leaned in and reported, her voice full of excitement. "I am overnighting tonight in Aomori. Where are you staying?"

"I don't know," he lied.

"I am at the JAL Tower downtown. Shall we have dinner?"

"Nami, I would love to. But some of the fellows are meeting me. We may be losing an important client. I have to go. Literally, I will be running off the plane. I don't know when I will be finished."

There was a loud ding. The plane slowed and began its descent; she reached out and held his arm to regain her balance. "I have to go," she whispered. "I'll see you when you deplane."

"Nami, that's not necessary. I told you. I have to rush."

She leaned forward, their faces almost touching. "Bye!" she said, turning and walking briskly up the aisle. The young man followed. She stopped mid-plane to speak with a colleague. Turning sideways, he slid past the two and took his seat in the business class cabin.

"You were gone a long time. Is everything okay?"

"Yes. I told you. I have an upset stomach. Must have been something I ate this morning."

"But we ate the same thing," she reminded him, "and I feel fine."

When the plane reached the gate, the young man quickly stood and looked back at the boarding door. Another flight attendant, not Nami, began to unsecure the door. He reached up, opened the overhead bin, grabbed their items. "Here," he said, handing her her jacket. Then he grabbed their two small bags and made his way to the door.

"Wait!" she said, surprised at this unusual behavior, but he ignored her. A couple of impatient businessmen stood between him and the door. A couple more stood between him and his wife. He looked past the two in front of him and saw her coming to assist her colleague. The large door opened and bent back, and soon the gangway was at the door. As he deplaned, she looked directly into his eyes. "Thank you! We hope to see you again!" she said warmly and bowed.

Once he turned the corner, he stopped a few feet up the gangway and waited for his wife.

"Do you know her?"

"Who?"

"The flight attendant."

"The flight attendant? Why would I know her?"

"She seemed awfully friendly," she replied, looking suspiciously at her husband.

"I did talk to her a little bit. I was waiting to use the bathroom. She told me there was another bathroom at the rear of the plane. But that's their job. To be friendly." He turned, and they joined the long line passengers as they made their way to the terminal.

Since the two had no luggage to claim, they quickly exited the arrival lounge and hailed a taxi. "The JAL Tower," he said to the driver.

As the taxi made its way, the young man calculated how much time he had. Certainly, they would arrive much sooner than she. Still, he was nervous.

"Are you hungry?"

"What? No," he replied.

"I am."

"Okay. Let's get checked in. If I am still feeling under the weather, maybe you can get something by yourself. I am sure the hotel has a restaurant. Would you mind?"

"Yes," she replied, reaching over a hand to take one of his. "We are a couple. We have to do things together. That's what couples do."

"But I told you. I am not feeling well."

On this Friday evening just before seven, the check-in queue was more than a dozen guests long. Slowly, they made their way to the front. After twenty minutes of waiting, and after the young man had glanced back at the entrance many times, he decided he couldn't risk staying any longer.

"Listen," he said, opening his wallet. "Here is my card. The reservation should be in my name. I need to go to the bathroom. Just get our room keys. I am sure you can sign. If there is any problem, I can take care of it in the morning. And then come get me. I'll be over there." He pointed across the crowded lobby, past some couches and chairs and coffee tables. Just beyond these items, a red "Toilet" sign glowed above a hallway that turned to the left.

"Now?"

"Yes."

"But I don't know what to say."

Without responding, he left her, making his way to the hallway that led to the bathrooms. He turned the corner so he was out of sight, but he stopped and looked back at the lobby. Sure enough, six JAL flight attendants—still in uniform, and she among them—entered with their roller bags and strode up to a special counter. They were handed room keys right away, and in good spirits, they made their way to the bank of elevators on the other side of the lobby from where the young man stood. When he saw them enter an elevator and the doors close, he looked back at his wife. She was at the counter, pen in hand, apparently filling out a form. Soon she had the keys. He stepped back so he couldn't be seen. He waited a few seconds, then emerged as if he were coming from the men's room. He met his wife in the lobby.

"Thank you," he said.

In the elevator, passing him the small envelope with the two keycards, she said, "I was thinking *sushi.*"

"Sounds good," he replied. "I may watch you eat—if that is okay."

She looked into his eyes with concern. "I am sorry you are not feeling well."

"Me too."

From a house phone in the lobby, he called. "Is it too late? I apologize, Nami. What a day it's been."

"I was just about to go to bed. But you can come up, I guess, if you promise to say and do nice things."

When he stood before the door a few minutes later, he knocked gently. He was about to knock again when she slowly opened it. For a long moment, the two stood facing each other.

"I didn't know JAL made pajamas," he said at last, looking her up and down.

"We do," she said with a smile. "You should check your duty-free catalog. Would you like me to buy you a set?"

He nodded.

"You look wonderful."

"Thank you. You look tired."

"I am. What a day it's been. Truly one of the strangest."

"I am a lowly flight attendant," she said, standing back so he could enter, "so my room is nothing special, but you are welcome to take a shower if you want. And I bought beer and peanuts, the kind you like."

As the door closed behind him, the two embraced. Then he turned her around and held her from behind, burying his face into the back of her head.

"My God, it's good to see you, to hold you like this."

"And you."

"You smell so nice."

"Thank you."

"Where is your uniform?"

"Is it going to be that kind of night again?"

"I would like it to be. Do you mind?"

"I guess not. As long as you use your gifted hands."

"I'll do whatever it takes to make you happy. I promise. Where is it?"

She pointed to a closet to her right. He freed his right hand, reached over, slid open the door. He saw what he desired, the various items hanging neatly on several hangers.

Slowly, while she still had her back to him, he began unbuttoning her pajama buttons. He pulled the top off her shoulders, letting it fall to the floor; he lifted and massaged her ski-jump breasts, rolled her erect nipples gently between his fingers, kissed her neck and ear. Still with her back to him, he reached into the closet and found her light-blue bra hanging on a hook. He slipped it on, cupped her breasts with it, and then attached the clasp. He kissed her neck and ear some more. Then he reached in and grabbed her white blouse, removed it from its hangar. Slowly, he guided her long arms into each sleeve. Then he turned her around. As they kissed, he did up the buttons.

"Stockings?" he asked as he bent over and slid down her pajama bottoms.

"Hanging in the bathroom. They may still be a little wet."

"Do you mind?"

She shook her head.

When she stepped into the bathroom, he entered the room and sat down at the end of the second single bed. She came out, sat down beside him, rolled up the dark-blue stockings, and placed each foot in them. Then, as she looked at him, she pulled them up slowly, carefully. When the stockings were at her thighs, she stood, bounced on her feet once, and pulled them the rest of the way. He leaned back, his hands on the bed, and watched her as she reached into the closet and pulled out the blue skirt. She stepped into it, pulled it up to her waist, tucked in the blouse, and then zipped it. There were three items left.

"Blazer too?"

He nodded. "And the scarf, if that's not too much trouble."

After she had put on her blazer—there was her name tag, Nami Yokoda—and after she had tied the red and dark blue scarf around her neck, she looked down at him.

"Finally, the cap."

"Of course."

She placed it on her head and adjusted it accordingly.

"What do you think?" she asked, turning to her right, then to her left, one hand on her hip, as if she were a model on a runway.

"You look fabulous."

"I guess I am ready for work."

"Please, Nami. I don't want you to think of it as work. I want you to think of it as pleasure."

"You know I didn't mean it that way. Now be a good passenger and take your seat. If you give me any more trouble, I will have to call the captain."

He stood up, took her hand, led her over to the room's small desk. He pushed over the lamp and phone so the desk was mostly clear. Then he bent her over so that she leaned on it with her elbows. Slowly, he lifted her skirt and carefully, using both hands, pulled down her stockings and panties at the same time. He reached down with his right hand. There was a large mirror attached to the desk, and the two looked at each other through it as he gently massaged her.

"You are a naughty girl. You are very wet."

She nodded.

"Here?"

She nodded again. He found the spot and began rubbing harder.

After a minute, she closed her eyes, and her face contorted. She was breathing much faster. After another minute, she shuddered.

She opened her eyes and looked at him again through the mirror. And though it was hard for her to speak, she asked, "Coffee, sir?"

He nodded.

"Cream… and sugar?"

"Here?"

She nodded. He rubbed harder and faster, then slowed.

"Did you ask something?"

"I asked… would you like… cream… and sugar?"

"Black, please."

She closed her eyes again, tilted her head to her right. "I want you… inside me…" she asserted.

"Young lady, I had better take my seat. I don't want to delay the departure."

"Don't talk."

As he massaged her vigorously with his right hand, he used his left to unbutton his belt and pants and to pull down his zipper. He pulled his pants and boxers to his knees. Gently, and very slowly, he slid his erection into her.

"Like that?"

She nodded.

"And now what, Nami?"

"That," she said. She reached down and adjusted his right hand slightly. "There."

"Are you close?"

"I already came. But I can again. Just don't stop.

"But don't," she insisted, "come inside me. And whatever you do… don't come… on my uniform."

Another minute passed. She shuddered intensely, and he felt her wetness run down his thighs. He couldn't take it anymore. He pulled out, exploding on the carpet and on the bedspread, and fell back on the bed. For a long time, neither moved, both panting heavily. "You know," she finally said as she leaned up and turned to face him, "I still have my high school uniform. It still fits."

A half hour later, at the door, still dressed in her uniform, she asked, "Did you get her number?"

"What?"

"The rich-looking woman who was sitting next to you on the plane. I could tell that she liked you," she said, giving him a teasing smile. "She was practically chasing you off the plane."

"When are you coming back to Aomori?"

"I don't know. When are you coming to Tokyo?"

"Maybe this weekend."

"I don't know if I like this."

"What?"

"Our staying in the same hotel but in separate rooms. It seems kind of strange, doesn't it?"

"I want to stay tonight here with you. You know that. But if the office calls early in the morning and I'm not in my room, it will look bad."

"I understand."

"What time do you leave?"

"My first flight is at 6:50. The bus will pick us up at 5:30. Should I call you then?"

"I wish you wouldn't. After Paris, after the long flight, I want to sleep in. At nine, someone from the local office is coming to take me to my apartment. It's going to be another long day."

He entered the dark room as quietly as he could, slipping in sideways and shutting the door behind him. After his eyes adjusted, he stepped inside and saw his wife's form on one side of the bed. Lying on her side, the sheet-and-blanket combination pulled up to her shoulder, she appeared to be asleep. He tiptoed past her to the shower room, sliding the door shut behind him. In the darkness, he ran his hand along the wall until he found the light switch. Quickly, he began removing his clothes, beginning with his tie and dress shirt, items easy to hang on the towel hooks. After he pulled down his trousers and yanked off his socks, he lifted the front of his T-shirt and sniffed it, the unmistakable scent clearly present. He pulled it over his head and tossed it into the deep sink and turned on the hot water. He ripped off the paper wrapper of a small bar of soap and tossed the bar into the sink. Last, he removed his boxers, adding it to the little washing machine that the sink had become, the water rising slowly, the soapy bubbles forming.

Just as he sat and turned on the hot water—the large, *sento*-style bathroom offered a small, wooden stool before a low, handheld shower head—he heard a timid knock on the door. Wasting no time, he snatched the body soap from the shelf and pumped it several times, filling one hand with the fragrant liquid; he vigorously began soaping his genitals and abdomen and thighs with both hands. The knock came again, this time a little louder; then the door slid open. Glancing over his shoulder, he saw his wife standing there in the doorway in one of his white T-shirts. She looked at him and then at the sink, where the faucet was still running, the hot water nearly overflowing. Stepping into the room, then reaching over, she turned off the tap.

"Let me help you," she said, coming closer, her feet and legs bare.

"I didn't mean to wake you."

"I wasn't sleeping. Here," she said, after a pause, "pass me the sponge."

As he filled a low, wide bucket with warm water and poured it onto his head and back, she lathered the sponge with body soap, and then careful not to get herself wet, she began scrubbing his neck and back and arms.

"We can't do it tonight," she said, stepping back, passing him the sponge. "My period just started."

"That's okay."

"I was hoping I would be pregnant already, but I guess we have to try again."

"We have time," he said, rubbing the soapy sponge vigorously over his face and head and chest.

"Do you feel better?" she asked.

"I feel much better," he replied, squinting at her with one eye, his head and face covered with soap. "Thank you. I went down to the bar, had a few drinks, then went outside for a long walk. It's incredible! The air seems so fresh. I think we are going to like living here."

He stood and, rotating first to his left, then to his right, used the showerhead he held to rinse off the soap. "And this shower," he added—turning it off, standing before her, dripping water, fully naked under the bright light—"was just what I needed."

"Why is your T-shirt and underwear in the sink?" she asked, pulling down a large towel from the rack and handing it to him.

"I didn't want to wake you," he said, unfolding the towel and using it to dry his face and arms, "so I undressed in here. They got wet, so I just threw them in the sink."

"You need to be more careful."

Still quite wet, rivulets of water running down his legs, he tossed the towel on the counter, walked past his wife into the dark room, collapsed on the bed. He lay on his back and threw out his arms, his head without pillow. Without turning off the shower room light, without closing the door, his wife followed him, crawled onto the bed, snuggled next to him.

"Aren't you cold?"

"Not at all."

"Aren't you going to put any clothes on?"

"Why?"

"Don't you want a pillow?"

"No."

"You're not angry, are you?"

"Angry? About what?"

"That we can't do it."

"No," he laughed. "I understand."

"But I want to try the oral sex."

"Mariko, that's not necessary. It's late. And can't you see? I am exhausted."

She reached down and touched his penis, a new experience for her.

"Mariko, please, let's just go to bed."

"Shouldn't it be hard?" she asked, running her fingertips over the shaft as it lay on his abdomen.

"Well, it's not like a light switch that goes on and off. But if you play with it a little, something might happen."

"Like this?"

"Uh huh."

"It's getting bigger," she reported a minute later, as it thickened and lengthened and began to lift. She slid down and, perhaps a bit frightened, took him into her mouth.

What she was doing felt good, and he was soon fully erect, but with the alcohol he had consumed, with what had transpired just an hour ago with the other, with his wife's inexperience and lack of technique, he knew it was going to take him a very long time to come.

After a few minutes, she stopped. "Am I doing it right?" she asked, turning her head to look at him.

"Yeah, it feels good. But when you take a break, rub it hard with your hand, like this." She did as he directed, and then her head went down again.

More minutes passed, her head going up and down slowly, perhaps too slowly. He closed his eyes and began to fantasize about the woman he had just left. He imagined the short high school skirt, the white blouse, another mirror, this one much larger.

She paused again and looked up.

"How long does it take? My jaw hurts."

"I am very close," he lied.

She rubbed him again, this time with both hands, and then, wanting to finish what she had started, down went her head.

⧗ ⧗ ⧗

She couldn't help herself. She called down to the front desk just after five. "I want to leave a message for a guest. I don't want to talk to him. It's too early, as you can imagine, to call. I just want to leave a message. Is that possible?"

"Yes, you can do that. What is the guest's name?"

"Tanaka-san, Makoto."

The caller waited as the front desk staff member punched her keyboard.

"We don't have a Makoto Tanaka. Wait. We do. Mariko and Makoto Tanaka. Is the message for them?"

There was a long pause.

"Ma'am?"

The pause continued.

"Do you still want to leave a message?"

"I do," the caller finally said.

"Okay. In a few seconds, you will hear a beep. You can leave your message. You have two minutes. When you are done, simply hang up. The message will be transferred to the Tanakas' room phone. Thank you."

The caller heard the beep. She had to gather her thoughts since what she had planned to say was no longer appropriate. Finally, and with conviction, she began: "Good Morning *Mr.* and *Mrs.* Tanaka. Or should I say '*Bonjour*!'? This is Japan Airlines. *We* like to take *care* of our customers. Yesterday, the *two* of you flew from Haneda to *Aomori*. We believe you left behind a *fashionable* Hermes scarf in the overhead bin. Perhaps it's part of a *uniform*. If this is indeed *your* scarf, please call us. If you describe it accurately, we will mail it to you. I am very *sorry* to have *troubled* you. Have a *very* nice day! And don't ever *do* anything you might *regret*!"

⧗ ⧗ ⧗

Just before eight, the young man was in the spacious shower room again, this time soaking in the deep tub, his head resting on the wall behind him. He had slept rather well. And as he luxuriated in the warm water, he found himself ruminating—and chuckling—over the previous day's escapades. All those close calls, all that incredible stress, he mused, was actually quite thrilling. But then his wife, still wearing his T-shirt, slid open the bathroom door with a loud bang.

"You have to listen to this!"

"Listen to what?"

"There's a message. From Japan Airlines. I just noticed the red light blinking on the phone. It's creepy. It's about a lost item, but it's like it's some kind of secret message."

Reluctantly, he pushed himself out of the warm water, wrapped a towel around his waist, and followed his wife to the disheveled bed where the two sat down on the edge, the phone there before them on a nightstand.

"It's not blinking anymore," he said. "How do I listen to it?"

"Press star 6."

He picked up the receiver and put it to his ear. He pressed the appropriate buttons and listened. Then he pressed the star and 6 again and listened one more time. Slowly, he replaced the receiver in its cradle and looked away from his wife. "Did you notice how she emphasized certain words like 'Mr. and Mrs.' and 'uniform' and 'sorry'?" she asked, reaching out to touch his arm. "And what kind of customer service agent would end with something about regret?"

"Well," he said, turning to look at her, a hint of anger in his voice, "did you forget your scarf?"

"No," she replied. "And if I did, who cares? I would just buy another."

After a long pause, she added, "Aren't you going to do anything? I think you should call and make a complaint."

He looked at her face for a long time.

"Why are you looking at me like that?"

Instead of replying, he stood and returned to the bathroom. When he stepped back into the tub and immersed himself, he found that the water had cooled considerably. He was breathing quickly, and his heart was beating fast.

BOOK 3

1 The Light-Blue Handkerchief

In the bedroom, the young man sat on the edge of the unmade bed leaning forward, his head bowed, his elbows on his knees. He was contemplating a light-blue handkerchief, the item he held in his right hand.

The high school girl startled him; he looked up to see her standing in the doorway. "Yuka-chan and I are…" she began, then stopped. In the ten days the two had known each other, she had spent three nights—none consecutive—in the apartment, but this was her first time in the spacious bedroom. The light was dim. Only one of the two bedside lamps offered a subdued light, and long, heavy, dark-blue curtains covered nearly all of the two sliding glass doors and held back most of the early-evening sunshine. She blinked a few times, letting her eyes adjust, and then glanced around.

On the wall above the king-sized bed hung a large, blue and black and red abstract painting. On each side of the bed stood two small nightstands, the same small, stylish lamp on each. And on one—the one with the light-offering lamp—stood a small blue, black, and white *kokeshi* doll. To her right were the two large, sliding-glass-door windows, and through the small gap in the curtains she could see what appeared to be a wide balcony outside. To her left, she saw two large closets, the fold-open doors to the first one fully open. Taking a few steps closer, she saw hangers and hangers of women's clothes—a boutique store-like collection of stylish dresses and fashionable skirts and colorful blouses and costly jackets. Many items were still covered in plastic, as if they had recently come from the cleaners or had never been worn. On one wall stood a high shoe rack made of wood, a few of the cubbyholes empty, others holding two pairs of leather sandals or house slippers; on the floor lay a jumble of more shoes and shoe boxes, some of them opened, still more boxes stacked to the ceiling in one corner. Could the closet hold more? She wondered. In between this closet and the other stood a tall dresser; several of the drawers had been pulled partially open. When she peeked inside the top drawer, she saw a variety of colorful, expensive-looking lingerie.

Trying to comprehend such excess, she looked back at the young man, on her kind face a frown of concern. "Are you okay?"

"I think so," he replied, turning to her and nodding. "I am sorry. I was gone a long time, wasn't I?"

"That's okay."

"As you know," he said, still maintaining eye contact, "I came to change, but then, for some reason, I started going through her things, her clothes." He sighed, and, holding out both hands, he gestured wearily to what she could plainly see.

"There is so much. I have no idea what to do with all of it. And then I found this," he said, holding up the handkerchief. "It was mine. She took it from me on one of our first dates. I had no idea she had kept it. I… Well…" Blinking back the tears, he sighed again, more heavily this time, leaned forward once more, took a few deep breaths.

She stepped around the corner of the bed and sat next to him, one warm shoulder touching another, the warmth and intimacy reassuring. For a minute, perhaps longer, the two sat in silence.

"I shouldn't be telling you this," he said at last, turning his head so he could see her face, see into her deep-brown eyes. "I apologize."

"I don't mind," she replied, slowly reaching out and taking the handkerchief from his hand. She neatly folded the nearly weightless item and set it next to her on the comforter. Then, with the tips of her small fingers, she wiped away her own tears.

"I am not asking you to be her."

"I don't think I could be her," she replied softly. "I want to be myself."

"Of course. The last thing I want," he insisted, taking her left hand into both of his, "is for you to be someone else." As he looked down at the small palm, he gently massaged it and the delicate fingers.

"I loved her," he continued, still looking down at the hand he held. "I did. You know that. But you must know this too. There were times when I treated her badly. I feel awful about those moments."

"Why did you treat her badly?"

"I have no idea," he replied, shaking his head. "I was selfish, I guess. And immature."

"If we stay together, are you going to do the same things to me?"

"I don't plan to. I am a better person now. I am certain of that."

She joined her free hand to the one he held, the four united hands caressing each other awkwardly, yet lovingly, and for another long minute, both stared into space, saying nothing.

"But," he said, taking a deep breath, releasing her hands and rising, "I need to do something with these things. I know it hasn't been that long, but I think it's time."

She looked up at him; in her face he saw that she agreed and, more important, sympathized.

"I have no idea how to begin. I could throw it all away, but it seems cruel—and perhaps a waste—to do that."

Still looking at him, the high school girl nodded.

"What did you do with the cosmetics I gave you?"

"I gave them to my friends. I hope you are not angry."

"Might your friends want the clothes and shoes as well? Everything? There are handbags too."

"I think so."

"Would you then? I mean, whenever you have time? A few items each week? But perhaps it's a good idea not to tell them where they come from."

Just then the little girl appeared. She stood on plump, unsteady legs in the doorway, her left thumb in her mouth. In her right, she clutched to her chest a small, red blanket that she had dragged after her. The high school girl pushed herself off the bed, stepped over to her, gathered her and the blanket. As she held and caressed the heavy toddler, she pressed her face against the girl's chubby face.

"Are you hungry, little loved one?" she asked, her voice exaggerated and child-like.

The little girl nodded, hiding her face in the other's long hair.

"Shall we eat then?"

Again, the little girl nodded.

The young man, unknotting his tie and letting it fall to the polished-pine floor, followed the two down the hallway to the kitchen. "Let's go out," he announced with a smile. "The fresh air will do us good."

Soon the three were dressed for the cool, late-winter evening. They took the elevator down to the lobby. Out on the sidewalk, they turned right, the young man holding his daughter to his chest as she pointed the direction, and walked toward the heart of Shibuya where they would find plenty of places to eat.

2 A Newlywed Couple
Have a Very Hard Day

The very hard day started at breakfast. The young husband liked to cook, and he was a good cook, but the young wife hadn't had much experience in the kitchen. He knew that, and since both had woken up later than planned, he wanted to be the one to prepare breakfast; however, she had insisted ("I have to learn how to do this," she had said), so he reluctantly sauntered into the living room still wearing his pajamas and turned on the TV. As he half-watched the news and half-read the Sunday paper, he heard her opening and closing cabinet doors and drawers and setting items on the small kitchen table. It seemed as if half an hour had passed. Then he heard something sizzling loudly in a fry pan.

When he smelled something burning a minute later, he stood up. "You need help?" he called.

"Maybe."

He stepped into the kitchen.

"What am I doing wrong?"

Just then the smoke alarm in the hallway went off; he was quite hungry, so the shrill, headache-inducing chirping—and her incompetence—irritated him.

"The heat. It's too high. And you need cooking oil. And you really shouldn't try to fry something that's frozen."

He turned off the gas. He picked up the pan with its long piece of outside-burned-black, inside-still-frozen mackerel and placed it in the sink. Then he grabbed one of the kitchen chairs, went into the hallway, and placed it under the smoke alarm. He got up on the chair, reached up, opened the alarm, removed the battery. When he returned to the kitchen, he saw two pieces of bread in the toaster oven. They were no longer pieces of bread. Both had blackened and had started smoking, yet the oven coils were still glowing a bright reddish orange.

"Did you forget about those?" he asked, nodding in the direction of the small oven.

"I did."

He went to the toaster over, shut it off, yanked open its glass door. With a fork, he stabbed a piece, then the other, carried them over to the sink, and dropped them into the pan that contained the burned fish. He wondered if bread could start on fire. Maybe it could. He turned on the faucet and let the water run onto the blackened bread and the burned fish. He turned and looked at her. Then he passed by her into the living room and opened the sliding-glass doors. The cold winter air rushed in.

Back in the kitchen, she sat on a chair and looked up at him, her face twisted in frustration and dismay.

"Don't worry about it. Let's get showered and go. We can get something on the way."

"I guess I have a lot to learn."

"We all have to start somewhere."

"I wish you would sound more encouraging."

"Okay. But what can I say? I'm hungry. And if we don't hurry, we're going to lose the day. Get in the shower. Please."

"Don't tell me what to do," she said, averting her eyes. But she stood up and walked past him and down the hallway to the bathroom.

He knew that she liked to take long showers, but after thirty minutes, he wondered, what could she be doing? Finally, he heard the water stop. He knocked on the bathroom door and slid it open. He slipped past her, pulled down his boxers, and got in the shower. Three minutes later he was finished.

"Is there another towel?" he asked after he had pulled aside the shower curtain and saw nothing on the vanity.

"I haven't washed them yet."

Naked, beads of water still running down his back and legs, he stepped out of the shower tub and walked past her into the bedroom. He found the T-shirt he had just removed and dried himself with it.

From the bedroom, he called, "Almost ready?" He tried to sound cheerful. She didn't reply.

He ripped off the plastic from the new pair of long underwear and donned them, a long-sleeve T-shirt, and a sweater. Then he pulled on some warm socks. He quickly made up the bed and threw on it the plastic bags that contained the ski wear they had purchased the previous day. He found his pair of ski pants and pulled them on. He set out her items, then grabbed his jacket and their goggles and gloves and their knit caps and walked down the hallway and set the items on the floor next to the apartment door.

As he passed her, he saw that she was still standing in front of her mirror with a large, white towel wrapped around her torso. It seemed she was carefully applying makeup. Her hair was still wet.

"Almost ready?" he asked.

"Do I look like I am ready?" she answered, the small eyeliner brush poised over her right eye.

"You look great! Just throw on some clothes. I put the items we bought for you yesterday on the bed."

"Can you shut the door in the living room? I'm getting cold." He went into the living room and did what she requested. Also, he got back on the chair and replaced the smoke detector's battery, the red light resuming its blinking.

He called out, "Shall I go down and start the car?"

"In a minute."

"As I said, your items are on the bed."

She stepped out into the hallway and glared at him. "If you are in such a hurry, why don't you go by yourself?"

He walked down the hallway and faced her. He smiled. "That wouldn't be much fun, would it? You said you wanted to learn to ski. Today's the perfect day. There isn't a cloud in the sky."

"But you are rushing me. I don't like to be rushed."

"Well, like I said last night, we should be there when the mountain opens."

"It's not like the snow is going to disappear."

"You're right. But for a beginner, you want to be there early when the trails are in good condition. And on a Sunday with the weather like this, I imagine the mountain might be a little crowded."

They arrived late. The main parking area, near the lodge, was already full. The second and third lots were full as well, so they were directed to the last lot, more than a half kilometer away. Since she was not used to physical exercise, and since all she had for breakfast was a few bites of bread and some orange juice they had purchased from a Family Mart, the uphill walk on the slippery, packed snow tired her.

Inside the lodge, they filled out the necessary forms, stood in line, collected their rental equipment. Since she had never worn ski boots before, he needed another fifteen minutes to get her comfortable in her pair and to get their shoes in a small locker. To make things easier for her, he carried both pairs of skis and poles as they made their way outside to the ticket counter. Still, she found it very difficult to walk in the heavy, bulky boots. As they stood in another line, he looked up at the lift-ticket prices. It seems the newlyweds had two options. One two-person, seven-minute chair would take them up a few hundred meters to a beginner's course. An unlimited day ticket for the chair cost 2,600 yen per person; a single-ride ticket cost 300 yen. The second option was the

40-person gondola; it would take them to the top of the mountain. A one-way gondola ride cost 1,000 yen. As he looked up at the trail map, he saw that from the top of the mountain, there were no beginner runs, just red for intermediate and black for experts. According to the posted information, it took a skier an hour to descend the mountain course. With my help, he thought, she'll be fine. So without consulting her, he bought two tickets for the gondola. He had hoped they would be there at nine when the mountain opened, but here it was nearly eleven. And as they made their way over to the gondola entrance, the little blue in the sky disappeared, and it began to snow.

They waited another twenty minutes in the gondola line. She was cold, so she leaned into him and slipped both of her ungloved hands into one of his jacket pockets. In doing so, one of her gloves fell to the concrete floor. In the crowded entranceway, neither they nor anyone around them had noticed, even when the gondola doors opened and all the skiers made their way into the car. The windows were heavily frosted, and inside the metal carriage it was meat-freezer cold.

As they ascended, the weather conditions worsened. The light snow became heavy, and the wind picked up. The gondola swayed. Soon they couldn't see where they were going, just up, higher and higher. She began to shiver.

When they arrived at the top twelve minutes later, the large gondola slowed and then lurched into its position, and its doors slowly creaked open. Even though the disembarkation area was covered and surrounded by three walls, small tornadoes of snow were swirling around inside. With an extended arm, an attendant guided everyone out. Then he loaded a few skiers, who, for some reason, were going down with their skis and poles. After they were inside, he secured the gondola's doors for its descent. As the newlyweds made their way outside, one didn't see the sign, "Due to today's conditions, Expert Skiers ONLY." The other saw it but ignored it.

Outside, the winds were howling, and it seemed the temperature had dropped significantly. At this altitude, the snow was mostly ice pellets, and they stung whenever they hit exposed skin. Most of the skiers—their faces fully covered and their goggles on—quickly and adeptly donned their skis and began their descent; a few others stabbed their skis into the snow piles outside the mountain-top chalet and made their way inside. The young newlyweds should have followed, but they didn't. Soon, they were the only ones outside in the blowing snow.

"I have only one mitten," she reported as he helped her step into her bindings.

"Where is the other?"

"I have no idea. I must have lost it."

"Here. Take mine." He slipped off his gloves and passed them over to her. He took the one she held out.

"I'm cold," she said.

"Me too. But once we get going, we'll warm up."

"Shouldn't we go inside?" she asked, turning to look at the door to the chalet.

"We'll be okay. You need to learn to ski," he said with a chuckle, nearly shouting so he could be heard. "Obviously, these conditions aren't the best. But we have to get down somehow."

There was just one groomed run from the top to the bottom, but it was narrow, and since it descended through trees, and since the young woman had never been on skis before, and since she couldn't see more than five or ten meters in front of her through her now ice-encrusted goggles, she never felt comfortable.

The trail was relatively flat at the top. Yet, they had gone only twenty meters before she fell. He quickly got her up, and they made it another thirty meters. But then she fell again. The angry wind blew cruelly. He got her up again, but she made it only a few meters before falling.

He skied up to her and shouted, "Hey, you're doing fine!"

"I can't do this," she said.

"What?" he asked, leaning over her.

"I said, I can't do this," she yelled, anger rising in her voice.

"Yes, you can. It's not that hard."

He looked at her. She lay on her side in the snow. "Come on!" He grabbed an arm and pulled her up.

"Where are we supposed to go?" she asked once she was upright.

"Down."

"Which direction?"

He lifted one of his ski poles and pointed. "That way."

She looked at where he pointed in the blowing snow.

"How far is it?"

"Just a few hundred meters more," he lied. "Then we can go inside and warm up." He had no idea where they were and how far it was to the bottom. The young woman tried again, but the course had gotten steeper, and the visibility remained just a few meters.

After twenty more minutes of this stopping and starting, of her constantly falling and of his helping her up, he began to hate her. He couldn't understand why she couldn't stand on her skis. After all, he had learned in an afternoon just a few years ago. And after a few days, he was sailing down the red and the even more challenging black runs. When he slid off a chair at the top of a run, he knew another adventure awaited him. After two years on the slopes, he loved every blissful moment. Some of his best Waseda memories were the ski trips he and his rugby mates had made. And even when the conditions were severe like they were today, he had been having fun.

But now he was not having fun. He found himself getting angry. And what angered him was that it seemed his wife possessed no will to fight. Instead of trying to contest each fall, to struggle each time she became slightly unbalanced, she simply gave up and fell into the soft snow. He had always been competitive. And he had taken to whatever sport he tried quickly and aggressively. Most sports, he felt, like life itself, were a challenge he accepted eagerly. She was complaining about being cold, and it was cold, even dangerous to be out on a ski mountain in such conditions, but wasn't he cold too? Wasn't he out in such weather with only one glove, thanks to her carelessness? Life was hard. One had to struggle. When a person got knocked down, he or she got back up. That's what he believed. In stark contrast, she didn't seem to possess such a spirit. Soon, she was crying.

As he stood over her, she wailed into the cold, indifferent wind, "I can't! I just can't!"

"Don't say that. You were doing just fine." Through the iced-over lenses of her goggles, he could see her eyes; he could see that she was scared.

"Come on. One more time."

He tried to pull her up, but he felt her resistance.

"If you can't do it, you have to walk."

When she didn't move, he quickly removed his skis, then hers. "Up, up," he shouted. "Let's go. Let's get down and get something hot to eat and drink."

After he got her standing, he pointed. "Just go down there. I'll follow with the skis." He quickly got his skis back on, shouldered hers and the four poles, and followed her. He was certain his exposed hand was nearly frostbitten; he made a fist and shoved it into a pocket. It was hard keeping his balance, what with her skis and the poles on his right shoulder and his left hand buried in a pocket, but he was able to ski down after her.

Gradually, they made their way. When she stopped, which she did often, he encouraged her and pointed which way to go. They had lost the groomed trail long ago, and he had no idea if they were going in the right direction, but as long as they were going down, he knew, sooner or later, they would find the lodge or, if they somehow missed it, the road. It was just taking longer than he had expected.

As they descended, the weather improved, even if only slightly. The harsh winds abated, and the hard snow pellets became soft flakes again. The visibility improved as well. He couldn't see any buildings down below, but at one point they came across a large trail sign. Though it was mostly covered in snow, they could read enough of it: a red arrow, pointing to the left, guided skiers to an intermediate trail; a black arrow, pointing to the right, guided skiers down an advanced course. "We're almost there," he said encouragingly, pointing to the left. "Do you want to try putting your skis back on?"

She shook her head and stumbled on. Soon she was thirty, forty meters down in front of him. The trail had steepened, so she was sliding on her rear more than walking. But the two were making progress.

Just then a skier shot by. Then another. Then three more. Then one stopped and pulled up alongside the young man. The young woman was sitting in the snow a few meters in front of him. Leaning in, the skier asked, "You two okay?"

"Sort of. How far to the bottom? To the lodge?"

"Well, if the lady is going to walk, it's got to be another hour. At least. You want me to send up the ski patrol? They have a snowmobile."

"Sure. Would you mind? My wife is a beginner, and as you can see, she's not doing too well."

"Will do." The kind-hearted skier, a middle-aged woman, dropped, made a few sharp turns, and soon disappeared into the swirling flakes.

The young woman had paused. The trail was steep, and she was sitting in the soft snow. The husband pulled up next to her on his skis.

"What did she say?"

"She said we're almost there. Are you getting hungry? What would you like?"

The young woman ignored him and started sliding down again, her outstretched hands at her sides to balance herself. He watched her. After she made it twenty or thirty meters, he skied down next to her. He waited as she paused and surveyed the hill below her.

When she made it another twenty or thirty meters, he skied down next to her. Very slowly, they were making progress.

Ten minutes later, he heard the faint *ee-aw, ee-aw, ee-aw* of a siren, the sound growing in intensity. Then a large yellow and black snowmobile with a flashing red light emerged out of the softly falling snow. It pulled up next to the couple. The driver, a fortyish-looking man with a small goatee, got off the machine and lifted his goggles. He wore red snow pants and a matching red parka with a white cross on the back.

"You've come from the top?" he asked, looking first at the woman, then at the man. "Like this?"

"Mostly. She skied a little. She was doing well, but with the wind and snow, she got scared. That's all."

"I am cold," the young woman said.

"You must be," the man said kindly. With both of his gloved hands, he lifted her off the snow and helped her stand. Then he threw an arm over her shoulder and guided her onto the back of the snowmobile. Finally, he took from him her set of skis and poles and slid them into a rack at the back of the snowmobile.

"How about you? You want me to come back for you?"

"No. I'm fine."

"You sure?"

The young man nodded.

"All right then. I'll have something to say to you when we meet up at the bottom."

In the loud, crowded chalet, the young husband found his wife sitting in front of the large fireplace. Even though the fire blazed in front of her and the bed of coals glowed red and orange and yellow, she was still wearing her ski jacket and hat, and a thick, wool blanket lay over her shoulders and back. As she peered into the fire, she held a cup of hot soup with both hands.

"That was crazy," he said with a chuckle, touching her on the shoulder to let her know he had returned. "Wasn't it?" Standing at her side, he removed his hat and shook the snow and ice off it.

Saying nothing, she kept her sleepy eyes on the fire.

"Did you get something to eat?"

Again, she didn't respond, didn't acknowledge his presence.

"I'll get you something if you want," he offered, unzipping his jacket and looking past her to the long line at the cafeteria. "What do you want?"

When she said nothing, he asked, "What did you do with your skis?"

"I returned them," the ski patrol guy said. He had approached them and stood face to face with the young woman's husband. "Her boots too." Then he turned to her. "Here are your shoes," he said kindly and placed them down on the floor next to her stockinged feet. Turning from her, he grabbed the young man by the back of his upper arm and led him to an empty counter where souvenirs were sold.

"Listen, hot shot," he began, his red, wind-burned face just inches from the other man's, "what you did today was incredibly reckless. Bringing up a beginner to the top of Hakkoda-san in weather like this? What the fuck were you thinking?"

"I…"

"You what?"

Not waiting for a response, the man grabbed the man's jacket with both of his hands. "You clueless fuck! I should call the police. You could have killed her. Is that what you wanted?" Then with an angry shove, he sneered, "Get the fuck back to the city where you belong!"

The drive home was miserable. For the first few minutes, the young man tried to make lighthearted small talk, at one moment even stupidly suggesting that they should give the skiing another chance when the weather was better, perhaps as soon as the next weekend; but his wife remained deathly silent, her leave-me-alone attitude colder than the strong winds that blew the snow across the narrow, winding road and kept the visibility to fifty meters at best. For most of the ride, she kept her eyes closed in utter exhaustion, resting her stocking-capped head against her window, her still-jacketed arms folded across her chest. He dug around in the small compartment between the seats, found a cassette of some John Coltrane, slid it into the deck. As he listened to the pleasant music, he cast her a sideways glance, deciding it would be best to ignore her; but doing so was impossible, her presence to him a negative force so strong that he began to feel a little ill. To make matters worse, the heavy snow began to fall again, the thick, wet flakes landing on the windshield and half melting as the wipers struggled to push the slushy matter off before it froze. His tired eyes began to burn as he followed the red lights in front of his SUV, the car in front of his following another set of red lights, that car following another, and the car behind following him in a similar manner—each car becoming part of a slow-moving, seemingly endless procession. The drive down the mountain, with its numerous twists and turns, with the necessary stops to let the snow-removal operators do their work, took nearly three hours instead of one. It was early-evening, winter-storm dark by the time they got to their neighborhood.

He drove by the entrance to the heated, underground garage that they shared with the other wealthy tenants of their building. She pulled her head away from her passenger window and was about to say something when he rolled the SUV into the snow-covered parking lot of their neighborhood *izakaya*, a place they frequented two or three times a month. "Let's get something to eat," he said, trying to sound cheerful as he turned off the engine. As he opened his door, she leaned back in her seat, her arms again crossed on her chest. "You go," she said, not looking at him.

"What?" he asked, turning to look at her, noticing that she was still wearing his gloves. "What's wrong with you?"

"I'm not hungry."

"How can you not be hungry?"

"How could you do that to me?" she hissed, looking askance at him.

He sighed deeply, closed his door, leaned back. With the engine and its heater off, the cold began to creep into the SUV.

"And what exactly did I do? You told me you wanted to learn to ski. So I took you skiing. Yes, the conditions were awful, and I am sorry about that, but I didn't know it was going to be that bad at the top. And then you lost your glove and had trouble staying upright. And with the wind and blowing snow, everything turned against us."

She glared at him with extreme hatred, but in the semi-darkness, he couldn't see just how angry she was. But he could feel her intense loathing.

"Do you want to hit me?" he asked, chuckling a little. "Would that make you feel better?"

"It's not funny."

"Listen," he said and sighed again. "We're not always going to have good days. That would be impossible. Today, like the time in Paris when we got lost, didn't go so well. Right? So let's eat and drink and put the whole day behind us."

"It's not that easy."

"Just stop it," he said, sounding and feeling drained. "You are being selfish. I love you. You know that." He opened his car door, stepped out, walked around the front of the SUV to her door. He lifted the handle and pulled it open.

"Are you coming?" As he waited, large, soft flakes drifted into the SUV and settled onto her lap, the falling snow quieting all city sounds.

Slowly, she lifted one stiff leg, then the other. When she was standing, he pushed closed the door and turned, and she followed him into the restaurant.

Inside, the place was Sunday-evening, family-night-out crowded. They had to squeeze in at the counter, their elbows touching.

Without looking at the menu, he ordered some *maguro sashimi*, the *tempura* set, two draft beers, and a small bottle of hot *sake*. When the waitress brought the sake and one small cup, he roughly told her, gesturing with his eyes, "Bring another cup for my wife." He waited until she did. Then he filled a cup of the hot liquor and passed it to her. He filled one for himself and held it out to her.

"Okay?" he said, turning to her, looking her in the eyes. "Are we going to talk now? Be friendly? Smile a little?"

"Maybe."

"What kind of toast is that?" he asked and laughed.

After he touched his small cup to hers, she took a sip; he emptied his and poured himself another.

The dishes began to arrive. He ate greedily as she took a few small, tentative bites; but then she too ate quickly, the warm, delicious food a salve for her physical and mental pains. They ordered more. Later, as they took their last bites, he ordered himself another beer and another *tokkuri* of the hot *sake*.

When he was full, he leaned back, rested his forearms on the counter, looked at his wife. She took another sip of the *sake* and then licked her dry, wind-burned lips. "Your face is red," he reported, reaching out to refill her cup. With her free hand, she reached up and touched her cheek. Her eyes half closed, she looked at him and nodded slowly.

That evening, after they bathed together, after he had finished a large tumbler of whisky, the young newlyweds retired to their large bed and there, in the lights-off, curtains-open semi-darkness, began to make love. He was on top, leaning over her, his hands flat on the bed, as usual, but for the first time, he got up on his knees. As he looked down at her, he reached out first one hand, then the other, and found her ankles. As he gripped each in his hands, he lifted her thin legs into a wide V, her legs straight, her feet high above her. Slowly, he pushed himself deep into her; then slowly he withdrew. He pushed himself into her slowly; then he withdrew.

"Look at me," he told her, his voice sounding a little rough.

She opened her eyes, squinting to look up at him. Once more, he pushed himself deep into her. "Oh, God," she moaned. "Just stay there."

"There?"

"Yes, there," she replied, nodding quickly, her eyes half closed in pleasure.

Ever so slowly, he slid himself out.

"Why?" she groaned. Her head lifting off the pillow, she reached down with both hands and grabbed him and tried to guide him back into her. But he let go of her ankles, pushed away her hands, turned her over, this too something he had never done before with her. With his two hands, he grabbed her waist and lifted her so that she was propped on her hands and knees. From behind, he slowly entered her and slowly withdrew. He did this again and again and again, all the time her sounds of pleasure increasing. Then, abruptly, he yanked her off the bed, walked her out to the hallway, stood her up against the wall as if he were a police sergeant and she a common criminal needing frisking. With his right foot, he kicked apart her legs and leaned her over, her head and hands on the wall. Standing behind her, his left hand clutching her shoulder, his right as a guide, he slipped himself back inside her.

"Listen," he said, in English, as he gently thrust and thrust and thrust, "the snow is falling. The snow is falling everywhere."

Since he was intoxicated, and since he was still more than a little angry, his orgasm was far away. With her hands high on the wall, and with him behind her, with him massaging her shoulders and neck and small breasts and erect nipples, this lovemaking went on for many minutes, one naked body slapping hard against another. Though the young couple had started in the mostly dark, he had reached over and turned on the hallway light. To his surprise, he found that she had arched her back and was meeting his thrusts.

"Yes?" he asked once, pausing.

"Yes," she replied, panting.

He increased his speed. He banged harder and harder. As she shuddered and cried out, he gripped her slim waist with his two hands. At last, deep inside her, he too came. As he rested his head on her back, he kept himself inside her for as long as he could. Then, sensing that she was about to collapse, he grabbed her from behind, lifted her, carried her back to the bed. When he playfully tossed her onto it, she let out a little scream. He collapsed next to her and rolled over onto his back, his arms outstretched.

"I am very sorry," she said, nestling into him, one arm thrown across his chest.

"I am sorry too. But let's not talk. Let's just sleep."

"Can I say just one thing?"

"No."

A minute later, their breathing slowed, the inhalation and deep exhalation joined. With his free hand, he reached down, found the overstuffed duvet that had been kicked earlier to the foot of the bed. He pulled it up and over them. The young newlyweds, exhausted by the hard day's adventures, soon fell into a deep, satisfying sleep, the hallway still brightly lit.

"Nami."

She said nothing.

"Please don't hang up. Not again."

Still, she said nothing.

"Did you get the note and flowers I sent?"

"Lost item department. Can I help you?"

"Nami, please!"

"Perhaps, sir, you are calling about a lost Hermes scarf. We have a nice one. Can you describe it?"

He sighed. "It's green and red with blue stripes. It looks brand new."

"That description doesn't fit. This one is rather well used."

"I am incredibly sorry you had to find out that way."

"Is there any good way to find out?"

"Of course not. But I was planning on telling you."

"Oh yeah? And when was that going to be? When you had me in my high school uniform? Principal," she added, her voice raised in mock flirtation, "I was a very bad girl today! I didn't finish my homework, and I was rude to the teacher!"

"Nami, please!"

She said nothing.

"Can't we meet? Just one time? Please!"

"And why should we meet?" she asked with rising anger. "So you can tell me more lies? I know a good one, 'Oh, Nami, she's as ugly as a wart. I married her for her money.'"

He didn't know what to say. She waited a few seconds. When he said nothing, she hung up. As he gently replaced the receiver, he felt overwhelmed with genuine sadness. There was no doubt he had been excessively selfish and cruel; he decided he would never call her again.

4 Trying to Do Something Good, Part 1

In the large shower room, as the young man sat on the wooden stool, the young woman stood behind him. Both were naked. She had long, brown hair, but it was tied up in a loose bun at the top of her head. Before she began, she tested the water temperature; when it was warm enough, she wet him with warm water from the shower nozzle. Then she applied liquid soap to his back and shoulders, and with her large breasts and shoulders and wrists and elbows, she massaged the soap around his torso. The young man closed his eyes. Occasionally, as she slowly moved around him, she would brush her nipples across his ears and face, as if she had done so by accident. Later, she sat down on the tiled floor and used the inside of her arms and her breasts to lather his thighs and calves, but she made sure her hands never touched his body. After twenty minutes of this, she rinsed him with warm water. Neither had said a word. Next, she applied a generous amount of soap to her small hands and crouched over in front of him so that her breasts hung right in front of his face. Slowly, she began soaping and massaging his genitals. Most customers were erect by this point, but to her, he seemed preoccupied.

Some people, no matter the indignity of the job, try to do it well, and he could tell that she was trying hard. She had a determined look on her face, as if what he wanted was what she wanted too. After a minute, he opened his eyes and looked at her. "Why do you do this?" he asked. It was a question he had wanted to ask since he had been shown the three available women and he had picked her.

She stopped what she was doing and looked up at him.

"This?"

"Yes."

She looked down again and resumed soaping his genitals. "What else am I supposed to do?"

"How old are you?"

"Twenty."

"How did you end up doing this?"

"I got pregnant my last year of high school," she said flatly. "Most of the girls I knew had abortions, but I dithered. Then it was too late. They threw me out the last semester."

"Wouldn't you rather be doing something different?"

She stopped and again looked up at him, her eyes filling with distrust.

"Like what? Adult films? I did one once." For a few seconds, she closed her eyes at the memory. "And once was enough. You have no idea how humiliating it is to have two guys—with all the lights and cameras and crew—do the things they do to you."

"I am not talking about anything like that."

When she noticed that his erection was waning, she began soaping him again.

"Don't you have a wife? Or a girlfriend?"

"I do."

"I am not supposed to date customers."

"I am not asking for a date. But I could help. In my line of work, I know some people, some clients. One is a manager. I could get you in at a department store. You know Seibu, yes? You could sell lingerie or chocolate or cosmetics. Pretty much anything, I think."

"And make what, 490 yen an hour? I'll make more tonight than what I would make there all week. And who wants to stand all day?"

He reached out and brushed a few loose strands of her hair from one eye. She pulled back her head, stopped what she was doing, and looked at him. "Sir, as you know, you are not supposed to touch me."

"I'm sorry."

"Anyway, thanks. But I don't need your help. I don't mind doing this." He found the assertion hard to believe. But he said nothing. She looked up at the clock behind him and saw that there were only fifteen minutes left. With both her hands, she rubbed him vigorously for a minute. When she saw that he was very hard, she rinsed him with warm water. Adeptly, she slipped on a condom, then repositioned herself so that she sat on the tile floor with her face in front of his groin. She took him into her mouth and began blowing him. She closed her eyes and was all business, her head quickly going up and down, her left hand holding the base of his erection, her right hand massaging his balls.

After he came, she slid off the condom, soaped his genitals again, then rinsed him. As they both stood, he said, "I saw a bunch of mailboxes down on the street level. One was for an electronics shop. If I am not mistaken, it's on the second floor. My name is Tanaka. I'm going to slip my business card in the box there. If you change your mind, contact me. I am not asking for anything. I simply want to help."

The young woman wrapped a towel around him and another around herself, then saw him back to the changing room where his clothes hung neatly on hangers, but she said nothing. It took him a few minutes to don his clothes, and after he had done so, she turned around and, without saying a word, walked back into the shower room. He exited through another door, walked through a dimly lit lounge where an older woman bowed to him and invited him to return, and took the elevator down five floors to the street.

5 Two Men Meet in Tokyo for a Drink, Part 2

"I must say, half of the traders don't think you warrant the number-one position. To be frank, they are jealous. You marry the old man's daughter. Six months later you're back in Tokyo as the number-one trader. An office to yourself and your own assistant, a rather attractive one at that. Some guys have been with us for years and they don't have half of what you have."

"And who might these revolutionaries be?"

"You know I am not going to name any names. That wouldn't be fair. In these difficult times when it's almost impossible to get new customers, we don't need any dissension."

His younger colleague picked up his whisky and took a sip. "I work hard. You know that, Nomura. The only guy who works harder is that fat slob Ito."

"I know your talents, Makoto. That Cisco buy has been paying off, paying off rather handsomely. Just this morning the old man gave the okay to commit another five million. And Apple? Who names a company Apple? Where do you come up with these finds?"

"Yeah. Strange, huh? Well, I don't care if it's a porno organization. As long as it's listed and there is the potential to make money, I'm interested."

The two were silent for a long while. Each sipped his whisky quietly.

"Anyways, how does it feel to be back? Do you miss New York?"

"It's nice, I guess. Junko is especially happy. We had a lot of fun there, and as you may recall, we traveled all over. It's such a beautiful country. But she never took to the city. And she's happy to have the kids in a proper Japanese school. Even with the private tutors, she was afraid that they'd never learn how to write and read *kanji* properly."

"And?"

"And what? Mary?"

The younger man shook his head. "No. If there is anything to know, I think it's best that I don't. I wish her only the best." He lifted his whisky, finished it, ordered another.

"I don't want to pry. Please forgive me if I am. But you're more or less my only confidant. What is marriage like after five or ten years?"

"I see," the other chuckled. "You mean the sex?"

His colleague nodded. "That. Everything. The day to day."

"Well, the first couple of years, the sex was very nice. And even when Junko got pregnant the first time, she wanted it all the time. I mean she wanted it more than I did, if that makes sense. Of course, on account of the baby, she would have to be on top, or I'd have to take her from behind. But she could never get enough. When I got home from work, we'd do it right there at the dining room table and then a minute later with my pants still at my ankles we'd sit down and eat. And then with her at the kitchen sink doing the washing up, she'd want me to do her again.

"But then the little one came," he said with another chuckle. "I didn't get laid for three months. Not even a hand job. She just changed. Like a light switch, she went from on to off. Spent all of her time with little Michiko. Of course, after a year, she wanted another one. But, at that point, it was like going through the motions. And when she got pregnant, I was hoping the good old days would return, but they didn't. Now, what, we've been married nine years, and she says she can live without sex. Fuck, I'm only thirty-six, and I live in a city with a million beautiful women." The man shook his head ruefully.

"You should find a girlfriend. Like her," the younger man suggested, nodding in her direction. As she approached, the young waitress hadn't heard what he had said. She set the new glass in front of him, picked up the empty, and bowed.

The older man laughed as the waitress retreated to the bar. "She's a piece of chocolate, but I don't need that kind of stress. Paying for it once or twice a month is okay with me. It's safer and a lot less expensive."

Again, the two men sat silently.

"I assume since you asked, things aren't all that swell in Shibuya."

"It's hard. I must admit. Now that she's pregnant, she's been sick a lot. The doctors tell her to eat more, to put on weight. I cook her whatever she wants, but she just picks at it. If the TV is too loud, if I leave the cap off of the toothpaste, if I forget to buy her her favorite fashion magazine, she snaps."

The younger man took a sip of his whisky and continued. "But it's not Mariko. She is trying very hard. I have to give her credit. With her upbringing, she never cooked a meal or washed a dish until we moved in together. She has come a long way. No, it's me. I can't tell you how much I miss my single life. I am beginning to think I am not cut out for marriage. It's like I have a problem, some flaw that I have had since my university days. I always want what I don't have, and then when I have it, when I hold it in my hands, I am not satisfied."

His companion nodded. "I understand. In a crowded room, with all the fake smiles and the mindless isn't-the-weather-nice-today conversation, most married couples seem happy. But at home, with all the needless bickering, one wonders if it's all worth it. It's amazing, isn't it? There was a time in my life when I couldn't stand being away from her. Now the littlest thing—for example, the way she chews her food—irritates the hell out of me. And the funny thing is, I'm sure she feels the same way about me. There is much love in this world that turns to indifference, even hate."

The older man lifted his hand and got the attention of the waitress, who made her way back to their table. He looked up at her and her nametag.

"Keiko-san," he said as he lifted his empty glass, "would you be so kind as to bring me another? I know you were just here, but then, as you stood before us, and as I looked at you and your lovely eyes, I was speechless. And then so quickly—and cruelly, I may add—you left without my getting a chance to order another."

Looking confused, and perhaps repressing a smile, the young waitress bowed, and then the two men watched her as she returned to the bar.

"You know, with your talents," the older man continued, turning his attention back to the man who sat across from him, "you don't need the old man. You could go it alone. Set up your own office. If you want, take Haruka with you. It's obvious how she feels about you."

"Obvious? What do you mean?"

"What do you want me to say?" the older man replied, shrugging his shoulders. Before he resumed, he thanked the waitress with excessively polite language, complimented her long hair, then took a sip of his newly arrived whisky. "Perhaps you and she should be a little more circumspect. Trying to get the office to let her accompany you to Frankfurt last month was not the brightest idea."

The younger man nodded. He picked up his glass and took a sip.

"Well, for some reason, I think my going out on my own at this time would not be a wise move. With Mariko due soon, the timing isn't quite right."

"But a year or two down the road—"

The younger man raised his hand, gesture his older colleague understood. For a few more minutes, each sipped his whisky quietly, as if in the liquid, somewhere, were the answers they were searching for.

"About six months ago, I let one get away. She might have been the one. I truly feel that now. I can't stop thinking about her."

"Yeah?"

"She's a flight attendant at JAL. And you know the craziest fuckin' thing? I met her the day I left New York. You know, the flight from JFK to Narita. She was working the first-class cabin. What with my leaving Mary so quickly, and with the lies I had to tell, I was a wreck. I got completely shitfaced. I don't remember much of anything, just glass after glass of brandy; but I guess I came on to her, this flight attendant. I was supposed to meet her the night we landed in Tokyo, but as I said, I don't remember anything about a meeting. Never showed up.

"She called me about three weeks later. I was curious, naturally. We talked a few times, but for weeks she played me off. She always had an excuse. Later, when we finally met, I wasn't impressed. I mean she was beautiful. Sure. But there was not much of a spark. But gradually, as the weeks went by, and as we spent more time together, I saw all of her wonderful qualities. She was playful, creative, funny. Spontaneous too. And her smile. Just incredible!"

"But weren't you and Mariko—"

"Of course. We were making the wedding plans. What a hassle that was. Believe me, I thought long and hard about breaking it off with her, with Mariko. But deep down inside, I knew that I loved her. But I loved Nami too. I did. I know that you think I'm an asshole, but I loved them both. Nami made me wait a long time— the first few nights we spent together we didn't have sex—but when we started, the sex was extraordinary. Some of the best I have ever had.

"As one would expect, she found out. You won't believe this. After Mariko and I returned from Paris, we flew to Aomori the next day. I had no idea—no idea whatsoever—but Nami was working the flight. Thank God she was in the back of the plane, and I was able to keep things secret. Then, incredibly, we were all staying at the same hotel that night. It was the lowest point of my life. Probably the worst thing I have ever done. I am ashamed to say I had sex with both of them that night. Just an hour apart."

"Holy fuck," the older man said, inhaling deeply and shaking his head side to side in wonder. "Somebody should write a book about you."

"Somehow—I don't know how—she found out. Early the next morning, she left a cryptic message on our room's answering machine, which Mariko heard. Thank God she wasn't forthright, and thank God Mariko didn't put two and two together."

Stunned, the older man just looked at his younger colleague.

"I tried—believe me, I tried very hard—to make it up with her. But she wisely—and rightly so—gave me the colossal fuck off.

"So that's the story of my life. I am married to a woman I love dearly. But I still think about Nami, the exquisite pearl I let drop back into the deep ocean. Every time I fly, I wonder if I will see her." The younger man lifted his glass and greedily finished it.

"Anyways, it's great to have you back. I mean that!" The younger man reached across the small table and slapped his older companion on the shoulder. "Shall we?"

The two got up, made their way to the counter by the front door, settled their bill. As they sauntered down the street to the station, the older one placed his hand on the other's shoulder. "Shall we go get soaped up?"

His younger colleague laughed. "I would like to. But I'll pass. I am trying to be a bit better these days. A bit more faithful."

"You?"

Since they were going in different directions, the two parted, and the younger one watched his companion go up the escalator to the station entrance. When he saw him disappear into the crowd, the young man turned and found a payphone. He slipped inside and unfolded the glass door so that it closed behind him. He picked up the receiver and inserted his phone card. He paused and looked at the buttons. After the story he had related, he felt incredibly guilty. Instead of stopping by Haruka's apartment and spending an hour or two with her, he thought about going home to his wife and her growing belly. She would be watching TV and paging through a fashion magazine. She would have something warm to eat waiting for him. He hung up the receiver and stepped out of the payphone. But after a few steps, he turned around, re-entered the phone booth. He inserted his phone card and dialed.

"*Hai*! Tanaka *desu*."

"Hi Sweet Apple Pie. I am leaving now."

"That's nice! Shall I prepare the bath?"

"I wish you would."

"You know, I measured my tummy this afternoon. I grew by half an inch. Of course, I still think I look the same. And if you call me fat, you know where you can sleep tonight!"

"Do we need anything?"

"No. I did some shopping this afternoon. I bought beer and *edamame* and peanuts, too, the kind you like."

"I love you, Mariko. I'll be home in fifteen minutes."

6 The Summer Party

The company's summer party would start in a few hours. It, like the *bounenkai* that came in December, was always a grand affair. The old man would rent a large room at a traditional *izakaya*, one long table where they all sat, the food and drink endless. Of course, somebody always drank too much and did something embarrassing. They could count on that. But such moments, and the stories they exaggerated later, made such evenings special. The young man looked down at his watch. He had a good excuse not to go. After all, his wife was in the hospital. But since he had started the affair with Kumamoto, he wanted to see if there was any fun to be had. He had heard that some of the older traders were trying to set her up with Ito, the only single guy in the office.

To the young man, Ito was a bona fide loser. Sure, he was a sharp trader who made the company a lot of money; but there were many good reasons why he was still single. Did he shower every day? The young man had his doubts. Did he visit a dentist once a year? He wondered about that too. And he was a little annoyed that the guy wore the same wrinkled tie and the same pair of worn-out shoes every day. Ito was fifteen years older than she, so he chuckled at the thought of them together; but then again, he had seen some odd pairings in his day. Money—usually, the lack of it—made people do strange things.

After he left the office, the young man stopped by the hospital. "Aren't you going? Father was here this afternoon. He's going."
"I don't really want to go."
"Why not?"
"I wish you could go too."
"Are you crazy? I am due any day now."
"I know. It's just hard not having you at home." He sat down on the narrow bed next to her, reached out, took her hand. The two chatted pleasantly for over an hour.

When the young man arrived, he was pleased to see that most everyone was already well lit. Even his father-in-law had the tell-tale red eyes, a glowing face, the warm smile. Leaning on an elbow, the old man sat at one end of a long row of several pulled-together tables that could accommodate all thirty-six members of the Tokyo office. He was ordering food and drinks for them at a regular pace. He looked happy. A quick glance told him that Kumamoto had been placed next to Ito. When she looked up at him, her eyes seemed to ask, "And where the fuck have you been?" She had a glass of red wine in front of her. It looked as if she hadn't touched it.

The young man stood at the opposite end of the long row of tables from where his father-in-law sat and raised his hands. As he waited for his colleagues to quiet, he slipped off his suit jacket and handed it to a waitress. "Ladies and gentlemen, fellow rogues, general delinquents all!" he began, scanning the room with a mischievous smile. "Please. Let me have your attention. I am late. I know. But I have some very good news. I have been searching all over Tokyo. It's not easy to find one on a hot, summer Friday evening. But I found one. What did I find? A liquor truck.

Refrigerated, of course. I just spoke to the driver myself. Actually, I helped him park his rig in the back alley. Shall we then?" Everyone laughed and cheered and clapped. Down at his end of the table, the old man looked pleased. He squinted and wagged a finger playfully at his son-in-law. Kindly, the young man gathered the three waitresses and told them to bring the table another round. Then the din resumed.

One of his colleagues passed him a chair, and he squeezed in so he was sitting across from Ito. "What's going on, old boy?" he shouted across the table. "You look like you haven't had a drop. And why are you ignoring that lovely lady sitting to your right?"

The "old boy" blushed and mumbled that he was quite in his cups.

"You know what Shakespeare says, right?"

"I never read Shakespeare."

"What does he say?" the young woman asked, her eyes on the newcomer, her boredom easing.

The fresh drinks arrived and were being passed down the table, the young man reaching out for a mug of beer. When everyone had something, each lifted it, and they all shouted, "*Kampai!*" The young man emptied his in three quick gulps. Ito, trying to match his much younger and more vigorous colleague, chugged his mug as well.

"What does he say?" the young woman asked again, seemingly intrigued.

"'It provokes the desire,'" the young man said knowingly as he leaned across the table at the two, "'but it takes away the performance.'" He laughed and raised his empty mug. "He was talking about this wonderful nectar," he said. "So be careful, you rascal"—he now gestured to Ito with the empty mug—"not to have a drop too much. You wouldn't want to disappoint any eager young lady."

"Who said something about Shakespeare?" Nakagami asked, turning to join the conversation. He was sitting to the left of the young man. "You know," he added, "he has a number of choice drinking songs."

Ignoring his neighbor's question, the young man asked the woman, "How about you, Haruka? Do you know any good drinking songs?"

"No," she replied, her bright eyes twinkling with fake innocence. "I am a very good girl."

"I bet you are," he said with a laugh. Another broker leaned over and replaced the young man's empty mug with a full one. He picked it up and gestured to Ito. "Well, a couple months ago when we were out, this tiger cat had us all in stitches. You recall, Naka, don't you?"

"You bet!"

The young man leaned in and began, careful to make sure his voice could be heard only by the three. "Row, row, row your boat, gently up the stream," he sang softly, "slide it in, slide it out, listen to her…"

The three men all started laughing. The young lady just smirked and rolled her eyes.

"What was the other one? Something about Jack and Jill, right?" The young man reached over, found a new mug, one of many that had just arrived, and placed it in front of Ito.

"I sang no such songs," the drunk man mumbled before he lifted the mug and took a swig.

"Don't be so modest, you scoundrel. You're a regular Falstaff once you get going. It went something like this: 'Jack and Jill went up the hill, we know what happened next. / On her hands and knees she went, they started having…' God, I can never remember the ending!"

When the laughter subsided, the young man continued, "See, you charmer? She's smiling. And look at that virginal blush! It's all because of you and your songs. I wish I had your wit and charm, you rogue!" He finished off his beer and gazed at the couple.

"God, Naka," the young man said as he threw an arm over Nakagami's shoulders and leaned into him, "look at her. She's my assistant, but she can't keep her eyes off him." The "old boy" looked down, began to speak, but instead took another generous swig. "If I weren't married," he said confidentially, "I'd make a play for her myself." The young lady laughed, picked up her glass, finished her wine.

"Look at you!" the young man said to Ito, reaching across the table to cuff the man on his shoulder. "She just finished her wine. Where are your manners? Have you ordered her another? She's dying of thirst!"

Ito's right hand shot up. He snapped his fingers a few times and yelled rudely to get a waitress' attention. "Another red wine for the lady," he slurred. "And I'll have another mug."

"What? Be a man!" the young man said jovially. "We'll have two tumblers of whisky. Neat. Make that three, one for ol' Naka here. And three mugs. And of course, the red wine for Ito's lovely lady."

Hayashi, the office manager, slipped over and whispered something into the young man's ear. "Of course," he replied, pushing back his chair and standing, his smile disappearing. "You must continue a few minutes without me," he said, addressing his three colleagues. "I am going to see Ueda-sama to his car."

Outside, the young man could see that his father-in-law had had perhaps one too many. "The doctors say it's any day now," he mumbled, nodding and reaching out to his son-in-law an unsteady hand, his eyes heavy.

"Yes. I stopped by before coming here. I'm going tomorrow morning too. Won't you come as well?"

"Of course."

Out on the street, Yuji helped the old man into the back seat and closed the door. As he walked around to the driver's door, he grabbed the young man's arm and led him to the back of the car. The two men stood inches apart.

The young man, feeling the courage the alcohol provided, leaned into him, their foreheads bumping. "Fuck you."

Yuji chuckled. "Never more confident, eh?"

"Fuck you."

"I haven't decided what to do with you."

"Go to hell."

"I've been there. I had a very pleasant stay. I'm back."

The young man stood his ground.

"I wonder," Yuji began, his eyes narrowing, his tone menacing, "if that lovely assistant of yours has had the pleasure yet of being gang raped. It would be a shame if anything like that happened to her. Once a girl gets stretched like that, she's never the same. The experience kind of fucks with her, if you know what I mean." With that, he stepped over to the driver's door, got inside, and drove off.

Back inside, the young man found his seat. Without addressing the others, without even looking at them, he picked up his glass of whisky and finished half of it. As he looked out at nothing, he seemed distracted. Finally, he glanced across the table and saw the empty space. "Where is the giant comedian?" he asked.

"He stumbled off to the bathroom just after you left," Nakagami reported. "He didn't look so good."

"How long has he been gone?"

"Too long."

"I'll go check on him. Naka, make sure the adorable Haruka doesn't drink my whisky. She often has her eyes on things that don't belong to her."

In the bathroom, the young man found Ito slumped against a wall in one of the stalls. There was a great deal of vomit in the toilet bowl and on the seat and on the floor. With his shoe, he prodded him once, then again harder, the befuddled man letting out a groan. "Doing just fine, aren't you?" The young man turned, found a sink, washed his hands. He wet his face and then examined his reflection in the mirror.

Out in the hallway that led to the bathrooms, he found his assistant standing before the door to the ladies' room. "How is he?"

"As expected."

"You didn't have to be so cruel."

"Fuck him. He deserves it."

"Still," she replied, her eyes holding his. "You were not very nice."

"I swear to God, Haruka, if you marry that fat bastard, I'll jump in front of a Yamanote train."

"I hear he has a lot of money," she said playfully.

"More than I do?"

"Perhaps. Your money is predicated on your maintaining a certain relationship with a certain someone."

"And I've shared a lot of that money with you, you know."

"I know. I am not being selfish. As your devoted assistant, I always have your best interests—and any special needs—in mind."

"That's more like it." He looked down the dark hallway and saw no one. "Here," he said, fishing out a room key card from his wallet and handing it to her. "I checked in this afternoon. Room 3811. I'll leave now. Go back to the table. Follow in about fifteen minutes. I'll be in the bath. Come join me."

Just before sunrise, the young man slipped out of the hotel room, careful not to make too much noise. He left his still-sleeping-peacefully, still-naked assistant and caught a cab back to his apartment. In the bedroom, he tumbled into the bed he shared with his wife and fell into a deep, rejuvenating sleep.

When he woke just after nine, he slid open the veranda door and stepped outside onto the balcony. In his pajama bottoms and T-shirt, he stood at the railing, stretching his arms and upper body and gazing at the city. It was a fine morning. Somewhere, the life-giving sun was shining, the sky a bright blue. He found the contrast between the long, dark shadows and the bright sunlight brilliant. For some reason, he felt fresh and full of energy.

Back inside, he ate some buttered toast and strawberry yogurt, then took a shower. After he dressed, he set off for the hospital. He spent the whole day there.

7 The King Enjoys His Castle

He quite enjoyed having the spacious apartment all to himself. The doctor and the nurses reported that the delivery had been lengthy and difficult, so instead of the usual week, the exhausted mother and the tiny, fragile infant had been instructed to remain two. He visited every day, often twice a day; and at work, he could come and go as he pleased. In many ways, he felt free again. As he walked the sidewalks, as he rode the subways and trains, as he gazed out taxi windows, he noticed things that he hadn't before. It wasn't that he had been unhappy, but he felt happier these past few days, a mountain climber having reached the summit after an arduous trek.

One evening, in the living room, he ate some *edamame* and drank his Asahi and watched TV, as was his wont, but for fun, he simply tossed the pods onto the floor. Soon the floor was littered with the empty green shells. When he finished his second and then the third and fourth can, he threw each on the floor as well. Later, he played some records—a little too loudly, it seems, for the next day the apartment manager phoned him at his office to report that a neighbor had complained. He felt bad about that, so after work, he bought some expensive boxes of chocolate. That evening, he knocked on his neighbors' doors and apologized. He mentioned the baby. "I may have been a little too exuberant in my celebrating last night," he said and bowed. "Please forgive me."

One Saturday morning he rented a few pornos and watched one as he ate his yogurt and toast. He fast-forwarded to the first sex scene, and as the young lady in the film was blowing two guys at the same time, he stood up and masturbated right there in front of the TV. He came on the glass coffee table. He fantasized about having someone lick it off—perhaps he could ask Haruka to do something like that?—but then he was engrossed in the film again and was soon masturbating once more.

He did consider asking Haruka to come. What, he mused, could go wrong? But he sensed that having her in the apartment would be a grave transgression. Instead, he rented a suite at the Shinagawa Prince. They had their sex there—in the large bathtub, in the armchair, on the couch, in front of the large floor-to-ceiling mirror. The energetic lovers could not get enough of each other.

All in all, with his wife and his baby at the hospital, he was having a grand time.

8 The Minders Get Rough

"Makoto, please!"

"Haruka, where the hell are you? You've been gone nearly two hours. I can't get any work done with the phone constantly ringing."

"You have to come," she wailed. "Right now." There was a pause as the receiver was passed from Haruka to another.

"Hey, lover boy," the new speaker said. "Recognize the voice? I got a bunch of swinging dicks here ready to fill her every orifice if you don't get your ass here pronto. They're ready to get pounding. You understand?"

"I understand."

"Now calm down. There's been no harm done. Not yet, at least, has there?" These last six words he addressed to the terrified young lady. "He can't see you nodding your head, stupid," the young man heard Yuji say. "Say something."

"Makoto, please!"

"That's a good girl. Now sit the fuck back down. Get your pussy good and wet. If your Romeo isn't here in an hour, I'll be the first. After I blow my load, I'll use a baseball bat on your tight little anus. Then the rest of the fellows will have their turns. It may take a few hours, but we'll go round and round until we're all good and satisfied.

"Sorry about that," Yuji continued, once again addressing the young man. "There are a lot of anxious people here. I am worried. Something bad might happen. Now where were we? Oh yeah, you were going to get 5,000,000 yen and make us a visit. That's what we were talking about, right?"

"Are you insane? I can't get that kind of money in an hour."

"Gee whiz, and I thought you were a magician when it came to making money. Boys," the young man heard Yuji shout, "you ready to get started? Get the video cameras ready too. We'll need a lot of close-ups."

"Listen," the young man said, speaking quickly. "It's half past one. The banks close at three. I'll need to get to at least two, maybe three. I'll be lucky if I have the money by then."

"Well then, you had better get lucky. Here's the address: 1-14-16 Kabukicho. The name of the bar is the Red Rose. Got it written down? Now you seem to be a little nervous, so repeat the address slowly."

After a pause, Yuji said, "That's right. You got it."

What the young man heard next truly unsettled him. "Makoto," the young woman wailed, "there's a guy masturbating!"

"For fuck's sake!" Yuji shouted. "I told you not to come in her hair." Then the phone went dead.

The young man jumped out of the taxi and ran down the narrow alley. When he found the number and saw the name, he pounded on the door. He tried the handle, but it was locked. He heard a bolt slide open, and the door opened a few centimeters. "Get the fuck in," said a guy he had never seen before. As he entered, the fellow held out a hand and gestured with his chin. Seeing what he wanted, the young man passed over the large envelope he had brought.

He needed a half minute for his blinking eyes to adjust to the semi-darkness, but what he saw shocked him. Several shady-looking fellows had their dicks out and were stroking themselves.

In the center, on a low, round stool, sat the woman he had been with the previous night. What were those stains he saw on her white blouse and blue skirt? A few seconds later, he had the answer: one of the fellows walked over and came on her shoulder as she grimaced and turned away her face.

"Well, my good friend," Yuji said, not at all sounding friendly, "I see we meet again."

For a minute, the new arrival glanced around the window-less bar. About the same size as a small hotel room, the entire place reeked of overflowing ashtrays and stale beer. Nothing pleasant could ever happen in such a place.

"Do I have your full attention?"

"You do."

"I never wanted it to come to this," Yuji related with a heavy sigh, sounding tired. "I mean that. I gave you a rather stern warning the other night. But then you had to go and play the tough guy. A real Clint Eastwood Dirty Harry. You know, you kind of hurt my feelings." Another fellow walked over to the young woman and blew his load on her back. He squeezed out the last bit of semen and then wiped the tip of his penis on her shoulder.

"Did you get it in her hair?" Yuji asked the guy.

"I may have. Just a little. I couldn't help myself."

"I told you not to. She's not exactly the guilty party, though she hasn't behaved properly either."

"I'll be more careful next time."

"You do that."

The young man glanced above the bar and saw the TV screen and below it a VCR—some kind of an orgy, six or seven naked bodies writhing in a tangled knot, the sound muted.

"Haruka," he said, turning to the visibly distressed woman. "I am very sorry. I had no idea something like this would happen."

"Oh, God," she moaned, her face full of fear and disgust, when another guy approached her. Stroking himself vigorously to finish, he too came on her.

"That feel good?" Yuji asked with a leer.

"It would have felt better with my cock in her mouth."

"That's nasty. Don't say such things. She's a good girl with a good heart, I'm sure. This has to be very hard for her."

Yuji moved near the young woman. Gently, he placed his hand under her chin and lifted it. "You don't feel so well, do you?"

"No," she moaned again, tears streaking her cheeks.

"You don't want any of these tough guys to put their big, meaty cocks in your mouth, do you?"

"No," she replied, shuddering.

"You want to go home, don't you?"

"Yes."

"I mean home home. As in Aomori."

The young woman nodded, her distressed face telling her interlocutor that she would do nearly anything to extricate herself from the rather unpleasant situation.

"That's a very good girl. I want that too. So does your lover boy. That's why he brought you some moving expenses. You've done that, haven't you?"

"I have," the young man replied, nodding his head.

"Is she taking the night bus? Or is she flying?"

"She can fly," he reported. "First class if she wants."

"You wouldn't put her on a plane dressed as she is, would you?"

"Of course not."

"So there's enough for some new clothes? I mean, she could go down to Takashimaya right now, if she wanted, and buy herself a new wardrobe, little pink panties and silk stockings and all that fine stuff young fashionable ladies are fond of?"

"Yes."

"That's good," the older man replied, nodding. "I like that. I like that very much."

He turned to the guy who had taken the envelope. As he sat at the bar, he was counting out the 10,000-yen notes. "Is at all there?"

"Seems so, boss."

"Good. Now if I had a beautiful daughter," Yuji said, placing his hand on the top of the young woman's head, "and a bunch of VD-infected assholes were blowing loads on her in some shit bar in Kabukicho, I wouldn't feel well at all. But this is what happens when people are selfish and disregard orders. Please," he said to the young woman, grabbing her hair forcefully, "stop crying." As he shook her head roughly, she whimpered only more.

Then he looked at the young man. "You have a wife, fuckface?"

"You know I do."

"And as we have this little rendezvous, this little heart to heart that is so painful to all of us, especially to the lovely Haruka, the lovely yet distraught Haruka who can't seem to stop crying, this wife of yours is lying in a hospital bed?"

"Yes."

"I understand a week ago she gave birth. Is that right?"

"Yes, that's right."

"And that little wonder of the world is probably suckling on her left breast right now, just like you suckled on this one's last night?" Still gripping the young woman by her long hair, he shook her head forcefully.

"Yes."

"And last night you spread this slut's pink pussy lips"—he shook her so violently this time that she cried out and nearly fell off the stool—"and then fucked her 'til she begged you to stop?"

"I guess so."

"I couldn't hear you."

"Yes."

"What the fuck," Yuji roared, "is wrong with you?"

For a moment, the young man said nothing. Then, his eyes on the floor, he mumbled, "I don't know."

"Haruka, dear, do you know?" he asked, giving her head another shake.

"I don't know," she sobbed.

Yuji turned to the half dozen men he had collected. "Do any of you know?" They remained silent. Yuji looked from fellow to fellow and then up at the TV, the naked bodies still in motion. He shook his head disdainfully. Motes of dust floated in the dimly lit bar.

After Yuji gave the sniveling young woman a final rough shake, he let go of her hair. Casually, he walked behind the bar, found the small refrigerator, pulled out a large bottle of Kirin. He looked at the bottle's label for a few seconds, then set it on the counter. He yanked open a drawer, found an opener, popped off the top. From a shelf behind the bar, he grabbed a small glass. Tilting it, he slowly filled the glass with the cold beer, then took a sip. "Good," he reported, nodding and looking around. "Very good. Just what I needed." After another sip, he said, sighing, "I apologize. I was getting a little hot and thirsty." He finished off the glass and, in no hurry, poured himself another.

"Now where were we?" he asked, looking around the room again. As she sat on the stool—hunched over, her unkempt hair covering most of her face, her eyes cast down—the young woman was still whimpering piteously. When he looked at her, the others did as well. Everyone seemed to be waiting. Finally, still holding the large bottle in his right hand, he looked directly into the eyes of the young man. "Let me be clear then."

Suddenly, and with great force, Yuji hurled the bottle. With a thud, it careened off the young man's forehead. He staggered, reaching out a hand that found the back of a chair, but he remained standing. As he leaned over, blood began to ooze from the wound. Meanwhile, when the bottle struck the concrete wall behind the young man and shattered, the young woman let out a scream and fell from her stool. On her side, her knees at her chest, she lay cowering on the dirty floor. One of the fellows walked over to her, grabbed her upper arm, yanked her up, set her back on the stool. As this man balanced her, another walked over to her, and, though she tried to cover her face and head with her hands, he ejaculated on one side of her head. This man reached down and grabbed the young woman's forearms. He tried to get her to stroke his still-erect penis, but she turned her head away from him and struggled to put her small hands behind her. "No," she pleaded, shaking her head, "please, no!" as the heavily tattooed man squeezed out the last of his ejaculate into her long, black hair. In brooding silence, his two hands flat on the bar, Yuji looked out at the scene before him. After a minute, he shook his head, reached out for the glass, lifted it. He took another sip before he continued.

"As I said, let me be clear, clear as the Hokkaido night sky in January." He raised his voice. "Haruka, dear lovely Haruka, this evening you will return to Aomori. I've already spoken to your landlord. This morning, he and I reached a mutual agreement." He stepped out from behind the bar. "If you return to our vast metropolis, or if you try to contact this asshole, I can guarantee that something much worse is going to happen—to you first and then to him."

"Boss, I don't think she fully understands," one of the fellows said. He was still stroking his large erection. "Let me bend her over this table and give her a nice, long drilling, one that she'll fondly remember."

"Let's have at her," another urged eagerly.

The terrified woman fell off the stool once again, crawled on her hands and knees a few feet, and prostrated herself in front of the indifferent man. "Please!" she begged, leaning on her elbows in front of him, one hand gripping his pant leg. "No more!"

Yuji sighed wearily and looked down at her. "See, Haruka? See what kind of cruel, selfish people live in this world? Their evil natures make me ill." He turned to the young man. "Fuckface, what do you have to say?" The young man was still bent over, his right hand at the wound. Blood, which he tried to stop with his handkerchief, continued to drop from the gash on his forehead.

"I asked you a question."

"We understand," he replied hoarsely. "We understand clearly."

"Do you?"

"I do. She does too."

"Now, dear, sweet, lovely Haruka, there is a bathroom in the back. I apologize that it's not up to your usual high standards for space and cleanliness, but go and try to make yourself presentable."

When the woman didn't stand, Yuji found a patch of unsoiled hair and pulled her up by it. "For heaven's sake, stop making those noises," he said to her. "It's over." He was about to pat her shoulders with both of his hands, but seeing the stains, he caught himself in time. "Put your cocks away, boys, unless you want to fuck fuckface here. He likes having his anus tickled."

Slowly, perhaps not getting what they had been expecting, the fellows let go and zipped up. One reached up a hand and pushed a button on the VCR, stopping the video. In the silence, the men stood awkwardly. Yuji, leaning an elbow against the bar, sipped his beer. A few minutes later, Haruka returned from the bathroom; hunched over, her eyes still on the floor, she made eye contact with no one.

"Be nice, fuckface, and give her your jacket. You probably have a half dozen just like it hanging in your closet."

Carefully, so as not to get any blood on it, the young man removed his suit jacket and draped it over Haruka's shoulders.

"Here is your purse, and here is your money," Yuji said, stepping out from behind the bar to pass her the two items. "Now where are you going?"

"Haneda."

"When are you coming back?"

"Never."

"Go," he said, pointing to the door, then shouted, "Now!" When she stood before it, her body still visibly shaking, the man standing there unbolted it and let her out.

Yuji turned to the young man. "Anything to say?" he asked.

"No."

"Any questions?"

"No."

"Good. Now just so you don't get any ideas of following her, Yuhei here will accompany you back to your office, which is where you intend to go, right?"

"Yes."

"We all know you have a reputation to uphold, so he'll follow you at a discreet distance. He's good at that. Aren't you, Yuhei?"

"You bet."

"Of course, if you need to stop by a hospital and get a stitch or two, we are not averse to that. I see the bleeding has mostly stopped. With any luck, the scar won't be noticeable."

Yuji and the young man stood looking at each other. Taking a last swig from the glass, the older man finished what remained. "Well, then," he said, looking satisfied, setting the empty glass on the counter, "I guess we're done then."

9 Albertina

"My God, Mariko! What's wrong? Why are you crying?" He had keyed in and entered the apartment. He had slipped off his shoes and had been making his way down the hallway when he saw her on the couch with her face buried in her hands.

"It's so hard," she sobbed.

"What's so hard?"

"Being a mother!"

"Hey," he said and sat down next to her. Embracing her as she wept, he glanced down and saw the sleeping infant, a folded red blanket underneath her. She lay on her back in a diaper only. With her face tilted toward her mother, her little mouth hung open, and her chubby arms were thrown out to her sides.

"You have no idea," she groaned, still sobbing. "You are gone all day. Often, you don't come home until very late. The littlest of things take so much time. Even going to the supermarket is a great burden. I didn't think it would be this hard."

"I see," he said, nodding as he comprehended what she was relating.

"And today little Yuka has had diarrhea all day. This afternoon she wouldn't stop crying. I was sure the neighbors would complain. She has been so fussy. She fell asleep just a few minutes ago."

"Hey," he said soothingly, reaching for her face with both of his hands. "Look at me. We'll get through this. First, we'll find you a helper. A nanny. Someone who can help you clean and cook too."

"These are things I should do," she said and started crying again.

"What? Who says that? Times have changed. And we have the money. You think the empress ever changed a diaper?"

"But I am not an empress."

"You're my empress. And my queen. And," he added, pointing down at the sleeping baby, trying to sound encouraging, "she's my princess. You two deserve the best. I insist."

He stood, reaching out both of his hands to pull up his wife.

"Now, go to the bathroom and get freshened up. I'll throw some clothes on Yuka-chan. Let's go out for a bite."

That night, even though the young man said he knew she was exhausted, his wife insisted on making love. "Do it as slowly as possible," she whispered as he leaned over her, her eyes fixed on his. "I want you inside me for as long as possible. Just don't touch my breasts. They are sore beyond belief."

The next morning, when he arrived at the office, he asked around discreetly, but none of his married colleagues had any idea how to obtain a nanny. It seemed their wives were more adept than his at mothering. Or they had an experienced mother or mother-in-law to assist. Or they didn't complain. Sounding casual as he related, "We just need a babysitter for a few hours a week," the young man didn't reveal the seriousness of the situation. Finding no help, he finally approached Kawasaki-san, the receptionist, and asked if the office had the Yellow Pages. She had the three-volume set under her desk. "Which one do you want?" she asked. "I'll take all three." Back at his desk, he found just one half-page advertisement and made a call. He spoke to a representative. Then he spoke to the representative's manager. "I don't think you understand. I need you to send someone today. Like I said, money is not a problem."

At first, he wondered if he had somehow entered the wrong apartment. In the kitchen, he found a short, young woman, standing at the stove, bouncing a baby gently on her hip. The baby was making happy, gurgling sounds. He saw that the young woman had dark skin and straight, waist-length hair. And he saw that the baby was playing with the hair. The young woman didn't seem to mind. Then he remembered.

"Where is my wife?"

"She is taking a rest," the helper replied, turning to face him.

"What smells so good?"

"I made dinner. If you are hungry, you can eat now."

"You're not Japanese."

"No, I come from The Philippines."

"You speak English?" he asked in English.

"Yes, sir," she replied in English. "I think my English is better than my Japanese."

She had a thick accent, but he understood her. "You are a wonder," he said and smiled.

"What is a 'wonder'?"

"You," he said. Since he was a little tipsy from his after-work carouse, he reached out and touched her face. He caressed her cheek and ran his hand through her long hair. "A 'wonder' is something great, something wonderful. You are that wonder."

With a big smile, the young woman blushed. "You lie," she said.

So, Albertina came to be the Tanakas' nanny and cook and cleaner and general all-around problem solver. The young man was paying the agency a ridiculous amount of money for her services;

when he got the first monthly bill, he was shocked at the number of hours and the amount he had to pay. It was like he had a second mortgage. But Albertina didn't seem to mind the long hours. And she was indeed a godsend. She had bonded immediately with the baby, and in many ways, she was more of a mother than Mariko. One day when Mariko tried to take her from Albertina, the baby started crying and reached out for the nanny. Mariko did her best to laugh off the baby's antics, but she was heartbroken. She retired to the bedroom for another tearful hour.

When the three adults were together, Mariko's jealousy was unmistakable. She hated that the two spoke English and often smiled and laughed at what she couldn't understand. Further, Albertina cooked and cleaned as if those activities brought her great joy. The apartment was always immaculate, and there was always something delicious to eat. Mariko tried to help, but it seemed she was mostly in the way. Indeed, if Mariko didn't want to do anything, she could have sat on the couch and watched TV all day. She could have read fashion magazines in the morning and spent long afternoons shopping. Instead, she observed Albertina closely and tried to learn from her. What bothered Mariko the most was that the young woman was slim and attractive. She smiled warmly and had large, lively eyes. The two women were the same age, but because of the vicissitudes of fate, they lived completely different lives. Mariko was confused, often wondering how it could be that Albertina seemed genuinely happy with her place in the world.

"You have a daughter too?"

"Yes, ma'am."

"How old is she?"

"She is five."

"Where is she?"

"At home in Cebu with my mother."

The two women were at the park on a glorious fall day. As they sat on a bench, little Yuka lay sleeping in her stroller.

"I make now money," she said in her broken Japanese. "I send it home."

Albertina withdrew two photographs from her small purse and showed them to Mariko. In one, Albertina was sitting in a chair, her shy-looking daughter standing next to her. The other appeared to be a school photograph, the young girl, a red ribbon in her long hair, wearing a school uniform.

"God loves us."

"I'm sorry?"

"God," she said, pointing to the cloudless sky above, "loves us."

Mariko looked up at where Albertina was pointing. "I see," she said, not fully understanding. There was so much more Mariko wanted to learn, but the language barrier made any kind of meaningful conversation impossible.

On Sundays, Albertina went to church with other Filipinas—the dozens of old and young women who functioned as maids and cooks and cleaners in the vast Tokyo metropolis. Some—the younger, prettier ones—worked as "entertainers," a rather vague term. This means that they worked in hostess clubs, sitting and drinking and chatting with businessmen. Most got propositioned every night. Some were willing to go if the money and the fellow seemed right. Or they would go one night and not the next. Fortunately, they had the option to say no. Others declined all the time. For reasons known only to them, they just didn't go. In any case, they all lived hard lives, often four or five or six of them crowded into a small apartment. They worked many hours, often for thankless or deceitful overseers. But they made money and sent most of it to family back in The Philippines. Some even married local men. No matter what had happened each week, however, they never failed to gather at church on Sunday. After the service, they would retire to a park. They all brought food and ate and gossiped. In many ways, they were strangers in a city that cared little for them, but they had each other, and they had their God. And this God had helped Albertina find the extremely generous Tanaka family.

When Mariko was in the hospital, Albertina was an incredible temptation. The young man was certain that if he simply reached out, she would willingly comply. He saw what her nearly black eyes conveyed to him. She had gotten pregnant at seventeen, she had been kicked out of her Catholic high school, she had no husband. Makoto knew all of this. Still, he thought about her often, feeling both unease and desire.

"Your going home so late doesn't make any sense," he said one night at the door as she stood in front of him in her too-big-for-her winter jacket. "Why don't you just sleep here? You can sleep on the couch. We have a lot of extra blankets."

When he rolled off the bed in the middle of the night and made his way to the kitchen to get a drink of water, he saw that the couch was empty. Had she gone home after all? As he made his way back down the hallway to the bedroom, he paused at his daughter's room. Gently, he slid open the door a foot. He could see from the faint glow of the baby light that Albertina lay on the floor on her side, her legs pulled up in a half fetal position; next to her chest lay little pajama-clad Yuka with her eyes closed, a futon underneath the two, a small blanket covering the baby's legs. "Do you need anything, sir?" she asked, lifting her head off a small pillow and turning to look up at him. He studied her, noting that she wore only white panties and a thin blue T-shirt. He thought for a moment, all the while her eyes on his. Shaking his head, he slid the door closed and returned to his empty bed.

10 Not Feeling Well

After the miscarriage, Mariko—weak, moody, distant—was advised to spend a few days, perhaps a week, in the hospital. She had always been thin, but in the past year, ever since she had given birth, she had lost a lot of weight. Now she was tired. She had no motivation. Nothing—not even her energetic daughter—seemed to interest her. "It happens," one specialist told Makoto privately. "She's been through a lot. Some women… well, they don't react well. She needs time. Let's see how she feels in a month or two."

One Saturday morning, the young man sat on the carpeted living room floor. He was watching the news and playing with his daughter, a pile of various colored wooden blocks between them. Albertina, who had let herself in just after seven, was cooking, cleaning, washing towels and the toddler's clothes. The young man's wife still lay in their bed asleep.

After an hour, he gathered a few items—a fresh croissant, some blueberry yogurt, some purple grapes, a pad of butter—and set them on a large plate. He added a small spoon and a butter knife. He carried the plate and a glass of orange juice down the hallway.

Quietly, he slid open the bedroom door with a foot, slipped inside, then closed it behind him. With the heavy curtains drawn, the room was very dark. He waited a half minute for his eyes to adjust, then made his way to the bed. He sat on the edge. She had been lying face down in the center, but she rolled over and looked up at him.

"I brought you a few things," he said quietly and smiled. "Won't you have a bite?"

She nodded.

"Sit up."

She leaned forward, grabbing a couple of large pillows from his side of the bed and setting them against the wall behind her back. After she settled into these soft pillows, he handed her the glass of orange juice; then he reached over and turned on the lamp that sat on the nightstand. By accident, he knocked over the *kokeshi* doll. After he righted it, he grabbed another pillow and set it on her lap. On the pillow, he balanced the plate. With both hands now free, he picked up the pad of butter and began unfolding the wrapper. Having accomplished that task, he tore the croissant into two pieces, and with the small knife, he applied some of the butter to one piece and then handed the piece to her. She took a tentative bite, then another. As she chewed slowly, he looked at her and smiled. After she swallowed, she took a sip of the juice.

"There is warm rice, too. Shall I bring some?"

"Aren't you playing golf today? I thought—"

"Not today. It's supposed to rain," he lied. "Some grapes?"

She nodded and took one. To him, her long, slim arm seemed longer and even slimmer, the bones fragile.

She chewed the grape slowly, then swallowed it. As he looked at her, he wondered, had the circumference of her neck grown smaller as well?

"I don't know why," she said. "I'm just so tired. All of the time. If you hadn't come in, I probably would have slept all day."

"That's okay. With more rest and more food, you'll be feeling better soon."

"No," she said, shaking her head slowly and looking out at nothing, "it's like something is wrong. I have no energy. And I feel so light-headed."

He pulled back the cover to the small container of yogurt and handed it to her. He picked up the small spoon and passed that over as well. She took a small spoonful, and then one more, then placed the cup and spoon back on the plate.

"More croissant?"

She nodded. He buttered the other piece and handed it to her. As she chewed slowly, she seemed to grow more alert, her eyes glancing around the room. She finished the croissant half, then the orange juice. She ate three more grapes.

"I feel better."

"You look great. Did you sleep well?"

"I did. What time is it?"

"Almost ten. More yogurt?" He handed her the cup. As she held the small cup in her left hand, she dipped three fingertips from her right into the creamy yogurt. She brought the tips to her mouth and began licking them. She did this again—dipped her fingertips into the cup—but this time she reached out to him. He leaned in and began licking and gently sucking on each yogurt-covered finger. When he paused to look at her, she dipped her fingertips once again, and this time she wiped the yogurt on his lips and face and neck.

"Take off your shirt."

"Are you sure?"

She nodded.

With the shirt off, she painted his chest and arms. "You are a purple monster," she said, smiling, her thin lips dry and slightly cracked. "Perhaps I should be one too."

She set aside the plate and pillow, leaned forward, and began to undo the long line of buttons on her short-sleeve pajama top. When she had it open, she began smearing the remaining yogurt on her tummy and breasts and neck and face. She got to her knees, and with her sticky, yogurt-stained fingers, she pushed him down on his back, his head at the foot of the bed. As she licked off some of the yogurt from his face and chest and ears, she pulled down his pajama pants and boxers. She reached over to the plate and found what remained of the butter; she rubbed the soft yellow cream onto his expanding erection and stroked him slowly. When he was hard, she slipped off her pajama top and bottoms and panties and climbed on top of him. Using her left hand and lifting her right leg slightly, she guided him into her. She straightened her back, placing her palms on his stomach, and slowly, she began moving her hips up and down. He closed his eyes. She had grown so thin and gaunt, her small breasts even smaller, the breasts of a still-growing adolescent, that he didn't like to look at her.

When she stopped suddenly, he looked up at her, his face a question. Casually, she got off him and the bed. She walked over to the bedroom door and slid it fully open. "Albertina!" she called down the long hallway. "Come here! I need you."

She waited a moment, then returned to the bed and climbed back on top of him. Once she had him inside her, she began moving again.

He could hear the TV from the living room. Skillfully, Mariko was moving her hips side to side, up and down. Having never seen her behave this way, he could not fully comprehend why she was doing what she was doing.

"Albertina!" she called out again. "Come here."

"I'm here." Her voice told them that the young woman was standing in the hallway, just outside the door.

"No, come in the room."

"I don't want to."

"I said, come in the room."

"I don't want to."

"Just watch," she said, breathing faster, increasing her speed. "This is what he likes. This is what he likes best."

11 Trying to Do Something Good, Part 2

Just after seven, he exited the office building, turned right on the crowded sidewalk, headed toward the subway entrance. Feeling the cold, he hunched over, buried his hands into his pockets. As he walked, a few drops of rain dotted the concrete. But lost in thought, he didn't notice them. And he didn't notice the young woman with long, brown hair until she stood directly in front of him. Blocking his way, she wore an ugly, heavy jacket; thin, tired-looking blue jeans; brown leather boots, knee high. "Hello," she said quietly.

"Yes?" he asked, pausing to look her up and down.

"You don't remember me?"

Narrowing his eyes, he examined her face more closely. "No," he replied, shaking his head. "I don't."

She looked down, turned, started walking away.

When he realized who she was, he shouted, "Wait!" and rushed after her. When he caught up to her, he grabbed the back of her arm. "Of course I do," he said, turning her body. "It's been a while. That's all. And I've had a long day. How have you been?"

With her tired eyes, she looked up into his but said nothing.

"I'm starving," he said, sensing that she needed comfort. "Let's go eat. On a cold night like this, we need something warm, don't we? You must like Korean barbecue!" With a small smile, the sad-faced woman nodded.

"You didn't eat very much," he said, leaning back, looking across the four-person table at her, his arm resting on the back of the empty chair next to his.

"Can I have more?" she asked, her hand at her mouth as she chewed and then swallowed the last piece of beef.

"By all means." He got the attention of one of the waitresses and ordered another plate of *kalbi* and bowl of *kimchi* and another mug of beer for himself. "Anything else?"

"One more bowl of rice, please."

"Absolutely. Another ginger ale too?"

The young woman nodded.

"I am very sorry," she related as they waited. "I called several times. But the lady never put me through. She wanted to take my name and number. What was I supposed to say? I just hung up."

"Hey, there's no need to cry."

"I would like your help," the young woman resumed after she collected herself. "I met someone. He doesn't mind that I have a daughter. But he doesn't know where I work. You can imagine what would happen if I told him. He thinks I work at an all-night *karaoke* shop. It's been only a month, but I think, with him, I could make a fresh start."

"What good news! Of course you can. It's never too late."

An hour later, he was walking with the young woman toward the subway. After he had told her what he can and would do, and after the delicious repast, she seemed to be in a much better mood. "Where do you live?" he asked.

"I am staying with my sister in Kawasaki."

"Kawasaki?" he said, pausing his step. "You are going all the way to Kawasaki tonight? That's an hour and a half."

She nodded.

"You go all the way from Kawasaki to Shinjuku every day?"

"Almost every day."

"That's not good."

As they continued, she slowed, then stopped. "What's wrong?" he asked.

"Can I service you tonight?" she asked, looking up at him. "You don't have to pay."

For a long time, he studied her face. With his right hand, he reached out and cupped her chin. "I could use a bath. Would you mind?"

At the elegant Shinagawa Prince, the young man leaned his elbow casually on the chest-high check-in counter. "We want a room with a view. Give us one of your double rooms on the 38th floor, that is, if one is still available. With breakfast, of course."

"Yes, sir."

The much older front desk clerk looked at the handsome, stylishly-dressed man and his unkempt companion dubiously, but he couldn't refuse them.

"How would you like to pay, sir?"

The young man set 20,000 yen in the money tray on the counter.

"Of course, sir. One moment, please."

Up in the room, the young man slipped off his shoes and walked past the king-sized bed to the enormous, floor-to-ceiling window. His companion stood awkwardly just inside the door. "What a nice view, huh? Come here." One at a time, she slid off her knee-high boots and did as she had been told. When she stood next to him, he gently laid one hand on her shoulder and pointed with the other. "Look! See those flashing red lights over there? That's the Rainbow Bridge. Rather impressive, huh?"

She nodded. For a silent minute, they both looked out at the marvelous night view.

"Shall I run the water?"

"I wish you would."

He walked back with her to the large bath and shower room, larger than the one in which they met several months ago. The toilet was in a separate room all by itself.

"Wow! Look at this bathroom! A young woman needing a night of relaxation could get lost in here. And that tub! It's like a small swimming pool. And look at all of these toiletries!"

She walked over to the tub, bent over, turned on the hot and cold water. After she reached down and checked the temperature, she made a small adjustment to the cold and put the stopper in place. She ran her hand through the accumulating water one more time to make sure the small waterfall from the faucet was running at the appropriate temperature.

"Jacket off," he said after she had turned and faced him.

She removed her bulky winter jacket and handed it to him.

"Next, jeans."

She unbuttoned her jeans, pulled down the zipper, slid them down her legs, handed them over.

"And those cute socks."

She removed her brown socks.

"Sweater."

She pulled her sweater over her head. She stood before him in her panties and bra, the panties a tired off-white, the well-worn bra a faded purple.

"Now," he said, placing his hands on her shoulders and turning her so she faced the tub. "Take off those last two items and climb in the tub."

With her back to him, she pulled down her panties, undid her bra, dropped the two to the tiled floor. Gingerly, she stepped

332

into the spacious tub. He scooped up her underwear and bra, slipped out of the bathroom, set all of her items on the bed. Then he withdrew 50,000 yen from his wallet and set the bills on the desk opposite the bed. When he returned, he sat casually on the edge of the tub and looked down at her as she sat hunched over, steam rising from the warm water and filling the room. He reached out and caressed her face with his fingertips and then ran his hand through her brown hair, pulling back behind her ear as much as he could.

"How is the water?"

"It's warm," she replied, nodding. "It feels good. All day waiting I was so cold. But after dinner and sitting in here…"

"That's just what I wanted to hear, little sunshine."

"Aren't you coming in? I don't mind if you don't use a condom. I'll do whatever you want."

"Let's review," he said, ignoring what she had said. "Like I told you at dinner, I am going to make a few calls tomorrow. Today is Tuesday. Tuesday night, that is. I imagine you'll be starting next Monday. First, you will need some interview clothes. For this, I have left you some money. It's on the desk. You want a black skirt and a black jacket and black stockings. Black shoes, too. What do you ladies call them? Pumps? Just make sure the heels aren't too high. Oh, and of course a white blouse. Perhaps a haircut would be a good idea too. It never hurts to look one's best. But go easy on the makeup." As he paused and looked down at her and smiled, he saw that her eyes began to swim. "Next, you and I are going to meet Saturday morning. You, little sunshine, are going to wear your new interview outfit. Where are we going to meet?"

"In front of the Tower Records in Shibuya," she replied, her voice a whisper.

"What time?"

"Ten."

"And what happens if I cannot make it? If I somehow fail to show up?"

"I'll come on Sunday at the same time."

"What a golden memory!" he said, beaming down at her. "With a mind like that, soon they'll have you in a management position. One day, I'll be asking you for a job. I hope you won't forget me."

As she looked up at him, the tears ran down her cheeks.

"There's no need to cry," he said, smiling again.

With her small, wet hands, she reached out and grabbed the hem of his suit jacket. "Please don't go," she pleaded. "Nobody has ever been nice to me like this, not once."

He took her hands and gently squeezed them. He leaned over and kissed them. But then he released them, first one, then the other, and stood. "My little sunshine," he said, looking down at her, "you have the room until noon tomorrow. Breakfast starts at seven. If you can believe it, the restaurant where breakfast is served is on a higher floor. Catch the sunrise if you can. And don't forget. I want to hear all about what you ate when we meet Saturday morning. You promise you will tell me?"

As the copious tears fell, she nodded.

"Well then, see you Saturday," he said with one last smile. Slowly, he backed his way out of the bathroom and quietly closed the door. Then, at the entrance, he slipped his feet into his shoes, pulled open the door, exited the hotel room. The young man had a lot on his mind, but as he strode down the hallway to the bank of elevators, he was genuinely happy with himself, a feeling he hadn't felt in quite some time.

12 Lies, Ever More Lies

"What's with the hag?" Nakagami asked as he chomped his *gyoza*.

"The hag? You mean Fukumoto-san, my new assistant? She's extremely competent."

As he stuffed another piece of *gyoza* into his mouth, Nakagami let out a chuckle. "Give me a break. No one chooses an assistant based on her competence. One must consider more important matters, like the size of her tits, the firmness of her thighs, the length of her skirts. And by all means, she has to be single. Let me guess, Fukumoto-san is married and has two kids."

"Actually, three."

"How old is she?"

"Forty-six."

With a mixture of doubt and disbelief, Nakagami looked across the table at the young man.

"What? I told you. Haruka—Kumamoto-san—had some kind of family emergency. I don't know the details. But it seems her father is very ill. She had to return to Aomori."

"You don't know the details? She gave up her well-renumerated position to take care of her father?" Nakagami again looked at his lunch companion dubiously. "That just doesn't make sense. Doesn't she have a mother? A brother? A sister?" He stuffed one more piece, then another, of *gyoza* into his mouth. As he chewed noisily, he asked, "Is she coming back?"

"For fuck's sake!" the young man replied, looking annoyed. "Don't talk with your mouth full." He sighed and took a sip of his tea. "She hopes to come back to Tokyo, to us, that is. At least that's what she told me."

"Let me see," he said, lifting his bowl of rice with his left hand, in his right a pair of chopsticks. "On Tuesday last week you take an afternoon flyer. Turns out Kumamoto-san—who used to be Haruka—is out as well. Quite a few office gossips have told me she left before lunch, you, in a rush, several hours later. Then on Wednesday when you come to work, you have a large bandage on your forehead and Kumamoto-san has mysteriously—and quite suddenly—returned to Aomori to be with an ailing father. There's something you're not telling me. But that's okay." With his chopsticks, he shoveled more rice from the bowl into his mouth.

The young man frowned and pushed his plate of mostly uneaten sauteed fish to the center of the small table. "It's just a small cut. Just a few stitches. I told you. I fell, slipped, on the subway stairs. They were wet, and I was a little drunk."

"And you hit your head? The front part of your head?"

"Yes."

"A little drunk because for some reason, the luscious lollipop Kumamoto-san left you. Or you broke it off with her. Let me see. You had a fight. She hit you with a glass ashtray. Am I getting close?"

The young man leaned across the table. "I wasn't having an affair with Kumamoto-san."

"That's not what some think. And some of those some think it's a very good thing she's gone. You'd be fucked if the old man found out, and those some would be sorry to see you go. I happen to be part of those some. But still some others of those some are sad to see her go. Those some wanted you to get caught, wanted the old

336

man to find out about the affair you were not having. Put it this way. You have your enemies. People are often jealous of the rising star. But sooner or later, the rising star implodes. Or crashes into something."

The young man didn't reply. Raising his hand, he got the attention of the waitress and asked for the check.

"Well, anyway, how is Mariko?"

"She's home now."

"How long was she in?"

"Ten days."

"Ten days for a stomach complaint?"

"All right, truth seeker," the young man said angrily, placing both hands on the table and leaning across it. "Here is what you want to know. She had a miscarriage. If you want to know all the fucking details of my life, it was her second miscarriage in the last year. She hasn't been well. Naturally, she's sad. I'm sad too. But I am more worried about her health." The young man stood. As he towered over the other, he looked as if he wanted to say something more, perhaps even strike his colleague, but instead, he withdrew a 1,000 yen note from his wallet and let it fall onto the table.

"Makoto, I'm sorry."

"Anything else you desperately need to know?"

"I am very sorry. I had no idea."

"Are you? At times, Naka, you can be an insensitive fuck." Without saying anything more, the young man threw his arms into his suit jacket and walked out of the restaurant.

"What if I die?" she asked softly, looking down at her hands where they lay in her lap.

"You're not going to die. Don't be foolish."

"But I have the same cancer that Mother had, and she died."

"It's a simple procedure. With the anesthesia, you won't feel a thing. Yes, there may be a little pain and discomfort for a few days. But that's all. And then afterwards, you will begin the chemotherapy. The doctors say that that will be the hard part. You may feel weak and nauseous, but Yuka-chan and I will be here with you every day. And when you come home, I can do most of my work from there."

"They are going to take my breasts," she said, in her voice and moist eyes a heavy sadness. "Do you want to see them one last time?"

"Mariko-chan, don't be this way! Please." The young man, sitting on the side of her bed, reached out and, with his fingertips, gently wiped away her tears.

"The doctor says," he continued, trying to sound more encouraging, even playful, "that once you heal properly, you can have reconstructive surgery. We'll get you a new pair. We'll get you some peaches this time. Wouldn't you like that?"

"Will you tit fuck me then?"

"Mariko! Please don't talk that way in front of Yuka-chan."

"She has no idea what we are talking about. Look at her. I don't think she even misses me. She loves Albertina more than she loves me."

"My God, how can you say that?"

Not old enough to comprehend where she was and why, little Yuka sat in an armchair by the room's front door. While the couple had been conversing quietly, she had been paging through a plastic picture book of animals, but now she closed the book and chewed one of its corners. The little girl yawned and rubbed an eye with a chubby fist. Then she pushed the book away and kicked it to the floor. As the two-year-old leaned back, seemingly trapped in the deep chair, she appeared sleepy but happy.

"I bet you tit fuck all your whores."

"Mariko," he groaned. "Please!"

"You want to tit fuck Albertina, don't you? But you can't. She has small breasts like I do. I bet the two of you are having sex now in our bed. Are you?"

"Mariko, your jealousy is too extreme. Please! You have to stop thinking such thoughts."

"I'm not angry," she said. "Just sad." She looked away and started crying again.

According to the oncologist, the surgery went very well, better than expected. He and his team took most of the lymph nodes as well. Mariko convalesced for a week and then began the chemotherapy. Naturally, she was depressed, irritable, fatigued. But the initial reports were promising.

"Things look good," Dr. Hirata said one morning to the young man out in the hallway.

"But she looks awful."

The doctor sighed. "Unfortunately, that's to be expected. The chemo can be hard. And your wife is naturally thin. She needs to eat more and get a lot of rest."

"But she won't eat anything," he countered, alarmed.

Opening the folder he held, Dr. Hirata looked down at her chart. He seemed to be checking some numbers.

"Doctor," the young man said, grabbing the older man's arm, "you have to do something."

"We are doing our best. Please believe me."

A week later, Dr. Hirata and his staff noticed something alarming. A routine follow-up scan found the cancer had spread to her lungs. More chemo and radiation were prescribed, but the new regimen didn't seem to bring any positive effects. Eight days later, another scan found small tumors in her pancreas and liver. The young man was despondent. He and the staff kept the very bad news from Mariko, openly lying to her, but from the looks on their faces, she could sense that something was amiss. The nurses came regularly to check on her, and they, like him, did their best to cheer her, but instead, she found their smiles and meaningless chit chat and good health irritating. She no longer wanted to bathe herself. She ate and drank just about nothing. Most distressing, Mariko lost all interest in little Yuka. She no longer cared to play with—even see—her daughter. She spent most of her last hours sleeping fitfully or, at night, in the darkness, staring out the window at the beautiful Tokyo skyline.

Except for her visits to other floors to receive her scans and treatments, and except for a few walks in the hallway and one early trip down in a wheelchair to the hospital's garden, Mariko had been sitting and lying in Room 651 for nearly seven weeks. No longer feeling or showing any emotion, she seemed resigned to her terrible, unfortunate fate.

⧖ ⧖ ⧖

A nurse was directed to give him an injection of fast-acting Methohexital. "Oh God," he sobbed, beating his head with his fists, "Oh God, what have I done?" Just after midnight, when his wife departed the world of the living, his heart-rending moaning and keening could be heard down at the nurses' station, and if these expressions of genuine, overwhelming emotion could be heard there, certainly they could be heard in the nearby patient rooms.

14 Trying to Do Something Good, Part 3

The young woman, conservatively dressed, stood in front of the Tower Records. The store was closed, and very few people were out and about at this hour on a Saturday morning. With her hands clasped in front of her, she looked nervously to her right and left. Except for a white blouse, she wore all black. Her shoulder-length hair was tied at the back of her head. She wore no visible jewelry and no lipstick and no nail polish, just a bit of eyeliner and cheek palette.

Exactly at ten, a young, slender man in a suit, his hands buried in his pockets, walked up to her. "Are you Tamamoto?"

"Yes."

"Follow me."

"Where is Tanaka-san?"

"Tanaka-san? I don't know any Tanaka-san."

The young man turned and began to walk away, but the young woman remained.

"Are you coming?" he asked, turning to look back at her. "I don't have all day."

She wished Tanaka-san had come. But what could she do? She hurried after the young man.

The following day, wearing the same clothes, she returned just before ten. Since the shoes she wore were new, her feet hurt immensely. She waited nearly two hours. But the man she was waiting for didn't turn up.

15 Makoto and Little Yuka Visit Kamakura and Have an Adventure

The young man and his daughter were making their way to Shibuya Station. They could have taken a cab, but since the sun was warm and the sky a vibrant blue, he decided that it would be nice to walk. They had all day, after all. Walking was a mistake, however, as the toddler continued to stop along the way to notice the world around her. She saw a discarded cough-drop wrapper on the sidewalk and spent thirty seconds examining it. He tugged her arm gently. A few minutes later, she sat down next to a flattened piece of green gum. When he said, "Don't touch," she touched and laughed and then put her chubby fingers in her mouth. A bit irritated, the young man scooped her up and carried the fidgeting child the rest of the way to the station.

From Shibuya, they took the Yamanote train to Shinagawa. At Shinagawa, they transferred to the Yokosuka line. While transferring, the young man bought three cans of beer, a small Pet bottle of pineapple juice, and a small box of animal crackers. Since it was a Tuesday morning, and since they were leaving the city, not entering it, the express train was mostly empty. When it left the station, he slipped off his daughter's shoes and set them by his feet. As he sipped on the beer, the little girl stood on the seat, a half-eaten cracker held tightly in one hand, the other smudging the window with her dirty fingers. While he looked blankly at the seat across from him and saw nothing, the child gazed out the window and watched the colorful world pass by. She seemed enchanted; she pointed her finger at this and that, but except for reaching out a hand to steady the toddler when the train occasionally sped up or slowed down, her father mostly ignored her.

At Kamakura, the two left the station, their first stop a Lawson. He was going to buy more cans of beer, but before he made it to the back of the store where the refrigerated drinks sat on shelves behind glass, he saw the 200-ml bottle. For a moment he hesitated. He wanted to go to the other place, the place of comfort, but he didn't want to go too far. But then he found himself at the counter. Passing over a 5,000-yen note and then collecting his change, he was about to walk out, bottle in hand, but the clerk insisted on placing it in a plastic bag. Then he half-walked, half-carried her through the still-quiet town down to the deserted beach. There, he let go of her hand and plopped her on the sand. Reaching for the bottle, he removed it from the plastic, balling up the bag and shoving it into his jacket pocket. Then he twisted it open, tossed the cap aside, took a long pull, the copper-colored liquid burning on its way down. As he watched his daughter, he wiped his lips with the back of his hand.

On her unsteady legs, she ran down to where the sand and ocean met. Gentle waves lapped the shore. With her small, inquisitive black eyes, she watched the water come in and then retreat. She screamed, the sound of a deliriously happy child. She took a step closer to the water and then pointed to it as it made its way to her and then submerged her shoes. She smiled, let out another joyful sound, sat down in the wet sand after the wave receded. The young man, somewhat annoyed, got up, went to her, carried her back to where he had stood the bottle in the sand. Dismayed, he realized he hadn't brought any change of clothes for her, not even a diaper. Nearby, he found a small stick, a worn branch from a tree that clearly had been washed ashore. He handed it to her, then sat down next to her. Out in the distance, the endless ocean shimmered brightly.

As she used one end of the branch to dig in the sand, as she grunted her happy-child sounds, the young man took occasional nips, the bottle resting against one of his legs when he didn't have it in his hand. As he looked out at the indifferent ocean, a tear, and then another, stained his cheek, and his vision blurred. With both hands, he pulled up the bottom of the T-shirt he wore and used it to wipe his face. But he could not hold back the oncoming tsunami. Rubbing his eyes with the cotton fabric, he sobbed once, then again, and the tears began to flow.

He needed the release, and he immediately felt better—not whole, but better—after the wave had passed. He wiped his now-burning eyes one last time and brought down the T-shirt to see that the bottle had tipped on its side, spilling most of its contents. In front of him, he also noticed a pair of dress shoes, black and shiny. Not far behind that pair was another. Glancing up—with the bright January sun in his eyes, he had to squint—he found two blue-capped men, one probably in his fifties, the other much younger, standing over him. "Sir," the younger man asked, "are you okay?" The two men wore matching uniforms, blue trousers and white, short-sleeve dress shirts. Each carried a gun and other accoutrements attached to his black belt.

"We are fine," he replied, glancing over to see that his child was still happily digging the fat end of the branch into the sand.

"Is this your daughter?" the older officer asked.

"She is."

"We had a report," the younger officer said, "that a man was drinking whisky on the beach with a toddler. The citizen who made the call was very concerned."

"There is nothing to be concerned about."

"But it's illegal to drink alcohol on this beach," the younger officer said.

"Is it?"

"It is, sir."

The young man lifted the nearly empty bottle and took a last yet very long pull. Then he tilted it, pouring out the little that remained. He pushed the bottle, neck first, into the sand. As he did this, the older officer turned and started walking away from the three, up towards the trees and the promenade that separated the beach from the city streets. As he carefully made his way, trying not to get too much sand in his shoes, he began speaking into his radio.

"No one is drinking alcohol on this beach," the young man reported, holding out and turning over his hands, as a magician would do, to show that they held nothing.

"Sir, are you okay?"

"I told you. I am fine."

"But why would you come to the beach with your daughter and drink whisky?"

"I have my reasons."

"And what are those reasons?"

"You wouldn't understand."

"I wish you would explain. I would like to help."

The young man looked up at the officer. Leaning slightly to his left, he had to put a hand into the sand to steady himself.

"Sir?"

"You want to know?"

"It would help me understand."

"Today is Tuesday, yes?"

"Today is Tuesday," the younger officer confirmed, nodding. He leaned over so he could better hear what the troubled man had to say.

"My wife died last Thursday," he said, his eyes now on the sand, his voice low and devoid of any emotion. "She was cremated last Saturday morning. We had the service that afternoon. There were nearly four hundred guests. And today is Tuesday, as you have kindly confirmed."

Leaning up, the younger officer placed his hands on his waist. He turned and, for a moment, looked out at the ocean. Then, inhaling deeply, he reached down, grabbed a bicep, lifted the young man to his feet. When he could see that the man could stand, the officer picked up the toddler, who started wailing. She was still holding the branch. As he cradled her in his left hand, he guided the father with his right. Soon the three of them had made it up the beach to a small parking lot where the shiny black and white police cruiser sat. The older officer was leaning against the car, his arms folded across his chest. The younger officer opened the door and showed the young man into the back seat. As he held the now-quiet child, he turned to his partner. "I am going to take them home."

The older officer nodded to his subordinate. "Don't worry about me," he said, looking up the cloudless sky. "The weather is nice. I'll walk. But don't be gone too long." He shook out a cigarette from a pack that he was holding. After he lit it with a lighter he fished from his front chest pocket, he sauntered off toward the town center.

The officer opened the front passenger door, and, using two hands, not minding that her bottom and legs were covered with sand, he carefully set the heavy child on the seat. He tried to pull the seatbelt across her, but seeing it wasn't going to do its job, he decided to break another rule and let it roll back into place. He went around the front of the car and got in. After he started the engine, he picked up a clipboard that lay between the seats and, with a pen, made a notation on the form it held. Then he turned to the young man. "Sir, I need you to pass up your driver's license," he said. "Do you have it with you?"

Out of habit, the one spoken to placed his right hand inside his jacket, but he found no inside pocket in the windbreaker he wore. So, reaching around to his back, and fumbling, his jeans seemingly not wanting to release it, he needed a moment before he lifted it to show the officer that he was a good citizen with a wallet. But since his fingers didn't seem to be working, it took him almost a minute

348

to open it and slide out the small, plastic card. When the latter finally had the license, he studied it. Then he asked, "Is this where you live? Shibuya?"

At this point, the young man was far away. But he nodded.

"When we arrive, will somebody be there to take care of your daughter?"

When the man didn't respond, the officer asked again, this time more loudly and more slowly. "Tanaka-san, when we arrive in Shibuya, will somebody be there to take care of your daughter?"

His head jerking up, the young man again nodded.

"And who will that somebody be?" Once more, he spoke slowly and loudly.

"The nanny."

"The what?"

"The nanny."

"You have a nanny?"

"Yes."

As the officer put the cruiser in gear and slowly edged it out of the nearly empty parking lot, the young man mumbled, "It was never my intention—"

"I am sorry, sir," the officer interrupted, his voice loud, his eyes now trained on the traffic in front of him, "but you will have to speak up."

"I said, it was never my intention…" But the man in the back didn't finish the sentence, or couldn't, and the officer no longer seemed interested in what he had to say. He was focused on the task at hand. Even though it was strictly forbidden to do so, he drove the man and his daughter to their apartment in Shibuya. In the stop-and-go traffic, the numerous traffic lights mostly red, the heavy trucks and crowded buses slow moving, the drive took nearly two hours. Ever the good child, she had stopped crying and, for the first hour, seemed engrossed with the branch, her new friend. Then, she fell asleep, her head hitting the door with a thud, the unusual sound surprising the officer since the bump of the head didn't wake her. Her father lay slumped in the back, his hands—the fingers interlaced as if in prayer—resting between his legs, his head and shoulder leaning on the door. Was he too sleeping, resting his distressed mind and tired body? No, though he had fallen into an unconscious state, he was visiting a no-joy place, a dark region full of dark, menacing shapes, dark shadows, an even darker night sky where no stars brightly shine.

16 Makoto and Little Yuka
Have a 10:00-p.m. Visitor

Just after ten, the appointed hour, he heard the "ping-pong" of the doorbell. He got up off the sofa, pushed the Off on the TV remote and dropped it on a cushion, went down the short hallway to the door. He turned the handle and pushed it open. The fashionable-winter-jacket, scarf-wearing woman standing there had her hands clasped in front of her; she was a little short, her skirt too, but what he noticed right away—and it bothered him—was that she seemed to be wearing too much makeup. As he studied the fake eyelash extensions, the painted eyelids, the excessive rouge, the bright strawberry red on her lips, she said nothing. She didn't smile. She just looked at him.

"Please come in," he said, stepping aside. In his right hand, he held his tumbler of whisky.

The woman wondered if the man was a little off, a little intoxicated, that is. She had done this only twice before, never at a client's home and never before with someone drunk. She wondered if that would change things and, if so, how. The last man hadn't been drunk, but she had found the experience so searing, still so eye-closing, make-the-memory-go-away painful, that she had needed a couple of months to mend. So, in the entranceway, as she used her heels to slip off her brown loafers, she hesitated, just slightly.

But she could see that the young man before her was muscular and handsome and well dressed in his tan trousers and dark navy Izod polo. And she knew that if she did what he wanted—at least some of it; she had limits, after all—she would receive what to her was a ridiculous sum of money. She decided to accept the risk. The kitchen was just a few steps from the entranceway, and soon both he and she stood on its wooden floor in their stockings, each examining the other, each perhaps wondering what was going to happen and when.

The man leaned back against a counter, to his left an open bottle of Glenfiddich. He reached for it, splashed a little of the auburn-colored liquid into his glass. "Want a drink?" he asked, holding out the bottle.

"Do you have apple juice?"

The man laughed. "Check the refrigerator," he replied, still chuckling. "I'm not sure if we have any."

She didn't move. She just stood there looking at him, the silence awkward, uncomfortable, long.

"How about your jacket and scarf? Are you cold, or do you want to take them off?"

She nodded, smiling for the first time, and he thought he saw her skin redden slightly into a blush, but he wasn't certain on account of all of the makeup.

She unwound the long, multicolored scarf, withdrew her arms from her puffy jacket, and then, not knowing what to do with them, she clutched them to her chest. He set down his drink. "Here," he said, smiling and reaching out a hand, "Give those to me." When he had them, he turned and stepped into the living room, setting both on the seat of an armchair.

Back in the kitchen, he resumed his place at the counter, and the two again stood and faced each other in awkward silence. To him, under the bright kitchen light, the skirt seemed too short, and her large breasts, perhaps held in a size-too-small bra, pushed against her tight, red sweater. He found that he was attracted to her—the shoulder-length hair, the shy smile, her large, expressive brown eyes that he felt were her best feature—but still, he inwardly frowned at the amount of makeup.

"How old are you?" he asked at last.

"Twenty."

"Really?

"Yes."

"You go to college?"

"Yes," she replied unconvincingly. "Yes, I do."

"Where?"

"Meisei."

"Meisei?"

She nodded.

"Where is Meisei?"

"What do you mean?"

"I mean, where is the campus? Where in Tokyo?"

He knew where it was, of course. So when she paused and averted her eyes, he also knew that she was lying, that she had no idea where in Tokyo one could enter the gates of the mediocre Meisei University. To her, it was just a name, probably something she had seen on a promotional brochure or on a train-station poster, and she couldn't say Todai or Waseda since those universities had such good reputations. "Listen," he said, feeling sorry for her, "I am not going to embarrass you, but don't lie. You don't go to university, and I don't think you are twenty." He picked up his glass and took another sip. Instead of replying, she bit her lower lip, her eyes still on the floor.

"The apple juice?" he said, pointing to the two-door refrigerator.

Slowly, cautiously, as if she were a puppy that had been severely scolded, she half-stepped, half-slid over on her stockinged feet to the refrigerator and pulled open the right door. After a half minute of searching, her body bent slightly at the waist, her head inside, she reported, "I don't see any."

"You're on your own then," he said cheerfully. "Help yourself to whatever you want."

"Can I have some tea?"

"Absolutely."

After she closed the door, she held a large, rectangular-shaped bottle of *mugi cha* in her right hand, her arm sagging under its weight. From the cupboard behind him, he withdrew a glass, the same design of tumbler as the one that contained his whisky. He passed it to her. Since she held something in each hand, she couldn't unscrew the cap, so she turned around to the kitchen table and set the glass on it. When it slid a few centimeters, she noticed that the table was not level.

"What happened to the table?" she asked, turning back to him, now holding the large Pet bottle of tea with both hands.

"A few days ago," he explained matter-of-factly, "I was drunk. I was upset, I guess. I kicked it, and, as you can see," he added, sighing, "the leg is badly bent. I'm not going to have it fixed. I never liked that table anyway. My wife picked it out. I ordered a new one. Chairs too. Everything is supposed to be here Friday."

He stepped over to her. "Here," he said, taking the bottle from her. As he held it in his right hand, he unscrewed the cap with his left. Then he nodded in the direction of her glass. With two small hands, she picked up the bottom-heavy glass and held it out to him.

"Listen," he said, as he poured the tea into the glass, the two standing tantalizing close, "I am going to fuck you. That's all. Maybe I will fuck you here in the kitchen. Maybe I will fuck you in the laundry room. I haven't decided yet. But, I will use a condom, and oh, I almost forgot, we can't make too much noise. My daughter is sleeping in her room."

"Your daughter is here?" she asked, sounding quite surprised and looking at him with questioning eyes. She held the half-full glass to her mouth but had not yet taken a drink. In her confusion, perhaps she had forgotten she was holding it.

"Yes."

"So you are married?" she asked, still looking at him, still holding the glass with two hands.

"I was married," he said, pointing to a large, nicely-framed photograph that hung on the far wall—lovely mother, handsome father, both fashionably dressed, both shoulder-leaning-into-shoulder on a photo-studio loveseat; a madly-grinning infant, the two baby teeth just emerging from the bottom gum, propped up and lovingly held by both smiling adults. The young woman's eyes looked where the finger pointed; when she saw the large photo, she took a step closer and squinted as she took it in. Then she looked back at him, her face curious, perplexed, her eyes full of questions.

"But don't worry about my wife," he said, taking another sip of his drink. "She isn't here."

"Are you two getting a divorce?"

"No."

"She's away?"

"I guess so."

"Did you have an argument?"

"Not quite," he said, and paused. Then, "She died a few weeks ago."

The tumbler the young woman held, the liquid still untouched, slipped out her hands and hit the floor with a bang. Fortunately, the glass didn't shatter, but the sound of it hitting the wood was loud, the noise strong enough to disturb the sleeping child in her bedroom.

As they stood and listened, each tilting the head to offer a concerned ear, the unsettling "Waaaaah!" grew louder and more insistent. He raised a hand in a don't-worry, stay-here gesture and, setting his glass down, turned from her and headed down the hallway. He slid open the third door and looked down at his daughter where she lay on the futon, her face contorted, her mouth open, the wailing loud and troublesome. Quickly, he bent down and scooped her up. As she screamed into his ear, he hugged her and stepped out into the hallway, nearly bumping into the young woman. "Here," she said, reaching out her arms. "Let me take her."

The young woman must have possessed some kind of marvelous magic. As soon as the child was passed and held, the screaming grew less insistent, the wailing now sobs of bewildered, young-child discomfort. "Oh, you little lovebug," the young woman cooed, touching her head gently to the child's forehead, "Did someone make a big noise? Are you grumpy now that your sweet sleep has been disturbed?" She bounced the child gently in her left arm, and with the forefinger of her right hand, she carefully dabbed away the child's tears. Without saying anything, she turned away from the man and made her way back towards the front part of the apartment; but instead of turning left into the kitchen, she turned right and found herself in the unlit living room. She sat on the front edge of the sofa, passing the child from her left arm to her right, still bouncing her gently. The little girl made happy gurgling noises, and soon her small eyelids became heavy. A moment later, she was once more fast asleep.

For a few more minutes, the young woman merely gazed out into the darkness and hugged the sleeping child to her chest, humming softly and rocking her slowly side to side. Behind her, not knowing she was being watched, the young man—deeply affected, stunned even—looked on in wonder.

As she glanced around the room, the only light coming from the hallway and kitchen, the young woman spied a red blanket on the back of the sofa. After she made a little nest of the sofa's cushions, and after she placed the sleeping child in this nest, the woman partially unfolded the blanket and laid it on the again-sleeping child. And after tucking the blanket in so only her chubby face could be seen, the young woman looked down, pleased that the child was safe and secure.

"I don't know—" the man said when she turned and stood in front of him.

"Quiet," she admonished, lifting a finger to her lips. Then, her small hands, first on an arm, then on his muscular back—the first of their human touch—she turned him and pushed him back across the hallway and into the kitchen.

"I have to pee," she whispered. "Can I use the bathroom?"

"Of course," he replied, nodding. "Just down the hallway, the first left."

"Thank you."

She wasn't gone more than a minute when he had an idea. He found, under the sink, what he was looking for, a wide-bottom, fold-open paper bag—with handles—from a local upmarket supermarket that specialized in French wines and cheeses. He grabbed it and went down the hallway. Outside the door, he waited. He heard the toilet flush, then the faucet run. When the door unlocked and slid open, she was startled to see him standing there. "I have something for you," he said quietly. "Come with me." He guided her down the long hallway past his daughter's room. He stopped at the next door, slid it open, slipped past her. Inside, he touched the light switch and turned back to where she stood in the doorway. "Please," he said. "Come here."

Pausing, the young woman glanced around the small, windowless room. What was it? It was too small to contain a bed, but it wasn't a closet. As far as she could see, all it contained was a small desk with a chair and a large mirror. Was this a dressing table? She had seen such furniture before only in Western movies. And what did he want with her here? "This was my wife's room," he related, seeing the confused look on her face. "She put on her makeup here. That's all. Okay?"

"Okay."

"Hold this," he said, gently shaking open the bag and handing it to her.

The lavender desk had two, large, side-by-side drawers. He pulled one open. With his two hands, he collected as much as he could—all of her lipsticks and eyeliners and face creams and other stuff he didn't know the names of, much of it still unused—and tossed the items into the bag she was holding. He grabbed more, removing everything. Then he yanked open the other drawer and emptied that one too. As far as he knew, all of his dead wife's cosmetics lay heaped in the fashionable paper bag.

"That was hers," he said, sounding satisfied. "Now it's yours."

"But I don't want these things."

"Then why do you wear so much makeup?"

"I thought I was supposed to look like this."

"It's not a good look," he told her, laughing a little as he now better understood her and her thinking. "Still. Take it. I don't want it."

Slowly—he gestured to her to go first—they stepped back into the hallway. As they stood there, her eyes fixed on his, he could see what she was thinking.

"I think it's best you go now. I changed my mind. I am not going to fuck you. My having you come was mistake, and I am very sorry about that. I don't know what I was thinking. But I will still pay you."

"I can stay."

"No, you need to go."

"Why?"

It was his turn to touch her. Placing his hand on the small of her back, he guided her back to the kitchen. After he had her there, he quietly stepped into the living room. Casting an eye on his daughter, seeing that she was still sleeping peacefully, he collected the young woman's jacket and scarf.

"Here," he said, passing first the jacket, then the scarf. "It's late."

"I think I should stay."

"No, I don't think you should stay."

As she placed first one arm, then the other, into her jacket, she looked down at the tumbler on the floor where it lay on its side, next to it the stain of dark tea. "I should clean this."

"I have a maid. She will take care of it tomorrow."

"But it's going to get sticky," she said, stepping over to the sink and looking for a place to set her scarf. "You need to use hot water and soap. The sooner the better. I will do it."

"No," he said. "I don't want to wake Yuka. Not again. And look," he said, pointing up at a clock. "It's nearly midnight."

At the door, the young woman seemed reluctant to go, taking a long time to slip on her shoes. "I don't know why you don't want me to stay," she said, reaching down to pull up a tired sock but still looking up at him with her big brown eyes.

"I know."

"But why?"

The man shook his head. He reached into his front pocket and took out a handful of 10,000-yen notes. "It's 50,000, right?"

"No," she said, shaking her head. "I don't want the money."

Ignoring her, he counted out the five bills, then counted out another five, and tossed them all into the bag she held that contained his wife's cosmetics. He leaned in, and for a moment, she thought he was going to kiss her, so she closed her eyes and lifted her mouth; but instead, he reached behind her and opened the apartment door. A second later, she took a step back and found herself outside in the cold. "Goodbye," he said, pulling the door shut and locking it.

17 An Old Gentleman Ruminates

The old gentleman sat at one end of the long, narrow dining-room table, in front of him an empty wine glass and a wine bottle. With an unsteady hand, he reached out and picked it up, the bottle nearly empty. He examined the label: "*Grand Vin Château Pojeaux Moulis-en-Médoc.*" There was a time when he had rather high hopes in regards to a certain individual and the French language, but now the foreign words irritated him. He tilted the bottle; what remained nearly filled his glass. He set down the now empty bottle and picked up the glass. He took a sip, then another; then he quickly finished the glass. But in his haste, he spilled some, the rivulet of red liquid escaping from a corner of his mouth and running down his chin and then his neck. Outside, a light, steady rain fell. It had been falling all day.

"Yoshiko!" he called out.

Quietly, but quickly, the old woman, house slippers on her feet, shuffled from behind the half wall that separated the kitchen from the dining room. She held a small, white towel. Keeping a watching eye on the man who had been paying her for over twenty years, the man who this late evening sat with his back to her, she had been polishing glasses and silverware. The kitchen was her space, and the floor and counters were immaculate, every utensil and dish and glass in its place. The breakfast items she planned to serve were in the refrigerator. At this late hour, there was nothing for her to do except look after her kind employer. Behind her, on a shelf, a small radio played *enka* softly.

"No more wine."

"That's very good, sir. You drank nearly two bottles." Frowning, she collected the empty bottle and the empty glass.

"No, I mean I want it all gone," he slurred. "Throw it away. Give it away. Drink it yourself. Just get rid of it."

"You have over a case, sir, in the pantry. Each bottle cost nearly 9,000 yen."

He gestured with his right hand, a gesture she understood. She bowed her head.

"Anything else?"

"Please. Warm up some *sake*. When it's ready, bring it and a cup."

"It's after midnight, Ueda-sama," she said softly, gently laying a comforting hand on his shoulder. "Wouldn't you rather be in bed?"

He looked up at her with watery eyes. "I'll sleep soon enough."

The old woman bowed and returned to the kitchen. It took her a minute to gather the items she needed, but soon she had the large bottle of *sake* and poured from it a small amount into the *tokkuri*. Carefully, she placed that smaller bottle into a pot of water on the stove and then lit the gas burner. As the *sake* warmed, she placed the wine bottle in the trash and then washed the glass. Next, she withdrew a container of mixed nuts from a cabinet and poured some into a small bowl. She filled a cocktail glass with ice and water. She carried the mixed nuts and the ice water out to the old gentleman and set both items on the table. The old gentleman had his eyes closed and his head tilted to the left. She wondered if he were sleeping.

Back in the kitchen, she watched the water and waited. From experience, she knew exactly when the *sake* would be ready. With her small towel, she lifted the *tokkuri*, dried the outside of it, and switched off the stove. She set the *tokkuri* on a small tray that already held a small cup. She carried the tray out to the table.

"Ueda-sama."

The old gentleman still had his eyes closed.

"Ueda-sama. The *sake* is ready. I brought some nuts too. And water." She set down the *tokkuri* bottle and the small cup. She nudged his shoulder.

"Ueda-sama."

Slowly, the old gentleman blinked open his eyes and looked up at the old woman. Then he glanced at the items in front of him. It seemed he needed a half minute to realize where he was and what he was doing.

"Thank you very much," he said, bowing his head slightly.

She poured some of the hot *sake* into his cup, which his thumb and forefinger found. Leaning forward, the hand shaking somewhat, he brought it to his lips. Though he spilled most of it, he was able to sip some of the hot rice wine. "Very nice, Yoshiko. Thank you."

"Would you like me to warm up some rice and fish? You haven't eaten anything all evening."

The old gentleman shook his head.

"Bring me the telephone. I want to hear the voice of my granddaughter."

"Sir, it's quite late," the old woman said softly, again placing a hand on his shoulder. "I told you. It's after midnight. I am sure little Yuka-chan is sleeping. You can't talk to her now."

The old gentleman pointed to the far end of the table where the black telephone sat next to a lamp.

After the old woman brought the phone to him, he said, "I want you to leave now. You may go home."

For a moment, the old woman remained, looking down at the old gentleman, her face full of concern. It seemed she wanted to say something, but instead she bowed and retreated behind the half wall. Quickly, efficiently, she returned all of the items to their places. She wiped the stove and the counters too. Her kitchen was immaculate once more. She removed her apron, turned off the radio and the light, walked past him, and made her through the living room toward the front of the house. But before she went down the hallway that led to the front door, she turned to face the old gentleman. Placing one hand over the other in front of her, she bowed deeply. At the entrance, she removed her slippers and switched off the hallway light. Except for a soft light that emanated from the lamp that sat on the dining room table, the house was dark. As she stood there, she opened the house door and then closed it. But she remained inside. Quietly, she sat down on the bench there and waited in the darkness.

So. The old gentleman wanted to hear the voice of his granddaughter. The two-year-old spoke no sentences, only words. After he heard the front door click shut, the sound bringing him back to the world of the conscious, he glanced around him with his not-fully-seeing eyes. His large, expensive house—perhaps his heart as well—was empty. With a shaky left hand, he reached out, found the receiver, lifted it. He looked down at the square of numbers. He needed a minute, but finally he was able to push one, then another, then more. But nothing happened. There was no ringing, only silence, and then the recorded announcement—a young woman's voice—telling him that if he wanted to make a call, he should hang up and try again. As he listened to this message, the receiver fell from his weak hand and bounced once on the table. With great difficulty, he found it and returned it to its cradle, his head hanging low. He spied the *tokkuri* bottle and reached for it, but in doing so, he knocked it over. It rolled across the table, spilling most of the *sake*, and fell to the polished wooden floor with a thud. The old man smiled—at what? his carelessness? the spectacle he made?— and then closed his world-weary eyes. He lifted his right hand and gestured with it, but there was no one there to see the gesture, no one there to understand what he meant or what he wanted or what, if anything, he needed.

From the bench, the old woman heard the bottle hit the floor, but she waited. After twenty minutes of silence, she stood up very quietly, donned her slippers, and made her way back to the dining room. She left the hallway light off. At the dining room table, the old gentleman sat precariously in his chair, his eyes closed, his entire body leaning to his left. Gently, she placed her hands on the tops of his arms. With her touch, the old gentleman woke. Once more he blinked open his eyes and glanced up at the old woman. She said nothing, but he understood that she wanted him to stand, so, with her help, he did, his legs weak. He understood that she wanted him to walk somewhere, so he placed an unsteady hand on her shoulder. She led him out of the dining room, past the living room, past the large photographs of his *kimono*-clad wife and daughter that hung prominently on a wall, and down a corridor. Fortunately, there were no stairs to climb. The two ended up in his room. The light from the dining room was very faint, but he saw his bed, and it seemed only natural that he should lie on it. After he had done so, and after she had lifted his head and placed a pillow under it, the old woman unfolded a blanket and covered him with it.

Back in the dining room, the old woman wiped the table and cleaned the floor. In the kitchen, she washed the *tokkuri* bottle and the cup and the bowl that contained the nuts. Once she had dried these items, she returned them to their places in the cabinets. She looked up at the clock; it was twenty minutes after one. She returned to the dining room, pulled out a chair, sat down; she folded her hands and placed them in her lap. She closed her eyes and soon fell asleep; she slept there fitfully until five. When she woke, it was still dark out, and still the rain fell. She stood and returned to the kitchen. She poured a glass of water, added ice, and brought it to the old gentleman's room. There was just enough light for her to see that he was sleeping, his mouth open, his head tilted to his left, his right forearm resting on his forehead. She placed the glass on the nightstand.

After she returned to the kitchen, she turned on the radio, adjusting the dial to locate the NHK morning news. Then she placed a filter in the basket and added coffee grounds. She added water and then turned the maker on. As she waited, she made her way to the large dining room window, pulled back the edge of the curtain, looked out; feeling melancholy, she listened as the heavy drops struck the glass, then watched as they slid down the pane like unending tears.

Just after nine, the appointed hour, he heard the "ping pong." Assuming the delivery guys had arrived with the new table, he sprung to the door. He couldn't get rid of the old one, and the memories that came with it, fast enough. But when he had the heavy door—steel with a long, vertical rectangle of clouded glass—open, he was taken aback to see a high school student in her dark-blue, skirt-and-blazer uniform, her hair dark brown, a black backpack hanging from a shoulder. She looked vaguely familiar.

"Yes?" he asked, studying her face.

She was about to respond when he heard two men—the delivery guys, each dressed in white overalls—talking loudly about a soccer game and approaching from the elevator. "Here," he said, his voice nearly a shout. For the moment ignoring the girl, he raised his right hand and waved to the men. When they stood at the door, the young man stepped outside, holding it open. Kicking off their shoes in the entranceway, the skinny fellows entered, followed by the high school girl, she too having removed her shoes.

"You're going to take the old one, right?" Makoto asked, turning to the leader of the two.

"Yes," the man replied as he glanced down at his clipboard. "We'll do that first. The chairs too. Then we'll bring up the new one. Shouldn't take more than ten or fifteen minutes."

"Great!"

Meanwhile, the high school girl had disappeared into the living room. After setting her backpack on the sofa, she removed her blazer and laid it on one of the arms of the sofa. With both feet to one side, she sat on the floor next to little Yuka. As if the two had already been acquainted, she held out a hand, which the toddler accepted, the tiny fingers of the child warm, sticky, sweaty.

"Hi, baby doll!"

At the sound of the voice, the toddler looked up, her eyes big, her large head a little too heavy for her thick neck. Seeing the new arrival, she smiled. The little girl—the high school girl too—was not concerned with what was happening in the other room.

"This is the one, right?"

"Yes. As you can see, one of the legs is badly bent. The table is no longer level."

Not interested in the damage, the two guys picked up the table and began carrying it to the entranceway. The young man rushed in front of them and held open the door. Stabbing their feet back into their shoes, and careful not to scratch the door with a wayward leg, they lifted the table, rotated it, and soon had it outside, where they set it down, their work quick and efficient. Then they walked past the young man back into the apartment, again leaving their shoes just inside the door, and gathered the four chairs, each man carrying two. "We'll take these items down," the leader said as he walked past the young man, who was still holding open the door. "Then return with the new table and chairs."

"Perfect!"

After they had disappeared, the young man returned to the combination kitchen / dining room. Happy with the men's progress, he leaned back, one hand on the counter behind him; but then, with a start, he remembered the high school girl. Where was she? He stepped across the hallway into the living room. He was surprised to see the two on the floor, his daughter resting comfortably in her lap, two ankle-high white socks covering the feet of the high school girl's otherwise bare legs.

"I'm confused," he began, looking down at her. "Did the agency send you? You're not Albertina, the usual nanny. And there's no need for you to be here until noon. I am not going to go to work until then."

With a kind, half smile, the high school girl looked up at him. When he saw her big brown eyes, he staggered back a few feet, reaching out a hand to search for something stable, a hand that nearly knocked over a tall lamp before it found the wall.

"Holy fuck!" he stammered, steadying himself. "You told me you were twenty. I knew you were lying, but I had no idea—"

"I'll be nineteen this summer."

"What do you want?" he asked after a long pause, using the half minute to reflect on what had and what had not happened two nights previously.

"Nothing," she replied and smiled again. "I just dropped by to see if you are okay. You were not okay the other night." With one hand, the other cradling the heavy child, she pushed herself up off the floor and stood looking at him. "I was worried. About you. And about Yuka-chan. And," she added, "I want to return the money you gave me." She bounced the little girl, who had one fist in her mouth and was drooling on the high school girl's white blouse, the stain spreading over her right breast.

"Shouldn't you be in school?"

"I don't have to go to every class."

"What high school do you attend?"

"Mitaka."

"Mitaka? My God! That's over an hour away. You came here from—"

Just then, he heard the delivery guys back at the door. "Excuse me!" one of them called out, opening it. The young man rushed back to hold it open. Once more heedful of the expensive-looking door and the surrounding walls, the two men carried the new table—made of oak, it was much heavier than the old table—inside and set it down in the empty space. As they began to remove the plastic and bubble wrap that protected the corners and surface and legs, the young man and the high school girl, still cradling the happy toddler, looked on from the hallway. Then the four chairs were brought in.

"Can you sign here?" the leader asked, picking up the clipboard from the floor where he had set it, his partner gathering the wrapping and leaving with it. When the man had the signature, he passed over a copy of the bill of sale, bowed quickly, wished them a good day. When the young man heard the click of the apartment door as it closed, he turned and looked incredulously at the high school girl. She was still gently bouncing the toddler she balanced on her hip.

"It looks nice," the high school girl reported, looking from him to the table and chairs, nodding her approval. "I like it." The child she held gripped a handful of her shoulder-length hair in her left hand and was trying to put the strands in her mouth. Casually, as if the task was one she had performed a thousand times, the high school girl reached up a hand, and, gently separating the fingers of the toddler's fist with her thumb, she pulled her hair back behind her ear.

Did the young man need to sit? Perhaps he did. He reached out a hand, found the back of one of the chairs, turned it away from the table, all the while his eyes trained on hers. He sat down, leaned back, rested an arm on the table. The high school girl shifted the toddler from one arm to the other. A moment passed, then another. He opened his mouth, but no words came.

"What?" she asked, with a smile.

19 Makoto and the High School Girl Talk, One Tucks in Little Yuka, and Then They Watch TV

"But why would you do such a thing?" he asked, looking at her with a frown of concern.

"I don't know," she replied, her eyes cast down at her hands where they lay in her lap. "I was curious, I guess. And bored. My friends were doing it," she added, after a pause, "so I thought I would too."

The young man sighed deeply and shook his head. But who was he to scold her? How many dozens of women had he paid over the years? If there was a problem, weren't men like him a large part of it?

"You have to stop," he said, reaching out to pull back some of her hair to look into her eyes.

"I know," she replied, lifting her head, her eyes meeting his. "I already stopped."

"It's extremely dangerous."

"I know," she said. "I told you. I did it only twice. And then look what happened? The third time I met you."

As they talked, little Yuka played happily with her plastic animal toys on the floor in front of them.

⧗ ⧗ ⧗

The high school girl and little Yuka were in the bath / shower room. The plan was for the high school girl to give the child a bath, not to take one with her; but when she stood in the room and saw how big the oval tub was—how spacious and clean and well-lit and well-provisioned the entire room was—she took off her uniform, folded the items neatly, set them on the vanity. Next, she removed her socks and underwear and bra, placed them on her uniform, stepped in to join the little girl in the large, deep tub, the rose-scented water warm and luxurious.

The two had been in the bathroom for so long that the young man began to wonder. He made his way down the hallway and stood listening outside the door. He heard all kinds of splashing and joyful laughter; both his daughter and the high school girl, it seemed, were in the tub. Sliding open the door, he peeked inside. He saw his daughter standing in the water, her smile wide and animated. As she faced the high school girl, she was holding aloft a yellow rubber ducky. "Ahhh!" the child screamed happily. And though the high school girl sat in the tub with her back mostly to the door, what he saw and heard was more than enough to set his heart racing—her I-am-a-monster arms raised playfully, her bare shoulders, the curve of one soapy breast, the large areola and its nipple pointing up slightly. "Oh," she growled to the child, the sound low and ominous, "I am a bear, and you are a jar of honey. I am going to eat you up!" Again, the child let out a scream of delight. He returned to the living room, his heart thundering in his chest, his hands trembling.

A few minutes later, a naked, screaming Yuka came running down the hallway and jumped on the sofa next to him. "Hey you little monster!" he heard the high school girl yell. "Where did you go? I'm gonna get you!" Pushing him slightly forward with her two small hands, the water-dripping child tried to hide behind her father. The high school girl—a large white towel wrapped tightly around her torso, a corner tucked in just above her breasts, a smaller towel wrapped around her wet hair—sat down next to him.

Without all that garish makeup, and smelling so fresh and lovely, he found that she was a marvel. "I wonder where she went," she said loudly, picking up a cushion and looking under it, pretending that she couldn't see the excited child. "She must be behind the TV." "Here, here!" little Yuka exclaimed and jumped up. "Here, here!" As the happy child jumped into her open arms, the high school girl leaned over and whispered to Makoto, "Where do you keep her clean clothes?"

Folding her legs under her, she sat on the sofa next to him. He passed her a soft blanket, one of many that belonged to his daughter, and she smoothed it out over her bare legs. She wore only her white blouse, her white bra, her white panties. "She's sleeping," she reported, smiling and reaching out to take his closest hand with both of hers. When she held this right hand, she interlocked the fingers of her left with his. She had combed her hair, but it was still wet, and he felt the moisture through his T-shirt when she leaned her head on his shoulder. They both looked at the TV; a young lady, earnestly discussing the low-pressure system that sat over the eastern part of the country, explained the next day's partly-cloudy, bring-a-jacket weather. Then the woman turned to the camera, bowed, said good night. A beer commercial followed. Smiling friends were camping by a river, barbecuing *yakiniku*, drinking silver cans of Asahi Super Dry. On the TV, the young people looked incredibly happy.

"I am sorry about the other night," he offered, muting the TV and breaking the long silence. "I wasn't myself."

"Were you drunk?"

"Just a little, thank God. I can't tell how glad I am that nothing happened," he said, turning to look at her.

"Me too," she said, returning his gaze.

"I am very sorry," she continued when he said nothing, "but I don't know what to say about your wife."

"There's not much to say," he sighed. "These things happen. I just never thought they would happen to me."

With the remote in his left hand, he changed the channel, then changed it again. Finally, he powered off the TV and the big screen went black.

"I know what you told me earlier about your home situation," he said, again looking into her eyes, "but you can't stay here."

"Why not?"

He started to reply, then stopped.

"May I come tomorrow?"

"And stay the night?"

She nodded.

"What will you tell your mother and father?"

"I will tell them that I am going to stay at a friend's house."

"They will believe you?"

"They will. They don't mind."

"What if they call this friend?"

"They won't.

For nearly a minute, he seemed to be contemplating this step and what it entailed.

"Okay. But you sleep with Yuka-chan in her room. Or you sleep here on the couch."

At the door, she stood before him in her school uniform, the backpack again hanging from a shoulder. "Will you kiss me?" she asked, looking up at him. This time her closed eyes and raised mouth met his, but the kiss was brief, just a light touch of his lips to hers. "Tomorrow, then," she said and smiled.

20 A Mother and Father Talk

"What's up with the slut? I haven't seen her around the past few days."

"How can you say such things about your own daughter?"

"Any girl who spends so much time away from home has to be up to no good."

"Well, she has good marks, doesn't she? And she's graduating. That's more than you can say."

"And why didn't I graduate? Didn't I get a job so we'd have money?"

"I was the pregnant one. I was thrown out. You could have finished. You quit because you're lazy."

"That's calling the kettle black. Who does most of the work around here? She does. Who looks after the other three? She does. If it wasn't for her, those kids would never eat. They'd never make it to school. You should be ashamed."

One of those kids ambled into the kitchen. "Mommy, I'm still hungry."

"Drink a glass of water," the mother groused, pulling out a cigarette from a pack that lay on the table and lighting it. As she looked at the skinny boy, she inhaled deeply, then exhaled, blowing the smoke up toward the ceiling. "Then shut up and go to bed."

The father pulled down a bag of potato chips that sat on the top of the refrigerator. He opened it and shook some onto the kitchen table. "Here," he said to his son, pulling him onto his lap. "Have some of these."

21 The High School Girl and
Little Yuka Listen to Music

When the young man returned to the apartment early in the evening, he saw nothing but the high school girl's backpack on the oak table. He slid his arms out of his suit jacket and threw it over the back of a chair. He glanced into the living room, but it was empty. He stood still and listened, but he heard no sounds. He assumed the two were out. Perhaps they had gone off to the park, as was their wont, or perhaps they were at the supermarket. But he noticed the toddler's stroller by the door. Perhaps, he mused, they went without it this time. With the high school girl's mothering skills, and with her incredible attention to detail, he wondered if he needed Albertina anymore. He certainly could call the agency and get her hours cut back.

The young man loosened his tie, grabbed a can of Sapporo from the refrigerator, found a bag of butter peanuts, hit the sofa. With the remote in hand, he pushed the ON with his thumb and ran through the channels. When he found nothing of interest, he returned to the baseball game, Hanshin leading the Giants by four. He muted the volume. He grabbed the can; lifted the tab, the sound pleasant, familiar; took a pull. Then, thinking it would be nice to have a half hour, maybe longer, to himself, he leaned back and threw his stockinged feet on the glass coffee table.

He had nearly dozed when a strange sensation roused him: someone—some presence—was in the apartment. He was certain. Setting down the can, he leaned forward, his elbows on his knees, and listened.

He stood and went to the front door. Nothing had changed. Still, he felt the presence. He turned around and looked down the long, dark hallway to the other rooms. Slowly, he made his way. The first door on the left was the toilet, but he opened it anyway and turned on its light. Nothing. The second door was the much larger bath / shower room. He slid open the door. This room, too, was dark and quiet. He reached in, found the switch, turned on the light. Leaning in, one hand on the doorframe, he scanned the room. Fresh, fluffy towels—folded neatly into squares—sat on the vanity, just as he liked. Nothing seemed to be out of place. He looked further down the hallway. Not counting the last door, the door that led to the master bedroom, there were three rooms left.

He entered next his daughter's room. The futon lay on the floor, and on it a pile of colorful blankets and small pillows. Under the wide, rectangular window on the far wall was a small-child's desk and chair, and next to it stood a low dresser, the second drawer pulled open to reveal a tangle of socks. A little messy, the room was its usual self.

When he slid open the next door and touched the light, he saw his reflection in the large oval. For a moment, he examined his appearance—had he lost weight?—then glanced around. The room had been untouched. Nothing lay on his wife's lavender desk, the matching chair turned away slightly. On the floor, the small wastebasket sat empty.

The final door led to his audio room. He had special floor-to-ceiling shelves built into one wall to accommodate his vast record collection. He had over 500,000 yen of audio equipment installed as well. There was a desk; a cushioned chair, with arms, on wheels; and a small bookcase crammed with English-language books.

The window, larger than the one in his daughter's room, offered a wonderful view of the Tokyo skyline.

He gently slid open the door, the room dark and shadowy; the small desk lamp, the bulb pointed down, seemed to be on its lowest setting. As his eyes adjusted, they moved to the stereo equipment. An album was spinning on the turntable, and the various green and red lights on the receiver were jumping up and down, showing him the volume levels, yet he heard no sounds.

With her legs spread out underneath her like the wings of a butterfly, she sat on the floor in her uniform, her back to the door, on her head a pair of his headphones. He could see that she held—with both hands—The Smiths' first album and, bent over, was looking intently at the cover. She turned it over and looked at the back. Other albums were strewn on the floor around her. She set down the one she had been holding and lifted another, slid it out the special plastic case that he had for each album, and squinted at the cover. What could the unusual montage mean? The cloudless sky, the two tall trees, the two fencers, one with the foil extended in a thrust, dressed in white. "Elvis Costello and the Attractions" was written in the top left corner; she assumed, correctly, those words comprised the singer's or band's name. On the bottom right corner, she read "Goodbye Cruel World." She was familiar with "goodbye" and "world," but with her limited command of English, she did not know the meaning of the word "cruel."

Next to her, he saw his daughter lying on her back, her eyes closed, her little mouth open, each hand a tiny, unclenched fist at her sides. She too wore a pair of headphones, but hers were much too big for her head, and when he followed the long cord, he could see that it wasn't plugged in.

Sensing him, she turned her shoulders and looked up at him. She smiled, lifting a small hand and waving. He returned the smile and slipped into the room. Finding the desk chair, he swiveled it around so he could watch the two of them. After a minute, and without waking her, he slipped the headphones off little Yuka and lifted them to his ears. Reaching over to the receiver, he plugged in the cord. As the gentle song played, she looked up at him. Then she set down the album cover she was holding and began to play the drums, her lifted hands holding the make-believe sticks and striking the make-believe snare and cymbal. He responded by playing the guitar. He held out his left hand, and with his right, he strummed the imaginary guitar slowly. As they played together, he gazed into her eyes, mouthing the words, "For you are all that matters / And I'll love you till the day I die / As long as the hand that rocks the cradle is mine." She closed her eyes, gently swayed her head side to side, and drummed. "Oh, your untouched, unsoiled, wondrous eyes," he mouthed, "I'm here and here I'll stay / As long as… As long as… As long as the hand that rocks the cradle is mine."

The song, the last one on the album side, faded out, and her gentle drumming gradually came to an end. The needle lifted and returned to its off position; the record stopped spinning. Silence filled the headphones. But still she had her eyes closed and her head tilted, on her face a serene, dreamy look. The young man looked down at her in fascination. Slowly, she opened her eyes and looked up at him. She smiled again. He nodded. She picked up the album cover once more and examined its cover. Then setting it aside, she crawled on her hands and knees over to where the phonograph player sat on the receiver. She lifted the needle and placed it back on the first track. Then she glanced at little Yuka; seeing that the toddler was sleeping peacefully, she turned her attention back to the pile of albums that were strewn on the floor around her.

22 Running into an Old Friend

"Makoto! Hey, Makoto!"

The young man who had been accosted paused and turned around. The wide sidewalk was crowded with early-evening foot traffic, but he saw a smiling face coming toward him, the face and slicked-back hair familiar; the only difference, it seemed, was the goatee.

"Satoshi! Wow!" he said, reaching out a hand that the other accepted and shook cheerfully, "How long has it been?"

"Years, it seems. Still buying records, I see."

He lifted the Recofan bag he was holding. "I guess so. Just found a couple I couldn't do without."

"More of that obscure UK indie shit?"

"Pretty much. But I listen to other stuff too. My tastes have expanded quite a bit."

"What's up with the suit and tie?" the old friend asked, nodding in appreciation of the fashionable blue jacket and its pin stripes. "What happened? You win the lottery?"

"No," the well-dressed man laughed. "My job."

"What are you doing?"

"I'm a… I work for a company. Near Tokyo Station. Got to look my best, I guess. Maybe one of these years I'll get promoted."

"With duds like that, you must be doing well. You always were one smart motherfucker. When you bolted without saying anything, the others thought you had gotten into some kind of mischief, but I knew you were simply onto better things. Good for you. So, you got a pad? Where you living?"

"Actually, I live here in Shibuya. On the other side of the station. I am on my way home now."

"Shibuya? Fuck! Well done! You must be loaded. You got a girl? Wait. Don't tell me," he added, giving the other a playful shove. "You married the only daughter of a billionaire!"

"Well, I was married."

"Didn't work out?"

"You could say that. It's complicated."

"It's complicated? Like she died or something? That kind of complicated?"

"You've always had a fanciful imagination, Satoshi."

Smiling, the two men stood on the sidewalk and considered each other, each perhaps recalling fondly the heady days when they toiled together at Rick's. A young, attractive, well-dressed lady approached from one of the narrow side streets. She sported a short, tight, black skirt; black fishnet stockings; black high heels. On top a soft-blue blouse and a matching black jacket. The fashionable Gucci handbag that hung from one forearm must have cost at least one million yen. As she passed—the clip-clop, clip-clop of the heels loud on the pavement—they both stared, the old friend raising an eyebrow and grinning, a small explosion of happiness in his eyes.

"Fuuuck!" he said knowingly and cuffed his old companion on the shoulder. "I kind of miss the old days. We had a lot of fun, didn't we?"

"We did."

"Plenty of those delights."

"Indeed."

"Listen, you should come to the club where I work. I manage the place. There's a steep cover charge, but that's to keep out the riff raff. All you need to do is to show the doorman this." The man pulled out his wallet, withdrew a business card, passed it over to his old friend. "This will get you in. Drink whatever you want. On me. Plenty of girls too. Plenty of tight pussy. Girls who will drool over a guy like you. They don't read the books you do—they probably don't read at all," he added, laughing at his own joke—"but they give very good head."

"You look good, Satoshi. Ever cheerful! Thank you!"

As the two shook hands warmly once again and then parted, the well-dressed, record-carrying man promised to visit his old friend's club soon, but he never did.

23 Trying to Do Something Good, Part 4

It was a long letter, and though the Japanese was somewhat ungrammatical at times, the sincerity touched him. When he finished reading it a second time, he looked again at the photograph. He smiled as he recalled her. There she sat in a kimono, her face and hair elaborately made up. She looked happy. The man, a homely-looking fellow, much taller than she, stood behind her in a black suit that seemed to be a size or two too large for him. He smiled proudly, his hand on her shoulder. In front of the couple stood a little girl dressed in a pink dress and shiny, black shoes.

Naked, little Yuka ran out from the bathroom, screaming happily. "Monster, come back!" yelled the high school girl from the bathroom. The naked Yuka crawled up onto her father's lap.

When the high school girl joined them in the dining room a minute later, she handed him a white towel. As little Yuka squirmed, he wrapped her in the towel and then tipped her upside down. "Oh, no," he called out, before righting her, "she's a rocket crashing to earth!" Then he freed a hand and with it slid across the letter and photograph. "I received this at work today," he said.

The high school girl adjusted the towel that she had around her, sat down, began reading.

After a minute, she asked, turning her attention to the photo, "How do you know them?"

"To be honest, I don't recall. Maybe at the golf club. Maybe she was one of the waitresses. But I am glad I was able to do her a good turn."

"You helped her get a position at Seibu?"

"The human resource manager is a client of mine. I simply passed on her name. It seems she is doing rather well there. And look, now she has married."

The high school girl nodded warmly. She read the letter once more, then laid it next to the photograph. She looked across the table at him. "The water is still warm."

"Thank you. And you," he said, loudly addressing his daughter, "still stink like a rotten pumpkin!" He began to tickle her. She screamed in delight. "We have to get you cleaned up. That is if the shark doesn't get you first!" Standing up, he threw his daughter over a shoulder. As he carried the giddy, still-squirming child down the hallway back to the shower room, she screamed in delight, "No shark, Daddy! No shark!"

24 The Young Man and the Old Man Play a Final Round of Golf

On the 12th hole, a 376-yard par four dogleg to the left, the young man drove his ball into the right fairway bunker. On the previous hole, a short par three, he purposely missed his three-foot, double-bogey putt so that he and the old man would tie.

His father-in-law bent over and teed up his ball. He looked down the fairway for a long time. He swayed a little before he addressed the ball. Then he turned to the young man and the caddie and said, "I think that's it for today. I am feeling a little lightheaded."

"Father," the young man said, frowning and approaching, "you have been working much too hard. You don't need to spend so much time at the office. Please. I can do what needs to be done." He took the old man's driver and helped him over to the cart. It was a chilly, late-winter, the-grass-still-brown afternoon; a light drizzle began to fall from the low, scudding clouds.

The middle-aged lady took her seat and radioed to the starter that the group was finishing early. In the back of the four-person cart, the young man climbed in next to his father-in-law, and the caddie pushed the gas and they began to roll. Perhaps they had forgotten, but no one picked up the old man's ball and tee.

"How is Yuka-chan?" he asked, his voice low and tremulous.

"She is fine. Would you like me to bring her around again this Sunday?"

"She must miss her mother terribly," the old man said, struggling to get the words out, his eyes welling up.

"We all do," the young man said, placing a comforting arm around the old man's shoulders.

Back at the expansive clubhouse, he guided the slow-walking man from the club storage area through the lobby to the front doors. The young driver, a new fellow, was already there with the Grande Mark II, the engine running, the back door open; he helped the old man into the back seat. As he walked around to the driver's door, the young man pulled him aside. "Listen," he said, looking the driver in his eyes and speaking earnestly. "He may ask you to take him to the office. Don't do it. Take him to the house. Tell Yoshiko-san to make sure he gets some rest. You understand?"

"Yes, sir."

The young man waved them off, and the two began the long drive back to the city.

But they never made it to Nishi Azabu. After fifteen minutes, just after the two entered the expressway, the old man made an unsettling, not-quite-human sound and leaned back. He appeared to be choking, his mouth hanging open, his arms and legs stiffening. With concern, the driver looked at him through the rearview mirror. "Ueda-sama? Are you feeling okay?" He called out again, but there was no response. He exited the expressway at the very next chance and continued speeding to a hospital, but the old man's face, his not-seeing eyes open, had already turned blue. He had made a few more unsettling, gurgling sounds, and then he was silent forever.

It had been an incredible turn of events. In eleven weeks, the young man had lost both his wife and his father-in-law. He went from being a millionaire to a billionaire. At 26, he was no longer one of the leading traders and advisors to the president of a small albeit distinguished investment firm; he *was* the president. He was in control of billions of yen and millions of dollars and pounds in investments and directed dozens of employees in small offices in Tokyo, New York, London, Hong Kong, Singapore. "Except for the child's inheritance, you control everything," the twice-his-age lawyer said matter-of-factly. "That's what the will says. You have acknowledged reading it. When the child turns twenty, the 500,000,000 yen my firm is holding will be released to her. You need to place your seal here, here, and here." He turned over another page and pointed. "And here. Do you have any questions, Tanaka-sama?" The young man carefully placed his seal where he had been directed and then, looking up at him, shook his head. The lawyer gathered the documents and bowed himself out of the conference room. For a little while, the young man sat and stared out at nothing. Then he stood and walked over to the floor-to-ceiling windows, the impressive Tokyo skyline stretching out before him—the sun setting, rays of bright light streaking through the rolling clouds, long shadows at play.

And just as miraculously, the young man had met the high school student. She was in the apartment when he keyed in later. At the oak table, she and little Yuka were eating dinner: apple wedges, white rice, small pieces of glazed *yakitori*. As he eased himself into one of the chairs opposite the two, the high school girl—the bib-wearing child on her lap—looked over at him and smiled.

"How did it go?"

"It went well," he replied with a sigh.

"Would you like something to eat?"

"Strangely," he replied, glancing away, one elbow on the table, "I don't feel like eating. To be honest," he continued, first looking down at his hands, then across the room at the wall, "I am not exactly sure what I should feel. Maybe I should go for a walk. Maybe I should…" Instead of finishing his thought, he seemed to have slipped into a reverie, his brows furrowing, the eyes open but staring at what. Mechanically, he reached up his right hand, grabbed the knot of his tie, loosened it. His mind clearly elsewhere, he nodded at the space in front of him, as if he were confirming something someone had said. Or perhaps he was seeing a situation in a new light. Or perhaps he had been looking for something and had found it. The high school girl said nothing. Patience was one of her numerous virtues. But she watched, a little concerned. And then, his eyes seeing again, the spell was broken. Inhaling deeply, he turned and looked into her big brown eyes. "I am sorry," he said, self-conscious of his odd behavior. "What was I saying?"

"Nothing," she said, smiling again, the fidgeting child trying to slide off her lap.

"I apologize," he said, laughing at himself. "It's been a very long and a very strange day. I am happy to be home."

25 Makoto Visits Mitaka on a Warm, Saturday Afternoon

The young man slipped into the back of the crowded gymnasium. All the seats for guests were taken, so he had to stand in the back. Most of the attendees—mothers and fathers, brothers and sisters, grandmothers and grandfathers, aunts and uncles and cousins—wore dresses and suits. Many held large bouquets of flowers. Others held small, use-once-and-discard cameras or large, bulky video recorders. It was a nice spring day, so the many doors to the gymnasium had been thrown open. As he found a place to stand, the band played the slow, sad Japanese national anthem.

The students sat in their uniforms in front of the stage, row upon row, many with their heads bowed. A teacher introduced the stolid principal, who, the young man felt, spoke too long and with neither conviction nor charisma. Then he and another teacher began. Each student, when his or her name was called, walked up the stairs to the stage, crossed it slowly, bowed first to the audience, and then turned to the principal. The principal called out the student's name, congratulated him or her, and then handed the diploma with both of his hands; in turn, the student accepted it with both hands and bowed deeply and slowly to the principal. There were no shouts from the audience. The guests simply applauded. The student walked off the stage and returned to his or her seat. The process repeated itself nearly two-hundred times.

When he saw a mother dabbing her eyes with a white handkerchief, he too teared up. He didn't know why, but he teared up so quickly these days. He could be watching a TV documentary on the plight of the African elephant, and that would set him off, especially if she was sitting by his side.

When the principal called out her name, and when he saw her walk slowly to the stage, and then cross it, he blinked back his tears. When one slid down his face, he reached up and rubbed his eyes with his thumb and forefinger, and with the heel of his hand, he wiped away the second tear that had fallen. He looked up at the ceiling to collect himself. She was indeed a marvel, for him some kind of undeserved gift from the heavens. Of that he was certain. With her, he felt, he was putting his somewhat chaotic and selfish past behind him.

When the event concluded, nearly three hours after it began, he slipped out quietly. He walked back to the station, caught an express to Shinjuku, transferred there to the Yamanote train, and rode the three stops to Shibuya. For the young man, it had been a most enjoyable afternoon.

26 The President Meets with His Tokyo Employees

As everyone quietly gathered in the conference room, the president walked around and greeted each worker by his or her first name. "Thank you," he said. "Thank you very much!" He bowed slightly to each individual and shook each hand warmly.

When Kobayashi, his secretary, told him all were present, he began. His booming voice, full of a maturity and a confidence that impressed them all, filled the room. "Good morning! I wish we had chairs for all of you. I am sorry. And I wish you hadn't had to come in so early, but we all needed to gather before trading commences at nine. I am sure we will have another busy day." He paused and glanced around the room. "As you all know, we have had a great deal of success here despite the market turmoil of the last few years. I attribute that success to your diligence, to your perseverance, to your close attention to the special needs of our customers. I sincerely thank all of you." The president bowed deeply.

"Effective today," he continued, "I am resigning. I have already spoken with Nomura-san, and he has agreed to assume my position. Those of you who reported to me now report to him. Otherwise, our mission remains the same." Pushing back his chair, Nomura stood and bowed to the president. He held the bow for a long time.

Then he turned and bowed to the others. "Be as kind and as helpful to him," the president resumed, "as you have been to me these past few months. As you all know, they have been incredibly difficult for me and my family." The president looked around the room and was, for a moment, silent.

"I recently realized I have more than I ever dreamed of. I need nothing, absolutely nothing. I hope you too can find what you are looking for. Sometimes it finds you." Many of his employees might have assumed he was referring to his recent inheritance, but perhaps the young president was talking about something else. They all envied him his money and his present stature, but perhaps they envied him for the wrong reasons. He bowed one last time. His employees all stood and bowed to him.

The previous afternoon, the same conference-room setting, the president had met with his old friend and confidant. "I am glad you are willing to take over, Nomura," he said as the two sat across from each other. "You will do well. Of that I am sure. I told you what I want done. How you proceed is up to you. Of course, I will drop in from time to time, and you can always call if you have any questions." The president stood. Nomura did as well. "Captain, the ship is yours!" he said, shaking the other man's hand firmly. "Steer her well!"

The president made his way to the door, but there he paused and turned around. "You already contacted the agency. Albertina has her money, yes?"

"I spoke to the manager personally a few days ago. She has received the letter you sent. She will receive a half-year's salary, to be paid out monthly, as you have directed."

"Good. Very good. One last item then. You will keep Yoshiko-san and the two drivers on the payroll until I tell you otherwise."

27 Makoto Hangs Out with the Minders, Possibly for the Last Time

Late on a fine Saturday morning, the young man decided to walk over to Recofan. "One or two records won't hurt," he mused. "Maybe there is something new." His daughter and the high school graduate were playing together in the living room. "Want to go for a walk?" he asked. The high school graduate shook her head. "We're fine," she said, looking up. He got down on his knees and kissed each one on her forehead.

As he exited the apartment building, he saw the Grande Mark II across the street, the two minders inside. They jumped out when they saw him. The young man waved to the two, waited for the light to change, made his way over to their side of the street.

"Planning to break my legs?" he asked with a smile.

"No, sir!"

"You used to call me other names."

"Only in jest, sir. Only in jest."

"No. I deserved those names." The three looked each other over. The young man chuckled.

"We were wondering, sir, if you would join us for lunch," Yuji asked, the commanding swagger of the old days gone.

"*Ramen?*"

"Whatever you want, sir. Our treat."

"Is the place still open?"

"Just barely. We'd be doing the old lady a favor if we stopped in."

"By all means, then, let's go. And stop calling me 'sir.'"

The proprietress still had the opener on the string around her neck. She was wiping the counter when the three slid open the door and entered. "Well, well, well," she said, looking at the three, smiling playfully, drying her hands on a hand towel, "look what the cat dragged in. A couple of gutter rats and a full-grown puppy."

"Now, Setsuko, don't insult our guest," Yuji said. Of course, she knew what was needed. She pulled out three large bottles of Asahi and three small glasses from the refrigerator. Once she had everything on the counter, she popped off the bottle caps.

"Three of the usuals?" she asked, pouring out the beer.

"We wouldn't have it any other way. Lots of garlic. And the *gyoza*."

During the gentlemen's early afternoon repast, they downed nine bottles of beer and were working on the tenth. After she removed the bowls and plates, Yuji told a dirty joke about a one-legged whore. When the laughing subsided, he coughed. He coughed again and looked uncomfortable.

"What is it?" the young man asked.

"What you have done, sir, for the two of us and old Yoshiko is an act of genuine kindness."

Smiling, he looked from one to the other. "What have I done?"

"Don't play the fool, sir. To keep us on when there is no work to do is—"

"I don't know what you're talking about."

Yuji looked at his companion. "He's a fucker," he said, shaking his head. "Through and through."

"He is," the other replied, nodding in agreement. "A mean-spirited, selfish cocksucker."

Laughing heartily, the young man lifted his glass and emptied it. He smiled, and again, he looked from one to the other.

"Sir, the beer bottle was never supposed to hit you."

"What?"

"The bottle. When I threw it, it was supposed to sail over your head. I wanted to frighten you. That's all. But it slipped." With this confession, Yuji shot to his feet and bowed deeply to the young man.

"Well," he replied, nodding appreciatively, reaching up his right hand to touch the scar, "you certainly got my attention."

When Yuji tried to say more—contrite, apologetic words about having overreacted on more than one occasion—the young man waved him off. "Sit down," he insisted. "You three were always good to Mariko and the old man. Very good. And you two delinquents were being good to me when you treated me roughly. I know that now, and I appreciate it. There's plenty to go around. You deserve it. My birthday is January 10. Buy me a box of chocolates every year."

"If ever you need us, for anything, all you have to do is call."

"I know that," he replied, rising and swaying slightly.

"Actually, I need you now. After I drain the radiator, I have a rather important job for you. I am a little drunk, so take me home so I can be with my family."

28 Makoto, Little Yuka, and the High School Graduate Visit the City Office in Shibuya; a Holiday on Oahu

A couple of months after her graduation, on a Tuesday morning, the young man and the high school graduate—balancing little Yuka on her hip—stood before a city official at the Shibuya City Office. The young man held various papers, and he passed them to the middle-aged man. The official accepted them and spread them on the high counter that separated the two parties. When he saw what they contained, he looked down at them more closely. He checked her birthdate. Then he checked his. He glanced at the toddler. He did a quick mental calculation, and the result surprised him. But he said nothing. He made a few annotations on one with his pen. He checked a box on another.

"You will need a witness. Did you bring one?" he asked genially, looking up.

"We were told you could provide one," the young man replied. His daughter had several of her fingers—some of the high school graduate's hair too—in her mouth and was making gurgling sounds.

"We can. Certainly. Please wait a moment."

The young official walked off, leaving them alone at the counter.

The high school graduate gently bounced the toddler, her face radiant sunshine, the cheeks ruddy, her large eyes small circles of black ink.

"Do you want me to take her?" he asked, reaching out to pull back from the child's face some of her long hair.

"No, she's fine."

The high school graduate looked at the child and made a funny face. "My little tulip," she said with great animation, their foreheads touching, "are you ready for your first big trip? The big airplane is going to carry us far, far away. Don't be scared!"

The official returned with three ladies, two women appearing to be in their fifties, the other about the same age as the young man. Smiling, the ladies introduced themselves. "Adorable," the young woman said, pointing to little Yuka with envy.

"Place your seal here please," the official said to the high school graduate. After passing the child to the young man, she inked her seal and placed it carefully on the form. After she did this, the official slid the paper over in front of him. "And you, sir," he said, pointing to the space with his index finger, "need to place your seal here." After the child was passed once again, the young man placed his seal where directed. Then the official asked one of the ladies to place her seal in the box for the witness, which she did, smiling. Then after stamping yet another seal, this much larger one from the city office, he acknowledged that all seals were genuine. "That concludes everything," he said. The three ladies clapped softly but happily. "*Omedeto!*" they all said. "*Omedeto!*" One of the older ladies reached across the counter to pinch one of the child's chubby cheeks. "*Kawaii!*" she said.

From the city office, the three caught a cab that took them to Narita. At the JAL check-in counter, the young man slid across the three passports and the three air tickets. The young, uniformed lady was surprised to hear they had no luggage to check. "Just a couple of backpacks," the young man said, turning his shoulder to show one. "At this point, they have everything we need. We'll carry them on the plane with us."

Just as the city official did a few hours previously, the ground staff agent looked closely at the birthdates of the two adults.

She also noticed that the passport of the high school graduate contained a different surname. Since she had been on the job only three months, and since this was the first time she had experienced a situation like this, she gathered the three passports, excused herself, went to confer with her superior. With a raised hand to cover her mouth, she whispered a few confidential sentences to her. The experienced manager looked at the passports, and then she looked beyond her subordinate to where the two adults stood at the counter, the young woman holding the child. Looking again at the three passports, she acknowledged the situation was highly unusual, but no regulations stated that the three couldn't board.

The ground staff agent returned and apologized for the delay, printing their boarding passes and directing the three to the security checkpoint.

In the JAL lounge, the three enjoyed pretzels, grapes, large wedges of sugary pineapple—and for the young man, a frosted glass of beer; for the other two, pulpy orange juice.

When they arrived in Honolulu, they jumped into a private car provided by the Hyatt, where the young man had reserved a suite for the week, the hotel's Japanese staff members there to greet them and to show them to their rooms. All along the travel route, everyone wanted to know how the three were related, but no one had the courage to ask. At the Shibuya City Office, at the JAL check-in counter, in the JAL lounge, in the first-class cabin, at the reception desk of the Hyatt, all parties wondered, could the two really be a couple? And could the little girl really be the young woman's daughter?

As can be imagined, the three enjoyed Oahu immensely. After they spent their first day at a mall shopping—a lot of new clothes, some toys, even a stroller—the young man rented a convertible, and they used it generously to explore the island. They took a long helicopter ride. They climbed Diamond Head. Little Yuka rode a pony. And of course, they splashed around in the beautiful ocean for hours and tanned handsomely. The people who saw them were pleased—a little jealous too?—with how happy the three appeared. "Everybody should be like that," one middle-aged woman said to her husband one evening at dinner, pointing with a dessert fork as the three sat at a nearby table and enjoyed their meal, seemingly oblivious to the outside world—the handsome man chomping his prime rib merrily, the radiant young woman enjoying her fried prawns and licking her buttery fingers, little Yuka gleefully wiping chocolate ice cream on her chubby cheeks with her chubby fingers. Though the wait staff and the other hotel guests around them couldn't possibly know, each of the three was beginning a new life. They were going to travel a long road, and they were going to travel it together.

29 A Rather Unusual yet Happy Ending

Was it completely unprecedented for a 26-year-old playboy billionaire to marry a young woman only two months out of high school? It was. And to do so less than five months after his wife died seemed, to the few who knew him, incredibly heartless, even cruel. But something had changed deep within this troubled man. The coming years would show that it was a positive change. He gave up his self-obsessed, philandering ways. He stayed home and played games with his daughter, and later, when she was ready, he taught her to read and write. As a family, the three strolled to the local supermarket and did the necessary shopping, and they enjoyed doing it. When they returned, they cooked together, and then later they did the washing up. When their city explorations took them away from Shibuya, they could have used the more expensive taxis, and they did occasionally; but mostly they walked or took the convenient, clean, inexpensive subways and trains and buses. Several times a year husband and wife took their daughter to the zoo. They went bowling too. Every summer they went camping. Every winter they went skiing. Together, they all learned to ice skate. The young man's transformation was truly astonishing.

Equally surprising, an attractive, intelligent, indepedent-minded high school graduate, in the full flower of her youth, exchanged all of the joys of young adulthood for those of instant motherhood. But Satomi—at this much-too-late point, let's share her name; we've disrespected her long enough—did this, and she did it well, and she did it happily. At first, some overly cynical observers were certain she did it for his money, never believing that such a union would last. But she never asked her husband for money. Of course, within days of their marriage, he had opened a savings account for her and had given her her own passbook. She had access to millions of yen. But she never bought gaudy jewelry or unnecessary items for the apartment. She didn't have a closet full of designer clothes and fancy shoes she never wore. Every day, she cooked and cleaned, tasks that she enjoyed, tasks that she performed well. Occasionally, they would go to a restaurant, but more often she bought *bento*, at times marked down, from the supermarket, and once a month the family could be seen at the local McDonald's. And naturally, she went herself to Tsutaya to rent the videos that she and he liked to watch at night after they put little Yuka to bed.

The young man kept the apartment in Shibuya. One day, early in their marriage, he asked his wife, "Would you like to find a new place?"

"Why?" she replied, looking into his eyes. "This is our home. I like it here."

One Sunday morning, he began to take down the large family photo that he and his first wife had hung in the kitchen, but she stopped him. "I don't mind," she said, placing a hand on his arm. "I think we should keep it. We can add more. I would like that. We can start with some of the photos we took in Hawaii."

He kept the house in Nishi Azabu as well. He didn't change a thing. The garden still retained its *koi*-filled pond. The Ueda family photographs still hung on the walls in the studio. And upstairs the furniture was covered, but underneath the white sheets, it was all the same. Once or twice a year, the young man would surprise the maid, calling first before he made his visit. In the early evening, he would sit in the garden room for an hour, sometimes longer, sipping the lemon-flavored water.

When the three welcomed Mika, little Yuka's sister, the young man considered moving into the house, but instead, the four simply moved into a much larger apartment on a higher floor in the building they presently occupied. On the 34th floor, they had a spacious ten-room apartment, one with a huge veranda that offered stunning views of the magnificent city. If they were up early, they could catch the sunrise; in the evening, the four often ate outside and watched the setting sun.

They were fortunate, certainly. They had been given much. But they hadn't wasted what they had been given. And when it would have been easier perhaps to use more, they were often content using less. So, the springs came, and with them the pink and white cherry blossoms and the longer, warmer days; the summers were hot and humid, as usual; the autumns were cool, and the gentle breezes blew the brown and red and yellow leaves from the trees; the winters were cooler still, and once or twice a wet snow fell on the city. In other words, the years passed. They had these years, and then later more years, and for them they were wonderful. In the vast metropolis that was Tokyo, in the other parts of Japan, in the many countries they visited, they were living a happy life together.

Acknowledgements

First and foremost, I want to thank Duane. Without his introduction, and without his persistence, this novel never would have been considered for publication.

Second, I want to thank Mikesch and Culicidae Press for publishing it. He and his team of editors were incredibly helpful, and patient. It's been a joy to work with him.

Third, I want to thank the following friends and colleagues. They were my first readers, and they were invaluable in pointing out minor errors and in suggesting improvements: Bill A., Greg A., Bill B., Jerry C., Beni F., Ken H., Tomas P., Ken S., Jodi S., Warren S., and Dave W.

Fourth, I want to thank Kyoko, who assisted me with some of the English-to-Japanese translations.

Finally, I bow deeply to Rie, my wife, who puts up with my many idiosyncrasies and my selfishness.

www.ingramcontent.com/pod-product-compliance
Lightning Source LLC
Chambersburg PA
CBHW061113100726

47911CB00013B/527